## "You're content with your upcoming marriage?" he asked

"I would not like to think it made you unhappy, but I did it for the best," her father continued.

"I know, Papa," she said quietly. "Stonor and I understand each other. You mustn't worry."

But once she was upstairs in her bed, the deep, burning ache inside her drove her mad, telling her to go to Wolfe, who waited outside. Dear Lord, what was she to do? What kind of life could she and Wolfe make together? His was a hostile world, and she would only burden him.

Yet she had to go to him, and in a few minutes she stood before him in the darkened woods.

Wolfe slowly pushed the silken hair back from her face. "You came."
It was all he needed to say.

"Wolfe!" Sophia whispered, as if his very existence were enough to make heaven real for her, as if without him the world would become a shadow for the rest of her life.

# About the Author

Sheila Holland lives with her husband and five children on the Isle of Man. Before 1970 she was a housewife who spent her days taking care of her children and occasionally writing poetry. Today she is known as Charlotte Lamb, one of the world's foremost authors of contemporary romance fiction. Her first book appeared in 1971, and since then more than seventy of her novels have been published, with sales exceeding seventy million copies.

With the publication of the contemporary *A Violation* in November, 1983, and now with *Secrets*, a two-part historical-romance novel, Sheila Holland demonstrates her remarkable versatility. Part One of *Secrets* was first published in 1980 under the title *Secrets to Keep*. The author has developed this compelling romance into an exciting and passionate saga sure to delight and intrigue readers everywhere.

# Secrets

## Sheila Holland

# W❃RLDWIDE

TORONTO • NEW YORK • LONDON • PARIS
AMSTERDAM • STOCKHOLM • HAMBURG
ATHENS • MILAN • TOKYO • SYDNEY

This edition published April 1984

Part One of *Secrets* first published in 1980 by Playboy Press under the title *Secrets to Keep*.

Part One and Part Two of *Secrets* first published in 1983 by Fontana Paperbacks.

ISBN 0-373-97007-2

# PART ONE

## CHAPTER ONE

He stood alone, his hands in his trouser pockets, watching the dancers with a faint, sardonic smile. A shrewd observer might have noted a tension within his body, a controlled but deadly violence that betrayed itself in movement: in the way he held his head, the flicker of his eyes. Graceful, wary, hostile, he trod among the other guests like a strange animal in dangerous territory, his eyes constantly watching for a challenge.

Sophia was not the only one to glance aside at him. His darkly handsome face drew other female eyes. Secret, almost furtive looks were stolen at him from behind fans, which fluttered faster if he returned the stare.

"He sends shivers down my back!" Sophia had heard one girl whisper to her friend.

"Don't look at him!" The other girl was blushing as the dark young man turned those strange blue-green eyes on them. "Mama might notice and take me home!"

The exchange had amused Sophia. Was the young man so dangerous? It was true that the impression he left was of a staggering insolence, as if he were daring them all to disapprove of him, but surely the most sedate mama could not fear a mere glance in a dance room?

Sophia lost sight of him as she was led out to dance by a stiff young man with a large Adam's apple, but a few moments later she saw him again, still alone, still wearing that air of mocking amusement.

The thick black curls that clustered on his head in a casually attractive tangle framed a face of power and intelligence, the hard lines of cheek and jaw arguing with the beauty of blue-green eyes set in a fringe of black lashes.

As Sophia stared at him, he turned and their eyes met. Even while her body went through the accustomed motions of the dance, she was aware of something in that direct stare that penetrated the normal social mask and went to the core of the personality. She felt stripped, the strange, compelling eyes boring through her head as though he could see the function of her mind. Sophia had never been so aware of herself in her life. It was as if by seeing her, he forced her to see herself from outside, throwing back to her the reflection of what he saw— no physical image alone, certainly not the girl she saw in the mirror when she dressed, but her whole self: mind, emotions, desires, mirrored for her by this stranger in one long glance.

She was both furious and awed. Instinctively, to hide herself from those alarming eyes, she jerked her gaze away, rather as an animal seeks cover from the eyes of man, fearing comprehension, and heard a soft laughter from where he stood.

Hot colour ran up her cheeks. Her partner looked down at her. Feeling her stiffen in his arms, he glanced around to discover the cause and scowled at the young man, seeing his eyes fixed on them. "Insolent puppy! I wonder James Whitley permits him to be present! I was never so surprised to see anyone in my life. It is beyond anything!" Then he broke off sharply, turned red and gaped like a landed fish, obviously afraid he had said something he should not have.

"Why should he not be here?" Sophia looked at him curiously.

He cleared his throat, stammered incoherently, "I beg your pardon, Miss Sophia. A slip of the tongue."

"What is?" Sophia was being mischievous now, amused by his unhappy face as he stared at her.

He was a city merchant with a receding hairline and lifeless eyes that it seemed only hostility could illuminate.

His desperate eye fell on Elizabeth and he gasped eagerly, "Why, how pretty Miss Elizabeth looks tonight!"

"So she does," Sophia agreed, sensing that she would get no more from him.

She suddenly saw her Aunt Maria staring across the heads of the dancers with a frozen expression. Turning, she realized that her aunt was watching the black-haired young man who, apparently at ease, was now leaning on a chair, his head cocked in mocking observation of the other guests.

Who on earth was he? Why did his presence seem to be unwelcome? Why was he here if everyone disliked him?

"I hope you are enjoying your visit to London?" her partner said.

She smiled politely. "Very much."

"Long journey from Somerset," he mumbled.

"Yes," she said. What a bore he was! Was this dance endless? Would she never escape him?

Her Aunt Maria was almost a stranger to Sophia, since her marriage twenty years ago had made her family cut her dead. It had infuriated the Stonors that Maria Whitley's husband had then become so wealthy that they were forced to regret their overhasty estimate of her choice of marriage partner.

Maria Stonor had met and married James Whitley during her third season in London, when her hopes of a good match had become so faint as to be mere ghosts of possibilities.

A silk merchant from Spitalfields in the East End of London, James had been the first real chance Maria Stonor had had of marrying a fortune, and the fact that he was in trade had only briefly weighed with her. Meeting him by chance at the house of a friend in better social circumstances, the surroundings in which they met had given James at first a spurious respectability in her eyes. By the time she realized his real social standing, she knew that, given encouragement, he would propose. The alternative seemed to her unbearable—a life of genteel spinsterhood in her family home in the country. She had accepted him and been cast off by her family in consequence, for the Stonors were an old family, short in the purse but long on pride.

Their home, Queen's Stonor, was one of the great houses of England, so beautiful that it cast a spell on all who saw it. Although time had laid a covetous hand upon it in recent years, wearing away the fabric in the relentless circle of the seasons, the wind and rain had made infinitesimal inroads upon its magical allure. The Stonor family had owned it since it was built. A passion for the house was bred in them. They grew up learning that life was short but Queen's Stonor was eternal. Maria Stonor had regretted leaving it ever since she married.

The decay of the house was gentle, an enhancement rather than a flaw, conferring a new beauty upon it in Sophia's eyes, making it finite, almost human. Small imperfections in a thing of beauty can breed new beauty, give potency to love, since the poignant threat of time's encroachment concentrates the heart.

Those years of Maria's marriage had, however, trebled James Whitley's fortune. He was a shrewd, hard man. He had built a handsome town house exactly in the latest admired fashion; his wife and children were dressed handsomely, and tonight Maria wore jewellery that dazzled the eyes, reflecting the candles in flashing brilliance as she walked about the room, as if she felt compelled to display the wealth for which she had sold her birthright.

Sophia was present tonight because of the decay of Queen's Stonor. There were no male heirs left, apart from Maria's eldest son Stonor Whitley, and eventually Edward Stonor had been forced through the humiliating procedure of approaching his sister to end the old quarrel.

Maria had been agreeable, indeed she had been eager, and after a long exchange of letters, it had been decided that Sophia should come up to London to visit her aunt and make the acquaintance of her cousins.

No attempt had been made to hide the idea behind this visit. Both Edward Stonor and Maria were hopeful that Sophia would marry Stonor Whitley, the heir to the house. It was a plan so convenient, so sensible that they shrugged aside the conventional dislike of marriage between first cousins.

Sophia was very young to be married, although early marriages were quite common in 1870. At sixteen her blue eyes were all Stonor, bright and wide beneath her dark brows. Her black hair would never curl in neat ringlets, flying out against all constrictions, especially when she had been riding hell-for-leather across the rain-swept autumn fields. Mud-streaked gowns or torn petticoats rarely troubled her. The only child of a vigorous, hard-riding father, Sophia had grown up in the saddle, loving the hours spent with Edward Stonor out in the fresh air. The delicacy and sweetness of her face conferred beauty on her; the passionate nature she had inherited was revealed in her smiles and glances.

Her mother had died when she was very young, and all her affections had been centred upon her father and her home. Edward Stonor took her everywhere with him. She was the darling of his tenants, a warm, smiling, loving little creature as a child, growing up into a young girl with the instant friendliness of someone who has been surrounded with love and concern all her life.

She had found it exciting to visit the dressmaker for the first time in her life and order new day dresses, new ball gowns, a new riding habit. Maria Stonor Whitley had sent the money with which these clothes were purchased. Sophia had to be dressed according to her station. Her trunks when she packed for London were therefore overflowing with lace-trimmed petticoats, nightgowns of stunning appeal, gloves, stockings, slippers and gowns. A cornucopia of bliss had been spilled for her. After years of making do it would have been surprising if Sophia had not found it thrilling.

The journey from Somerset had provided further excitement. She had never ridden in a train before. Travelling with a neighbour who had occasion to visit London, she sat in a window seat, staring out at rolling green fields that seemed to flash past alarmingly. The noise, the smell of smoke, the rattling of the wheels gave her a headache eventually, but she found it all enthralling, and Sophia had a great capacity for enjoyment. She entered upon pleasure with enthusiasm, eager to be pleased, still childlike in her simplicity of reaction.

She was unaware of being stared at by some of the men she met on that journey, too absorbed in her own impressions to be conscious of the impression she made on others. The fashionable clothes she wore gave her a new and unexpected allure, enhancing the rounded curves of her slender body, throwing into dramatic relief her warmly coloured features, the smooth skin, the large vivacious eyes, the generous pink mouth. Her nature was written in her face, but of that Sophia was totally unaware.

It was her first visit to London. The size, the noise, the foggy atmosphere overwhelmed her. She had driven past narrow, dark alleys, along roughly cobbled roads, before arriving at an elegant, modern square.

Queen's Stonor had set her ideas of beauty in one gracious, elegant mould, and she regarded the tall, handsome red-brick house of her aunt with curiosity and no admiration.

London was spreading fast in ever-increasing circles, outward from the central core, the hub of the city. New estates sprang up like mushrooms daily, their raw brick an eyesore under the grey skies.

Even to Sophia's innocent eyes the power of England's capital was obvious. She could almost hear the throb of London's heart as she stood in the Spitalfields square. Victoria had been on the throne for over thirty years, twice Sophia's lifetime, and in those years the industrial sprawl of English life had changed the whole landscape. Men had deserted the land in droves to labour in the growing towns. The green fields were empty, while the city streets were full. The ports resounded with the cries of dockers loading ships bound for foreign parts. Trade dominated the life of the nation, and to protect the trader, the English army went out across the seas guarded by English ships, to enforce the domination of the world. Trade followed the flag, and in 1870 much of the world map was coloured pink to indicate that England had a stranglehold on other nations.

Apart from minor skirmishes and the humiliating tangle of the Crimean War, England had been largely at peace throughout Victoria's reign and this was reflected in her prosperity. The men responsible for her wealth were men like James Whitley, merchants who bought and sold, who invested shrewdly and bargained hard. His success was visible in the raw newness of his fashionable town house.

Sophia had looked up the steps at the varnished front door and lifted her chin in what was, although she did not know it, a characteristic gesture of defiance, straightening her back as she did before she took a difficult fence.

Her first impression of her aunt's family had been of a strangely formal gathering in the elegant drawing room, as faces turned towards her as the footman announced her, faces which had a similar look to them.

"Welcome to our home, Sophia," her aunt had said, advancing with a rustle of black silk, holding out a pair of thin white hands whose delicacy betrayed her breeding.

Sophia had thrown aside her brief anxiety, her whole face lighting with the unconscious charm which made her instantly memorable. She had kissed her aunt and turned to face the other members of the family, who had risen to their feet to greet her.

"This is Stonor, my dear," Aunt Maria had said.

The tone of Maria's voice had been coy and Sophia had felt herself blush, but she had held out her hand to her cousin and smiled.

In fact the two boys, Stonor and Grey, were close in age and alike in appearance. Both had thin, pale faces and hair of a dusty shade of brown-gold that gleamed in lamplight. Their eyes were cold, grey and unsmiling. Stonor, she knew, was nineteen, but his manner gave him the gloss of maturity. He was totally self-possessed.

Holding her hand, he had looked into her face with narrowed eyes, studying her as closely as she studied him. Sophia could not help the appearance of her betraying dimple as she looked back at him, amused because she knew he must be thinking, as she was, that one day they might be husband and wife. It seemed so odd!

"You and your brother are so alike!" she had said. "How shall I ever tell you apart!" He had smiled, but later she had noticed that Grey had a white scar running down the side of his left cheek. Later she would come to recognize in him an uncontrollable temper and to learn that that scar was the physical revelation of Grey's emotional instability. When he was angry, it would seem to writhe as though it had a life of its own.

The girl, Elizabeth, was tiny, like a blonde doll, with Stonor eyes; bright blue, open, easily filling with tears. Her ringlets had a fairy-tale sheen. Her figure was well rounded despite her low height, and her lower lip had pouted as she kissed Sophia, as though she resented the other girl's obvious beauty.

When Sophia would come to know them better, she would realize that Elizabeth's easy emotions were shallow. Her real nature was akin to her brothers' coldness. She assumed poses that she supposed would be admired. It came easily to Elizabeth to pretend to possess the fashionable sweet modesty. Only the occasional avid gleam of her blue eyes betrayed her.

That evening Sophia had also met James Whitley, finding him polite but withdrawn, a short stocky man with the pale hair he had passed on to his sons, his eyes as cold and grey as theirs. He had made a few chilly remarks to her and then vanished. Sophia had noticed that his disappearance had left an unaccountable gloom upon the rest of the family and wondered if he had left because he still bore a grudge against her family for the twenty years of estrangement suffered by his wife.

Whatever the cause of his abrupt departure, his going had brought a tension into the room, which she had felt, and she sensed that tension now, watching Maria Whitley's face as she looked at the young man with black hair. There had been that same white anger in her aunt's face on that first evening as James Whitley left the room.

Suddenly the music came to a halt, and her partner stepped away from her. She smiled and curtsied, then laid her fingers on his dark sleeve so that he might lead her to a small gilt chair at the side of the room.

"May I procure you a glass of lemonade, Miss Stonor?" he asked, bending in a formal bow, his figure stiff in his evening clothes.

She thanked him, wondering secretly if she would ever escape from his intolerable dullness, and he slipped away through the throng that was passing into the supper room to search out the refreshments. Sophia amused herself by watching some of them, grateful for a few moments of relaxation.

Suddenly her eye travelled up a pair of highly polished evening pumps, along narrow dark evening trousers whose seams were braided with thin ribbon, past a cream waistcoat across which a gold chain glittered, and found herself looking into the dark face of the young man who had attracted her eye earlier.

"So, you're the cousin," he said, and she felt a peculiar excitement at hearing his voice for the first time. It was a voice as original as his appearance—cool, hard and charming. It betrayed the owner to be oddly aware of his own personality, more controlled and self-assured than someone of his age usually was, an almost wilful certainty in those tones.

She looked back at him, as open as he in her manner. "Yes, I'm Sophia Stonor. We have not been introduced, have we?" She knew they had not, but the rules of society dictated that she ask.

"So you don't know who I am? I saw you watching me, and I thought you knew."

His tone was curiously thoughtful, almost calculating, as though he were considering some course of action.

"I'm Wolfe Whitley," he said, observing her closely.

"Then you're related to Uncle James!" A smile lit her face, giving her the sudden, flashing beauty that she herself had never seen. She thought then that she understood why he was unwelcome here. Aunt Maria probably resented her husband's city relatives.

"You might put it like that!" His lip curled, although his eyes lingered on her with narrowed interest.

"So we're cousins of a sort?"

She patted the little gilt chair beside her, smiling at him, her blue eyes filled with amused enjoyment. She would show Aunt Maria that she was happy to acknowledge Uncle James's relations!

"Do sit with me! I'm so afraid that that dull young man will come back and bore me to death."

His laughter rang out. "Don't you like Bingham?"

"Is that his name? Isn't he a bore?"

"Deadly," he agreed, gazing at her. "My God, are you sure you're a Stonor?"

"You mustn't judge us all by Aunt Maria," she whispered, dimpling.

He laughed again. "I hadn't expected anything like you!"

"That's what Stonor said!"

His smile went. "Did he?" He stared at her sharply.

"Tell me about the Whitley family," she invited. "Are they nice?"

He gave her an intent, incredulous stare. "Oh, you must not ask me," he drawled. "I'm what one might term a prejudiced witness."

She laughed. "As you're a Whitley, I suppose you might be, but I'm open-minded."

He laughed again, his white teeth showing between his lips. Again he gave her that long, searching look. "I saw you arrive."

"I did not see you," she frowned. "I suppose you live nearby?"

He grinned but did not reply to that. Instead he said, "You got out of your cab and looked at the house with the most rebellious expression."

"I was dreading the next few moments," she admitted. "And wishing I were home again."

His mouth quirked sardonically. "Ah, yes, Queen's Stonor. We have all heard so much about it."

"Queen's Stonor is not a house anyone could forget. It was very hard to leave it." Her face was passionate, the colour flying into her cheeks, the conviction of love in her voice.

"Your aunt has been talking about it since the day she left, like Eve turned out of the Garden of Eden." He sounded cruel suddenly, his voice biting, and there was a contemptuous amusement in his eyes. She sensed that he did not like her aunt. Family loyalty made her bristle.

"You have not seen Queen's Stonor or you would not dismiss it so lightly. It has great beauty; everyone agrees so. Why, people come from miles around just to see it. There are places like that, you know, places with so strong a sense of their own that they leave an indelible impression on everyone who sees them."

He was watching her oddly. "Not just places. There are people like that too."

"Yes," she thoughtfully said, eyeing him, thinking that he was one.

For a while they were silent, staring at each other. Sophia was unaware of everything but him during those moments, unconscious of the effect her presence with him was having upon the other people in the room. The attention of the whole gathering was now focused upon them. There was something about the two young people that drew and held all eyes.

They were much of an age, Sophia still below seventeen.

Wolfe Whitley perhaps a year above it. He was a head taller
than she, his body lean and muscular, but they bore a certain
faint resemblance to each other as they sat, their dark heads
so close together, staring at each other with all the natural
curiosity of two young people meeting for the first time. It
was a resemblance not of feature but of nature, as though two
animals met in passing and recognized their own characteris-
tics in each other. Vibrant health, energy and confidence dis-
tinguished both of them. They shared a common force of
personality, as if a radiance encircled them, and if Sophia was
as yet unaware of herself, Wolfe gave an impression of controlled power that his youth could not quite disguise. He wore
an impression of maturity in the self-willed strength of his
face.

A sudden hush fell upon the crowded room. Sophia looked
up in surprise as Aunt Maria descended upon them with a
flurry of petticoats, her arm jerking Sophia to her feet.

Open-mouthed, she stared at her aunt and saw a white face
in which small nerves leaped and quivered. At that moment
the musicians struck up another waltz. The couples moved
onto the floor and began to sway to the music, but beneath
their bright, fixed smiles the whispers ran like the pattering of
mice, and they kept their excited eyes upon the little tableau
being played out in the corner of the room.

"You must not sit out a dance, my dear," Aunt Maria said
in a falsely bright voice. "Come, here is Stonor eager to dance
with you." She pushed Sophia somewhat ungently towards
Stonor, who slid his hand around her waist, his face unreadable, and moved her away into the swell of the dance.

Sophia kept a puzzled, alert eye upon subsequent events.
James Whitley joined his wife. A taut conversation began,
their voices never raised, Aunt Maria wearing a fixed public
smile. Her eyes moved away among her guests from time to
time, acknowledging those whose curious eyes met hers with a
gracious nod here, a little wave there, but all the time her
pallid lips moved acidly, as though the words issuing from
them tasted bitter on her tongue.

Behind the host and hostess, ignored by both but watching
them, lounged Wolfe Whitley, his manner still that odd con-
junction of power and lazy insolence. Whatever was being
said, it appeared to have no effect upon him but to amuse him.

Sophia glanced away and looked up at Stonor, finding him
watching her with an impassive expression.

Some might think him almost handsome, Sophia thought. Those perfectly formed features, the straight nose and fine-boned face, the hard pale mouth did give an impression of understated good looks, but his reticence and enigmatic courtesy somehow chilled her. Sophia's own open, warm nature responded more naturally to the casual, assured charm of Wolfe Whitley.

"Are you enjoying the party?" he asked in his cool voice.

"Oh, very much," she agreed lightly. "I am very fond of dancing and music."

"You have a great capacity for enjoyment, I imagine," he said considering, as though accusing her of something, and she felt an odd revulsion of feeling against him. She had already decided that Stonor was given to making enigmatic statements that held the seeds of hidden criticism.

His eyes were pale, cold, expressionless. She wondered what he was thinking and longed to shatter his composure, to ask questions about Wolfe Whitley, perhaps, since the subject obviously disturbed his mother, but even her superb self-confidence could not rise to such an effort. She felt sure that Stonor would freeze her with a glance. She had seen him reduce a servant to stammering shame with one word. She had no wish to feel the ice-cold sting of his tongue.

Instead she asked the question that had been puzzling her ever since her arrival. "I imagine you are named for our family, but why is your brother called Grey? It is an odd name."

"After my mother's cousin, Lord Grey of Strybourne."

"Is he related to us? I did not know."

Stonor's lips twisted. "Strange, my mother often mentions him to us!"

For some reason her ignorance of the relationship seemed to amuse him. Stonor had a way of smiling that she did not care for; it disturbed her. His face hid thoughts that she suspected she might not like. There was too much secret intelligence in his cold eyes.

"You make an interesting addition to our family, Cousin Sophia," he said now, watching her with that secret smile. "You are not at all what I had been expecting."

"What had you expected?"

"I'm not certain. Someone resembling my mother, I suppose. But you are nothing like her."

"I'm sorry," she said, hardly bothering to conceal her annoyance.

"I'm not," he said, and for some reason the way he said it threw her into confusion, her cheeks growing pink.

She looked down and longed for the music to end and release her from the circle of his arms. He danced quite well. She had to admit that. He was the best partner she had had all night. It was a pity she found him so unlikable.

"What are you thinking?" Stonor asked, watching her.

"Nothing," she said, looking at him through her long lashes.

"How small your waist is," Stonor said, tightening his arm around her. "Don't stop smiling, Sophia. I like to see you smile."

Sophia had never felt less like smiling in her life.

Maria Whitley knit her thin fingers together as if to still their trembling and spoke in a low voice, her tone made uneven by the effort to keep smiling as she spoke, conscious as ever of watching eyes. "How long must I suffer it? Is it not enough that I am humiliated in my own house, before my servants? Must you publish my shame to every soul I know in the whole wide world?"

"Maria, you exaggerate," said James Whitley with a weary sigh, rubbing a hand across his face.

"Exaggerate? How can you say so? I told you how it would be if you forced me to permit him to be present tonight. He has always been insolent, but tonight he surpassed himself. To approach my niece, my brother's child, to take advantage of her innocence in order to make mischief, to make her a public laughing-stock! He knew what talk it would make, he did it deliberately. Never tell me otherwise! Look at their faces." She swallowed, her thin throat moving in a convulsive fashion. "Every one of them burning to leave our house so that they may spread the tale around London! They all know who he is, everyone knows. Had he kept out of the way there would have been no scandal, but no! He had to stir up trouble, and he enjoyed doing it."

James Whitley looked over her head at his son, whom he had named Wolfe in honour of the famous British soldier he admired more than any other man in the world; Wolfe, the hero of Quebec, who had died at the very hour of victory. Within the quiet, blunt exterior of James Whitley's face emotion seethed whenever he thought of his bastard son. He felt no part of himself in his two legal sons, begotten as they had been—respectably, upon a shrinking woman who had sold herself into matrimony of her own volition and yet resented honouring her bond. Maria had always behaved as though his touch defiled her, lying stiff and cold in his bed, making James Whitley feel each act he committed to be a shameful crime.

Stonor and Grey were physical counterparts of their father for all the world to see, yet James emotionally rejected them. They were their mother's children in spirit, not his, and he was never able to look at them without remembering things he preferred to forget. For the first few months of his marriage, he had been genuinely in love with his wife. It had been some time before he had realized how she felt and began with pain and anger to realize that she would never alter. Her physical revulsion towards him had killed that love, leaving him with a need that he had satisfied elsewhere. Maria had been almost pathetically grateful when he ceased to visit her bed, but her gratitude had not remained once she knew about his mistress.

Towards his bastard, born of mutual love, he felt all he had never been able to feel towards his other sons. In his relationship with Wolfe, James Whitley, the hard-headed, shrewd businessman, was vulnerable.

"And what was he saying?" Maria was demanding in a shrill whisper. "What mischief has he sown? If Sophia has heard the truth from his vile lips, she will be dreadfully shocked, poor child."

"She seemed quite taken with him, it seemed to me," James returned rashly. He had noticed the way the Stonor girl had smiled at Wolfe, and it had pleased him. He had meant to dislike the girl. Her family had done him nothing but ill. All that had changed suddenly when he saw how Sophia smiled at Wolfe. The boy got few smiles in this house. Never had his father seen him show such interest in anyone. Normally he prowled the house like a savage dog in a house where they do not like dogs, the only smiles he gave and got a mere baring of teeth, meant for offence.

Maria was speechless with rage. Words trembled on her tongue but she was afraid to open her mouth for fear of losing all control. She had learned discretion in a hard school. She looked at her sturdy, quiet-faced husband and hatred filled her eyes so that they shone brilliantly in her white face.

James winced from that look. It was not pleasant to see such emotions directed at oneself. Maria usually wore a mask whenever they met, the politely smiling mask convention demanded of her. Maria would always wear whatever mask society dictated. For so many years they had lived apart, strangers and enemies beneath one roof, and their relationship was a tortuous one, the roots of it snaking out of sight and only the fruit visible to the eye.

Once one has loved, there is always this legacy of unforgotten feeling.

For a moment the two of them stared at each other across the great abyss dividing them.

"I insist that he leave at once," Maria said thickly. "He is ruining your daughter's birthday party."

James hesitated, then gave a curt nod. It was true, and although he felt little love for his daughter, who was too much her mother's child for his taste, he could not but admit in fairness that she had a right to enjoy her party.

It was true, too, that Wolfe had been mischievous in approaching Sophia Stonor. James would not concede so much to his wife, but he knew his son too well to doubt that her assessment of the situation was accurate. Wolfe had been up to something. He loved to see the sparks fly. It had surprised James when Wolfe had asked to be present at Elizabeth's party, but he rarely refused his son anything he asked. Wolfe could always twist him around his little finger.

James Whitley was half-aware of his own hidden reason for giving in to Wolfe's demand. For years he had used Wolfe as a weapon against Maria. It pleased him to force her to recognize his son. He got a form of satisfaction out of the situation, as though he were still punishing her for her rejection of himself all those years ago.

He moved away from Maria, joining Wolfe. "You'll have to leave," he said abruptly.

Wolfe smiled, showing his teeth in that attractively sardonic smile. "Blistered your ear, did she, Father?" It was typical of him that he never used the more formal Papa, as did the legal chidren, as if he knew instinctively that James got more pleasure from hearing him call him Father. Young as Wolfe was, he knew far more about James than his father realized. He had an instinctive understanding of human nature, a gift he had been born with, and he had needed it in this troubled household.

"You were bent on making trouble!" James eyed him with wry understanding.

"Was I?" Wolfe lifted one brow quizzically and met his father's hard stare head-on in a mocking smile.

"If you were younger, I'd give you a damned whipping!"

"You've never whipped me in my life!"

"I dare say it would have done you good if I had."

"I'd have hated you."

James looked at him and sighed. "Aye." There was a force in his son's face that he recognized and respected. Although Wolfe was younger than himself by nearly thirty years, the boy was already a considerable personality, one James Whitley would not care to take on in battle. There was a self-willed arrogance, a raw power in those bright eyes, as though Wolfe was the possessor of a strength he had not as yet learned to discipline. The potential in his face impressed on sight. James did not imagine he could ever have tamed the fierce spirit in the boy. He might have made him hate him, as Wolfe said, but he had instinctively backed away from confrontation and, although it might be said to be weak, his policy of pandering to Wolfe's every whim had made their relationship a happy one. Sometimes, James thought, Wolfe almost patronized him, as though it were he who were the elder.

"Well," he sighed, "you must leave. I wish you had not played the fool and brought this bee swarm down about our ears, boy. I had trouble enough in getting her to agree to your presence tonight in the first place." Maria had been shrill, well nigh hysterical, but in the end, as always, James had beaten her down. "If she'd not been so eager to see Stonor married to that niece of hers, she would never have agreed. She wanted to keep me sweet. I was surprised she said yes until I saw why." He stared at Wolfe. "I was even more surprised that you wished to come. Why did you suddenly take it into your head to be here tonight?"

"I saw her arrive," Wolfe said, his eyes moving in search of Sophia.

James looked at him in dismay. "My wife and her father mean to marry her to Stonor. Don't get ideas into your head."

"Beautiful, isn't she, Father?" Wolfe said, his blue-green eyes on Sophia's bright curls as she moved to and fro, the light turning the black hair to an iridescent gleam. Her skirts billowed around her as she was swung to the lilting waltz music. Her enjoyment of the dance emerged in laughter, vivid and alive, in a flash of excitement that died as she looked up to meet Stonor's close stare.

James Whitley watched Wolfe anxiously. The boy sauntered away towards the door, arrogant, casual, followed by stares of which he seemed unaware, and vanished without a backwards look.

Sophia grew increasingly weary. At Queen's Stonor they were abed early, waking with dawn's light to breakfast on cold meat and be in the saddle by eight. She looked at the blaze of candles and wondered afresh at them. She had rarely seen so many. Her aunt's household was equipped with modern lamps for everyday use, but tonight they had abandoned those for the more romantic candles. They were sinking now, their flames flickering as the guests began to depart. People yawned and looked pale as they drifted towards Aunt Maria to make their farewells. Elizabeth, at her mother's side, was flushed with dancing and excitement, kissing the women as they left, having her hand kissed by the gentlemen.

When Sophia listlessly joined her, Elizabeth wound an affectionate arm around her cousin's waist. "Oh, I did enjoy the party!" She leaned her head towards Sophia, whispering, "Did you like him? He danced with me twice. I did not dream he would stand up with me again after the first time. Mama was watching and she frowned at me, but I do not care!"

Sophia was amused. She had not particularly noticed Elizabeth's partners, being quite enough absorbed in her own, but she did have a vague recollection of a pleasant, open-faced young man in brown who had blushed on being presented to her, and whom she fancied she had seen gazing at Elizabeth with a look that might have signified particular regard.

"Tom Lister?"

"Yes," Elizabeth sighed rather than said, making the name sound magical.

How strange, thought Sophia, that each separate person who had attended tonight would carry away a totally distinct and different impression of the evening. She, for her part, would always remember it as the evening on which a darkly handsome young man had said to her, "So you are the cousin." Elizabeth would remember it as the evening on which she had danced twice with Tom Lister.

"He is a very pleasant young man," she offered, realizing that her cousin waited for her to make some comment on him.

"Oh, isn't he?" Elizabeth agreed enthusiastically.

"Does your mama not approve of him?"

Elizabeth pouted. "She does not think he would make a good enough match for me. She wants me to wait. I will be a shrivelled old spinster if she has her way."

Sophia eyed her with amusement, her pink lips parting in a grin. "Somehow I doubt that."

Elizabeth gave a giggle. "So do I," she whispered, and then since everyone had departed and the house was empty, they slowly made their way upstairs, leaning upon each other like weary swimmers, arms around each other's waist.

A yawning footman snuffed out the candles. The windows were opened wide to let the cool night air blow through the overheated rooms. Maria Whitley watched her daughter and her niece vanish, then turned and looked at her husband.

"Tomorrow, Maria," he said flatly. "For God's sake, let it be tomorrow. I'm for bed."

"Her bed," Maria whispered thickly.

"When was I ever welcome in yours?"

"I'm your wife!"

He laughed in bitterness. "My God, do you think that excuses you? I'm a man, not a lap dog. If you deny me affection, why then, I must look elsewhere."

"Affection?" It was her turn to laugh, her face contorted in a sneer. "Is that what you call it?"

"It's what I receive," he said in sudden calmness. "You should be grateful to her. She has made my life in this house possible. Had she not been here, I swear to you I'd have left it long since; and so you know, or why have you blinked a blind eye at her presence all these years?"

"After tonight they both leave this house!"

He glanced at her with half-pitying amusement. "My dear Maria, you must be tired or you would not make such a ludicrous demand. They stay here, or I leave with them. If you do not wish to share this roof with us, you've an alternative. You are always talking of your ancestral roof! Doubtless your brother would offer you shelter beneath it."

The irony of his tone hit home. "You know very well that my brother..."

"Is on the point of financial collapse?" James smiled icily at her. "Yes, Maria; hence the arrival of his daughter in our house. You do intend her for Stonor, don't you? She is bait for my money. I know you've dreamed of seeing your son in splendour at Queen's Stonor. Well, I've no wish to stand in his way. I won't pretend I like him, but he'll have the money he needs. He'll inherit the estate anyway, under the entail, but he'll need my money to bring the estate back to life, won't he, Maria? You'll need my consent, my agreement. My money's not entailed. I may leave it where I choose."

She looked at him sharply, going even whiter. "You would not cut our sons out of your will?" He had been ruthless enough in the past for Maria to find that a terrifying possibility, one she had dreaded a long time.

"I recognize my obligation to them, my dear," he said, smiling blandly at her, enjoying the alarm in her white face. "Your sons will inherit sufficient for their needs, if, as I say, they show themselves obedient, dutiful sons." He looked at her out of his pale, cold eyes and the smile died on his lips. "To me, my dear. . . dutiful to me."

He had abandoned their children to her almost since their birth. James had made no attempt to win them, no attempt to show them affection. All his affection had gone to that other boy, openly, almost defiantly.

He turned away and walked towards the stairs, and Maria stared after him, trembling, hating him. In some recess of her mind, she knew that James was punishing her for her coldness to him in their marriage. He was a man who gave back hurt for hurt, and he had a long memory. In that, she dimly sensed, Wolfe Whitley took after him. The strange, proud boy had always returned with interest everything done to him.

James turned along a corridor on the second floor and went up a small, winding stair to a private apartment set apart from the rest of the house. Opening a door, he stood watching a woman who sat before a dressing table, brushing her hair with one pink, naked arm raised in a graceful curve above her head. She wore only a lacy petticoat that left her rounded bosom half-exposed.

She smiled at him in the mirror. "James."

He shut the door and went slowly over to her. She watched him approach, tracing the weariness and pain in his face.

Without a word she swivelled and put up a hand to his neck, pulling his head down so that his mouth touched hers. James fell to his knees and kissed her hungrily.

"What is it?" she asked him later as they lay in bed together in the warm glow of a dying fire, the lights extinguished and the bed curtains drawn back because Lucy loved to watch the reflection of the flames on the ceiling.

"Hmm?" He was unwilling to talk. She had eased his pent-up emotions and soothed him to a form of content. He had no desire to dwell on a subject that only angered him to no purpose.

"Where is Wolfe?" She turned her head lazily, her silken flesh touching him as she moved. "I expected him to come in and see me after the party, but I suppose he has gone off prowling again. I wish you would put a stop to it, James. He will end in trouble. Where does he go on these night excursions of his? Whom does he visit? The pair of you will shut me out, I know, and never speak of these things in front of me."

He gave her an ironic smile. "Believe me, you'd rather not know."

She sighed. "Did he enjoy the party?"

"He did in his own peculiar fashion. He was mischievous."

"What did he do? Don't say there was another quarrel with Grey?" Lucy gave him an alarmed look, her face tensing.

"Worse than that. He paid too much attention to my wife's niece. He knows very well that they intend the girl for Stonor. Wolfe will always do what makes the most trouble. Of course, the girl wasn't to know. She had no more idea who he was than a babe in arms. Wolfe took advantage of her."

Lucy sat up, the sheet falling away, exposing her magnificent body in all its naked beauty. "Was there a scene?"

"The making of one." James's face tightened. "Stonor was quick to create a diversion, but everyone in the room stared, and Maria was furious." He put a hand to her back, stroking her warm skin. "For a woman of your age, you're indescribably lovely, my dear."

She ignored that. "What did Wolfe do then?"

"He was saucy to me, laughed and left." James gave a bark of sudden amusement. "He's a cool hand, Lucy, for a lad of eighteen. Damn me if I didn't feel less in command than he was! I dare say he went off in search of more accessible petticoats."

Lucy looked indignantly at him. "And you did nothing to deter him, I suppose? What if he takes the pox from his pleasures?"

"Why, how d'you suppose I could deter him?" James had a wry look. "I wish I could. Wolfe has always been a knowing one. But better we should be aware of his pleasures. Wolfe is at least open in his pursuits. I hate a secret lecher. I suspect

Stonor of having a penchant for such pleasures, but he hides it too well.''

"Stonor makes me shudder," she muttered. "He's sly and cold and full of secret hatred. Whenever he sees me, he looks through me, yet I always feel as though he spat at me."

James didn't reply. His frown deepened and the weary look returned to his face. His feelings for his eldest son were complex, even more tangled than those for his wife. Stonor was a mystery to him. He did not understand him at all and he did not like him, either. His treatment of him as a small child had made their relationship barbed. They spoke politely to each other, and beneath the ice moved dark waters. Stonor puzzled and alarmed James Whitley.

Looking sideways, Lucy was filled with remorse. "Dearest," she breathed, enfolding him in her arms. "Forget them."

A coal fell through the grate. The shadows flickered on the ceiling. James slowly drifted into sleep, his head pillowed on her warm, naked breast.

Wolfe Whitley stood in a narrow alley running down to the dark Thames, fumbling in his breeches pocket and cursing. "Damned whore," he said aloud. "Cleaned me out! I'd swear I had a handful of silver when I met her." Then he laughed, throwing back his dark head, the sound bouncing back off the clammy walls of the houses. "Why, damnation take all women! She did as I needed, so she's welcome to the money."

He stumbled as a rat slid past his foot, skidded on a foul-smelling pile of rotten food left there by a householder and banged his head on a warehouse door. The pain lifted him temporarily from his drunken stupor. He cursed again, rubbing his head.

For a moment he leaned against the wall, fighting down a wave of sickness and pain.

Through the haze of his clouded mind a sound penetrated, the sound of running footsteps and shouts. He peered ahead to where the moonlight gleamed briefly on the waters of the river.

Silhouetted against that bright gleam he saw a huddle of figures. Two or three men seemed to waver, struggling together. Then there was a splash, a strangled cry and the men left on the wharfside stood for a moment, staring at the river, then turned and ran back along the riverbank.

Their footsteps faded into the distance. Wolfe shook his

head to clear his thoughts, then he began to run, too, towards the water.

When he arrived on the wharf, he saw a figure struggling blindly against the running current. Wolfe flung off his jacket and shoes and jumped into the cold water, which hit him like pain and made him wince in shock. He was a strong swimmer and he needed to be. The tide was running fast, trying to sweep him away. Somehow he reached the drowning man and began to take him under the armpits from behind. The man hit out in panic. Wolfe struck him once, hard, and the body went limp in his hands. He towed it carefully towards a rotten flight of wooden steps.

It was not easy to drag the body ashore without help; it was heavy as lead, the water ran from it constantly and the arms hung and impeded his progress, but at last he laid the man out on his back and began to squeeze life back into him, his strong young hands thudding down on the limp body.

At last the mouth opened and belched muddy Thames water. Wolfe grinned and sat back, panting, hearing the gasping of air in the man's sodden lungs.

A few moments later he helped the other to his feet, supporting him as he swayed unsteadily.

"You're a big fellow," he said, wheezing as the great, powerful frame sagged against him.

"You're not small yourself," the other whispered hoarsely, his throat obviously still sore from his experience. Wolfe noted the London accent, familiar to him from his adventures in Ratcliffe Highway. The other pushed him away and stood on his own two feet, breathing thickly. "Curse it, I'm as weak as a mouse."

"There's the Black Dog a hundred yards off," Wolfe suggested. "A jug of home-brewed will put new strength into you."

"Not the Black Dog," said his new friend. "I've no wish to go back into the river."

"Oh, like that, is it? Are you safe at the Turk's Head?"

"Safe as houses."

They steered a silent course through a maze of tiny, dark alleys pervaded by the rotten odours of river and decaying wood. London's dockland lay all around them, the haunt of seamen from all parts of the globe, with every vice possible and all for a very small outlay. The Ratcliffe Highway was an ancient route running along the north side of the Thames, crammed with dozens of decaying streets from which the poor spilled day and night in foul, ragged clothes. A century earlier it had been worse because there had been no attempt whatever during the eighteenth century to cleanse the cesspool of the vice that had swirled here even then, but now, in the last quarter of the nineteenth century, reforming hands were at work, although as yet the dockland showed little sign of it.

Reformers had begun to fight to rid the city of constant outbreaks of typhoid and cholera by cleansing the water supply. They had begun to force unwilling parents to send children to school. They had made it legally impossible for a man to employ a child below the permitted school-leaving age. The reforms were slow, hard-fought and not always successful, but they had begun.

Of course it was still possible to find child prostitutes in these streets, to be knifed and die in a gutter, to drink oneself to death on cheap gin. Poverty is a powerful motivator. It was better to be corrupt than starve to death. Men living with despair had no scruples.

Wolfe Whitley had found his way here because his nature drew him to the dark, dangerous streets, and he had survived in them because he was dangerous himself. They were a jungle, but Wolfe was a wild animal, the more dangerous because he knew what he was about. He had no illusions and he enjoyed the very risk itself.

When they came to an ancient, tumbledown inn overlooking the river, lights still gleamed within although the night was half-done, and voices raucously bellowed a bawdy song.

When they staggered into the taproom, silence fell as they were closely observed. Then someone said, "Eh, it's Black Strap Smith. Been for a swim, Black Strap?"

Laughter roared, then died as Wolfe's sodden companion glared around at them all, his blackened teeth bared in a snarl that gave him an unpleasant look.

"I'll take your private room, Rummy," he snapped to the bloated barman. "Is there a fire in it? If not, light one."

He turned back to Wolfe. "Take a drink with me, friend."

Wolfe hesitated, shrugged and nodded. "Thanks."

They went up the private stairs, watched by the whole of the crowded public bar, and only when they were out of sight did the noise recommence.

The tiny room above had an odour of tar, rope, and coal smoke. The table was ringed with wet stains. The barman cleared a fistful of empty mugs in a deft sweep of one fat arm.

"Bring us a bottle of Jamaica," Black Strap told him.

"Aye," the man growled.

Wolfe was impressed by the assiduity with which the barman served his companion. Clearly Black Strap wasn't a man to argue with or cross. Why, then, had he been thrown into the river, and by whom? Enemies who had caught him unawares, perhaps? Many men from these dirty streets ended up in the river, even in the year 1870. The prim respectability of Victorian society ended at the outskirts of the slums.

The rum came and Black Strap heated it over the fire in the long-handled metal container kept handy for the purpose, then poured it steaming into pewter mugs.

"Here's to yer right arm," he grunted, toasting Wolfe. "What name d'ye go by, lad?"

"Wolfe."

Black Strap eyed him. "Wolfe, eh? You're a mighty pretty wolf, ain't yer? How d'ye earn yer bread? Got a woman to earn it for yer? A face like yours fetches 'em in, I'll lay."

Wolfe knew better than to answer that question. He had learned the necessity of discretion early. He grinned, his eyes audacious, and the other man slapped his knee and roared with laughter.

"Yer young dog. Live around here?"

"Around," Wolfe said vaguely.

"That's right. Keep your lip buttoned. I like the cut of your jib, lad. If you ever need a berth, come to me. I owe you a favour. You can always find me here. If I'm not around, Rummy'll know where to lay hand on me."

"Thanks, I'll remember that," Wolfe said, holding out his hand.

The other stared at it, surprised, then grinned, his jowled face splitting with amusement. He spat on his grimy palm and clasped Wolfe's fingers, almost wringing them in his huge grip.

"I must be getting off," Wolfe said a moment or so later. Black Strap tried to persuade him to stay, but after a cheerful farewell Wolfe clattered down the stairs and out into the dark night. As he stepped along the muddy cobbles, avoiding foul pools, he whistled softly under his breath, barely aware of his damp clothes and hair. It had been an eventful night.

# CHAPTER TWO

On the morning after the ball, Sophia awoke later than was her custom, despite the rumble of traffic in the London outside. Flushed, lazy, she lay stretching under her fine linen sheets, considering at her leisure what had happened the night before, the strange sequence of events like a series of lantern slides seen by a flash of light; baffling, fascinating, full of unanswered questions.

She had become aware of the tension that pervaded the Whitley household, and perhaps she should have been aware of it before the party. Looking back over the time since her arrival in London, she realized that she had been given clues before but had not understood them. Behind the careful courtesy she had seen the basic unhappiness of her aunt and uncle, and it disturbed her, remembering that she had been sent to London for the express purpose of marrying Stonor.

That thought chilled her and her smile died, but she pushed away the thought of Stonor as another face imprinted itself on the inner backcloth of her blue eyes. Wolfe Whitley. Now, she thought, mischief in her face, he was another matter.

With a wild leap she flew out of her bed, her slender young body tangled in her long white nightgown, and rang violently for the maid whose services she was sharing with Elizabeth. She had already realized that her aunt would be deeply shocked if she knew that Sophia managed perfectly without a maid at Queen's Stonor. Maria Whitely had grown up during the earlier years of the house, when servants thronged the rooms, and she would not believe the changes the years had wrought. The heyday of the Stonor family was over. They had to manage with a bare minimum of service these days.

She waited impatiently for the stiff female to arrive, wishing she could merely do as she did at home—dress rapidly and run downstairs to eat a plain breakfast served only with the sauce of appetite, listening to Mrs. Buffell complaining of the weather or the price of meat while she shuffled around behind her. The stately observances insisted upon by Aunt Maria frustrated Sophia's quick, impulsive temperament. But she wished to please her aunt as much as she could, for her papa's sake, and so she waited, tapping her small feet, while the maid slowly proceeded to find her clothes for the day and dress her.

"Are my aunt and cousin down yet?" she asked, watching the elegant reflection of herself in the mirror.

"Oh, no, Miss," the woman replied primly, her voice conveying somehow that Sophia, in rising before she was expected, had committed some social misdemeanour. "Not after a party, Miss. I doubt they'll be down before noon."

Sophia grimaced secretly. She gave herself a last glance before she left the room. She was wearing a green-striped walking dress with a short train that rustled as she walked, the black ribbons at shoulder, waist and sleeves fluttering as she moved. The present fashion for a small bustle gave her outline a more rounded, feminine look, and the length of the hem at the back forced her to walk swayingly.

She sat down at the long, highly polished dining table and was ceremonially served by the haughty butler, his face expressionless although he somehow contrived to indicate that her arrival downstairs before any other member of the family had been an irritant to him and his staff, still busily engaged in clearing up after the evening's pleasure.

Her meal over, Sophia wandered upstairs again for want of other occupation and began to stroll about the corridors of the house, inspecting the decor and furnishings with curious eyes. Everything was so new, so beautifully kept. It lacked the shabby beauty of Queen's Stonor, but it breathed an air of wealth.

Finding herself in a corridor she could not remember having seen before, she went up a winding stair and stopped in surprise as she came face to face with Wolfe.

His eyes narrowed, inspecting her shapely young body, then lifted to her face, probing it intently. "Well, well, well, how do you come to be up here, Miss Sophia?"

She was flushed, excited by the sight of him, her eyes very blue. "Do you live in the house, then? I thought you were a guest," she said, with her customary direct manner of speech.

His mouth curled derisively. "You lack subtlety. You should draw out your information piecemeal, Sophia. I gather you're still unaware of my status in this house."

"There's some mystery, I know that." She gave him a grin. "I saw as much last night."

His hand lifted her small chin and he stared into her face as though memorizing it in all its detail. "And they'd marry you to Stonor," he muttered as if to himself.

She grew pink under his stare, her lids wavering. To cover her embarrassment she asked, "Do you object to talking about yourself?"

He shrugged, releasing her. "Why should I? You'll learn soon enough, and I prefer you to hear it from me." He patted the top stair and sat down, his long legs stretching out lazily.

Without hesitation Sophia joined him, her slender body squeezing in beside him so that his hard, muscled thigh rested along her skirts in intimate touch.

Wolfe turned his head and looked down at her unconscious face, intensely aware of the warm touch of her body against him. He could see that she was as unaware as a child. Confiding and trustful, she rested her hands on her lap in an easy attitude.

She looked around invitingly. "Well?"

He watched her. "I'm James Whitley's bastard," he said.

Her blue eyes opened wide, brilliant as sapphires in their dark-lashed setting. "Oh," she said softly, her pink mouth a circle of astonishment. She had not even suspected that.

Wolfe waited, his face intent, no expression in his eyes but a hard wariness about him as he waited to discover her reaction.

"How very awkward for my aunt," she said at last.

Wolfe began to laugh, his teeth very white against his curling mouth.

She looked at him indignantly. "Well, I dare say you see it differently, but she can't like it very much."

Wolfe stopped laughing and leaned forwards with a snarl on his mouth. "You stupid little girl, have you thought what hell life is for my father in this house? Married to a woman who despises him and avoids his very touch? He loves my mother dearly, she's given him all the happiness he's ever had. If it were not for her presence in this house, he'd have left it long ago."

Sophia's eyes rounded. "She lives here?"

"My mother and I have apartments up in this side of the house. For the sake of social pretence, they give out that my mother is the housekeeper, but the very servants know the truth. My father's wife pretends that my mother is invisible when she passes her. Her children do the same, although when I was younger, they taunted me as far as they dared, especially

Grey, who always gave me a string of obscenities when we met. His scar twitches when he thinks of me, I dare say."

"His scar?"

"Haven't you noticed it? I gave it to him."

"Why?" she asked curiously.

Wolfe's dark face contorted. "He called my mother a name I'll not repeat. He was fouler than usual, so I hit him. He fell and cut his face open on the edge of a table."

"Were you whipped?"

"I was never whipped in my life," Wolfe said with dry satisfaction. "No, his mother flew at me, screeching, and began to hit me, but my father took me away. Grey has hated me more than ever since. I've marked him for life." He seemed well pleased with that thought. "He'll not tangle with me in a hurry. He keeps his foul tongue to himself, although I see in his eyes what he wishes to say to me when we meet."

"Poor Grey," Sophia said with a suppressed note of laughter in her voice.

Their eyes met and the smile came out into the open. Sophia did not like Grey, either. She looked down, her fingers stroking down the broad green stripes of her skirt, and Wolfe watched. Slowly he put his own hand over hers and pushed her fingers down against her warm body. She looked at him, unafraid, yet surprised by the movement.

"Are you shocked, Sophia?" he asked, his voice deep. "Does the fact that I'm a bastard disgust you?"

"Should it?" She left her fingers under his, eyeing him with a mischievous smile. "I'm afraid it doesn't. My father's had a woman in the village since my mother died. She's a nice woman. She has three children, two boys and a girl. I don't know if they are all my father's, but Nan is, she is the youngest. She has Stonor eyes, bright blue. She's a pretty little thing. I'm very fond of her. I gave her all my old dolls last Christmas."

Wolfe's hands tightened upon her fingers, his eyes fixed on her smiling face.

"I'd thought you would be shocked and horrified," he said deeply. "A delicately reared young lady would shrink away on hearing of my birth."

Her brow wrinkled. "I imagine that that is why Aunt Maria did not tell me."

His lips twisted. "She had other reasons."

Sophia tried to look grave and failed. She was sorry for

Aunt Maria, but what she had seen of her so far did not inspire warm affection.

"It is all very sad. I wonder if my papa knows?"

"I doubt your aunt will have told him a word," Wolfe grunted. "She's not proud of it."

"I don't suppose she is," Sophia agreed. "But if she does not care for her husband, I wonder she minds that he has another woman."

He burst out laughing at this practical attitude, eyes dancing, and whispered, "You darling," before he bent his dark head to kiss her on her surprised mouth.

She drew back and said nervously, "How long have you lived here?"

"As long as I remember," he told her, smiling in an odd way, his eyes watching her. "We all grew up together, Stonor, Grey and I."

Her smile died as he mentioned Stonor. "Did you quarrel with Stonor too?"

Wolfe's lips tightened. "Stonor wouldn't lower himself. He is the sort who hates from cover, but of the two, he's the more dangerous."

"He frightens me too," she said involuntarily, shivering, and Wolfe leaned slowly forwards to find her mouth again.

"I didn't say he frightened me," he murmured, brushing his lips against hers. "And if he dares to frighten you, I'll cut his throat."

She laughed, then Wolfe's hand slid around the back of her head, searching for the white nape beneath her hair, and the sensation of his caressing fingers was so extraordinarily pleasant that her lids abruptly shut, as if she needed to concentrate on the delight of feeling him touch her. His hard lips softly teased her lips to open. Still uncertain of what was happening, Sophia slowly parted her mouth, and then Wolfe's kiss blazed into intense passion.

Golden fire seemed to explode beneath her closed lids. She trembled, agitated, feeling pulses awakening where she had never known them before, his exploring fingers now trailing over her body, lighting an explosive sensitivity wherever they touched. Drowning in him, she felt an insistent need to get away, not because his lovemaking was distasteful to her, but because it was the first time in her life that a man had touched her, and Sophia was already finding it far too enjoyable.

She pushed at his chest, gasping, "No, Wolfe."

He pulled away reluctantly, breathing in an erratic fashion, and they looked at each other in the shadowy light. He gave her a slight, crooked smile. "I don't want to frighten you myself, Sophia."

"It was not that," she said, honest as ever, and Wolfe's eyes held that increasing warmth that was altering them minute by minute from the sardonic insolence they had first worn when she saw them to an expression Sophia found hard to pin down yet very attractive.

"I think," he said huskily, "you had best come and meet my mother now. If we stay here, I couldn't promise not to do it again."

Still flushed and trembling, she smiled back at him. "Then perhaps we should not stay here," she agreed.

He touched her hot cheek with one long finger. "You are quite the loveliest thing I've ever seen. How lucky you woke up before the rest of them and came exploring."

"I always wake early," she smiled. "And this morning I was excited. I hoped I would see you again."

The blue-green gaze searched her face. "Are you always this honest, Sophia?"

She bit her lip, dimpling. "I shouldn't have said that, should I? Papa is always telling me I'm too direct. It comes of spending so much time alone with him. We say what we think to each other and damn the consequences."

His laughter roared out at that. "You swear too, delightfully, which no well-brought-up young lady would."

"Oh, did I? It must have slipped out." She was lightly indifferent to that. "Papa swears all the time. One can't help but pick it up. Does it shock you?"

"Never in a million years," he said deeply. "Nothing you can say or do will ever shock me, Sophia."

"Ever, Wolfe?"

They looked at each other very gravely, their eyes held, and Wolfe gave that crooked smile again. "Never," he said in a husky voice.

Then he waved her along the corridor at the top of the stairs and opened a door, standing back for her to enter. She paused, looking around the room curiously. It had a totally different feel from any other room in the house, and that atmosphere seemed to emanate from the woman who sat in it, her fingers resting upon the wicker bars of a bell-shaped birdcage in which a canary hopped and sang. Sophia, staring at her, received an impression of golden ripeness, firm high breasts, glinting ringlets and a smooth, warm face.

The sun streamed in through a window behind the woman's head, lending her a halo so that she seemed all radiance and light.

Compared with Aunt Maria, thought Sophia, who could blame James Whitley for turning to this woman? Even Sophia's innocence could visualize a man preferring the mature beauty of Lucy to her aunt's refined coldness.

The woman was staring back at her, her lips parted in silent astonishment.

Wolfe took Sophia's hand, enclosing her small fingers with a gesture the meaning of which the girl was blithely unconscious but which made his mother stare sharply.

"Mama," he said, "this is Sophia," as if he were making some momentous announcement, and for a second or two they were all frozen as in a tableau, looking at each other.

Then Sophia, impulsive as ever, dropped a little curtsy, offering her hand. "How do you do, Ma'am? I am happy to meet Wolfe's mother." She did not know what to call her since Wolfe had not mentioned his surname. He called himself Whitley, but presumably that was not his legal name.

Lucy's eyes searched her face incredulously. "Good morning, Miss," she said stiffly. She was so accustomed to receiving snubs and biting coldness in this house that she seemed unable to believe that one of the Stonor family was actually being friendly to her.

Wolfe smiled lazily, watching his mother, his eyes full of warm laughter. He realized the meaning of her expression, but she would soon, he thought, come to realize that Sophia's warm smile was the outward sign of a nature every bit as warm, a nature he was increasingly beginning to find irresistible.

Sophia looked around the sunny room. "How cheerful you have made your home! It reminds me of my own."

Lucy blinked. "It does?" She glanced at her son drily, her eyes conveying that she thought Sophia a fraud.

"How could this remind you of Queen's Stonor?" Wolfe asked sharply, a sudden dark brooding coming into his eyes, his mouth hardening as he regarded her. It enraged him to believe that she had lied, to begin to wonder if that sweet, impulsive friendliness was all pretence.

Sophia laughed. "Ah, you've been listening to my aunt.

She remembers it as it was in her youth, no doubt. We were a rich family then. We've come down in the world. Queen's Stonor is shabby and homely now, I assure you, and to my mind the better for it." Her face glowed with love as she thought of her home, and Wolfe, his eyes fixed on her, seemed suddenly to reflect that glow in his own eyes. His mother noticed the way he was looking at the girl, and an anxious frown began to crease the smooth, creamy skin of her forehead.

"Your aunt gives a very different picture of it!" Wolfe spoke with a biting amusement.

"Don't we always love the place where we were born? I remember when I was a little girl, I thought the world began and ended at Queen's Stonor. It surprised me very much the first time I left the park and found there was a world outside it."

He laughed. "I'm glad you did leave it. Imagine if we'd never met!"

Her blue eyes smiled into his. "Oh, I'm sure we would have. Somehow."

The canary lifted its beak and gave a little trill. Her eyes drifted to it and she frowned. "It's pretty, Ma'am, but it is sad to keep birds in cages. A boy in the village once had a thrush in a cage. It pined and never sang."

Wolfe frowned, watching her with a strangely sombre face.

Sophia gazed at the canary for a moment, then shrugged off her darker mood, giving him a little smile. "You will love Queen's Stonor when you see it, Wolfe."

"What makes you think I ever shall?" he asked drily.

"You must. I want you to know it. There's a special feeling about the house. All the people who lived there before us sometimes seem to be there still. One can't help feeling their presence. The house is happy. Do you know what I mean? As though they are just out of sight, just out of hearing, but if you turned a corner too quickly on the stairs or in the garden, you might see them. Very old houses are magical. Anything can happen in them."

Wolfe scowled, listening to her, peculiarly jealous of the deep note in her voice yet thinking with excitement that if she could love a house like this, she would blaze with life when she fell in love with a man.

"If that's true of all houses, I shudder to think what this one will be like to those who come after us," he said cynically.

His mother winced. "Wolfe!"

"Come, Mama, don't be hypocritical," he said, half-teasing.

Sophia was distressed by the expression on his mother's face and intervened to change the subject. "Such a strange name—Wolfe. Ma'am, how did you come to choose it?"

"My father named me after General Wolfe," he said before Lucy could reply. "You know him from your history books, Sophia? Some other generals complained to the king that Wolfe was mad, and the king said that if he was, he hoped he would bite the other generals."

Sophia laughed, never having heard the story before. "Well, it suits you. You look like a wolf—a savage, shaggy creature that may bite if provoked."

His eyes narrowed and he moved closer, speaking as if they were alone, his voice intimate. "Try it, Sophia. Provoke me."

Her breath came a little faster, her cheeks warm. "If you ask me, you need no provocation."

He moved even nearer, smiling. "No, none," he said, and she sensed that he would kiss her if she stayed close beside him and, blushing, moved away. He laughed at her sudden withdrawal, and Sophia laughed back at him over her shoulder.

Lucy stared from one to the other of them, her eyes alarmed. She had never seen her son look at anyone the way he was looking at this girl, and, remembering her lover's words about Wolfe's behaviour at the party the night before, she was dismayed. What was he at? Was he mad to try to come between Stonor and the girl chosen as his bride?

Her son had grown up faster than most boys of his age. For years now he had gone his own way, leading a secret life of which she could guess a little, but of which she actually knew nothing. He frightened her at times. He was devil-driven, a man already despite his few years, with powerful, stark desires and self-willed arrogance. She blamed herself. She had brought the boy into a household divided among itself, and he had grown up in it like a savage little animal, constantly sniped at from cover by the two legitimate sons, never at home in the house, always aware of hostility.

She had never been able to interfere with his life. Wolfe had made that impossible. From an early age he had gone his own way, ignoring complaints, pleas and anxiety. She had once thanked God for his strength of character. His life in this bitter house would have been hell for him without an iron nature, but now she wished vainly that he were not so headstrong. His pursuit of Sophia Stonor could only lead to disaster for all of them. The seeds of hatred had been sown long ago. Wolfe might precipitate violent harvesting.

"It was good of you to visit me," she said to the girl stiffly. "But I've no doubt your aunt will be looking for you."

"I've no doubt, either," Wolfe said drily.

"Yes, I must go," Sophia said regretfully. "I hope I'll see you again, Ma'am."

Lucy sighed. She hoped to God she would never set eyes on the girl's friendly, charming little face again. Any danger to Wolfe disturbed her. She was a loving mother, and she sensed that this girl threatened whatever security Wolfe possessed at this moment.

"I'll walk you down the stair," Wolfe offered, opening the door.

Sophia went out, smiling up at him, and Lucy was left alone, staring at the bright little canary in its wicker cage. Her face was sombre. Before meeting James Whitley, her life had been hard. He had given her comfort, happiness and love, but everything had to be paid for, and Lucy had had a deeply religious upbringing. She was afraid of the wrath of God, which might one day demand that she pay for her sin in becoming James's mistress. She felt a premonition of disaster in her bones.

On the stairs, Sophia was saying goodbye to Wolfe. "I liked your mother. She is very beautiful." Her eyes teased him. "Not like you at all, though."

He grinned, white teeth showing against his strong mouth. "Little tease. Aren't I beautiful?"

"Not a scrap," she told him wickedly.

"When will I see you again?" Wolfe asked, taking her hand and looking at her small fingers with intent interest.

"Tomorrow?" she asked, not even pretending to be surprised by the question, let alone shocked.

"How early?" he asked.

"I wake up at dawn," she admitted cheerfully.

"Good God." Wolfe made a face. His normal habit was to go to bed at dawn, but he did not say so to her, although she guessed something of that from his wry face. "I'll meet you here at seven," he said quickly. "On the stairs, where we met before. No servants ever come up here, so we'll be safe. I tell you what—I'll take you out to look at the streets before the city wakes up. London's a different place at dawn."

She knew that all the men of the household went off to work during the day. Stonor and Grey both worked for their father and drove with him in the carriage, returning the same way each evening. During the daytime, therefore, she was forced to spend most of her time with either Elizabeth or her Aunt Maria, and of the two she had decided she preferred Aunt Maria.

As in most human relationships, she found it most pleasant to be in the company of someone whom she knew liked her. Aunt Maria did not take to many people, but she had taken to Sophia from the first, probably because Sophia was a Stonor and, like herself, the daughter of the house that still figured in Aunt Maria's dreams as a lost paradise.

The obsessive passion for Queen's Stonor that ran through the Stonor family had become a dark growth in Maria, and she was happy to have someone with whom she could indulge her obsession. There was another factor in their relationship: Elizabeth despised her mother and showed it. Sophia felt pity for her aunt and, since her nature was so open, her sympathy shone through, and Aunt Maria turned to it like a cold flower to the sun.

Elizabeth's only interest apart from Tim Lister appeared to be shopping. She was content to spend hours walking around the busy London streets, comparing prices and materials, musing over a bonnet here or a ribbon there. Although Elizabeth would have been annoyed if she knew, it occurred to Sophia that her cousin had a gift for bargaining. She haggled sharply with tradesmen, her eyes hard. In another level of life she would have been a very efficient shopkeeper herself, but Sophia knew better than to hint at her view. Elizabeth would have been offended.

That evening Aunt Maria took pains to leave Sophia alone with Stonor after dinner, deliberately removing Elizabeth and Grey from their company. Sophia looked anxiously after them as they departed and caught Stonor's cold eyes on her.

"How have you been amusing yourself today, Sophia?" he asked, and she looked around at him with a flushed face.

"Aunt Maria and I talked."

"Of Queen's Stonor?" Again that dry, sardonic tone, the voice she was beginning to find familiar in him.

"Yes," she said defiantly, tossing back her head.

His glance lingered on the silken fall of her black hair. "You love your home very much."

"Yes." She found it difficult to talk to this young man. His nature was the opposite of her own, closed where hers was open, secretive where she was frank.

He watched her moving restlessly on the velvet buttoned sofa. "Would you play for me?"

The request was a relief to her and she rose at once, betraying her eagerness to get away. Stonor followed her to the piano and leaned upon it as Sophia broke into a gay waltz. While she played she thought of Wolfe, seeing his dark face reflected in the polished wood of the instrument. Her face softened and the music beneath her fingers changed to a dreamy, romantic melody. She played with unconsciously revealing depth, her mouth curved in a faint smile. Stonor watched the expressive motion of her face; the brightness of the blue eyes, the warm pink lips. Looking up once, she caught his stare. Stonor's face was oddly blank.

She retired to bed early, pleading weariness, and fell asleep almost at once, waking in the grey light of dawn to leap out of bed at once and dress herself hurriedly. When she rounded the corridor that led to the private stair, she met Wolfe face to face and they looked at each other with immediate pleasure. It seemed to Sophia that she had not seen him for days. Time had gone so heavily since they last met.

Wolfe took her out through a side door into the silent London streets. They walked from the elegant new square through narrow, grimy alleys to the river, where Sophia gasped in excitement to see one of the sharp-nosed paddle steamers that plied the river to Greenwich, the tall black funnels solid against the sky. Her eyes fell from it to the shoreline and watched in shocked disbelief as an old woman in a ragged shawl waded waist deep through the filthy water spewing from the mouth of a sewer and began searching for something, her thin lips mumbling as she probed the foul depths in which she stood.

Wolfe was watching Sophia as her eyes took in the old woman's appearance. Slowly Sophia turned to look at him. "What is she doing?"

"She's a tosher," he said indifferently. "A shore worker."

"What does that mean?"

"She's looking out for coins or little trinkets," Wolfe shrugged. "They're swept down the sewer now and then."

Sophia shuddered. "Poor soul, surely she could find something else to do?"

"If she could, no doubt she would," Wolfe said through his teeth, eyes angrily bright. "But in this year of grace eighteen hundred and seventy, old women like her have to take what they can get." The blue-green irises sparkled with sardonic rage. "We all have to take what we can get. The strong survive, Sophia. It is the weak who go to the wall."

Sophia shivered, and Wolfe looked at her with a sort of regret, as though wishing he could have said something else to her. "I should not have brought you here."

"I'm glad you did. Glad I saw her. Poor old thing." Sophia fumbled in her purse and brought out a handful of coins. She was about to call the old woman when Wolfe caught her wrist, shaking his head.

"Put your money away," he said sharply.

Sophia's eyes were surprised and shocked. "Wolfe! It is so little, and I have so much!"

He took a guinea from his own money and flung it in a glittering arc. The old woman's eyes, like those of a scavenging crow, followed it, and her skinny body moved fast, falling to her knees to find the coin where it sparkled in the mud. Wolfe took Sophia's arm and led her away without a backwards glance.

On the way back to the house, they paused in a street market. Wolfe bought Sophia an apple, and the stallholder, grinning, teased Wolfe about her, making it clear to Sophia that Wolfe was well known around these streets. She could not imagine Stonor or Elizabeth becoming the butt of vulgar jokes.

"You keep 'im in at nights, lady," the man shouted after her. "'E'll catch something going down after the Ratcliffe ladies."

Chuckles came from the other stalls and Sophia glanced sideways at Wolfe. "What does he mean?"

Wolfe's lips twitched in amusement. "We must take a look at the highway some time," he said. "Then you'll see."

Sophia was not sure she did not see already. "I suspect you are a wicked young man, Wolfe," she said, laughing, and Wolfe looked down at her with laughter in his own eyes.

"Does it shock you, Sophia?"

"Horribly," she said, dimpling.

"Liar." He took her hand and kissed it, his mouth moving on her warm palm.

"I wish I were a man," Sophia said thoughtfully. "How much more free men are. What fun they have."

Wolfe roared, his head flung back, the strong throat moving in a deep laughter. "I'm damned glad you're not, my darling. We will have much more fun together as we are, believe me."

She had a narrow escape when she slipped back into the house, almost being caught by Stonor as he came down to breakfast in his formal city clothes, his face as shuttered as ever.

He looked hard at Sophia as she entered the breakfast room ten minutes later. "You're very flushed, Sophia. Are you well?"

"Very well, thank you," she returned, the brightness of her eyes betraying her happiness. Stonor stared as she began to eat, his brows knitting.

At Aunt Maria's suggestion that evening, Stonor took her out to dine in a restaurant. They were leaving as Wolfe sauntered into the house. Stonor turned his head aside, ignoring his half-brother. Sophia gave Wolfe a little secret glance, delighted to see him, and as he passed her, Wolfe brushed his hand against hers in a private caress that she carried with her as she followed Stonor into the family carriage.

Wolfe stood on the step watching as they settled themselves before the carriage moved away. Stonor was watching Sophia's bright, unguarded face as she looked back at Wolfe. Suddenly he turned his pale gold head, and across the pavement his eyes met Wolfe's. Wolfe regarded him, his eyes sharply narrowed. The carriage drew away, but Stonor stared from it, his features drawn into a hard, cold mask.

Over dinner Stonor asked her about her home and her father, listening intently to her answers, although Sophia found it hard to be as frank and open with him as she was with Wolfe. Something in Stonor held her at arm's length, chilled her, alarmed her. His eyes watched her as though they read everything about her, yet he showed her nothing of himself. She felt as though there were a wall between them that Stonor had no intention she should ever pass, and this secrecy increased her unbidden feeling of hostility towards him.

She met Wolfe again the following morning. They wandered slowly together in the wakening London streets, the cobbles

piled with rotting refuse, passing a policeman in a steeple hat
who eyed them suspiciously until Wolfe grinned at him. Then
he grinned back and said, "Good morning, sir, out early."
And then with a twinkle, "Or home late, eh?" His amused
eyes touched on Sophia, who smiled back at him. Then he
trod on with heavy feet, and Wolfe looked down at her with
that deep warmth in his eyes that came only when he looked at
her, tucked her hand into his own and squeezed it.

They talked freely, passing from one subject to another, almost unconsciously laying themselves open to each other;
hiding nothing because with them there was no need for any
of the social masks custom imposed, no necessity for self-
protection.

Sophia watched Wolfe when he spoke to people they met,
seeing the light charm that made them respond, and seeing,
too, the underlying hardness of nature that made them keep
their distance all the same. Wolfe was a more complex
character than she had ever met, but Sophia felt more at ease
with him than with anyone in the world. Even her love for her
father, which had until now dominated her life, was gradually
passing into second place.

The London that he was revealing to her was a very different one from the city Stonor and Elizabeth knew. Wolfe
loved the life and gaiety of the dockland streets, a walk away
from the square in Spitalfields. The people were knotted in in-
escapable poverty but they worked and lived hard; noisy,
cheerful, warm, singing loudly, bellowing ribald comments to
each other.

Stonor took her to a polite musical evening at a friend's
house that night, escorting her in his usual cool fashion, his
fingers barely touching her elbow as he walked with her. Sitting among the well-dressed, civil ladies, Sophia remembered
the people she had seen that morning and suppressed a little
smile. Tonight their talk was all of servants, bonnets, the price
of fish. Sophia was so bored that she had difficulty suppressing a yawn.

Stonor took her home early, and as they got down from the
carriage, Wolfe emerged from the house. Sophia looked at
him sideways, a mischievous smile around her mouth, guessing at once that he had waited until he saw them arrive before
coming out.

She deliberately dropped her gloves and Wolfe bent to
retrieve them, handing them to her with a little bow.

"Thank you," she said in a soft voice, letting her fingers linger against his before she withdrew them.

Stonor moved nearer her, paler than ever, and Wolfe gave him that hard, piercing look that was as much his nature as was his charming smile. Stonor looked odd, Sophia thought, suddenly worried in case he had guessed something of her secret relationship with Wolfe. She had been playing with fire deliberately when she smiled up at Wolfe like that, not imagining that Stonor would notice anything.

The two young men eyed each other like dogs squaring up for a fight, silently bristling, an obsidian glitter in their glance. There was a curious silence. Then Wolfe strolled away, swinging a cane, his footsteps dying away on the night air, and Sophia moved towards the house with Stonor just behind her.

# CHAPTER THREE

Two days later Elizabeth took Sophia to visit the Tower of London, surprising Sophia, since she had not expected her cousin to show much liking for sightseeing. Sophia had seen little of the famous London attractions since she arrived, and she was eager to view the old citadel.

"You will wish to drive through the prettier part of the city, Cousin," Elizabeth said as they drove away. "I am afraid the route to the Tower is not a pleasant sight. They really should do something about the slums. Tom says it is time we had another fire as they did when London burned down." Her eyes had a shallow glitter as though she found the idea exciting. "That would be thrilling to see."

Watching the driver's shoulders, Sophia caught a muscular flicker of anger in them. She saw him turn his head as if to scowl backwards at Elizabeth's blonde head beneath its ravishingly pretty bonnet.

"Not very thrilling for the people who live here," Sophia observed drily.

"Oh, the poor always find another rat hole to go to; there are too many of them in London. It is all the fault of these radicals who whine about conditions. It never seems to occur to them that nobody asked these people to crowd together in squalid little tenements. They could go elsewhere. They are there because they like living hugger-mugger like rats in a sewer."

"You think they enjoy it? Would you, Elizabeth?" Sophia asked crisply.

Elizabeth gave a peal of laughter. "Oh, I wouldn't put up with such filth and squalor for a second."

Sophia eyed her. She could believe that. Elizabeth, beneath her pretty, blue-eyed femininity, was as hard as nails, capable of fighting tooth and nail for what she wanted.

"With your lovely face, Elizabeth, I'm sure you would soon find yourself in comfort," she said drily, and the driver's shoulders began to shake with silent laughter.

Elizabeth sat upright, angry colour in her face. Then she put a hand over her mouth, suppressing a giggle. "Sophia, that was not the remark of a lady," she said in prim tones belied by her expression.

"It was common sense," Sophia said, unabashed.

They had passed through the narrow, choked streets that led down to the river. Sophia saw gulls wheeling and diving above the waterfront, fighting for scraps flung to them as women sorted baskets of newly landed fish. The white wings and cruel yellow beaks flashed through the sky. Small boys in ragged jackets and torn trousers rolled to their knees were wading through the shallow water, searching the shoreline.

"Mudlarks," Elizabeth yawned. "They make a living selling any old bottles or coins they find."

"Poor children," Sophia said, her mouth quivering. Their muddy faces were pinched and wan beneath the grime, and some of them looked no more than six years old.

She had never seen poverty like this in Somerset. The villagers on the whole were clean and healthy, all with a trade of their own to follow, having a place in their society. They had gardens filled with vegetables, some kept hens or even a pig, and they caught game on the common land, where they could trap as they pleased. There was no great variety in their daily diet, it was true. They lived on bread and cheese some days, but most of them had fresh meat once a week if not more often, and eggs and milk were cheaply available to them.

Her father could no longer afford to maintain his coverts as he had. The gamekeeper did his best, but poachers were rampant on the estate, and many a villager ate the squire's pheasants or rabbits at his own convenience.

Edward Stonor seemed to accept it all. He turned a blind eye to the poachers, chucked the village children under the chin and said happily: "Well, they're a fine-looking crew."

Judging by the look of the mudlarks, London children never saw meat from one year's end to the next.

The driver touched his whip to his tall black hat as Elizabeth ordered him to leave them at the Tower and return in two hours.

Behind Elizabeth's back Sophia ran a loving hand over the sweating backs of the two greys that drew the carriage, grinning at the driver, who winked back at her.

She felt a chill in the air of the old grey fortress as she walked into it with Elizabeth over the dry moat. The stone walls had a grim obduracy that reminded her oddly of Stonor.

"Up from the country as you are, I've no doubt Stonor seems very different from the other men you've met," Elizabeth said patronizingly.

"Yes, very different," Sophia said truthfully, not adding that he perplexed and disturbed her.

On the well-known lawns great ravens waddled like venerable clergymen under the beneficent eye of red-clad beefeaters with their gold buttons. They saluted politely as Elizabeth and Sophia passed, hopeful of a tip, she suspected.

"I took a great deal of trouble memorizing some facts about the place," Elizabeth said with a bored air. "This is the White Tower, where Queen Elizabeth was kept a prisoner along with a lot of other tedious people whose names escape me."

Sophia laughed. "Pray do not trouble yourself, Cousin. I shall enjoy just looking around. I doubt I shall remember anything you tell me, anyway."

"Oh, it is dull, isn't it?" Elizabeth agreed with relief.

They came out onto the green riverbank, where a line of ancient cannon pointed across the Thames as if expecting an invasion at any time from the dreary wharves on the south bank. Sophia, whose feet ached, sat down on a bench with a sigh and the next moment caught sight of Tom Lister striding towards them.

Elizabeth said quickly, "Promise you will not tell Mama a word about meeting Tom, Sophia."

"I'm not a telltale," Sophia said with a grin.

"I knew I could rely on you," Elizabeth said with satisfaction. "It is not often I can contrive to get out of the house alone, and if Tom calls on us, Mama sits there like a sphinx, watching us, never leaving us alone for a second."

"I wondered at your seeming so eager to escort me on a sightseeing expedition," Sophia rejoined, her eyes dancing.

Elizabeth gave her a cunning little smile, her china-doll's eyes bright. "You don't mind, do you, Sophia? Mama is much more lax with you and Stonor, you know."

Tom Lister joined them a few seconds later, and Elizabeth gave him a fluttering, flirtatious look.

"What a coincidence to meet you here," Sophia said mischievously, and the poor young man blushed scarlet.

"Shall we walk?" Elizabeth asked, giving Sophia a meaningful glance.

"I couldn't," Sophia groaned. "My feet ache so. Please excuse me, Mr. Lister. Why don't you take Elizabeth to see the rest of the Tower?''

He made a brief pretence of hesitation, and then the two of them moved off together and Sophia relaxed, watching the crowded waters beyond the bank. The river curved like a grey snake between wharves and mud banks, the gulls shrieking overhead.

A lean figure suddenly dropped down on the bench and, startled, she looked around into Wolfe's dark face.

"What are you doing here?" she asked breathlessly. "Someone might see us together."

"The coachman told me you were here. I saw Tom Lister walk off with Elizabeth, the shallow little bitch. I wish I could believe he would wake up and see the real girl beneath those pretty blue eyes, but poor Tom is blinded by them. When he realizes what she is, it'll be too late."

"You shouldn't be here, Wolfe," she said anxiously. "It will cause trouble if we are seen together."

His eyes smiled at her. "So it will," he said without caring.

She looked down the river, sighing. "You know I'm to marry Stonor," she said. Their secret meetings were all that was making her London visit bearable, but she could not close her eyes to the facts of her situation.

He sat upright, watching her. "You said you would never keep birds in cages, remember? If you married him, you'd be shutting yourself up in a cage from which you would never escape."

"It is not so simple. My father is ruined. I have to marry Stonor."

"Stonor inherits the house anyway," Wolfe pointed out.

"But Stonor does not love it as I do," she said seriously. "It is not only money the house needs, it is love."

"You would sell yourself for a house?" His eyes flashed savagely.

"You don't understand," she said, biting her lower lip. "Stonor is my father's choice for me. Queen's Stonor is dying, and I have to save it. It is my father's wish, and I love my father. I love Queen's Stonor."

"And me?" Wolfe asked in low, harsh tones.

She stared at his bitter face, seeing a look in it she had never seen before, a strength and purpose that frightened her. He moved forwards and caught her arms, his mouth brutally parting her lips, forcing her surrender without any of the ten-

derness he had shown her at other times. The driving demand
of his mouth went on until she ceased to struggle, and then his
hands moved down her arms to close over her breasts in a
gesture of silent possession to which Sophia found herself
weakly yielding.

Wolfe groaned, brushing his mouth against her white
throat. "You mustn't think of Stonor," he whispered huskily.
"You're mine. We'll find a way, believe me. My father will
smooth our path for us. Trust me, my darling. I'll speak to
my father, get him to settle some money on you so that we can
be married soon." His arms caught her closer, his hands
fondling her body passionately. "Soon," he repeated. "I
don't think I can bear to wait."

Voices drifted to them from a distance, and both recognized
them. Wolfe leapt away from her, gave her a brief, passionate
glance and vanished.

Elizabeth and Tom joined Sophia a moment later, Eliza-
beth giving her a sweet, insincere smile. "Here we are again,
Sophia. Not bored, I hope? Oh, I'm so glad you came to stay.
I've always wanted a sister."

Tom Lister gave her an adoring smile, believing every word,
and Sophia felt sorry for him.

After dinner a day later Aunt Maria sat talking to Sophia in
the drawing room, her gown rising and falling over her thin
bosom as she spoke eagerly of Queen's Stonor, her white
hands clasped eagerly together on her lap.

"Oh, the balls we had in those days! Half the county would
be there, and the rooms would be lit with hundreds of
candles."

No wonder the money had vanished, thought Sophia drily
as her aunt talked of visits to Bath, where she had danced with
eligible bachelors and drunk from the bitter spa waters with
the other visitors.

"Your grandmother, my dear, once danced with the Duke
of Wellington," Aunt Maria said, her voice reverent.

Old Hooky, Sophia thought, suppressing a grin. The tale
was one she had already heard from her father, with bawdy
laughter, after one of his long sessions with the brandy bottle.
The duke, he claimed, had made an indecent proposal to her
grandmother, who had most politely refused. "But that's my
mother's version," Edward Stonor had grinned. "And meant
for my father's ears. I wouldn't hazard a guess at how she
really replied. It was a great compliment, after all. Old Hooky

had a score of triumphs to his credit. He won as many battles in the bedroom as he did on the battlefield, kept mistresses like horses keep flies.''

Sophia sat with her eyes cast down to veil her amusement while her aunt talked of the duke with awe. ''A great man, Sophia—he stood between England and defeat and won the day.''

Had he won the day with her grandmother? Sophia wondered. She smiled at her aunt and got a returning smile of affection.

''It is good to see your pretty, smiling face around this house, Sophia,'' Aunt Maria said with a sigh. ''It has not been a happy house, but you are making it one. I hope it will be even happier soon.'' Her eyes were filled with meaning and a coy pleading.

Stonor strolled into the room, and Aunt Maria said with a quick smile, ''Has Stonor shown you the ferns in the conservatory? They are very rare.'' She gave her son a coy glance. ''Take Sophia to see them, my dear.''

Stonor bowed, his face expressionless. Flushed and confused, Sophia had no choice but to follow his tall figure. He closed the conservatory door behind them, catching her nervous glance at the action.

''We have to keep the temperature high for the sake of the plants,'' he explained coolly.

She moved around the long, glass-roofed building, staring without interest at the scalloped leaves of the ferns in their red earthenware pots. The scent of leaves and earth came to her nostrils. Stonor leaned against the door, his arms folded across his chest, watching her out of his queer pale eyes. In his dark clothes he looked remote, unreachable.

Her skirts dragged on the tiled floor, making a soft, silken sound. Nervously, she turned to face him. ''They are very interesting, Cousin,'' she murmured.

The cold, handsome face was suddenly sardonic. His pale mouth indented and his eyes flickered over her flushed face. ''You know we did not come out here to admire plants, Sophia.''

She turned away quickly, trembling. Sightlessly she stared at the dark green ferns.

Stonor moved to stand just behind her shoulder. She felt him there intensely and shivered, as if his cold eyes had impaled her.

"My mother expects us to return to her as formally betrothed lovers," he said in a stilted, calm voice.

Sophia put out a shaking hand and ran her fingers down the deep indentation of a leaf, feeling the coldness of it on her skin with a little shock.

"Do you want me to make a formal declaration, Sophia?" Stonor asked, watching her averted profile.

She thought of Wolfe, her body wrung by a spasm of such pain that she almost gasped aloud with it. Her trembling tongue sought her lower lip as she tried to answer, an image of her father flashing through her mind. He had sent her here to marry Stonor. It was his wish, his hope of leaving Queen's Stonor in loving hands, of knowing that her children would one day inherit their old family home. Edward Stonor was unhappy knowing that the Stonor name must die out once he died, his heir being a Whitley. The only comfort he had was that Sophia would be Stonor's wife.

"Say something, Sophia," Stonor said with sudden sharpness. "This cannot be a surprise to you. You came here knowing it was expressly what was expected of us."

She turned reluctantly. Her long, dark lashes lifted to meet his cold eyes. She felt his gaze narrow on her and straightened her back in that characteristic unaware movement of defiance.

"You have surprised me by asking so soon," she said quietly. "We barely know each other, Stonor. Can you not give me more time?"

"Why should you need more time?" he asked unanswerably. "This is no love match, Sophia. Your father sent you here to marry me."

Her cheeks bloomed with a dusky pink; her eyes challenged his angrily. His cold, precise tones flicked her ego. She might not care for Stonor, but she did not care to be treated like a piece of merchandise he was prepared to buy but towards which he felt no enthusiasm.

"You might pretend a little more interest, Stonor," she flung at him.

His thin brows lifted in an ironic query. "Are you disappointed by my honesty, Sophia? Curious; I fancied you were inclined to like frankness, but if, like my sister, you prefer to dress the truth up in pretty ribbons, I am ready to play the hot lover for you."

She had barely comprehended his words when he took hold

of her elbows, holding her effortlessly between his thin, strong hands, and bent his coldly handsome face to find her mouth.

Sophia froze, repelled and furious. She pulled her head aside, pushing back to evade him. "Don't touch me!"

She heard his intake of breath. Looking around, she saw his pale eyes illuminated by rage. He caught her back against him, his hands this time trapping her head, the thumbs pushing into her hair, his palms flat against her hot face. He forced his cold mouth down against hers, bruising her trembling lips, crushing them back upon her small teeth so that she felt her inner lip split and blood trickle into her mouth.

Sophia began to struggle in earnest, striking at him with clenched fists, kicking his shins, with her skirts flying upwards. Far from dissuading him, his breathing quickened, and she was terrified to sense a growing excitement in him. His arms slid down her back, bending her inexorably until she would fall if she attempted to struggle free. Then he forced her mouth to open for him, his tongue thrusting between her weak, parted lips, the intrusion catching her by horrified surprise.

Half-fainting under his onslaught, she swayed so that he held her against his thin, hard body. Her head fell back limply and Stonor followed the movement, his mouth now sliding hotly over her exposed throat.

Her head was dizzy, her body shaken by fear and repulsion. Through the mist that was engulfing her, she realized that Stonor was now fondling her breasts, his breathing fast, the rapid acceleration of his heartbeats racing against her own while his mouth was exploring behind her ears, under her chin, over her closed eyes.

"Stonor!" Aunt Maria's voice was torn between satisfaction and reproof. "My dear boy, even an engaged couple have no licence for such behaviour!"

Stonor stiffened and straightened, breathing as though he had been running, releasing Sophia. Swaying, she put a trembling hand to her bruised, hot mouth as her eyes filled with tears.

"There, you have frightened the child!" Aunt Maria looked at her with genuine anxiety, putting an arm around her. "Come along, my dear child, you must lie down. Why, you look so pale! Stonor, I am very cross with you!"

Standing in the conservatory among the dark green ferns,

Stonor adjusted his collar, his face thickly flushed, his eyes brilliant. He watched his mother lead the trembling girl away, and Sophia wept softly as she went.

In her bedroom Aunt Maria helped her to lie down, sitting beside her, patting her chilly hands. "There, there, do not look so shaken! It is a shock, I know. I felt the same myself. You have no mother to warn you, poor child. I should have done so. I blame myself. Men are disgusting brutes—even my Stonor, though he's my son." Her mouth was wry with distaste. "Women have to bear these things, Sophia. We have to do our duty. It was the same for me. So frightening and distasteful. Suddenly out of the blue." She broke off, her eyes filled with sour memory. "My wedding night quite horrified me...believe me, I know how you feel. We do not imagine such things."

Sophia turned over onto her face and cried as if her heart would break, and her aunt patted her shaking shoulders with a helplessly sympathetic look. Nothing Sophia could have done would so have moved Maria Whitley. Her growing affection for the girl was deeply strengthened by these moments. She saw in Sophia a reflection of her own shock and disgust the night she went for the first time into James Whitley's bed and found herself clumsily assailed by a man who had not understood her complete innocence about marriage. She had been too carefully trained in discipline to cry out, but she had lain in shaking pain as her husband used her body without understanding just how much pain he was inflicting on her. Maria had never recovered from those terrifying moments. From that night her husband was fixed for her as a crude animal without feeling.

Sophia wept, and Aunt Maria stroked her black hair gently. "Try to bear with Stonor, my dear. He is a good son. Men are to be pitied. Their nature is more animal than ours."

When she had finally gone, Sophia slowly undressed and looked at herself in the dressing-table mirror with sick eyes, seeing clearly the marks of Stonor's mouth and fingers upon her. She shuddered. Oh, God, she thought, I cannot bear it. She had found Stonor's cold, formal courtesy unattractive, but those moments in his arms had been a revelation to her of depths beneath his chill façade that terrified her. Facing a lifetime of marriage with a husband whose lovemaking repelled her sent shivers through her. What am I to do? she asked herself despairingly. Her father wanted her to marry Stonor. She had no real choice. When she came to London, though, she had not expected to find herself actually loathing the man her family had chosen for her.

Wolfe had spoken so blithely of getting his father to support them, but Stonor was James Whitley's son, too, and his legitimate son. Was there really any hope for them there?

She barely slept at all that night, tossing and turning in her bed, and when she came downstairs she stopped dead, seeing Stonor alone at the breakfast table. He lifted his pale, cold eyes to survey her. Straightening her back, she walked to the table and sat down. She would not have him see how afraid she was, so she began to force herself to eat the food the maid served her.

"All right, Lucy," Stonor said abruptly.

The maid curtsied and withdrew, giving them a curious look. All the servants knew that Sophia had come to London to marry Stonor.

Stonor drank some tea, his eyes on the table. She could hear every breath he took as if it drove nails through her scalp. After a moment he said, "I am sorry, Sophia." His voice made her jump, but she couldn't look at him. "I lost my head," he said, his voice oddly husky.

Her throat felt dry, as if it were filled with the dust and ashes of her future with him. He made a low, rough sound and pushed back his chair. She tensed as he walked around the table towards her, her fingers freezing on her knife and fork. She stared at her partly eaten food, her gorge rising at the sight of it. She felt she might be sick.

Stonor put a hand under her chin, lifting her head, forcing her to look at him, her black lashes fluttering against her cheek.

"Look at me," he said under his breath.

"Do I have to scream for help before you will leave me alone?" she asked bitterly.

His intake of breath sounded loud in the silent room. He slowly released her. Aunt Maria came rustling into the room, and Stonor turned away to stare out of the window. His mother looked shrewdly at his averted back and then at Sophia's pallor.

"Sophia, my dear, how would you like to visit Kew Gardens today? The weather is fine, and it is a pleasant drive."

"Oh, thank you, Aunt," Sophia said gracefully, thinking that this would mean an escape from Stonor and a whole day out of the cloistered atmosphere of the house.

"The carriage will be around in the next ten minutes," Aunt Maria said. "Run and put on your bonnet, my dear child."

Sophia fled up the stairs and got ready, coming down again in her pretty green bonnet trimmed with white flowers and fluttering ribbons, kissing her aunt warmly as she parted from her in the hall. She went down the front steps and then stood still, her face white with panic as she saw Stonor alone inside the carriage.

He got down, seeing her halt, and put a hand under her elbow, his grip compelling. The coachman turned a curious head, as though scenting trouble. Aunt Maria watched intently. Stonor's cold eyes rested on Sophia's face. Slowly she allowed him to assist her into the carriage.

For a while they drove in silence, staring out at the narrow, busy streets. Then Stonor made a few cool remarks about places they passed, giving her little snippets of history or pointing out the houses of friends. The little streets gave way to broader avenues and at last to small country roads. She could sense the driver's curiosity. He was a friend of Wolfe's, she remembered, and might repeat to him anything he heard. Stonor was being careful to say nothing much, and so perhaps he, too, knew that the driver was Wolfe's informant.

Although he spoke rarely he managed to sound quietly collected, his face impassive, and Sophia strove to match her manner to his.

When they arrived at Kew they found it quiet and half-empty. The driver went off to find an inn to drink at while the horses rested, and Stonor strolled beside Sophia, his arm lightly resting under her elbow.

Looking at his thin, straight figure, she found it hard to believe the fear and sickness that had possessed her in his arms last night. The cool-voiced young man with the unreadable face was back. The mask was firmly in place.

The Botanical Gardens were carefully maintained, with gardeners working everywhere, but Sophia, although she paused when Stonor indicated and stared where he pointed, barely noticed a thing. At last he paused beside a seat. "Shall we sit down? You must be tired."

Reluctantly she sat, staring at her full skirts. She wore white kid gloves, which she fidgeted with nervously.

Stonor leaned back, his long legs stretched out, and glanced at her. "You have hardly spoken to me all day, Sophia."

She could not speak; she averted her face.

"Did I frighten you so much?" asked Stonor in a voice that held a feeling she could not quite grasp.

The question brought red colour to her cheeks. She twisted her gloves between her hands. "Yes," she muttered.

He leaned forwards abruptly and put his hand over her nervous fingers. She jumped, flinching. Stonor said something under his breath that sounded like a curse.

After a pause he said, "I shall not frighten you again, I give you my word, but may I speak of it? I know you have been carefully brought up and you are very young."

"Your mother said. . ." Sophia began shakily, and he cut her off with a sudden, bitter gesture.

"Don't listen to my mother, Sophia."

"She's very kind!"

He laughed coldly. "My mother's attitudes on the matter are not those which I would wish you to share, Sophia." He stared at her flushed face as he spoke, and inadvertently she looked around, eyes widening.

"I've heard my mother's lectures to my sister on this subject," Stonor said, smiling grimly. "You're not like either of them, Sophia. Don't let my mother mislead you into seeing things her way."

She looked down, knowing that she shared none of Maria Whitley's attitudes but not willing to say as much to Stonor for fear that it would precipitate another demonstration of unwelcome passion from him.

"You have a strong, uncluttered mind, Sophia," he said. "You lack the hypocrisy, the shallow stupidity of my sister. On the night of her party, I watched you dancing, and your gaiety and spirit of enjoyment was brighter than the candles. My mother would snuff it out of you if you let her. Close your ears to what she says. Don't listen. Rely instead upon your own instincts."

She gazed at him, fascinated. He was speaking firmly and coolly, his voice frank, and she responded to that. "You should not speak of your mama like that," she reproved all the same.

His cold face twisted. "Oh, Sophia, are you listening to yourself? You're mouthing social hypocrisies and you know it."

"I would never breathe a word against my own father," she said angrily.

"Perhaps there is nothing to say," Stonor replied drily.

She laughed suddenly, her face changing. "No, that's true. Papa is a darling."

"Is he?" Stonor's voice was odd. He looked at her in a baffling way, smiling. "Is that where you get it from, I wonder?"

She blushed at the compliment, and Stonor lifted her hands to his mouth in a swift gesture, pressing his lips to the backs of each in turn. Her fingers jerked in his grasp and he looked at her from under his pale brows.

"Are you still frightened of me, Sophia? Do you want my word of honour that I will not lose control again when we're alone? And will you give me your word in exchange that you won't let my mother's hatred of men weigh with you for an instant?"

She lowered her lashes. "I promise," she said, knowing it was a promise easy for her to keep, since he had not understood her reactions at all.

She looked at him through her black lashes secretly and found him watching her in a curious fashion. He still held her hands, and again he kissed them, his mouth tickling her skin, moving over her palm to her wrist now, pushing back the frilled cuffs of her gown so that the intimacy of the caress made her acutely aware of him. "Is that more to your liking, Sophia?" he asked, shooting her a look, his eyes narrowed in cool speculation.

She could only look back at him helplessly, wishing she could say that she found it repulsive.

His mouth continued to play over her hands, planting kisses on each of her fingers, his lips parted slightly so that she felt intensely the inner moisture of his mouth on her skin.

"Will you marry me, Sophia?"

She froze, eyes wide. "Give me time, Stonor, please. Don't press me for an answer yet."

He smiled almost gaily. "A little time then, Sophia, but don't keep me waiting too long, will you?"

"I promise," she said, and he gave a husky laugh.

"How submissive and sweet you sound at times. You are a feminine creature. When my mother pretends to feminine sweetness, she cloys the throat. It's all an act to cover her ruthless sickness towards men. With you one feels the sweetness goes all the way through." Something in his eyes made her jump up hurriedly and move away, but Stonor followed her, catching her under a lime tree. The pattern of the shadowy leaves was cast darkly on his face as he looked down at her.

"I won't hurt you, Sophia," he whispered, and then his mouth found hers, his lips teasingly sensitive, as they had been against her hands. She stood passively, waiting for the disgust to fill her as it had before, but she found his kiss too gentle to cause distaste.

He lifted his head, the pallor of his face lost now in a flush, his eyes bright between those pale lashes. "Tell me that frightened you, Sophia," he said with a soft laughter. "That didn't disgust or repel you, did it?"

She could not in all honesty say that it did. Very pink, she lowered her eyes before his gaze. "Shouldn't we be going, Stonor? It is getting late."

"Not yet," he said harshly. "First I want you to tell me the truth. I've lived with lies all my life. I want the truth from you, now and for the rest of our lives. What did you really feel just now when I kissed you? Do you share my mother's belief that what happens between a man and woman is vile and disgusting?"

Her face was hot. "No," she whispered threadily, not meeting his eyes.

He forced her chin upward so that their eyes met. "Prove it. Kiss me, Sophia."

She stared at him, confused and off balance.

"I want to be sure of you," he said in a harsh voice. "Do you think I want a marriage like my father's? A wife who offers as a duty what should be a pleasure? Has it occurred to that innocent mind of yours that men driven out of their wives' beds by icy submission must find what they need elsewhere?"

"As your father did?" The question was forced out of Sophia before she knew what she was going to say, and Stonor stared at her, his mouth twisting.

"As my father did," he admitted.

"Yet you hate Wolfe," Sophia said accusingly. "Is it his fault if your mother froze your father out of her life?"

Stonor's face turned to ice. His eyes skinned the bright flush from her face. "Wolfe? You use his damned name easily." His eyes were hard, his voice sharp. "What did he say to you the night of the party?"

She looked away, confused, aware that she had betrayed herself.

"Look at me," Stonor said, forcing her head around. "You've seen him since, haven't you? How often? Where? What has happened between you that you speak of him so familiarly?"

Sophia thought fast and recognized that she could not tell Stonor the truth. "I've seen him on the stairs once or twice," she said. "He told me who he was."

Stonor listened, his eyes merciless as he watched her. "My father's bastard had no right to speak to you, and you had no business to listen."

She lifted her chin rebelliously, her back straightening in her most characteristic gesture. "I like him!" She would not betray Wolfe by lying about that.

Stonor was very still, his eyes probing her face, trying to read the thoughts hidden in her eyes. "Do you?" he asked thickly. "Do you indeed, Sophia? But that was apparent at the party, wasn't it? Do you think me blind that I shouldn't see the way the two of you looked at each other from the first? Oh, he's an attractive fellow, my bastard half-brother. Since he was old enough to go off by himself, he's been chasing women. He learned his way with women in the alleys off the Ratcliffe Highway. Do you know where that is, Sophia? Have you heard of it? It's where my father found his mother, the haunt of whores who ply for custom in the gutters and do their way against the walls of dark courts."

"I won't listen," Sophia cried angrily. "You call your mother sick? What are you?"

"I'm not sick," Stonor said icily. "I told you that between us I'll have nothing but the truth, and the truth about my father's bastard is that he comes from a whore and he learned about women from them. If you let him, he will treat you like a whore, Sophia."

She faced him bitterly. "As you did last night?"

His face ran a dark colour. He drew a sharp breath, almost as though protesting, then said in a low voice, "As I did, Sophia. Do you think I didn't feel your reaction when I tried to kiss you? If you hadn't turned away like that, things would have been very different. I told you when a man meets such treatment, he can be driven mad. What I did was done in anger and hurt. Wolfe will act deliberately."

She did not believe him. Wolfe had always been gentle with her, even when he was most passionate. Those blue-green eyes held warmth, unlike Stonor's pale glance.

"Why should he?" she asked him contemptuously.

Stonor shook her, a sudden passion lighting his face to anger. "You blind little fool, because he hates me," he said. "Why do you imagine he went out of his way to meet you at the party? He wants to harm me if he can, just as he harmed Grey, but the scars he wants to inflict on me aren't physical."

He wants me for himself, she thought secretly, remembering Wolfe's eyes, his smile, his passion.

Stonor saw the secret, blind, sensual smile on her mouth and he stared at her, his breath catching. "How often have you seen him? When do you meet him?" His questions had bitter coldness as he watched her face. "Do we have to watch you like a straying child, Sophia? I'd thought you safely chaperoned every minute of the day. How have you contrived to meet him?"

"I told you, we met on the stairs," she said nervously, aware of a threat in his voice. "The morning after the party, when everyone was asleep. I did not know he lived in the house until he told me."

"You're not to see him again," Stonor ordered. "Do you hear? Your father sent you to London to marry me, and marry me you will. In three days' time we'll announce our betrothal."

"And if I refuse?" she asked angrily.

He was calm now. "You will not refuse."

"You cannot make me marry you!"

"You're under age; you'll marry as your father decided," Stonor said coolly. "You've no real choice, Sophia. We both know that. And keep away from my father's bastard or you'll force me to deal with him."

She was disturbed by that veiled threat, staring at him, seeing a grim light in his pale eyes that indicated that he meant it very seriously.

# CHAPTER FOUR

Several days later Sophia and Elizabeth went shopping together, their excuse being that Sophia needed gloves, but their real reason being that Tom Lister had made a rendezvous with Elizabeth in the busy shopping arcades of Regent Street. Beneath Elizabeth's sweet docility, Sophia had discovered, was an iron-hard determination to get her own way, and although her mother did not frown upon Tom Lister, the constant chaperonage to which the girl was subject made her fret.

"How can Tom and I talk with Mama listening to every word?" she asked Sophia, pouting.

Sophia smiled agreeably, wondering if it were really Tom's conversation which Elizabeth found so inviting. After one of these secret meetings, there was a soft bloom upon Elizabeth's small, pouting mouth and a redness around Tom's neck. Beneath Elizabeth's childlike chatter of gowns and bonnets, Sophia sensed a hectic sensuality, a quality of which her mama would certainly not approve.

The more Sophia grew to know her aunt, the more she realized how distastefully she viewed relations between men and women. She was eager to see her daughter married, but the idea that Elizabeth could respond to Tom with anything but prim submission would horrify her. Sophia's terrified reaction to Stonor had convinced her that Sophia shared her views, and Aunt Maria was made increasingly fond of the girl.

Talking of the Lime Walk at Queen's Stonor, or the Lower Wood, Aunt Maria became free to wander in the world of her childhood, knowing Sophia understood without needing to have the names explained, and this freedom in her illusory Eden grew more and more precious to her.

"When you and Stonor do up the ballroom, it must be in blue and gold," she would say, her eyes shining. "Just as it used to be, my dear. And the stables...."

"They're in good order," Sophia said, laughing.

"Ah, Edward's a true Stonor," Aunt Maria sighed. "The

horses always came first. One of the things I missed most in London was the hunting season. A ride in the park is so tame.''

Sophia's eyes brightened at that. Here was something she could understand and honestly sympathize with, and she agreed eagerly. ''I doubt if I could bear to live in London; the smell of the stables haunts one.''

For a second Aunt Maria looked doubtful, shocked by the directness of the remark, then her face dissolved, as though Sophia had touched a secret spring in her. ''How very true, dear child. There is nothing like the Stonor stables. Oh, how fortunate you are, Sophia. Stonor will keep you at Queen's Stonor forever.''

Sophia felt a curious restless sensation. Was that truly what she wanted now? Once her life had been entirely bounded by her home and her father, but Wolfe had changed all that.

But she said aloud, ''And you will come and visit, Aunt Maria, and hunt on winter days, so that when we ride home, we will see the lights of Queen's Stonor through the trees as we come back and know the fires are lit and the servants busy in the kitchen.''

All her childhood there had been days like that, when through the soft twilight she and Papa had ridden home, wearily triumphant after a day in the saddle, watching the mellow lights of the house come closer through the trees.

Aunt Maria's eyes glistened as though with unshed tears. ''My dear,'' she said, kissing her gratefully.

Although she could not see everything as her aunt did, Sophia found a warm affection for her growing inside her as the days went by. Maria Whitley was a woman devoted to her sons, her home. Although her manner in her husband's presence was cold and stiff, once he had gone she became a different creature. The careful elegance of the house was due to her. She kept her servants in order without raising her voice. She made a beautiful home for her children, and her husband could have no criticism of her behaviour towards his city friends when they visited. Maria was all courtesy, all smiles, even in her husband's company.

James Whitley rarely sat with his family in the evenings. He still maintained a polite fiction with Sophia, excusing himself with a plea that he had work to do as he left to go upstairs to Lucy. Maria looked after him with a set, cold face but she said nothing. She had still not spoken to Sophia of the woman upstairs, and since the two households were quite separate, Sophia might never have known of her existence if it had not been for Wolfe.

Once when Aunt Maria was talking to her with a vivacious face, her eyes sparkling, Sophia caught James Whitley staring at his wife in a strange way, his features oddly like Stonor's, and wondered if she imagined the expression of regret that passed over his face.

Talking to Wolfe later, James Whitley said: "That little Stonor girl has a queer effect on my wife. I've never seen Maria so animated since we married. She gets her talking of that damned house morning, noon and night. Maria's shed years since the girl came here."

Wolfe made a wry face. "She needed to," he said indifferently, wondering if now was the moment for him to broach the matter of Sophia to his father.

"She was pretty when she was young," James Whitley said, his mouth twisting. "A little delicate, of course. The girl takes after her there. Maria had small bones. Like a little bird." He broke off and his eyes held anger. "Oh, damn it. Why think of that now? What point in thinking of it? The past is past."

Wolfe eyed him curiously, wondering if his father had once loved the cold, dry old stick downstairs. As he had married her, Wolfe thought, supposedly he had. He must have been hit badly when he found what manner of bird he'd netted. Nothing of Sophia in her aunt on that level, thank God. She was all warmth, and his heart beat faster as he tried to bring up the subject, but James Whitley was in a taciturn mood now, his eyes hard. Wolfe knew when to leave well enough alone, so he went off, meaning to bring the subject up some other day.

James Whitley stood at the window, jingling some coins in his pocket, remembering the shock he had had seeing Maria smiling at her niece like that. For a second she had looked as she had when they had first met. He had fallen head over heels on sight, overjoyed to win such a prize, impressed by her birth, her manner, her looks.

He had been so much in awe of her that he had come drunk to their wedding bed and lost his head within minutes, his hunger for her driving him blindly. Their marriage had ripped apart as he had forced himself on her shivering little body. James had believed that she would change as she grew used to it, but she had never changed. She had lain ice-cold in his arms, hurting and angering him, and gradually he had ceased to go near her because he could not bear to see that look come over her face.

What had she got in her veins? Vinegar? They had lived together and apart for years. Mostly he hated and despised her. Now and then he found himself angry because the hatred did not run as deep as he wished it would. The feelings he had killed would not quite die. They were submerged but present, and now and then they emerged into the light, and James found them unbearable.

He walked downstairs again to fetch something from his study and found Stonor there looking for a book. His son glanced around at him with that formal, frozen mask that James had never penetrated. Stonor was his mother's son, James thought, giving him a curt nod.

"You look tired, Papa," Stonor said, surprising him. "Are you well?"

"Perfectly," James Whitley said with a grunt. He hesitated. "Is this marriage settled yet?"

Stonor gave him a quick glance. "Yes," he said firmly. "I have been thinking, Papa, that when we are married, I should like to open a new branch in Bristol. I could then live at Queen's Stonor and work from there. Grey could stay on in London."

"As you please," James said indifferently. Stonor watched him, reading his mind with anger. James Whitley did not care whether Stonor stayed or went. All that concerned him was his bastard, the son who did not even bear his name. As a boy, Stonor had sometimes wished to cry out, "Papa!" and make his father look at him, really see him, but he had ceased to believe it possible for people to change. There had been times as a little boy when Stonor had run to his father eagerly when he came home from work, only to find himself shouldered aside while James Whitley ran up the stairs to the room where that woman and her child waited for him. Stonor had learned to hate early.

He understood very well the needs that had driven his father to find love outside his marriage, but Stonor's own feelings had been hurt too often for him to forgive his father—not for taking a mistress, but for turning to the woman's child and ignoring Stonor.

James Whitley in discarding his wife had discarded his children, too, and in that lay his crime so far as Stonor was concerned.

Stonor walked quietly from the room without another word, and James barely noticed his son leave.

Wandering along the shopping arcade with Elizabeth now, Sophia was thinking of Stonor. She would have to give him his answer tonight. What was she to do?

"You're so patient with Mama," Elizabeth said brightly. "She must be boring you to death. Poor Sophia." She only troubled her head with her mother's feelings when she wanted something from her, and it was convenient for her to have Sophia to take her mother's attention from her.

"I am very fond of her," Sophia said, not liking the way in which Elizabeth spoke of her mother.

The shared memory of hunting days that she had exchanged with Aunt Maria had been so clear, a tiny crystal image at the end of a dark tunnel, and her brow wrinkled as she considered the distance in time between that day when Aunt Maria had been young and the woman who now remembered it.

Brought up in a more tolerant world by Edward Stonor, in a house decaying comfortably, with little money and no desire for status, Sophia cared nothing for the social conventions Aunt Maria seemed to find so important. It mattered nothing to her that the coachman winked at her behind Elizabeth's back, or that James Whitley had a bastard son and a woman shut away upstairs. Many times Sophia had listened, forgotten, while her father and his hunting cronies talked drunkenly of things that, she sensed, Aunt Maria would find horrifying. The whole atmosphere in which she had grown up had been free of constraint, and it had made Sophia reckless, brave, carefree in her attitude to life.

Yet she did feel a fondness for her aunt. Her very tolerance made it possible for her to view her aunt's small snobberies with compassion, if not comprehension, and the pity she felt for a woman so clearly wrenched out of her own society and regretting it all her life made it easy for Sophia to be kind when Aunt Maria poured out her memories of a past she clearly supposed Sophia to share. If Aunt Maria found out the reality of life at Queen's Stonor now, she would be deeply wounded, Sophia realized.

Impulsive, warm, Sophia learned to hide her true nature from her aunt as a gesture of kindness, cloaking her real values in order not to wound or offend. If it pleased Aunt Maria to see her as a demure, well-bred young lady, Sophia had no objections, although she found the restrictions such a pretence placed upon her maddening.

Elizabeth too, found them annoying, despite her outer conformity, since she had a strong sense of her own needs, which she resented having to hide or indulge secretly. At the moment it was Tom Lister whom she wanted, but Sophia could not help but suspect that Elizabeth's passion for the cheerful young man was destined to be a brief one, although in all probability she would marry him. She wanted Tom because he had appeared when she was passing into a realization of her own needs. Three months ago such an idea would never have entered Sophia's head, but today she knew exactly how Elizabeth felt, because it was very close to her own feelings.

Desire had been unknown to her until Wolfe awoke it. She followed Elizabeth's swaying figure, saw her smile up at Tom, her passion for him visible in the very dip and sway of her full skirts as she inclined towards him, speaking softly. Sophia looked into a milliner's window. Lacy confections of feathers and flowers swam before her, and on the glass the shadows of Tom and Elizabeth moved like creatures trapped inside a bottle. Sophia felt her own body pulsating beneath the stiff material of her clothes. Ever since she had met Wolfe, she had been tormented by sensual feelings against which she had no defence.

When Wolfe's glance stripped her body and mind that first night, he had exposed her personality not only to himself, but to Sophia, causing some chemical reaction within her of which she had become restlessly aware. Oddly, it had not been Wolfe's lovemaking that had made her own feelings clear to her. It had been Stonor. Had he never kissed her as he had, spoken to her so frankly about the needs of men and women, she might merely have passed without understanding it into a passionate love affair with Wolfe.

Stonor had been strangely direct, talking to her as if she were an equal. Although Aunt Maria might have been shocked by his frankness on the subject, Sophia had found it attractive. She had a nature that was repulsed by oblique coldness, hypocrisy, lies. Frank, impulsive, warmhearted herself, she valued those qualities in others. She had been flattered when Stonor spoke to her so honestly. It had been the first thing she had seen in him to admire. Looking back on those moments in the conservatory, she could even forget her sick distaste for him, seeing his behaviour in a new light.

He was right. Uncle James had obviously been driven to find consolation elsewhere by Aunt Maria. Stonor had said he wanted nothing but the truth between them and that statement had chimed inside her head. She had looked at him properly for the first time, seeing a man who had grown up surrounded by hatred, secrecy, hypocrisy and coldness, and who rejected them all, wishing to build a totally different life for himself.

Her rapidly seeding affection for Wolfe had been halted by Stonor's honesty. It would have been so easy to turn finally to Wolfe, but now she seemed to have achieved a new understanding of herself and her emotions. Watching Elizabeth and Tom, she saw them in the grip of a human need that was outside the control of reason. When a tree broke into leaf in the spring, there was no reasoning behind the fact but a general law that governed all of nature. The time had come for it to happen. For Elizabeth, too, the same held true. She had come to that stage in life when she looked for the fulfilment of her destiny as a woman. Sophia guessed that Elizabeth's true character would reassert itself as soon as her driving need as a woman had been fulfilled in marriage. God help poor Tom then!

Elizabeth, under her frills and lace, was hard. Tom Lister, from what Sophia had seen of him, was a soft-shelled creature. Instinctively Elizabeth had looked for a man whom she could dominate, and certainly she would not find it hard to rule Tom. Society and nature both now demanded marriage for Elizabeth. Once that was achieved Elizabeth would turn her greedy little brain to other things, and Tom would become one of her possessions, of no more importance to her than her horses, her maid, her jewels—one of the trappings she required to demonstrate her own importance in the world.

Sophia was capable of seeing all this because of the freedom in which she had grown up. Her mind had not suffered the constriction that Victorian society placed upon the minds of young girls. Although she was herself intensely feminine, she had grown up in men's society, hearing them talk as though she were not present. When their farm tenants visited Edward Stonor, they talked of crops and lambing, taking a mare to the stallion, all the natural processes of their world, and Sophia in her corner had heard it all, often without understanding what she heard. Now the lessons flowered in her mind. She knew what was happening to her.

Her father had sent her to London to marry Stonor so that

she might one day be mistress of their family home and her children heirs to it. Sophia loved her father deeply. She loved Queen's Stonor. Yet she was divided in her mind.

Was she going to have to choose between satisfying her own nature and satisfying the dictates of conscience?

It was so tempting to think of marrying Wolfe, in the teeth of all opposition. He was in many ways her own reflection. They bore the same hallmarks. Alone with him she felt as easy as if she were alone with herself. Being a man, he had a tougher, harder mind. He was years ahead of her in experience. She did not doubt the truth of Stonor's accusation that Wolfe had learned his way with women among the whores of the Ratcliffe Highway. Wolfe had as good as admitted it. Sophia did not despise him for that. She had not had the sort of upbringing that bred disgust for such subjects. She was curious, half-fascinated by the world Wolfe had been showing her on their secret dawn walks. Whatever he had done, that queer likeness persisted. She seemed in touch with him at a level deeply below that of the reasoning mind. Their bodies seemed to speak to each other, their eyes to flash silent messages. The unspoken conspiracy between them was oddly exciting, satisfying.

Stonor had been honest with her. He had said he valued honesty, wanted it above all else. What if she told him frankly how she felt? Would he still force her to marry him? Or would he step aside and let her marry Wolfe?

Even as she asked the question of herself, Sophia guessed at the answer. Stonor's hatred for Wolfe and Wolfe's for him were as clear as crystal.

Elizabeth suddenly broke in on her thoughts. "Stop loitering, Sophia! We've done our shopping. Let us go."

Sophia grinned at her. "Oh, has Tom gone? I did not notice."

"You're my favourite friend," Elizabeth said.

"I wonder why!" Sophia gave her a dancing look, her eyes teasing.

In the carriage on her way back to the house, Sophia asked her: "Why does Tom not propose at once and put an end to all this secrecy?"

Elizabeth tossed her head, mouth satisfied. "He has, of course! But I'm not ready to say yes yet."

She was enjoying her courtship, Sophia thought. The conspiracy was part of the pleasure for her. Well, Sophia could understand that. She found her own conspiracy with Wolfe very rewarding. There was a delight in knowing one had a secret from the rest of the world.

Her smile died as she reflected that for several days she had been unable to see Wolfe. She had risen at dawn each morning in the hope of doing so, only to find a maid polishing the stairs she would have had to negotiate to reach his rooms. She half-suspected that Stonor had given orders to that effect.

After dinner that evening Sophia discovered that she was to spend time alone with Stonor. Tom Lister was taking Elizabeth and Aunt Maria to the theatre. "You will not mind sitting quietly in the drawing room with Stonor," Aunt Maria said coyly. "You can play to him." She gave her son a stern glance, silently warning him not to frighten Sophia again.

When they were alone, Stonor sat down beside Sophia on the buttoned sofa and turned, his arm resting along the back, staring at her averted face.

She jumped up. "Shall I play to you?"

He caught her hand as she moved towards the piano. "Sit down again, Sophia."

"Your mother said . . ."

"Sit down," Stonor repeated, and unhappily she obeyed.

"You know what I want to hear you say," Stonor told her quietly.

She looked down, pleating her skirt with nervous fingers. "It is too soon, Stonor."

"I want my answer," he said in even tones.

"How can I decide so quickly on something that will shape my whole life?"

"You know you have no decision to make. It was made for both of us by circumstances beyond our control."

That gave her a tiny flare of hope. She looked at him eagerly. "Stonor, I am a woman. I may have to submit to what my father wants of me. But you could refuse. You're free. They cannot make you marry me."

For a moment the straight, cold features of the handsome face were expressionless. Then he smiled faintly. "I don't wish to refuse, Sophia. The marriage suits me very well." His eyes surveyed her as if he wanted to say something yet could not quite bring himself to speak. At last he said, "Before you arrived, I admit I was in half a mind to refuse to marry you.

My father wouldn't have insisted, and I can afford to ignore my mother. But I've changed my mind.''

The little hope died. She looked down, biting her lip. "When we talked at Kew, you said you only wanted the truth between us.''

"I do," he agreed gravely.

Sophia drew a long breath. "Then the truth is that I do not think we could be happy together.''

She waited for his reply anxiously.

After a long pause he asked, "Why?" The monosyllable was spoken quietly, yet she sensed restraint behind it, although what it was he restrained she was not sure.

She twisted her hands on her lap, searching for reasons that would not sound forward, wanton or unkind. "I . . . I am not in love with you, Stonor," she achieved at last, her voice trembling.

"I did not ask you to fall in love with me," he said after a long silence. His voice had a controlled calmness that made him sound remote. "I asked you to marry me.''

"But when we spoke at Kew you. . ." She could not finish that sentence, her cheeks scarlet.

"Made love to you?" There was wry humour in his voice now. "Are you still so innocent, Sophia, that you imagine lovemaking goes always hand in hand with love?''

"If it is to mean anything, it must," she said, her blue eyes enormous in her flushed face.

Stonor met her glance with a slight twist of his hard mouth. "When I made love to you at Kew, you did not seem to find it unpleasant. You told me you did not, anyway. Yet you say you are not in love with me.''

She could not deny that. She had found nothing revolting in his gentle, sensitive kiss.

His hand moved slightly along the back of the sofa, and she felt it slide beneath the black hair that fell down her shoulders in a scented riot of ringlets. The cool fingers caressed her nape gently, pushing up into her hair. Stonor looked at her with a strange little smile.

"You liked it. Did you think I couldn't tell? You didn't turn away from me with distaste the way you did in the conservatory. Don't fret about feelings now, Sophia. Give yourself time. I can be patient.''

She was not finding his slow caress along her nape distaste-

ful, either. The gentle rubbing of his fingertips made her want
to arch herself like a cat being stroked. The soft murmur of
Stonor's voice had the same effect, as though he were deliberately gentling her, soothing her.

"There are women with lovely faces and cold hearts," he
said. "My sister is one. My mother was not beautiful, but she
was cold. But you, Sophia, you're a passionate woman. It can
be read in your face, in the way you move, in your response to
other things. Sooner or later you will need to satisfy the de-
mands of your body."

"But not with you," she found herself crying involuntarily,
wincing as though with pain.

His face changed. He sat up, his hands withdrawing from
her, a cold tension in his whole body. "With whom, then,
Sophia?" The question came out sharply, fiercely.

She looked away, shivering, unable to answer, realizing
what she had said.

His hand gripped her chin, turning her face towards him.
"With whom?" he repeated in a savage voice.

She stared at him helplessly.

"Have you been seeing my father's bastard?" Stonor asked
in slow, harsh tones.

"No," she denied weakly.

He searched her face, probing her eyes. "Then is there some
other man? Someone you know in Somerset?"

She shook her head, almost eager now to deny that. "No,
Stonor!" She dared not tell him about Wolfe. Her faint
dream that Stonor might release her had died as she saw his
face just now. Stonor was dangerous. He might harm Wolfe.

"God help you if you're lying to me, Sophia," he said now,
watching her with bleak eyes. "Although even if you do care
for someone else, it makes no difference. You'll marry me.
And you'll forget whoever it is you're hankering for."

She was angry suddenly. "You say you want the truth, but
you mean to offer me no choice. How dare you ask me to
share my thoughts with you? Do you share yours with me?
Are we equals, Stonor? You tell me I've no choice but to
marry you, become your possession, a chattel that in law you
own body and soul, and you demand not merely that I open
my body to you but also my mind. You may have the power to
enforce my acceptance of our marriage. You know I love my
father dearly. I want to please him. But although I may have
to marry you, you cannot force me to let you into my mind."

Stonor had grown paler than ever as she spoke, his cold grey eyes fixed on her vivid face. "At least you now admit you've no choice," he said at last when she was silent.

She bowed her head, all her fierce eloquence gone. She might wriggle helplessly to escape, but she knew she had no hope.

"Our parents made this marriage for reasons that have nothing to do with either of us," Stonor said. "We marry for the sake of Queen's Stonor."

"Yes," she said wearily.

"Then we understand each other."

"It is as far as we ever will," she cried rebelliously.

"Oh, Sophia," he said, suddenly sardonic. "You lie to yourself if you think that."

"No! We're poles apart, Stonor."

"There's no point in arguing the toss. We have years ahead of us to do that." The thought seemed to please him. He smiled.

She flinched.

He saw the movement and his face hardened. "Don't look at me like that," he said in sudden anger. "I've told you. I won't bear it. You've no cause to look at me as though I were a monster."

Looking at him beseechingly, she said, "Then will you at least agree to wait six months, Stonor? Give me time."

"I'll wait three months," he said after a short pause. "No longer."

She sighed. It was better than nothing. The clock on the mantelpiece chimed and she looked at it, wondering how many evenings in the future she would sit like this with Stonor, bitterly aware of the cold passage of time. He seemed to enjoy the prospect of the years when they would be shut up alone in a loveless marriage. What went on inside that pale cold head? She had no means of guessing at his thoughts. He was a total stranger to her.

"Time you went to bed," he said, standing up. "My mother made me promise not to keep you up late."

Under his sardonic eyes she could not hide her relief at getting away from him, almost running from the room.

She could not get to sleep for hours. She lay awake, listening to the clocks downstairs chime the long night away, staring into the dark with miserable eyes. The darkness began to streak with grey, and she knew dawn was approaching. Every-

one else had long since gone to bed. She had heard Aunt
Maria and Elizabeth laughing mutedly as they went to their
own rooms, and Stonor's slow, careful tread had made her
heart stop in a sort of dread before he went on to bed. Now
outside the birds began to give sleepy calls in the trees in the
square.

When the door began to creak open she turned. Astonished,
alarmed, she gave a gasp as Wolfe's head showed through the
shadowy half-light from the stairs.

Sitting up, she whispered anxiously, "You can't come in
here, Wolfe!"

He was wearing evening clothes, a cloak slung from his
shoulders with crimson silk lining showing, his black tie half-
undone, his hair dishevelled. A wild laughter filled his strange
blue-green eyes.

He moved unsteadily towards her, and she suddenly realized that he had been drinking. The aroma of brandy and
cigars drifted to her nostrils. Amused reproof filled her face.

"Go away, Wolfe," she whispered, smiling tolerantly.
"Have you been out all night again?" She was reminded of
her father after an evening spent carousing with his hunting
cronies; the same odour had accompanied him when he kissed
her good night. "You're in no condition to know what you're
doing!"

He sat down on her bed heavily and the springs creaked in
protest, sending a shiver of alarm through her. "Ssh!" She
listened but heard nobody stirring in the other rooms.

"Why haven't you met me for three days?" he asked thickly, pushing back his cloak. "I've waited for you."

"I couldn't. There has been someone about each morning."

He stared at her fixedly, his hand fumbling with the clasp
on his cloak. It came undone and he shed it, and Sophia heard
it slither to the floor in a silken rustle.

"Did you try? Did you, Sophia?" He sounded accusing, his
bright, drunken eyes spearing her face through the darkness.
"You've spent the evenings with Stonor, haven't you? The
days, too. He'll have made the most of his chance. You
haven't forgotten that you promised to marry me? You
haven't given him any promises?"

"I had to, Wolfe!"

"Had to!" He wrenched at his collar with one hand as
though it stifled him, and his tie fell to the floor to lie beside

his cloak. "You aren't going to marry him, Sophia. I won't have it. He'd stifle you, shut you up in a lifeless tomb of a marriage, as his mother did my father. I won't have that happen to you. It would be blasphemy."

"How can I disobey my father?" she asked unhappily. "You know I don't want to marry Stonor. I told him I didn't love him."

Wolfe sat still, his mouth curling suddenly in a smile of enjoyment. "Did you? What did he say to that?"

"It seemed to make no difference," Sophia groaned. "He still insists on marrying me! He says the marriage suits him."

"I'm sure it does," Wolfe said in those thick tones, grinning. She did not understand the look on his face, the peculiar brightness of his eyes.

"Do you think Stonor is as incapable of love as his mother?" Sophia asked him in a hurried whisper. "I'm beginning to think that's true. He wants to marry and he's decided that I will do, but he has no more interest in me than if I were a piece of furniture."

Wolfe gazed at her, smiling. "He's a cold bastard," he said. "I know him better than anyone in the world. We've made a special study of each other. Hatred can be as strong a bond as love. I've always been able to read Stonor's feelings, and he knows it. When we were boys, he was sick with jealousy of me. Father took me everywhere with him. We used to go to cricket matches together on a Saturday afternoon. Stonor never came but he would sometimes look out the window as we left, and I'd look up and see him staring at me. I think if Stonor had had the chance, he'd have stuck a knife in my back."

His amusement at the thought made her frown. "Oh, no, Wolfe. Poor Stonor. You must see how that must have hurt him!"

Wolfe scowled, as though he did not like her to sympathize with Stonor even for a second. "Stop talking, damn you," he said. "That's not what I came for."

She gave a little cry of protest as he pushed her back against her pillows, but his mouth found hers a second later, and at the first touch passion flared between them and Sophia forgot everything but the flame running through her.

Wolfe's hard, desiring hands pushed down her bedclothes and moved over her, warmly intrusive, shaping her body beneath the material of her nightgown as though he were a sculptor. Her lips clung heatedly to his, her arms around his neck.

Wolfe suddenly sat up again, his hands at his shirt, fumbling with the buttons. Cold common sense doused Sophia's own desire as she realized his intention. She leaped out of the bed on the side farthest from him, and Wolfe spun, his shirt now open, catching her as she tried to get to the door.

"No, Wolfe!" she cried, struggling to get away.

Their bodies swayed together. His mouth came down on hers and she felt the warmth of his skin striking through her nightgown as he pulled her hard against his body. Her head tilted back weakly to receive his kiss, her hands curling in to grip his shoulders. Wolfe's hands slid down her body. He moaned as he kissed her, their heartbeats racing together. Sophia did not even notice when he began to lift her nightgown. His mouth held hers, exploring her with such hungry thoroughness that she was unconscious of everything but him.

Suddenly light spilled over them from a candle. A woman's voice began to scream hysterically.

Sophia was wrenched out of her deep concentration upon Wolfe. She pulled out of his arms and turned, shaking, to find Aunt Maria standing in the open door, staring at them, her mouth open, her eyes wild, screams coming shrilly from her white face.

For a moment neither Wolfe nor Sophia moved, too stunned by her arrival at that second. The high-pitched screams split the silence of the house. Doors banged. Feet ran. Suddenly Stonor appeared in his nightgown, his brown hair ruffled from sleep. At the sight of Wolfe half-dressed beside Sophia in her nightgown, his face turned into a mask of stone.

At the next moment James Whitley appeared and halted, staring. He looked from Wolfe to Sophia and then at Maria.

She was still making those animal noises of disgust and rage. Stonor suddenly walked over and slapped his mother's face with an open palm. The shrill cries stopped dead and she gave a loud gasp, beginning then to cry.

Elizabeth, her hair in papers, her face smeared with white cream, stood behind her father, staring, a look of astonishment, glee, and lasciviousness on her face.

The servants were running down from their remote attics. Stonor turned to his sister and said coldly, "Go back to bed, Elizabeth." He pushed his mother into Sophia's bedroom,

glanced at his father in his usual expressionless, icy fashion
and said, "I'll send the servants back to bed."

James Whitley slowly walked into the bedroom and closed
the door. Sophia stood beside Wolfe, shivering, her arms
around her waist.

Maria Whitley turned to her husband, her pale mouth moving convulsively as she said in a sick voice, "That animal!
This is all your fault! He is a criminal."

Before James could speak the door opened, and Stonor
walked into the room. At the sight of him Sophia shrank, feeling guilty and afraid. She had lied to him about meeting
Wolfe, and now Stonor knew it. His eyes flashed icily towards
her, and Wolfe at once moved to stand at her shoulder as
though protecting her. He gave a drunken, mocking smile to
Stonor, who looked back without a sign of feeling, his features so stiffly empty that she thought perhaps he did not care
what had been happening except that she and Wolfe had
caused an uproar in the house.

He had been to his room, she saw, and dressed in the sombre formality of his working clothes. He looked oddly neat
beside the nightclothes of everyone else but Wolfe.

James Whitley gave Wolfe a weary look. "Well? What the
hell have you been up to?"

Before Wolfe could answer, Aunt Maria burst out: "What
do you think he's been up to? Isn't it obvious? You know
what he is—you've always known. He makes no secret of his
disgusting behaviour."

"Be quiet, Maria," James Whitley sighed.

"Not this time, James," she flung at him. "I've been quiet
for too long in order to spare my children the pain of knowing
what sort of father they have. . . ."

"You spared them nothing," James retorted. "You spared
none of us. Be quiet now and let Wolfe tell me."

"Oh, you'll listen to him, won't you? Your darling, your
precious bastard—he always has your ear. You've never cared
a straw for either of your legitimate sons. They might as well
not exist."

Stonor put an arm around his mother. "Don't upset yourself, Mama. You must be calm."

"How can I be?" she asked almost wildly.

James looked at Wolfe, a peculiar white line around his
mouth. "What is all this about? What were you doing in
here?"

"Can't we talk about it without an audience?" Wolfe asked. "I've nothing to hide, Father, and I wouldn't harm a hair on Sophia's head. Look at her if you don't believe me. Does she seem frightened of me?"

James looked at her, and Sophia felt hot colour rolling up her face. Her eyes dropped away. Stonor was staring at her, and although she did not look in his direction, she felt those eyes like spears lancing her body.

James raised his brows at Wolfe, silently questioning, and Wolfe gave him a level glance.

Maria was staring at Sophia, too. Sophia hung her head, feeling the heat in her face increase.

"I heard her cry out," Maria protested. "I tell you I heard her struggling with him. When I came in here, she was fighting to get away but he was dragging her nightgown off her in his drunken lust...."

"There was no fight," Wolfe said to his father, ignoring Maria Whitley. "Good God, Father, I love her!"

James Whitley looked sharply at him. Wolfe smiled at him, all his considerable charm in his face. "I mean it. I love her."

"He's lying," Maria accused hoarsely. "That poor child is so innocent she almost fainted when Stonor laid a finger on her. I tell you, he was trying to rape her, James, and she was terrified."

Sophia was shuddering with fear and guilt. She put her hands over her face, her head bent.

"Thank God I came in time," Maria Whitley said.

"Did she, Sophia?" The question from Stonor was dropped like icy pebbles into the little silence.

Wolfe laughed insolently.

Stonor's hands went for Wolfe's throat. The speed of his movement took them all by surprise. Maria Whitley screamed. James Whitley leaped forwards, his face congested with dark blood.

"Stonor, for God's sake!" He sounded almost pleading, but Stonor's hands were like a vise around Wolfe's throat, and his father could not make him release Wolfe. "Wait until you know the facts," he muttered, trying to pull Stonor away.

Sophia could hear Wolfe's breath coming raggedly. He was threshing to and fro as if in mortal agony, his hands clawing in an attempt to break Stonor's hold on his throat. He kicked viciously, his strong body unable to break free of the lock Stonor had on him.

"You'll kill him," James Whitley gasped.

The two young men seemed oblivious of everything but their own hatred, their eyes fixed in a bitter stare, Wolfe's back against the wall so that he could not move.

He was purple in the face now, breathing hoarsely. James Whitley put out a hand to him, choking as though in the grip of sobs, then he slowly crumpled to the floor. "Wolfe," he grunted as he fell, and Stonor, turning his head, loosened his hold on Wolfe to turn and look in consternation.

He knelt beside his father, his face white. James Whitley lay on his back, breathing with a whistling hoarseness that could be heard clearly in the still room. His eyes were flickering, and all colour had gone from his face.

"What's wrong with him?" Maria asked in a whisper. "What's wrong, Stonor?"

He is dying, Sophia thought, staring down at him.

"Send a servant for the doctor, Mother," Stonor said, opening his father's shirt. He put his head down against the panting chest. A little white froth crept from the corner of James Whitley's mouth and lay on his stubbled chin, drying.

Maria stood there for a second or two, staring, then she turned and hurried out.

Wolfe knelt on the other side of the supine body, his hand on his father's wrist. "A heart attack," he said heavily.

Stonor looked up. "A bad one," he said through pale lips. "He's dying."

Wolfe's face grew a deadly white. A brightness sparkled in his eyes as he looked down at his father. The tears that caused it slid from his eyes, but he did not sob aloud. He put his hand to his father's face. "Father," he said pleadingly. "Father, it's Wolfe."

The whistling sound thickened to a gasped panting. The lids rose and they all saw James Whitley's eyes rolling, his parted lips moving. Wolfe brought the hand he held up to his lips. A tear trickled from his cheek onto the limp fingers. The heart-rending sounds stopped, and Wolfe said wildly, "No. No, Father."

Stonor leaned forwards and silently drew down the lids, his face stony. He stood up, looking down at Wolfe, who still knelt beside his father, holding his hand, staring at the dead face. A peculiar contortion passed over Stonor's face.

"As for you," he said clearly, "you can take your whore of a mother and get out of my house."

For a moment Wolfe did not move, and Sophia thought he had not even heard. Then he gently laid his father's hand on his unmoving chest and stood up, turning to face Stonor with a wary look on his face.

"You think you're master here now, I suppose?"

"I know I am," Stonor said.

"What makes you so sure?" Wolfe's brow rose mockingly, a smile on his mouth. "Better wait for the will, Stonor."

"I have it in the safe," Stonor answered quietly. "Everything goes to me, apart from a legacy each for Elizabeth and Grey."

Wolfe's face betrayed his shock and disbelief. "There must be another will somewhere. There has to be."

"That shook you, did it?" Stonor laughed coldly. "Oh, I've no doubt he meant to change it, but he never did."

"Or have you destroyed it?" Wolfe burst out. "I wouldn't put it past you to burn any other will."

"Don't be a fool," Stonor said contemptuously. "My father may have thought the sun shone out of you, but he wasn't stupid enough to believe he could leave his property away from his legal heirs and hope to get it through the courts. No court would uphold such a will, and he knew it. I'm his legal heir. He merely complied with the law. I've no doubt he meant to settle money on you in his lifetime, but he never did, did he? He never expected to die so soon."

Sophia had listened incredulously, her face shocked. "How can you talk like this when he lies there on the floor? He's barely stopped breathing! Can't all this wait? Does it matter, any of it? Your father is dead. That's all that matters."

Stonor turned his cold face towards her, his eyes determined. "He spends no more nights under my roof. I want him and his mother out of here tonight. Do you think I'll have them following my father to the grave with the rest of us? They've no rights now. We're the ones with the right to mourn him, not they. That woman's usurped my mother's place for years. She'll do so no more."

"We'll go," Wolfe said harshly. "Take the house and the money. Sophia's right, what difference do they make? We had him while he was alive. What he's left doesn't mean a thing."

Stonor looked levelly at him and moved to open the door. Wolfe turned with a sober look to hold out a hand to Sophia. "Come with me, my darling. You can't marry him. Remember, birds in cages never sing. Get dressed and come with me and my mother. I'll look after you.''

Stonor closed the door, turning back towards her. Sophia was staring at Wolfe with a white face, biting her lip.

"If you go with him, you'll break your father's heart," Stonor said. "You could never go home again, you realize that?"

"Don't you want to be happy, Sophia?" Wolfe asked her with a husky voice. "You won't be if you stay with him."

"Don't ask me now, Wolfe," she said desperately. "Not with Uncle James lying there. It must wait. I can't think about it now. It isn't the right time."

"It's the only time," Wolfe said harshly. "If you wait, he'll fence you in. He won't let you go."

Stonor's lips barely moved as he spoke. "You're right. I won't," he said.

Wolfe laughed brusquely. "You think you need to tell me that?"

For a moment the two young men stared at each other. Outside the room Aunt Maria was weeping somewhere. The door opened and Elizabeth came running in, still smeared with cream. "What's happened? Mother says. . ." Her voice broke off as she saw her father on the ground. "Papa!" She moved to go to him and Stonor pushed her towards the door again.

"Comfort Mama! Put her to bed. Stay with her."

"But Papa," Elizabeth said. "Is he. . .?"

"He's dead," Stonor said flatly.

Elizabeth gave a cry and put her hand to her mouth.

"See to Mama," Stonor told her, his face unmoving. "She needs you. And try to be kind, Elizabeth. Try to be kind, for God's sake."

Elizabeth backed out, staring at her father's body. Stonor looked around at Sophia with a level gaze, his face the expressionless mask she was accustomed to seeing.

"You barely know him, Sophia," he said in his precise tones. "What sort of life do you think he could give you? Without money or a home; how could he look after you? You'd hamper him, drag him back. You're both too young to know what you are doing. And then there's your father. He wouldn't forgive you. He wants you to marry me, he wants to see you as mistress of Queen's Stonor before he dies. You couldn't ever see your father again if you went with him. He wouldn't have you in the house."

"Don't listen to him! Listen to me!" Wolfe cried in bitter, protesting anger. "None of that matters! None of it!"

The pain in his eyes made her wince. She moved involuntarily and his arms closed around her in a gesture of possession, his hand covering her head, stroking her hair, pushing her face into his shoulder. Like a child in her white nightgown, her dark hair loosely straying against his naked skin, she stood sheltered against him, feeling safe. His arms were where she belonged. They were her home.

But it was not that simple. Stonor had made her see that. Wolfe had nowhere to go, nowhere to take her. He was homeless now, penniless. She would be a nuisance to him. Wolfe needed to be free of burdens if he was to make his way in the world. They were both still so young.

She looked up, tears in her eyes, and he read her face with grim understanding.

"I'm sorry, Wolfe," she whispered, the tears falling faster.

He kissed her forehead lightly, then looked at Stonor over the top of her head. "You may marry her, but she'll be mine all her life. She loves me. She'll always love me. You can't change that, Stonor. Can you live with her, knowing that? Let her go, for God's sake."

"No," Stonor said harshly.

He stepped forwards and pulled Sophia out of Wolfe's arms, holding her elbow in a vise. Wolfe stared at him with white hatred, then he turned and walked out of the room while Sophia cried silently, her whole body shaking.

# CHAPTER FIVE

The Turk's Head was crammed with customers when Wolfe sauntered through the door. Heads turned to survey him. Narrowed eyes read the expensive clothes, the casual, assured air, and glances were exchanged. Wolfe was under no illusions. A visit to such a place alone was dangerous. He would be a tempting target for many of the desperate men here. The landlord was moving about, his large arms sweeping up mugs from the tables, shouting oaths at anyone who got in his way.

"Rummy!"

Wolfe's cold authority penetrated every corner of the room. A silence fell.

"What d'yer want?"

The bloated face turned to stare at him. The man eyed him unpleasantly with unfriendly eyes.

"Black Strap."

The faces watching him altered. A low whistle came from one man. Rummy chewed his lower lip. A faint grin came to his face.

"I see you with 'im before, ain't I? He's upstairs." The thick thumb jerked upwards. "Got a ladybird with him. Black Strap might not like to be walked in on at his work."

A roar came from the customers.

"Perhaps he'll need some help," Wolfe said gravely.

Another roar went up. Drunken hands banged mugs on the tables.

"Just try it!"

The voice came from behind him and Wolfe turned, grinning. Black Strap stood on the stairs, his huge, brawny frame half-dressed in dirty breeches, his chest bare.

Wolfe went up the stairs. Black Strap slapped him on the back, laughing.

"I wondered if we'd ever meet again, you young dog! Come in and meet Moll."

Wolfe followed him into a low-ceilinged room in which a well-rounded girl lounged on a dirty, unmade bed, her blonde hair spilling over her naked shoulders, her skirts pulled back over her thighs. She made no attempt to move or straighten her clothes. From under her lashes she studied Wolfe, who gave her a brief, disinterested glance.

"What can I do for you, young wolf?" Black Strap asked, scratching his chest lazily and suddenly nipping a flea between finger and thumb. "The little bastards get everywhere," he said, brushing blood from the insect along his hips.

"Introduce me to your pretty friend!" Wolfe murmured lazily.

Black Strap lifted a ragged brow. "Want some skirt, d'yer? You're welcome. Comes with the house, Moll does. This is Wolfe, Moll. Suits him, don't it? A mighty pretty fellow with sharp teeth. Fancy a throw with him, Moll?"

Her pink tongue caressed her lips but she made no reply, smiling as she ran her eyes down Wolfe's lean body.

Wolfe grinned at her, then turned to Black Strap. "Get her out of here for a while. I'm here on business."

Black Strap's eyes narrowed in speculation. He jerked his head to the girl. "Out!"

Her mouth grew sullen. Slowly she rolled off the bed, her skirts falling down to her ankles. She gave Wolfe a look as she passed him, her blue eyes nasty, and he slapped her hard but indulgently on the bottom, making her jump.

"Later, darling!"

His grin taunted her and her eyes spat rage for a second, then she went out. Black Strap sat down on a chair, his feet on the bed, gesturing to Wolfe to sit down.

"Business, you said?"

Wolfe went to the door and jerked it open suddenly. There was the sound of a blow. A body crashed down the stairs and a roar of laughter came from the bar as the girl landed at the bottom, her skirts flying everywhere, her legs sprawling as she lay on the sodden floor.

"I don't like eavesdroppers," Wolfe said.

He propped the door open with a chair so that he could see anyone who approached along the landing, then he sat and looked at Black Strap, who was grinning broadly.

"The Whitley warehouse," he said.

Black Strap eyed him curiously. "What about it?"

"It will be full of sugar and rum tomorrow night. An East Indiaman docked today and is unloading now. There are nightwatchmen guarding the doors, of course, but one of them is a friend of mine.''

Black Strap went to a cupboard, got out a jug and two mugs and poured brandy.

Wolfe took one and said softly: ''Well?''

''To crime,'' Black Strap said, lifting his mug with a grin.

''To crime,'' Wolfe said, clinking his mug against the other.

''Now, let's have the details,'' Black Strap said as he sat down again.

Later Wolfe lay on the dirty bed, his hands sliding over the blonde girl's open thighs, his mouth playing with her breasts. She was making a soft moaning sound, her eyes closed. Wolfe abstractedly took her, felt her pull him closer, heard a smothered sob in her throat. He had used her with tenderness, and Moll couldn't believe her luck. Wolfe thought of Sophia in Stonor's arms, and the girl beneath him cried out huskily: ''Oh, God!'' at the savagery of his movements. By the time he had finished, she was almost fainting at the driving force of his body, but she was crying, her hands stroking his hair. Sagging forwards, Wolfe lay with his head pillowed on her naked breasts. He had not even heard the wild cries of pleasure she had given beneath him.

''Oh, Wolfe,'' she groaned now. ''Wolfe.''

He lifted his head and looked at her in faint pity. Beneath the grime she wasn't an ill-favoured girl, and her reactions to his lovemaking had shown him that her usual customers were dirty, rough or old men.

''Was it good, Moll?'' he asked, teasing her, his bright eyes filled with the charm he could use when he cared.

''Bloody marvellous,'' she whispered. ''I won't charge, Wolfe. If Rummy beats me, I don't care.''

''Oh, you're Rummy's, are you?''

He thought of the fat, bloated old man downstairs and grimaced. Moll couldn't be more than twenty.

''He took me in,'' she explained. ''I get my own room and my food. He's not so bad. He only takes half what I get.''

''If he beats you, I'll cut his throat,'' Wolfe said casually.

Her eyes shone. ''I'd work for you, Wolfe. I earn enough for two. You'd never have to do a hand's turn.''

Wolfe laughed at that, yet his brows met darkly at the same

time. "You tempt me, Moll, but no. I've another future ahead. Thank you for the offer."

Her face was sick with disappointment. "You'll come again, though? I'd never charge you."

He gave her a kind, careless smile. "I'll be around, Moll."

She watched as he sat up and began to dress. Her hands lovingly touched his muscled back, running over the hard, handsome young face as though she could not bear to have him go.

"Was it good for you too, Wolfe?"

He heard the nervous note in her voice, as though she was afraid the answer would be no, and he looked at her, his eyes narrowed, bent and kissed her mouth. Her lips clung hungrily to him.

Had she never known kindness before, he wondered, that she mistook it for love? Her world was far from the world in which Sophia had grown up. He himself was the only point at which those two worlds touched.

"It was what I needed most," he said against her mouth, and heard her sigh with pleasure.

In the small lodging house where Lucy sat, her face white, tears dry on her cheeks, the canary sang and hopped in its wicker cage as Wolfe strolled into the room. He looked hard at his mother, jingling the coins in his pocket.

"I've been to see the solicitor."

She didn't look at him, staring like a dead creature at the little yellow bird.

"He made a will years ago leaving everything to Stonor. There was a codicil added later leaving legacies to Elizabeth and Grey, but he left us nothing. He must have put off changing his will. I've no doubt he meant to see to it some time, but he never did."

Lucy gave no sign of having heard.

"Mother, do you understand? There's nothing for us."

The golden head slowly turned. Her eyes were blank.

"How could he do this to you?" Wolfe was suddenly angry, seeing the shocked misery in her face.

Lucy's mouth quivered. "Does it matter? He's dead. I can't think about anything else just now."

"We're alive. We have to go on living and we're penniless, Mother. We only have what we stand up in. Do you realize that?"

"Wolfe, be quiet!" Lucy stood up, trembling. "Don't you see I don't care?"

He stared at her, opened his mouth to speak harshly, then changed his mind, his face taut with anger.

After a moment, he asked her gently: "Then what will you do? Where will you go?"

She gave a queer laugh. "The river, maybe."

"Don't say such things!"

"Life's over for me. James was my life. He's gone. I can do no better than follow him."

"You're still a young woman. How can you talk like that?"

Lucy stared at him, her mouth quivering. "Have you ever asked yourself what it cost me to live as I have? I sacrificed my life to James. I gave up my good name for him. I was strictly brought up, Wolfe. My family are Wesleyans, stern religious people. Living with James as I did, I put my soul in jeopardy. It wasn't easy for me to agree to what he wanted, but I loved him. I'd no choice once I knew he mattered more to me than anything else I'd ever known. Now he's dead and there's nothing for me to live for."

"What about me, Mother?" Wolfe asked, his voice curiously hurt.

She looked at him and her face changed, softened, warmed. "Oh, son!" Her hands were stretched out, and he knelt beside her chair, laying his head on her lap. For the second time that day, a woman comforted him, her hands gentle on his black head, and he closed his eyes.

Later Wolfe asked her: "Mother, your brother lives in Bristol, doesn't he?"

She grimaced. "Josiah? Yes, but he would not take me across his threshold, Wolfe. He's a Wesleyan, remember. He sees me as a fallen woman who would contaminate his house."

"You haven't seen him for nearly twenty years. Maybe he has changed."

"Josiah won't have changed. He always reminded me of one of the standing stones we have down west, a grim grey thing that stands up to time and weather without budging."

Wolfe grinned. "I want to go down west, Mother. Come with me to Bristol. We'll take a look at Uncle Josiah, see if he is kinder than you remember. We're blood kin, after all. He can't be all bad."

"Why Bristol?" Lucy asked, suddenly alarmed. She stared into his strange, changing eyes. "Why do you want to go down west, Wolfe?"

He avoided her gaze. "You can take ship for America in Bristol," he told her coolly, yet she suspected there was more to it than that.

"America?"

"I've a fancy to see the place."

"We haven't got the fare."

"We'll have it."

Wolfe's mouth was hard, his eyes coldly determined, and Lucy was worried, but she knew better than to ask him questions when he looked like that. Wolfe's secretive nature frightened her. Ever since the night when they had been turned out of the Whitley household just in the clothes they stood up in, she had been living in a cold nightmare. Stonor had sent two footmen with blank, wooden faces that hid malice to see that they took nothing of any value with them. The jewels that James had given her had been left in their box. All she could take, she was told, was her own clothes and the canary.

Maria Whitley had stood on the landing and looked at Lucy with hatred as she slowly came out in her bonnet and cape. "Remove all the furniture from those rooms and burn it in the garden," Maria had ordered a servant. "All the linen and curtains, too, especially the bed and all its hangings."

Lucy had winced at the note in her voice. A doctor in a tall black hat had stood in the hall with Stonor as she had come downstairs. Lucy had heard the man's polite, even voice say: "There would have been nothing I could have done, even if I had been here when it happened. Death must have been almost immediate. Still, it's a quick death, with little pain, my boy. I'd not be sorry to go the same way myself. A few moments and all is over."

Wolfe had not halted as he passed Stonor, but Lucy had seen the naked hatred flash between the two young men. Wolfe had given her no explanation at the time. All she had known was that James had died of a heart attack. It had been sufficient grief for her at the time. Only the next day did she drag from him what had caused his father's death, and then she had known that her premonitions of disaster had been fatally accurate. Wolfe's passion for the girl had caused his father's death.

Looking at her son now, she thought: Oh, God, I wish the girl had never come here. Why is he planning to go down to the West Country? Had it something to do with Sophia?

Queen's Stonor lay only a few miles from Bristol; Lucy could not believe that to be a coincidence. She dared not ask Wolfe. Between herself and this strange son of hers lay a gulf she could not cross. She might guess at the depths behind his hard young face, but she could not speak of them to him. He had not been a child for so long. He was a man in experience, and she felt helpless before that look on his face.

Lucy Hunt was a woman whose simple, affectionate nature did not match the physical magnificence of her body. It had been the combination of these things that had drawn James Whitley to her in the first place and that had kept him faithful to her for years. Lucy's childhood had been narrow, threaded with the dark menace of her father's religion. She had fled from that revengeful God to London under the curse of her brother Josiah and gone into service as a domestic servant. Then she had met James Whitley, who had fallen in love with her and seduced her. James had persuaded her to live in his house with difficulty. Lucy had been terrified of Maria Whitley's hatred, but James had shielded her from it, forcing Maria to keep away from Lucy by the simple expedient of threatening his wife that if she did not leave Lucy alone, he would take Lucy and their son and abandon Maria altogether.

Although her life had been a strange one, Lucy had made of her little apartment a warm home for James and Wolfe. She was a domestic creature, soft and kind, busy and contented. The circumstances in which she had lived with James Whitley had been alien to her. She had been born to be a happy wife and mother. She yearned for respectability.

"America is so far away," she said now. "If you got a job in the city, Wolfe, I could keep house for you. We could find a little place that didn't cost too much. I'm sure some of your father's friends would help, give you a position in a good firm. You've been well educated. You could clerk for a merchant."

Wolfe's teeth bared, white and sharp. "You think I'd settle for a life of skimping and slaving? No, Mother. I've other plans."

Sophia sat in the drawing room in a new black dress, staring at her hands on her lap. Aunt Maria lay upstairs on her bed, as she had all day, silent and white, as if the funeral yesterday had drained her of energy. The arrangements had all been made by Stonor. A line of carriages had followed the stately hearse with its four black horses, their heads tossing under black feathers. James Whitley had had a magnificent funeral. Many London merchants had attended. Of course, the women of the family had been in black from head to toe, their faces hidden by heavy veiling, and Aunt Maria's weeping body had been guided by Sophia throughout, since Elizabeth found her mother tiring after a short space of time.

Elizabeth was in the conservatory with Tom Lister now, whispering to him. Sophia could sense their glances through the window every now and then, but she ignored them.

Grey stood on the hearth, thinner and paler than ever, staring at his highly polished shoes. He was rarely at home, preferring to lead his own life away from the unhappy domestic circumstances in which he had grown up, but his father's death had kept him chained to the house, and he was looking bored.

Sophia had seen little of him during her visit. He passed a few stiff remarks whenever they met, but she knew nothing of him except that he had a violent temper and hated Wolfe as much as Stonor did.

Now he looked up and said to Stonor: "Unless you object, I think I'll take the private suite for myself."

Stonor, who had been deep in blank thought, started. "What?"

"The apartment," Grey said. "Now that they've gone, what will you do with it? You've no use for it, have you? It would suit me down to the ground. I could come and go as I choose, without Mama prying into my affairs."

Stonor eyed him coolly. "As you wish, but for God's sake, Grey, don't play the fool now Papa's no longer here to watch you."

"Don't cant at me," Grey said unpleasantly, the white scar on his face livid.

"I won't back your bills as Papa did," Stonor warned him with an inflexible ring to his voice.

"I've my legacy."

"Once that's gone, there's no more where it came from!"

"The will was damned unfair. Why should you get more than me? There's barely a year between us, and I work as hard at the firm as you do."

Stonor's pale brows lifted ironically. "You do? When do you do all this work? Normally you spend most of your time out of the office."

Grey's lips thinned in an ugly sneer. "Oh, I'm no office slave as you are, I admit. You have your nose in an account book morning, noon and night. It's meat and drink to you. But I do my share."

"You'd better," Stonor said, his lips closing in a thin line. "I won't have you sneaking off the way you did with Papa. You'll work the same as everyone else. If you must paint the town red, you can do it in your own time at your own expense."

"My God, there's no red blood in your veins, Stonor," Grey said with a glance of dislike. "You're not a man. You're a machine for making money. You can keep your lectures to yourself. I've no intention of letting you rule my life. Now Papa's gone, I'm free of all that." He walked to the door and slammed out of the room.

Sophia had heard all this without listening, without caring. She was not even aware of Stonor sitting opposite her, his body stiff in a black suit, his face as pale as the shirt he wore. They sat together in silence. He did not look at her or speak. She heard the clock behind her chime melodically. The sound made her start.

Stonor got up. She felt his glance on her bent head. Her body grew more rigid. He walked to the conservatory and drew the curtains, shutting Tom and Elizabeth out of sight.

Sophia's body tightened. She stared at her hands, swallowing. He walked back and stood in front of her. She did not look up.

"Obviously since I shall be in mourning for six months, our marriage must be postponed. My mother would consider it unseemly if we did not wait, and I wish to give her time to get over my father's death. I have decided, therefore, that you should return to Queen's Stonor."

She looked up then, her pale lips parted in surprise and relief. He saw the expression on her face and irony deepened the lines around his mouth. "You look tired. You must go up to bed now," he said.

She rose quickly, and Stonor crossed the room to open the door for her. She moved to pass him, her eyes on the floor, her black train making a soft, whispering sound against the carpet as she walked.

"Sophia!" He spoke softly as she drew level with him.

She halted, waiting, trembling.

He put a hand under her chin, felt the flinching movement

she made, and turned her face upwards. Apprehensively her wide blue eyes met his stare. She had not looked at him all day.

"When you leave me each night you will kiss me," he said, his tone level.

She moistened her dry lips with her tongue, and his cold gaze watched the movement. Before she realized his intention, his head swooped and his mouth covered her lips so that she tasted his flesh on her tongue. She gasped, hurriedly trying to close her mouth against him. Instantly his mouth was removed.

"Good night, Sophia."

She walked quickly into the hall, her legs trembling under her, and escaped up the stairs, shivering. The deliberate intimacy he had forced upon her had unnerved her. She found the combination of cold formality and hidden sensuality in Stonor quite terrifying. Since his father's death and Wolfe's departure, she had been in a state of shock, barely knowing what was happening around her. Aunt Maria's need of her, her weeping dependence on her, had been the only support Sophia herself had had during that period. She had contrived to remain calm merely in order to comfort her aunt.

Now she threw herself on her bed and began to sob, her whole body trembling in a convulsive misery that took total control of her. All the grief she had been suppressing rose to the surface.

Suddenly she felt a hand upon her hair and stiffened, terrified of finding Stonor with her.

"My poor little girl!"

It was Aunt Maria in her loose white nightgown, her hair pushed under a frilled nightcap. She sat down on the bed beside Sophia and looked at her pityingly.

"I heard you crying. Poor little girl, I know you must be feeling sick and frightened. It has all been a shock to you. But you mustn't cry like this! You will make yourself ill."

Sophia covered her face, moaning incoherently. "How shall I bear it? Oh, God, what am I to do?"

Aunt Maria stroked her hair gently, sitting on the bed beside her. "You must forget it all. Put it out of your mind. Thank God I came before that vile animal had had time to do you any lasting harm. It is over, thank God. That creature has left this house forever. When I think of him laying his filthy hands upon you, trying to..." She shuddered and broke off. "I know how terrified you must have been, and thank God you're still innocent. If I hadn't heard him!"

"Poor Uncle James," Sophia said, barely having heard. "It is all my fault he's dead."

The thought had been in her mind, tormenting her, ever since it had happened. She would always blame herself for James Whitley's death.

Aunt Maria's mouth set like stone, reminding her of Stonor.

"James Whitley died because his sins found him out. God struck him down. The Bible tells us what we may expect. Our sins are made the instruments of vengeance. That boy was James's sin."

"Don't," Sophia cried wildly, her voice ragged with sobs.

"You mustn't blame yourself," Aunt Maria said, becoming human again, the stony look leaving her face. "Nobody in this house blames you, my dear. We love you too much. We all know who was to blame. You are an innocent child, and that animal tried to take advantage of you."

Sophia wept while the thin hand gently stroked her hair, and neither understood the other.

Wolfe walked along the Ratcliffe Highway through the crowded midnight streets, ignoring the whispered invitations of street women, the curious dark stares of sailors, the drunken oaths of workmen who pushed past him. The street was notorious for the spilling, teeming life that spread into it from the dark alleys and courts behind. At night one could buy anything there, from a pair of shoes to a woman. Men sprawled across the gutters, their empty pockets pulled out by thieves or whores, snoring off their drunken haze while passersby ignored them. If the police came down the Ratcliffe Highway at night, they came in pairs. It was dangerous for them to walk alone.

A small girl with a crudely painted face clutched at Wolfe's trouser leg as he passed a shop doorway, murmuring automatic words of invitation. He looked at her grimly, pushing her away without unkindness. Children could be bought here like dolls. One saw them taking clients into dark corners everywhere. Wolfe thrust a coin into her dirty little hand, his eyes bitter. For all his amusements in the highway, he had never liked to see the child whores at their posts. In the more select parts of London, as he was well aware, there were special houses for those wealthy gentlemen whose tastes ran to children, but here the vice was out in the open and no worse for that, in Wolfe's opinion. He found the secret vices of the rich far more depraved than the rough pleasures of the poor.

In a dark alley later he stood with Black Strap and a few other men, talking softly out of reach of the lights from a nearby house. The gang had their faces blacked to escape detection. They carried cudgels and had pistols through their belts.

"The wagons will be outside the side alley," Black Strap told them. "If all goes well we'll have shifted the stuff and be gone before the cops get here. You, Leather Face, you know where to stash it, do you? Jackie will drive one wagon. Monkey takes the other. The rest of us will scatter once the job's done and meet up at the Turk's Head later."

"Sure about the chap inside?" asked Monkey in a rough voice.

Black Strap looked at Wolfe.

Wolfe nodded. "He's as safe as houses. I've known him for years."

"Can we trust him, though? How d'we know he isn't in with the cops?"

"We can trust him." Wolfe spoke sharply.

"Who says so?"

The men stirred, sensing Monkey's dislike of Wolfe.

Wolfe eyed him, his teeth white in his bland face. He had not blacked up like the rest, although Black Strap had urged him to do so.

"I do," Wolfe said. "Want to make something of it?"

Monkey was a small, bowlegged man. He stared at Wolfe, then shrugged. "All right. I hope you're telling the truth. I'm not risking my life on the say-so of a nark. If you've lied to us, I'll get you, my fine gentleman."

Wolfe stepped closer and stared down at him, his eyes bright with temper. "We'll see each other later," he said threateningly.

Black Strap intervened, smiling. "Now, now, boys. No fighting. We've got work to do."

They moved off through the black alleys, walking silently, attentive to every sound. The Whitley warehouse lay in a cobbled alley above the river, the great barred doors twice as high as a man. Wolfe tapped three times on a small door within the gate. After a pause they all heard someone inside tap back three times. Wolfe replied with a single tap. Silently the door slid open.

Wolfe tied a scarf around the mouth of the man who let them inside, then he whispered, "Hope this doesn't hurt much, Joe," and struck him once on his head with a loaded stick.

The man's body crumpled. Wolfe laid him on the floor, arranging his body to look as though he had fallen.

The others spread out in the darkness, their feet silent because they had socks over their boots. Wolfe heard muffled sounds as they crept up behind other watchmen and struck them down.

Suddenly there was a flash and a resounding sound.

"Oh, God Almighty," Black Strap muttered.

One of the gang stood staring down at a man who lay on the ground, blood covering the back of his head, his body sprawled face down.

"He grabbed my pistol and when I grabbed it back it went off! I couldn't help it!"

"That's a topping job," Monkey moaned.

"Shut up!" Black Strap turned on him. "It's done now. Scatter and get on with loading. Nothing we can do about him now."

"Someone may have heard," Monkey said, his small dark face twitching.

"Get on with it!"

They worked busily, carrying the great bags of sugar out of the open side door and loading them into wagons that stood there. Barrels of rum came rolling out and were rolled up a plank into the wagon to stand beside the sugar. The horses moved restlessly, their feet wrapped in sacking to deaden the noise of the stamp of their feet on the cobbles. From the dark river below came the hoarse moan of a ship's hooter.

Wolfe was helping the others, his face tight with excitement and the smell of danger. His eyes glittered as he grinned at Black Strap. "All out!"

"Whip 'em up, Monkey!" Black Strap ordered.

The wagons were whipped up and the horses began to pull away. Wolfe felt laughter in his chest as he looked at the Whitley name painted on the warehouse door.

"We've got away with the lot," he said triumphantly. "The bastard will feel this loss. A small repayment on account, Stonor."

The gang left behind began to run lightly, spreading out into the darkness. Suddenly a loud voice hailed them from the corner of the road. Wolfe saw a pair of policemen in the shadows.

"Stop or we shoot!"

"Damn!"

Wolfe ducked as there was a red flash in his direction but felt a sharp, burning pain in one arm just as he flung himself out of range. Running fast, wincing at the pain in his arm, he turned into a small court. A solid wall ended it, and Wolfe had a little difficulty scrambling over it and into the garden beneath. Across that he stumbled, climbing another wall into a little alley. He heard the shouts of the policemen as they followed him.

He was winded now, breathing harshly, his chest and lungs hurting. Blood trickled down his hand. He winced as he banged the wounded arm on a stone post set in the end of the alley to stop carriages from mounting the pavement. The alleys and courts seemed endless, their dark walls sometimes occupied by couples who paused in their movements to stare around at him as he ran past.

Once as he turned a corner he ran full tilt into a man and woman. For a second the ragged sound of Wolfe's breathing cut into the breathy moan of the man, and Wolfe ran on, followed by a string of curses.

He laughed as he ran, his right hand now gripping his left elbow to support it, and turned down the street of the Turk's Head, his heart pounding as though it would burst.

Flimsy wooden stairs led up the side of the building to the room above. Wolfe fell in through the creaking door and Moll, her legs wide, stared over the thrusting body of a rough-set sailor.

"Don't let me interrupt!" Wolfe gasped mockingly, then slowly crumpled to the floor.

When he opened his eyes, Moll was kneeling beside him, slitting his sleeve with a knife.

He grinned at her. "Sorry to ruin your night's work."

"Lie still, do!"

"Was your customer angry?"

"He got what he wanted." Moll looked down, wincing, at the dark red mass of blood and tissue. "Oh, God, Wolfe! What happened?"

"Worse than it looks," he grunted, his face taut as her fingers gently began to wash the wound.

Black Strap came into the room abruptly, flushed and breathless. He looked down at Wolfe, who grinned at him.

"Hurt bad?" The older man looked worried.

Wolfe shook his head. "A flesh wound. It will heal. Did the wagons get away?"

"No danger. We all did. You're the only one who got hit."

Black Strap watched as Moll cleansed the wound, seeing the young face whiten to a total lividity. Opening his cupboard, he brought brandy over to Wolfe.

"Take a swig."

"Will you get me drunk before you take the bullet out? I can feel it in there."

Black Strap's eyes were indulgent. "Drink, you young fool."

Wolfe drank a mouthful. Black Strap seized his jaw and yanked it open, pouring the brandy into his open mouth until it swished down his shirt.

Wolfe choked, gasping. "Goddamn you," he muttered. "There was no need for that."

Black Strap watched the hot colour come into the boy's face. Wolfe stared blindly at the ceiling, beginning to laugh. "Goddamn the lot of them," he said. "Get on with it, then."

Black Strap took his knife and began to heat it in the flame of a candle. Moll looked over her shoulder at him, shuddering. Wolfe was laughing, muttering drunkenly.

"Get out of the way," Black Strap told the girl.

"I'll hold him still. He might jump as you cut."

Black Strap nodded. The girl flinched but held Wolfe's body still as the other man began to work. The lean young body was sprawled easily, his legs thrown wide. She looked at him passionately. His lips moved in that drunken muttering, his face deeply flushed. She bent to kiss him and heard him moan. "Sophia." Moll's jealous eyes speared his handsome face.

Some hours later Wolfe turned restlessly upon the filthy pillow. His eyes opened to look at Moll's anxious face. For a few seconds he looked at her blankly, then a slow grin spread over his features. He looked down at his bandaged arm.

"Get the bullet out?"

"You're to lie still," Moll told him, covering him again.

"Am I?" He surveyed her from under his long black lashes, a little smile on his hard mouth. "Come here, Moll. I'm a sick man and must be comforted."

Moll hung back, her blue eyes hungry on him, shaking her

head. "You're too ill, Wolfe. Black Strap said as you was to sleep."

"There's no sleep sweeter than the sleep that comes after what I'm going to do to you," he said mockingly.

"Wolfe! We shouldn't! Wait till you're better."

He grinned coaxingly at her. "Comfort me, Moll, there's a good girl."

She lay down reluctantly and he moved. "Lie still," she said almost angrily. "I'll do what is needed."

He laughed, lying back. "What's needed? Oh, God."

"You're half-drunk still," she fretted.

"Not drunk enough." Wolfe was suddenly harsh, his brows dark.

"You don't want to drink," Moll said thickly, her hands caressing him, her eyes adoring his handsome face. "Oh, Wolfe, you're the best-looking man I ever saw. I love you, Wolfe. I'd do anything for you. Just lie still and let me love you. I'll do whatever you want. Just tell me."

Wolfe felt a qualm of pity. He stroked her dirty blonde hair back from her hot face, kissing her cheek as if she were a child. "Sweet little Moll," he whispered in her ear, and she smiled as though he had said he loved her.

Sophia sat with her head bent, disinterestedly pushing food around her plate while Elizabeth ate her way solidly through her usual breakfast of porridge, bacon and egg and toast. Grey had eaten his own meal and left before the two girls came down, but Stonor's place was untouched, his napkin still thrust through the painted china napkin ring. Aunt Maria was breakfasting in bed again.

Suddenly Stonor came into the room, his pale features set. Elizabeth glanced up, dabbing her mouth with her napkin.

"You're late this morning, Stonor."

"I have been out," he said, taking his seat. "Is the tea still hot?" He tested the temperature of the pot and then rang for the maid. "More tea, Joan."

"Where have you been at this hour?" Elizabeth asked, preparing to leave the table now that she had satisfied her appetite.

Stonor picked up his napkin and spread it on his lap. "A gang raided the warehouse last night."

"Good heavens! Were they caught?" Elizabeth's eyes opened wide, her face expressing dismay.

Stonor glanced at Sophia. He took a slice of lukewarm toast and spread it with butter, his movements precise and studied.

"They killed a watchman and knocked out the others. Then they escaped with wagonloads of goods."

"Was much lost?" Elizabeth asked, looking appalled at his crisp recital of the facts.

"What do you think?" Stonor's face was icy.

"What was in the warehouse last night? Wasn't there a ship in only the other day?"

"Sugar and rum from an East Indiaman," Stonor replied curtly, his eyes fixed on Sophia's bent black head. "Whoever was behind the robbery knew exactly what they were looking for and how to get into the warehouse. It was a carefully planned operation, timed to perfection, and there must have been inside cooperation. Someone let them into the warehouse."

"Who?" Elizabeth demanded, her jaw set squarely in irritation. "We must find out and see that they pay."

"We will," Stonor said grimly.

Elizabeth's bright blue eyes had a calculating glint. "How much did we lose, Stonor? Was it a good deal?"

"Hard to be certain yet, but it wasn't a small amount. It will have hit us hard," Stonor said.

"It was insured, though?"

He nodded curtly. "Of course."

Elizabeth sighed with relief and got up with a swish of skirts. "I must tell Mama."

"No," Stonor said abruptly. "She has enough to worry about. Leave her alone, Elizabeth."

His sister gave him a little shrug. "Oh, very well." She flounced out of the room, and Stonor turned his eyes back to Sophia. She got up, still not looking at him, and began to steal away, but his cold voice stopped her in mid-step.

"Aren't you interested in our robbery, Sophia? You ought to be. Some of the details are fascinating."

Some not-quite-hidden malice in his voice caught her attention. She did not look up, but listened, her head still bent.

"Most of the gang had blacked their faces to avoid being recognized, but one of them hadn't bothered. Either he was too reckless or too stupid to bother. He wore rather good clothes for a common thief, as well. The police noticed that particularly. They noticed his height, his hair colour, his gold watch chain. . ."

Sophia froze at that, her face turning white. Stonor's hand shot across the table and caught her wrist in a cruelly tight grip. She looked up, gasping. She could not bear to be in the same room as Stonor. The air around her seemed to stifle her.

"Did you hear what I said, Sophia?"

"Yes," she whispered.

"There's more," Stonor said, watching her lips tremble. She tried to stiffen them, but her eyes betrayed her fear.

"The policemen were armed," Stonor said softly.

The agony that flashed into her face rewarded him. Her eyes widened until he saw the white skin around them seeming to be stretched to the point of pain. She was breathing carefully, and Stonor made her wait, his eyes on her face, reading every glance, every flicker of her blue eyes.

"They shot him," he said at last, deliberately.

He rose as he spoke, moving around the table, his strides rapid, as though anticipating what would happen. Her body crumpled like that of a rag doll just as he reached her and caught her in his arms. He lifted her, her black head falling limply over his sleeve, and carried her up to her bedroom. Laying her on the bed, he got some water from a jug and loosened the neck of her gown. Then he dipped her handkerchief into the water and let the coolness slide moistly over her forehead.

Her lids began to stir. Stonor sat back and watched her. Slowly the white lids lifted. She looked at him, her eyes a wild blue between her black lashes. Stonor watched full consciousness return to her white face.

"Yes, your lover is dead," he said, a flat harsh tone to his voice. "Shot dead in the streets like a wild dog after robbing our warehouse. It seems a fitting end. If I were my mother, I'd say it was the hand of God that struck him down. But I'll not mouth such stuff to you, Sophia. My one regret is that it wasn't my hand that pulled that trigger."

Sophia neither moved nor spoke. Her blue eyes stared at him as though she were deaf.

"No tears, Sophia? Surely you should weep for the man you loved?" He sounded as though he were mocking her, but his face was taut and icy. She still sat there with a totally blank face, too shocked even to cry. Her mind was empty, as though she were without thought or feeling.

The fact that Wolfe was dead had penetrated her brain, but

she was refusing to accept it. For the moment she dared not accept it or she might go mad.

"Weep, you little bitch," Stonor said thickly, bending over her. He slapped her hard across the face. "Let me see you cry for him!"

When she still showed no sign of grief or understanding, he hit her again so fiercely that her head flew back at the blow, her black ringlets tumbling in disarray.

"Now tell me the truth," Stonor said hoarsely. "Did he have you? How many times had he been to your room at night? Is that where you met? Tell me, Sophia. I mean to know the truth. Was he your lover already that night my mother interrupted the two of you?"

The empty, uncomprehending stare of the blue eyes did not alter. Each harsh question passed over her head. Stonor watched her, pausing after each question, waiting for an answer and getting none.

He breathed as if he were drowning, the deep rasp of his intake of air painful. When she merely lay there with that fixed stare, he gave a deep groan, then he lifted her into his arms, his hand cradling her black head. His cheek came down against her hair. He rocked her like a baby. "Oh, Christ, you little bitch," he said in a thickened, bitter voice.

# CHAPTER SIX

The druggist's shop in the narrow, salt-blistered street was darkly lit and lined with rows of heavy oak drawers upon whose façades yellowing cards showed the names of the drugs within, their dark curlicues faded with time. Wolfe stood, his powerful shoulders back, as the sound of the doorbell faded and a short, bowed man came out in the faint light from a room behind the shop. The druggist eyed Wolfe politely without warmth, his thin, sour face pallid.

"May I help you, sir?" The courtesy of the words was as thin as watered milk, a mere pretence of service.

"Mr. Josiah Hunt?" Wolfe asked, staring penetratingly.

"Yes." Pale blue eyes regarded him without interest.

Wolfe moved aside and his mother slowly came forwards. She was wearing severe black, the rich yellow hair hidden beneath a plain black bonnet.

Josiah Hunt looked at her blankly for a few seconds, then recognition came into his face, followed swiftly by distaste and anger.

"Don't you know me, Josiah?" There was the merest thread of hope in Lucy's husky voice; her eyes pleaded.

"Get out of my shop." The druggist's voice rose, a full richness coming into his throat, as though he intoned in a pulpit.

"Josiah!"

"How dare you come here?"

"I'm your sister," Lucy whispered, her hand extended, a tremor in the fingers. "Josiah, let me talk to you. . . ."

"I have no sister! I had one once. She became a whore and was lost to the company of the elect forever." His nostrils flaring, Josiah Hunt spoke with a white sickliness around his thin mouth.

Wolfe saw his mother flinch. He moved abruptly, grabbing the older man by the throat. His strong hand jerked him off his feet, choking him, a spasm of rage making Wolfe's handsome young face look older and grimmer.

"No, Wolfe," Lucy whimpered, tugging at his arm. "I knew how it would be! I told you. Come away. There's no point in talking to him."

Wolfe seemed not to hear her. His rages since the day of his father's death had begun to possess him as if they were a drug he was addicted to, a sweet bitterness he could not turn from. He shook the old man as if he were a rat, and the old man gasped out, "You don't frighten me! I am saved."

Wolfe's quick eyes caught a movement at the lace curtain that was draped across the window of the door leading from the shop to the private room behind. He wondered who was watching. Then his eye went back to his uncle. With a casual gesture of cold contempt, he threw the older man away from him, turned on his heel and walked out behind his mother.

Josiah Hunt fell, shuddering, across the counter of his shop, his thin hands clutching at his throat. The door to the private room opened and a girl ran towards him, moving to lift him with her thin arms around his waist.

While she was helping her father into the other room, a young man in a cheap dark suit and stiff white collar slid discreetly around the shop and followed Wolfe and his mother into the shadowed street.

Coughing, a bitter anger in his face, Josiah Hunt leaned on his daughter's thin shoulder. The cold, bleak lines of his face turned to a shaking rage. He shifted his pale eyes to the girl, who shrank back, fearing his temper. When he was aroused, Josiah Hunt was terrible.

"If ever I am not here and that...that woman...or the man who was with her comes here, do not let them cross the threshold, Eliza. Do you understand? They are not fit to speak with decent folk. They are sinners."

"Yes, Father," the girl whispered obediently. Despite her plain attire and pulled-back hair, she had a delicate beauty of her own, a frail sweetness of mind that was reflected in her eyes.

Josiah Hunt pushed her away. "I can stand alone. Get back into the shop."

Eliza scuttled away, relieved to be free of his bitter presence, and her father stood staring at the bare, tidy little room. "Whore," he muttered beneath his breath. "Whore."

Wolfe and his mother walked back towards the inn at which they were staying. Running feet behind them alerted Wolfe.

He whirled, pushing his mother behind him, his lean body prepared for a fight. In the streets of London he had soon learned to defend himself against thieves who snatched and ran away, and his tough face still showed the marks of pain left by the slow healing of his bullet wound.

The young man approaching slowed, holding up both hands to demonstrate that he bore no weapon and intended no harm. Wolfe eyed him curiously, seeing the poverty of his cheap clothes and his neat, respectable appearance.

"I overheard what my father was saying in the shop," the young man panted, halting in front of them. He was thickset, in his early twenties, stockily built, with pale blue eyes and an obstinate, determined chin. He stared at Lucy before giving her a short bow. "I gather you're my Aunt Lucy. My mother often spoke of you when my father wasn't by. I'm sorry he turned you away, Aunt. My mother would have wished to see you if she had been alive."

"Nan's dead, then?" Lucy's voice was harsh. She shivered. "I didn't know."

"These four years." The young man spoke harshly. "She died because my father dosed her himself and wouldn't pay for a doctor. Had she seen one a year earlier she might have lived, but he wouldn't listen, even when I offered to pay for one myself."

Lucy looked at him compassionately, seeing the pain in his face. "I'm sorry. So sorry. I was fond of your mother."

"She was fond of you," he said.

"You're Luther, then." Lucy's mouth quivered. "I remember the day you were born. I wasn't even the age you are now."

Luther's jaw clenched. "My mother told me how you sat with her while I was born, and how my father refused to pay for a midwife, saying birth was an act of God and needed no human help." His voice was deep and bitter. "He said the same when she bore her last child. The birth took two days and the baby died before it was delivered. My mother almost died, but I fetched a doctor just in time. My father beat me for it. I'd disobeyed him, and he never forgave me for it."

"Did he want her to die?" Wolfe asked, shocked.

Luther smiled acidly. "You don't know my father. No, he takes the view that we shouldn't interfere with the will of God. If my mother had died, it would have been because God willed it so."

"Why do you stay with him?" Wolfe asked angrily. "I'd

choke the life out of the old bastard if I were in your shoes.''

Luther's pale eyes gleamed. ''I stay because he's dying,'' he said softly. ''I want to be at his deathbed.''

Wolfe looked at him alertly, cocking his head.

Lucy laid a hand upon the young man's arm, sighing. ''Oh, you're a good boy, Luther.''

Wolfe's eyes stayed on his cousin's face. He grinned suddenly, that wild, reckless grin which came when he was excited. ''Shall you enjoy watching him die?''

Lucy looked horrified. ''Wolfe!''

Luther's teeth bared. ''I shall kneel at his bedside and whisper in his ear that he's damned for all eternity,'' he said. ''It will be a long, painful death. I think he knows it's coming. The grey shadow of it lingers in his face. I pray it will be more than human flesh and blood can stand, and that I'm there to watch it.''

Wolfe held out his hand. ''Cousin, I'm happy to know you.''

Lucy was shivering, her shocked, bewildered eyes on them both as the two young men shook hands firmly.

''You'll need a lodging,'' Luther said. ''Are you in Bristol for long? I know where you can find one near here. It's no palace, mind, but they are honest and it's cheap.''

''We're at the Star, but I'd be grateful for a cheap lodging for a few days while my mother decides what to do.'' Wolfe turned a slightly troubled glance upon Lucy. ''I'm planning to sail to America, and she is reluctant to come with me, so I was hoping to leave her in good hands here.''

Luther glanced at his aunt, frowning. He lowered his voice, turning away from her. ''There's just the two of you, then?''

Wolfe met his glance frankly. ''My father's dead and we're left homeless and almost penniless. I can't go to America until I know my mother's safe.''

Luther smiled at him understandingly, approvingly. ''Look, I can't stay now or he may miss me. I'll slip out early tomorrow and meet you at the Star. These people are Irish, Catholics.'' His glance shrewdly probed their faces, seeing no hostility. ''My father detests them, of course. He hates the Church of Rome. I dare not let him know I visit them.''

''If they're honest, I don't care what they are,'' Wolfe shrugged.

Luther grinned. ''We're of one mind, then. I must go. I'll see you tomorrow, Cousin.'' He moved off, and Wolfe stared after him.

Lucy said wearily, "I'm so tired, Wolfe. I'd like to lie down."

Wolfe put an arm around her, his eyes concerned. "Don't look so worried, Mother. I won't leave you until you're in good hands."

"What hands, Wolfe? You're all I have in the world. If you go, my life goes with you."

Wolfe looked darkly frustrated, a seething tension in his eyes. "I won't leave you alone, Mother," he said again, his voice filled with unspoken reservation.


The Star was a dirty, crowded inn full of sailors, and rough bearded men who stared at Lucy fixedly as they passed up the stairs. She shuddered under their eyes. "Why did we have to come here?" she asked Wolfe.

"We've little money for lodgings," Wolfe said, as he had said a number of times. "Lie down, Mother, and get some sleep."

"What will you do?" she asked him anxiously.

"Take a look around Bristol. I shan't be gone long. Lock your door when I go."

Lucy locked the door and lay down on the grimy bed. The tears ran down her face as she abandoned herself to her grief and anxiety.

Wolfe walked through the narrow, crowded streets towards the port, shrugging past stumbling sailors with drink-glassed eyes, men lounging against walls, women on doorsteps. He stood out among the floating scum of the old city because of the dangerous, wild look on his handsome face and his clothes of a gentleman, although the gloss had left him slightly since he had been thrown out of the Whitley household to fend for himself. Pain had toughened his features. A desire for revenge had cut deep into his features. Anyone who saw him now would see a dangerous opponent, a man to be reckoned with, someone capable of anything to achieve his ends. He had always been ruthlessly unscrupulous, but now it showed in his face.

He found a grimy little inn on the corner of a wharf and spoke to the barman softly. The man jerked a thumb into a back room, and Wolfe walked into it. The men looked up, wary as cornered rats, trying to read his face.

"Black Strap told me I'd find friends here," Wolfe said, poised on his toes, ready for any necessary movement if the reaction were not friendly. A silence followed. The men looked at each other. A small, rat-faced man in sailor's jersey and loose trousers spat thoughtfully.

"Any friend of Black Strap's is welcome here," he said.

"Take some rum with me, friends?" Wolfe asked, pulling up a chair.

"We'd take rum with the Devil if he was paying," the other said, grinning. "What name d'we give you? I'm Link."

"Wolfe." The white teeth were bared in a not-unfriendly grin. "And I can bite."

"London too hot for you, Wolfe?" Link asked as the rum was served and the men lifted their mugs.

"I've a fancy to see America. I'm looking for a berth."

"Sailed before?"

"No, but I can turn my hand to anything."

Link grinned, showing yellow teeth. "I daresay you can! Especially if it isn't yours, eh?"

"Or if it's female," Wolfe said, grinning back.

Luther called for Lucy and Wolfe the next morning and led them through the narrow streets. The smell of salt and fish, the cry of gulls, the endless rows of chandlers' shops and sailors lining up at the doors of shippers laid the whole life of the city open to them at a glance.

Emigration to America had slackened since the lean and hungry years in the middle of the century, but many boards leaned outside the shipping offices, advertising sailings to the States, giving the tonnage and the cabin accommodation of the ships together with the name of the captain and the price for passage. With the nineteenth century almost three-quarters completed, life in England was becoming easier for the working man as reformers fought for better conditions for himself and his family. The terrible famines of the 1850s had become a bad memory. Bread was much cheaper and wages were much higher, and employment was easier to find.

Luther halted outside a flight of narrow, cracked steps. He knocked loudly and the door jerked open. A thin, pale girl in a dirty gown stared at them, her hair untidy around her face. Her brown eyes ran over Lucy and Wolfe, then returned apathetically to Luther.

"Good morning, Maveen. Is your father up?"

"He is not," the girl said in a soft Irish voice which sounded like rain. "Did ye need to be speaking with him?"

"I've brought you some guests. This is my Aunt Lucy, Maveen, and her son, Wolfe. They need rooms. Could you take them in?''

Maveen looked doubtful. ''Maybe.''

Luther said quietly, ''We'll come in and speak to your father.''

The girl's brown eyes looked glumly at Lucy, taking in her neat attire and clean skin. ''This is no house for the likes of her.''

Wolfe's lean body tightened. Luther caught the look on his face and laid a restraining hand on his arm, shaking his head. To the girl he said, ''The lady will not be troubling you, Maveen.''

''She looks too fine for us,'' Maveen said sulkily. ''I'll not have complaints made. I do what I can.''

Wolfe relaxed, seeing that the girl merely feared that his mother might look down on her. Lucy wrinkled her nose as she stepped into the small, dirty hall, offended by the rank odour of the house. Dust and grimy paintwork, the lingering smell of food and the stench of beer hung upon the atmosphere like smoke, tainting everything. Slowly Lucy untied her bonnet and turned to the girl.

''Who does the work in the house?''

''I do, when I'm able.''

Lucy looked her up and down, seeing the fragility of the bones beneath the pale skin, the querulous weakness of eye and mouth, the listless, dragging frailty that came from ill health.

''You need a strong pair of hands to help you,'' she said, her lips tightening. ''How old are you, child?''

''Fifteen,'' Maveen said dully.

''Fifteen!'' Lucy clicked her tongue. ''And where's your mother?''

''Dead these ten years.''

''And you've been coping with all this for how long?''

Maveen looked vague. ''Sure, I've no idea. So long as I could.''

''With nobody to help you?''

''How would I pay them?'' Maveen sounded indifferent.

A stumbling sound came from the narrow, yellowing stairs. An empty bottle rolled down to lie between them. A man swayed into view, peering as though unsure he saw them, his ruffled dark hair standing on end in a filthy cockscomb.

He was unshaven and as grimy as his daughter, but beneath the black stubble of his face the lines of his features were not unpleasant. Drink had given him a pouched look about the eyes and a jowl to his chin, but it had not yet quite destroyed the remnants of a certain good looks.

"Who's that below?" he asked, hanging onto the banister.

"Luther."

"Is it you, Luther? Come in and be welcome. Maveen, girl, send out for some beer."

"You've had enough by the look of you," Lucy said tartly. "A few minutes under the pump would do you no harm."

In his surprise at the sound of her voice, the man let go of the banister and lurched to squint at her through the shadows, then slid suddenly, bumping at every stair, until he sat at the bottom, his legs stuck out before him, a hoarse crow of laughter on his lips.

"Sure, that's one way to come down."

"Father, would ye be after shaming me?" Maveen moaned, looking at Lucy fearfully.

Lucy bent and yanked the man to his unsteady feet. He glared at her. "Woman, be out of my house! This is no place for a lady."

Wolfe took him in an iron grip. "The pump, you said, Mother?"

Maveen gave a little moan as Luther, grinning, helped him guide the Irishman towards the back of the house. "What are they after doing to him?"

"Washing him," Lucy said crisply. "Now, let's see the house." She walked away, skirts rustling over the dirt-roughened floors, and Maveen followed miserably, her eyes resentful.

"I do what I can!" she said, as she had said before. "I get so tired and then there's my cough."

Lucy had noticed the frequent dry little rasp. She glanced at the girl now, frowning. "Have you had the cough long?"

"I can't remember when I didn't have it."

Lucy's eyes were pitying. "And is it only you and your father who live here, Maveen?"

"There's Patrick," the girl said, brightening.

"Patrick?"

"My brother. He's off to work the morning, but he'll be back come dusk."

Luther and Wolfe guided the older man back, grinning. His face was streaked where cold water had made gulleys through the grime. His eyes were blearily awake, however, and he was capable of giving Lucy a bow.

"I forgot me manners, ma'am. Jack Duffey, at your service."

"Mr. Duffey, I'm looking for rooms. Your house isn't clean and your daughter is not well. If I run the house for you and nurse your daughter back to health, will you give me free room and board?"

He blinked. "Free room, is it? And board?" He looked at Luther. "She drives a hard bargain. What would a woman of her sort be wanting in a house like this? I may be drunk, but I know a lady when I see one."

"I've no money and I need somewhere to live," Lucy said. "You need a housekeeper. What do you say? Why beat about the bush? We can do each other a favour."

He stared at her, then grinned. "I say, give it a maiden voyage. If it isn't seaworthy, we'll turn to the breaker's yard."

"Does that mean you agree?" Lucy asked, smiling.

"Sure it does," he agreed.

Wolfe was delighted. For the first time since his father's death, his mother was showing signs of life. The challenge of this filthy, shabby little house, the pathetic ailing girl and the drunken father had fuelled a new interest in the future in her. Lucy needed to be needed.

"Have you a clean apron?" she asked Maveen, rolling up her sleeves with an air of determination.

"Are you going to clean the house?" Maveen asked in amazement.

"No time like the present. Mr Duffey, we'll need hot water—lots of it."

"Where would we be getting that?" he asked blankly.

"The pump," Lucy said. "You can pump the buckets of water for me and I'll get them boiling in the copper kettle. You have a copper, I suppose?"

Wolfe moved to the door, and she looked at him anxiously. "I've business to attend to, Mother," he said. "I'll be back."

Her face paled. "Don't go near that girl," she whispered so that the others shouldn't hear. "Promise me, Wolfe."

"I'll make no promises I wouldn't keep," Wolfe said grimly.

"Oh, Wolfe! If Stonor finds you near her, he'll kill you."

Wolfe grinned. "Stonor's in London. I am here."

He turned to the door and went out. Lucy stared after him, her eyes filled with deep anxiety for a moment. Then she went into the kitchen and began to work, sinking all her worries in the activity that best expressed her. Soon a great tub of boiling water steamed the air, and Maveen, sulkily huddled in a chair, watched as Lucy began to clean the grime from the walls and floor.

Wolfe reined in his horse and sat staring through the open gates of Queen's Stonor, amazed by what he saw. He had heard so much about this house, but nothing he had been told had prepared him for what he saw now. Queen's Stonor had a mellow beauty that was partly born of its surroundings, partly given by the centuries that had laid a loving hand upon it, washing away all hardness of colour and line, granting a unique harmony to the generations of building that had merged with time into a unity of impact.

It stood on a rise of green turf in the middle of a great, oak-filled park. The walls that surrounded it had been softened by wind and rain until they seemed as natural a growth as the trees within their circle. Sheep cropped the turf and ambled beneath the green frilled leaves of oak, their placid backs shedding tufts of wool on the scrub beneath the trees. The autumn sun gave a brightness to the windows and the soft rose of the brickwork.

The house was Tudor, built with great barley-sugar twists of red chimneys. The haphazard line of the building swayed with ivy here or moss there, the unified movement making Queen's Stonor a living organism as real and individual as any human being. Even the hint of decay seemed to add to its beauty. Age could only heighten it, although the moth of time ate day by day into the structure.

So, Wolfe thought, this is what Sophia was prepared to sacrifice herself to preserve! How he would like to take a torch and watch the house burn to the ground. He had come here intending to hate this house, and it angered him to see how beautiful it was, even to his hostile eyes.

He turned his horse into a line of trees that sheltered him from observation from the house and made his way into the park. Reaching a safe viewpoint behind some holly trees, he watched the red ball of the sun sink slowly behind the house, casting a final radiance upon it.

The scent of wood smoke drifted to him on the warm breeze. The sheep cropped ceaselessly, their teeth tearing at the turf. Wolfe thought of the raw red brick of his father's

London home and the dirty, narrow streets surrounding it. No wonder Maria Whitley had dreamed of Queen's Stonor ever since she left it. The great, ancient house seemed to sleep gently in the last rays of the sun, the peace of its green setting enhancing its beauty.

The sound of hooves attracted his attention. He turned and stared as he recognized Sophia's slight body riding beside that of a middle-aged man on a tall bay stallion. For a moment Wolfe stared hungrily at her, his face flushed dark red.

Then he forced himself to look at her companion. The man was wearing muddy, dishevelled clothes that had seen better days but that had once been well cut. His shoulders stooped. His thinning hair fluttered in the wind. The weary droop of his body proclaimed his long day in the saddle, but suddenly he and Sophia, as one, lifted their heads to look at the house. Wolfe could vaguely see their expressions, the look of love with which they greeted the house.

Wolfe slid down from his mount, looped the reins carefully around a low branch, patted the horse and left him grazing contentedly in the soft-falling dusk. Moving quietly, Wolfe made his way to the stable block on the east wing of the house. He stood in the angle of the wall, watching from the shadows as Sophia and her father dismounted.

A groom came out to take their horses. Edward Stonor walked slowly into the house, while Sophia patted her mare's long neck. The groom led the horses away, and Sophia turned to follow her father.

Wolfe moved out into the entrance to the stable yard. His footsteps on the cobbles made Sophia turn in surprise. He heard her harsh intake of breath. She stood still, staring at him. Wolfe moved back out of sight into the shadows outside and waited, his heart racing.

The next moment she came running around the corner, her eyes parting the shadows for him. She stopped as she caught sight of him, and he heard her breathing quicken.

For a few seconds they stood still. Then they both moved at the same time, their bodies clinging, their hands clasping each other's heads. Wolfe lowered his face, and their mouths met in a passionate explosion of such violence that it was more pain than pleasure.

At last he moved his lips along her face to kiss the warm white neck intimately, feeling the pulse of her life beating under his mouth.

"Wolfe!" she whispered hoarsely. "Oh, God. He told me you were dead."

He stood very still, his arms tightening around her. The agony in her voice reached him as agony of his own. He groaned, looked into her white face.

"I have thought all this time that you were dead!" she said in a whisper which shook with remembered anguish.

"My darling," he murmured, kissing her again.

"Why did he lie to me?"

"All's fair in love and war and this is both, my darling," Wolfe said with a sardonic twist to his mouth. "No doubt Stonor wished I were dead. God, how he must have hoped that shot killed me."

"Then you were shot? Oh, Wolfe, then it was you at the warehouse?"

He looked down at her recklessly. "I only took back what was mine. I'm James Whitley's son, too, and they knew my father meant to leave me provided for! For all I know, he left a will that Stonor destroyed. I wouldn't put it past him."

"You might have been killed!" She was aghast, staring at him.

"I was winged, that's all. And it has healed now; there's barely a scar."

She heard a footstep and stiffened. "They will be looking for me. I must go in, Wolfe."

"We must see each other," he said, holding her hands.

"It's too dangerous!" Sophia was trembling, her eyes disturbed. "We're bound to be seen."

"Not at night," Wolfe said quickly, whispering. "I'll wait out in the park all night, Sophia. By those holly bushes over there. Don't fail me, my darling." He kissed her mouth hungrily, but she broke away and ran back into the stable yard.

Wolfe leaned against the wall, breathing slowly, staring up into the autumn night. A pale, shimmering moon rose through a wreath of pearly cloud. The sound of the sheep cropping came to his ears, but far louder was the beating of his own heart as he waited for Sophia to come to him.

# CHAPTER SEVEN

Edward Stonor leaned back in his chair, the gleam of candle-light on his thin hair, watching his daughter across the table with a faint query in his eyes. She had hardly spoken during the meal, although that was not unusual since she had returned from London. The visit seemed to have oppressed her spirits, and her father was disturbed by that, wondering if his insistence that she marry her cousin Stonor might have made her unhappy. Now he sighed, thinking that since she went to London, she had become almost a stranger to him. Whatever it was that was occupying her thoughts was giving a new cast to her features, making her face an adult mask that shut him out.

She had felt ill during their day in the saddle. He had noticed her unusual flush, her abstracted air, and now he hoped she was not going to take sick. She was the only human being on earth for whom he cared really deeply.

"Are you still feeling ill, Sophia?" he asked.

She stared at him as though amazed to see him, her cheeks hotly flushed. "I am rather tired, Papa," she admitted.

"Perhaps you had better go to bed early, my dear," he suggested.

"Yes, I think I may," she agreed, rising.

"Have you heard from Stonor lately?" he asked, watching her for some sign that might betray her feelings to him.

He saw the flicker of her lashes as she looked away. "He is very busy with the firm since his father died."

"Does his silence distress you?" He tried to probe her masklike face.

"No," she said, and he wondered if he imagined the echo of a bitter irony in her voice, but dismissed the idea. Sophia was too direct and warm for such a feeling.

"You are content with this marriage, Sophia?" he asked, watching her. "I would not like to think it made you unhappy, but I did it for the best. You would not be happy away from Queen's Stonor, would you, my dear? This is where you belong. I want to think of you and your children living here when I am gone.''

"I know, Papa," she said quietly, her eyes meeting his in an unrevealing glance. "And Stonor and I understand each other very well, dearest Papa. You must not worry over me."

She left him drinking port, knowing that her lie had eased his mind, aware that her father's eyes had been worried and disturbed ever since she had come back from London in a grey, silent mood of despair. Tonight, knowing that Wolfe was alive, she felt able to lie to her father. Wolfe's disappearance and her belief that he was dead had left her too numb, too grief-stricken to be able to rouse herself to hide her unhappiness from her father.

She had cared little what happened to her since she had returned home. Day after day she had ridden in mist and rain, getting soaked to the skin and never caring, indifferent to her health, thinking that Wolfe was gone.

In her bedroom now she undressed, her fingers clumsy, shivering as she got into her nightgown. She could not go out to meet Wolfe, she told herself. It was madness. She knew she was beginning a chill; she had been feeling hot and cold alternately all day, and her head felt light and cloudy. Yet she stood at the window, looking into the dark park, aware of his presence, guessing that he watched her and feeling her body leap with desire.

She washed her face with water from the ivy-patterned basin that stood on a marble washstand, trying to restore herself to some semblance of calm. Drying her hands and face, she blew out her candle and slid into bed. Out in the dark park an owl hooted, a slow, melancholy sound that sent a shiver down her back. Wolfe was out there, waiting for her. She heard the distant row of feathered wings, the tiny shriek of a mouse or vole caught in the talons, and her heart closed with dread. When Stonor looked at her, she felt like that—a helpless creature trapped and waiting for him to consume her.

Yet if she went to Wolfe what life could they make together? He was a man with his way to make in a hostile world, and she would only burden him.

The deep, burning ache in the centre of her body was driving her mad, though. She rolled fitfully, trying to sleep, the heat inside her keeping her wide awake, nagging at her to get up and go to him, to douse this engulfing fire before it devoured her. She put her trembling hands to her hot face as the room swam around her. What was she to do?

Out in the park Wolfe moved to and fro, his eyes on the house. The dark sky was drifting overhead as if it were flowing in an ocean bed. The wind drove the clouds softly, covering and uncovering the moon so that shafts of light shone down from time to time, illuminating the park and turning the leaves of the holly silver, bringing the leaden windows of the house into a glittering fire.

The horse cropped languidly, shuffling its feet, puzzled by the long inactivity of the rider yet indifferent to everything but the pleasure of the cool grass and the empty, breathing silence around it.

Hot, aching, tormented, Sophia slid out of bed and padded to the window, peering out into the darkness. A shaft of moonlight showed her Wolfe's dark figure by the holly trees and even at that distance revealed to her the fires consuming him. Her body shook in answering passion. She turned, snatched up a cloak and wrapped it around herself and stole out of the room.

She went down the back stairs to the stable door. The horses were stamping restlessly in their stalls. The wind blew wisps of straw across the cobbles. She ran, ignoring the hardness beneath her bare feet, the cold wind blowing through her gown, her heart aching now to reach him.

Wolfe did not see the slender figure flit from patch to patch of shadow. On the smooth turf her feet made no sound. She halted a foot away in the darkness, and Wolfe, suddenly sensing her presence, swung around. She slowly walked forwards, dignity in her slender body. The wind blew back the cloak, showing him the white nightgown underneath.

Her dark hair streamed loose, blowing softly in the wind. She stood in front of him like a child awaiting punishment, submissive and resigned.

Wolfe slowly lifted his hands and pushed the silken hair back from her face. His long fingers trailed down the side of her face to lift her chin. He looked at her for a moment. "You came." It was all he could think of to say, all he needed to say.

"Wolfe!" She said his name as if it explained everything, as if his very existence were enough to make heaven and earth solid realities for her, and if he were removed the world would become a shadow for the rest of her life.

He lifted her like a child and carried her away into the sheltered hollow beyond the holly trees. When he laid her down on the damp grass, she shivered, but Wolfe barely noticed.

Their mouths met with that rush of need that drove them both, her soft lips parting to let him take what he wanted of her, the moist inner warmth open to his exploration. His hands framed her face, holding her tenderly. His hard mouth demanded and aroused a deep sensual yearning between them.

"It's been so long," Wolfe said huskily.

Sophia had forgotten the scene of his father's death, her own guilt and grief, her promise to Stonor, her love for her own father, all the reasons why she should not be here in Wolfe's arms. She only knew that she was floating on air, her head empty of everything but passion.

Her fingers moved along his warm neck, sensitively following the line of his dark hair. Wolfe pushed his own hands through her hair, sliding his fingers under the silken weight of it, finding her nape, stroking it with possessive pleasure.

Both of them seemed to have been waiting for this moment all their lives, yet now on the brink of it they were reluctant to approach each other, like two runners who, after pushing themselves across country to meet, slow to a crawl within sight of each other as if the journey had been the object rather than the meeting.

Their caresses were a deliberate prolongation. They stared into each other's eyes; silently touching, each caress precise and restrained, unhurried, yet with each one the hunger grew.

Wolfe's mouth went to her throat, crawling an infinitesimal speed over each smooth inch of it, his hands pushing back her head to expose the soft underside of her chin. She ran her fingers through the dark head moving against her, her eyes wide open, staring dazedly at the clouds in the dark sky.

He moved upwards to kiss her ears, his tongue insinuating itself into the coiled crevices, needing to touch, taste, know every part of her body. He had never experienced such a profound desire for any woman. His adventures in the Ratcliffe Highway had been a purely physical search for relief. Now his heart, his mind, his body all urged him on to take possession of Sophia, and Wolfe knew that nothing like this would ever happen to him again.

His tongue flicked over her closed eyes, playing with her long lashes, the silken feel of them tantalizing him. Then his mouth moved down to find hers again, and the deep, drugging, sensuous exchange began again, his tongue on hers, his breath mingling with her own, as if their lives flowed into each other without barrier.

His hands moved, deftly opening the nightgown, sliding in to find the warm, soft little body beneath. Her skin felt silken to his palms, her slender shoulders fine-boned. He defined each delicate curve with his fingertips as though he counted them, his hands stroking downwards, deliberately elongating the moment before he found the small, high breasts. Sophia began to breathe shallowly, her eyes shut tight, totally responsive to his caresses. She slid the buttons out of the buttonholes on his shirt and touched his bare chest with the same absorbed attention he was giving her.

Then Wolfe deliberately cupped both breasts, his fingers teasing the small, hardening nipples, and a cry burst from her, her slender body arching. He looked at her in the darkness, enjoying the revelation of her totally aroused state.

Slowly, making her wait until she was shuddering with the sweetness of anticipation, he lowered his head and Sophia gave a wild cry of pleasure as he began to take each nipple into his mouth, moving from one to the other slowly.

She twisted from side to side, moaning, now mindless, only aware of Wolfe and the sensuality of his caresses. Her hands caught his head and pushed it down against her body, waves of desire rushing through her.

His hands slid downwards, finding each warm curve beneath her nightgown, shaping her body, learning its contours. Sophia was moving restlessly now, her voice muttering his name, coming to him from a distance. He had totally unveiled her body and the night air rushed over her naked flesh, making her shiver. Wolfe lay looking down at the white gleam of it beneath him, then began pulling off his own clothes.

Sophia stared up at the sky, chilled and yet deeply flushed, the dew-wet grass against her naked limbs seeming to increase her fever. She had ceased to think a long time ago. All memory of Stonor had gone from her as if he had never existed. She no longer weighed the cost in terms of the future she would sacrifice, the loss of her father's approval and love, the loss of Queen's Stonor. The only thing that mattered was the life force driving her. She sensed the completion of her life, the ultimate expression of love. She waited for Wolfe to finish their lovemaking with total content.

The instant of possession was violent. Wolfe made no concessions to her innocence, offered her no gentle initiation. He fell on her and the hard, driving thrust of his body entered her. She gave a choked cry of pain, arching violently. Wolfe silenced her with his mouth, lying without moving on her, as if the need for urgency had gone now that he had merged with her body. Softly, expertly, knowing that the pain of entry had driven pleasure out of her, he began to caress her again, and slowly her body relaxed. Little gasps came from her. The rough pressure of his thighs against hers increased.

"Come to me, darling," he whispered. "Move with me."

Untutored, trembling, eager, she began to respond as he taught her, and the deliberate seduction of his experienced hands and mouth went on while he drove into her. She met each movement with an increased excitement, her own hands making constant pilgrimage over the taut paths of his body, bringing groans of pleasure from him. Suddenly the world seemed to be coloured with fire. She was groaning at each erotic movement, moving and breathing faster, but he deliberately slowed her pace, silencing her whimpering protest with a hard kiss.

"Slowly, slowly, my dearest." This time has to be perfect, he thought. To hurry it was to blur the fine edge of the agony. He wanted it to be so high-pitched that they would die of it. All their lives they must have this night at the back of their minds.

Wolfe knew the risk of separation still existed for them. Life was uncertain. Whatever happened, though, they would have this night. It must be the high point of their existence.

Sophia twisted reluctantly at his careful pacing of their love. She felt as though she were slowly approaching the edge of a cliff, eager to plunge over into receptive air, and Wolfe were holding her back. He had slowed to such an extent that she was whimpering with each movement. The acute, bitter spiral of tension in her body was being wound to an unbearable pitch. Her head fell back, her mouth open in a long moan. Wolfe watched her, seeing her now unfamiliar and unrecognizable; the girl forever lost in the new-made woman, her face stiff in a wild, primitive, frenzied mask of total desire.

His eyes travelled up to the house, as if calling it to witness what he had done to her; as if the dark outline of it on the sky made a ghostly third to their long lovemaking.

Then quite deliberately he turned the screw of pleasure one notch higher and released the cord on which he held her and himself, so that at the same instant each fell into an endless abyss of mindless pleasure, their voices mingled in sobbed satisfaction that was almost agonizing, startling the grazing horse into an anxious, puzzled movement.

Afterwards Wolfe lay totally still against her sweating white body, his dark head pillowed on her breasts, hearing her breath gasping under him, as though the sound were the sound of his own life. He felt languid and at ease. He had achieved what he had set out to do. He fractionally moved his cheek to feel the smooth skin of her breasts rub his skin and sighed in contentment.

Sophia began to shiver again. The coldness of the wet grass struck up at her naked skin. Wolfe seemed impervious to the night air. She tenderly stroked his head, her hand trailing down the long, lean back, following the faint prickling line of hair along the spine.

"I have to go back before dawn," she whispered.

"Not yet," Wolfe groaned, reluctant to end his night of triumph.

"I mustn't be seen," she said, shivering again.

"You're chilled!" He sat up anxiously. "Dearest, why didn't you tell me?" He gently dressed her again in the night-gown and cloak, then rapidly put back on his own clothes, pulling her close to him, his own thick cloak around them both.

"Before you go in, we have to talk."

"I love you, Wolfe," she said softly, leaning all her weight against his hard body.

His arm tightened. "My darling, that is what we have to talk about. I couldn't leave you behind now. You have to come with me. We will be married and go to America together. I've enough for the fare for both of us. We won't be rich, my darling. I can't promise you a secure life. Somehow I'll manage to get a home together, though, and we'll be together. That's what matters, isn't it?" He looked at her anxiously, still unsure whether she would agree.

She curved her body into the strong shape of his, her head on his shoulder, hearing the strong beat of his heart under her hand. "Wolfe, darling."

"You'll come?" His voice was rough with urgency.

"Yes," she whispered.

"You know it means you must leave your father and Queen's Stonor, perhaps forever?"

"Yes."

He sighed, deeply content. Into her hair he whispered, "I cannot take you tonight. You could not travel in a nightgown, love."

She laughed. "No."

"The wisest course would be for me to arrange our passage to America before I take you away with me. Then we can marry just before we take the ship."

"How long will that take, Wolfe?"

"I don't know, at present," he said heavily. "A week or maybe two."

"Two weeks?" She looked disturbed. "It seems so long."

Wolfe looked at the soft, dark head pillowed against him. "Are you afraid your father will find out? Or Stonor?"

Mention of Stonor increased her sense of chilled uneasiness. "Stonor won't like it."

Wolfe smiled secretly above her head. "No," he agreed. "Thank heavens America is a vast country. If he follows us it will take him years to find us. I've no intention of letting anyone know where we are."

Sophia looked at him in shock. "You think he will follow us? Surely not. Stonor wouldn't travel so far just for revenge."

"To the borders of hell if he had to, Sophia," Wolfe said, eyeing her curiously. "Don't you know why?"

"He hates you," she sighed.

Wolfe gazed into her face. His mouth twisted. "Oh, he hates me," he said. "And the way he feels now will be mild compared to how he will feel when he knows I've got you."

"He frightens me," she muttered. "He's a strange man. When he told me you were dead, I think it gave him pleasure. He tried to make me cry. He hit me and then he behaved so strangely, holding me almost tenderly, as though he loved me instead of hating me. I don't understand him at all. He can be so cold and cruel, yet he sometimes makes me feel I don't know anything about him."

Wolfe's face was averted so that she did not see the bright, cruel gleam in his eyes, the look of intense pleasure. "You dislike him, don't you, my darling? Let him hate us. What does it matter?"

"It's so unfair of him to hate you just because you're his half-brother. I told him so."

"What did he say?" Wolfe asked curiously, smiling still.

"He got angry. Oh, take me away soon, Wolfe. I couldn't bear to have to marry him. I belong to you, not Stonor."

"Yes," he said thickly. His mouth came down to find her own, the hard, arousing pleasure of his lips deliberate, sending shivers of response along her. She wound her arms around his neck and forgot the approaching dawn. When he withdrew she was shaking, burning again with desire, and Wolfe touched her cheek with one hand, frowning.

"You're so hot, my darling. You must go in now. I'll come again two nights from now, and don't fret in the meantime. What happened tonight is as much a sacrament as marriage, Sophia. I meant it as seriously and so, I think, did you."

"Yes," she whispered. "Oh, yes, darling Wolfe. I'm your wife now."

The first white rays were streaking across the dark sky and the birds were flying through the trees, their calls melancholy as they greeted the dawn. Sophia looked at him lovingly, then turned and ran across the grass towards the house. He watched her until she disappeared, blowing him a kiss before she went through the stable gate.

Heavy with weariness and relief, Wolfe rode back to Bristol. He had achieved more than he had actually hoped to and he was at peace. In a few weeks he and Sophia would be on the high seas on their way to America. Once in that new country they could vanish into the great continent, and Stonor would never find them.

His conscience briefly pricked him that he should be leaving his mother alone, but he felt he had no choice. He had this one chance to snatch Sophia away from Stonor and he must take it. Jogging along the tiring road to Bristol, he enlivened the journey by imagining Stonor's face when he heard that Sophia had eloped with him. Oh, that I could be a fly on the wall that day, Wolfe thought! If I could only hear the cry he gives, see the look on his face when they tell him. He will not know which agony is worse—that I have her, or that he has lost her.

# CHAPTER EIGHT

Sophia ate breakfast the next morning with her head bent over her plate, a burning flush in her cheeks as she glanced towards the windows, from which she could just see the dark branches of the trees in the park. Every time she remembered what had happened the night before, her body seemed to fill with heat, but she forced herself to go on pretending to eat, pushing her food around on her plate with a languid hand. It seemed incredible to her that her father had not noticed any change in her, read in her features what Wolfe had done to her. Yesterday she had still been a girl. Today, she knew, she was a woman. Surely it should show.

Edward Stonor was thinking of other things. They would ride across the fields, the tall grass brushing his boots, the scent of wood smoke in his nostrils, all the familiar sweet sights of his own country stretching around him. He was a man for whom the established pattern of his days was necessary. He wanted nothing but to go on as he was for the rest of his life, his world narrowed to the round of quiet days in the saddle. I am getting old, he thought without regret.

I hope I shall not be alive when Stonor begins to make his mark upon my house, he thought, thinking of the letter he had received from his nephew that morning, which had calmly outlined Stonor's plans for bringing the house back to life. Stonor seemed to take it for granted that his uncle would be grateful to him for bringing workmen to Stonor, redecorating, renewing, altering the shabby rooms.

Edward Stonor, on the contrary, had been offended. Who does he think he is? Young puppy, he thought, I'm not in my grave yet; and he had crushed the letter angrily. Later, with a wry grimace, he had smoothed it out, recognizing that Stonor was merely doing what he hoped he would do after his own death—taking Queen's Stonor into his care and giving it new life.

The slow decay and neglect of the house would be reversed. There would be a new flowering in the old wood, the fresh wine of Stonor's money poured into the cracked old bottle of the house.

Glancing across the table at Sophia, he frowned, suddenly seeing her look of feverish lassitude. "Child, you're ill," he muttered, getting up.

Her eyes lifted, his voice bringing her out of her absorption in thoughts of Wolfe. She looked at him absently, the fine-boned shape of his head shimmering across the table at her as though he were haloed in mist. "I am very well, Papa," she said.

He got up and came around the table to put a worried hand on her forehead. She felt as though she were floating in warm air; a dizzy, light sensation possessed her.

Edward Wolfe swore under his breath as his palm felt the burning, dry heat of her skin. "God in heaven, Sophia! You are ill! Why did you get up this morning?"

He shouted for the housekeeper, Mrs. Buffell, who came reluctantly, grumbling under her breath.

"Fetch the doctor," her master barked.

"I am perfectly well, Papa," Sophia insisted, suddenly afraid. "A chill, nothing more," she stammered, standing up. Her father's face came and went peculiarly while she stared at him. Her eyes glazed, then he disappeared into a blackness as Sophia slumped forwards into his arms.

One of the grooms rode down to the village to fetch Dr. West. He stood at her bed, his fingers on her high-beating pulse, shaking his head. "It may be nothing more than a chill, but the fever runs very high. It may be the start of something worse."

"What?" Edward Wolfe demanded hoarsely. "Don't mumble your nonsense at me, Ben. Tell me the truth."

The doctor had known him all his life. He gave him a thoughtful look. "At this stage I've no idea. It could be anything." He smiled. "Or nothing. She's young. Young people get these fevers. I've known a child to lie at apparent death's door one day and be running around the next."

Edward Wolfe stared down at the small, flushed face on the pillows, framed in that tangled web of black hair, the lips dry and cracked as they endlessly mumbled words he couldn't understand.

"Why does she keep talking about wolves?" the doctor asked, bending to listen. "She cannot have seen any, surely?"

"Some nightmare," Edward Stonor said anxiously.

"A book she has read, perhaps," the doctor shrugged. "Well, bear up, Edward. We'll put her through. She will need careful nursing. In a fever like this the danger is to the heart. Sophia must not be permitted to move. She must be kept very quiet."

Wolfe sat in the well-scrubbed little parlour of the Bristol house, watching his mother deftly patch a shabby but clean shirt, her fingers turning the collar to make the shirt seem less worn. Jack Duffey, shaven and clear-eyed, was pretending to read the newspaper while watching curiously around the edge of it.

"Ye're a marvel, ma'am," he said as he sat forwards and lowered his paper. "Sure, ye should have thrown the old rag away."

"Waste not, want not," Lucy said. "You cannot afford to throw away wearable shirts, Mr. Duffey."

"Indeed not," he agreed with a sigh.

Wolfe watched him. He had not failed to notice the fact that Jack Duffey admired his mother. It did not surprise him. Wolfe was too experienced to be unaware that his mother was deeply attractive to men. Her rounded body, warm smile and rich, golden hair were invitations men did not fail to notice. Wolfe was unsure about his mother's reaction to the Irishman. She wasn't a woman who showed such things, and his father's death was too recent for her to have any desire to find another man.

It would relieve his mind of one anxiety to know that he would be leaving his mother safely in Bristol among friends who would care for her. She would not be cast adrift if he went to America. Apart from the Duffeys, she would have Luther, and even on so short an acquaintance, Wolfe had recognized his cousin's solid integrity.

Luther had political views of burning conviction, which Wolfe shrewdly recognized as those fanatical principles that Josiah Hunt had sown in his son, but that, in Luther, had become an angry desire to shape a world in which man was born equal and granted equal opportunities. There was nothing new in this, Wolfe realized. The same change was taking place all over England at this time. A generation bred in chapel-going sobriety was turning to socialism eagerly. The education reforms were giving them a chance to read and learn, and they devoured books like starving children, discovering for themselves ideas which circumstance had previously hidden from them.

Luther's dreams were based on a view of mankind, an image of man formed by the biblical language of his childhood. Wolfe listened to him and seemed to Luther to agree, but Wolfe wanted a free world so that he could pursue his own ambitions. Luther had no real understanding of the young man he talked to with such excited earnestness, but Wolfe saw his cousin very clearly.

Wolfe glanced at the window. He stood up, and Lucy looked anxiously at him. "I have to go out," Wolfe told her.

"Don't, Wolfe," she said unhappily.

Jack Duffey watched them around his newspaper. Lucy put out her hand, and Wolfe bent to kiss her.

"I must go, Mother."

Lucy knew where he was going. He had said nothing of Sophia, but she knew. Her face was pale as she watched him walk out.

"Young dogs will roam," Jack Duffey told her quietly.

Lucy did not answer. She picked up her work and got on with it, biting her lower lip.

Dusk fell rapidly. Grey moths flitted on powdered wings beneath the oaks in Queen's Stonor park. The evening midges danced in dark swarms. Wolfe nudged his way through the holly trees and sat on his mount, staring at the house with a fast-beating heart. The warm walls faded into a dark outline; the night sky was moonless as yet but filled with a glittering light.

For the first time in his life, he knew himself to be in love, and the impatience with which he waited for darkness was a measure of the deep-seated passion he felt for Sophia, a passion like a cancer in the centre of his being, growing daily, feeding on itself; spreading through heart and mind and body, strengthening with each breath he took.

He had planned before she returned to London to seduce her if he could. It had amused him to picture Stonor's rage if his bride were stolen from him. Wolfe had not planned for his own emotions. The moment he had set eyes on her, he had felt a change taking place in himself. The first night they met, Wolfe had found her delightful. The next day he had known he was falling in love. Now he was so much in love he wondered how he had lived before they met.

She was his mirror, his reflection, his other self—female to his male, his mate, the point to his whole existence. Wolfe had never known himself to be romantic. He had had quite a different picture of himself, treating women with amused and callous lightness, a cynical disregard for their feelings buried in his charming smile.

All that had gone. He knew now that Sophia was necessary to him, and he would move heaven and earth to take her away from Stonor.

Leaning over his saddle, the leather creaking as his weight shifted, he frowned at the house. The moon was rising. She was late in coming out. He had expected her to be possessed by the same eagerness he felt, and a queer hurt pricked at him as he watched for her.

A man suddenly rode out of the stable yard. Wolfe watched him bend over his horse's neck, urging more speed, and a flicker of premonition ran through Wolfe's body.

The rider turned out of the park. Wolfe waited, frowning. Horses came galloping back from the village and vanished into the stable yard again.

Lights sprang up in the house. The curtains were drawn upstairs, and through the windows Wolfe saw a procession going upwards, lighted candles moving with them. One of the men was carrying a black bag in his hand.

Wolfe froze. A doctor? At this hour? He saw the gleam of candlelight move on Sophia's curtains. She was ill, he thought with shock. What was wrong with her?

Remembering the haste with which the first man had ridden to the village, he sensed that this was no mild ailment. She must be very ill for her father to send for a doctor in the middle of the night.

He could no longer sit still. Sliding off his horse, he paced to and fro under the trees, brushing aside the powdery moths that clung to his damp face and hair. The night dragged on and the lights still showed in the house. When dawn's light broke, it brought an orange glow to the sky. Wolfe saw the doctor leave the house, riding slowly, his shoulders stooping. Mounting, Wolfe quietly rode through the trees to reach the gate before the other man. He waited in the road, pretending to be adjusting his stirrups. When the doctor appeared, Wolfe looked around and asked politely if he was on the road to Bristol.

Eyeing him suspiciously, the doctor nodded.

"You're about early, sir," Wolfe murmured casually.

"I've been up all night," the doctor yawned. "A patient—I'm a doctor."

"I hope your patient is better," Wolfe said with a pretence of calm.

The man sighed, his weary face lined. "We live in hope, but she is very ill. I've done what I can. The rest is up to her own constitution. She has a fever. If her heart can stand up to the strain, she may pull through."

"What sort of fever?" Wolfe asked, unable to maintain his air of polite indifference any longer.

The doctor looked surprised at his tone. "She caught a chill. Riding in the rain in wet clothes, I've no doubt. Poor child, she's paying dearly for her recklessness."

Wolfe winced. He muttered something incoherent, nodded to the doctor and rode on, barely aware of what he was doing. Had their lovemaking brought on this illness? Miserably he wished he could turn the clock back. If only he hadn't persuaded her to come out to see him! Suppose she dies, he thought, and whitened. It couldn't happen, he told himself. Life could not be so cruel. He could not bear it if Sophia died, and Wolfe was still ignorant enough of the inescapability of fate to feel that something so terrible could not happen to him.

He found a quiet country inn in the next village and put up there for the night. He returned to Queen's Stonor after sunset and waited all night, watching the house, feeling that by being there he was holding back death's hand, projecting his own willpower through the darkness to force Sophia to remain alive.

In the silent dawn light the park looked misty and tranquil, as though the life of one human inhabitant was a matter of indifference to the orderly procession of the seasons day by day. From the dewy grass white mist rose up in shivering veils and stole silently through the trees, wreathing itself around stark branches like wedding veils upon bare dark limbs.

The house caught the first rays of the rising sun and threw back redoubled light. The walls seemed to absorb the sun, holding it in the old red brick like honey in a comb.

The chimneys began to smoke. A groom walked across the cobbles of the stable yard, and the horses stamped noisily in their stalls.

Wolfe, his eyes raw with lack of sleep, turned to catch the reins of his horse, realizing that he must leave before he was seen. The sound of carriage wheels broke the silence. Standing stiffly in the shadows of the trees, Wolfe glanced at the approaching vehicle and his heart dropped like a stone as he saw Stonor's face at the window. Even at this distance he recognized the white, rigid lines of his half-brother's face.

The carriage stopped in front of the house. Stonor descended quickly and disappeared into the opened door. He must have been summoned, Wolfe thought. He would have got a train to Bristol and hired a carriage. My God: he had made fast time.

Aching fury dragged at him. I'm too late, he thought. So near, and it is all snatched away by my own greedy carelessness. If I hadn't made love to her that night, she would never have taken a chill. Now Stonor's here and he'll make sure I don't get a second chance. Wolfe rode out of the park and turned towards Bristol with a set, white face.

Edward Stonor came down the stairs to meet his nephew as he entered the hall, his hands outstretched, surprise in his pale face. "My dear boy! So you are Stonor! I had not expected you to come down here. It is very good of you...."

"How is she?" Stonor's voice cut into his words abruptly.

"She's alive." Edward Stonor spoke on a sigh. "I thought for a while we were going to lose her, but somehow she held on."

He surveyed his nephew curiously, noting the cold grey eyes the shade of bluish slate in rain, the hard straight mouth and rigidly controlled bone structure.

"I'm sure you will wish to eat and wash before you go up to see her," Edward Stonor said, feeling a distinct lack of fondness towards this chill young man.

"I will see her now," Stonor said, barely moving his lips.

His uncle would have argued, but he caught those grey eyes and shrugged. "As you please."

He led the way up the stairs, saying flatly over his shoulder, "You must not try to rouse her, of course. The doctor is still afraid the strain will be too much for her heart."

"Heart?" Stonor repeated, as though catching the word suddenly.

"I am afraid so." Edward Stonor gave him a sober look. "There may be sad consequences from this even if she lives, I'm afraid."

"What consequences?" Stonor asked sharply.

"The doctor will explain all that to you," Sophia's father said unhappily. He opened the door to Sophia's room, and Stonor followed him into it. A nurse sat by the bed. Heavy red curtains hung around it to keep out the light. Stonor walked at once towards the bed, his set gaze on what he could see of Sophia.

The nurse rose and curtsied. Stonor briefly glanced at her, inclining his head without speaking. Then he halted at the bed, staring at Sophia.

Her black hair strayed loosely across the tumbled pillows. Her face was filled with the heat of fever, her lashes flickering restlessly on her hot cheeks. Her mouth moved in constant, incoherent murmuring, a frown on her drawn forehead, her tongue occasionally moistening her dry, cracked lips.

Stonor bent towards the girl, his eyes on her face. His hand touched her cheek, feeling the burning heat of her skin strike into his cold flesh.

"Wolfe, Wolfe," she moaned.

Stonor froze. He straightened and glanced at the nurse. "How long will this fever last?"

"The doctor cannot be certain, sir. She is very ill."

"I can see that," Stonor said bitingly.

"Come down and have breakfast, my dear boy," Edward Stonor said quickly. "You look played out. It's a long journey from London. I'm surprised you came so far. It's very good of you. I hadn't expected it, I admit. I only let you know because I felt you should be warned." He broke off with a grim look and Stonor's eyes flashed to his face, reading what he had not said.

Over a breakfast he barely touched, Stonor asked him: "How did she get this fever? Is it some disease?"

"Ben West isn't sure what caused it but he thinks she caught a chill, which has gone to her lungs. She could not breathe at one point. That was the worst moment."

Stonor's face showed no reaction to this news. Edward Stonor watched him, marvelling that this cold, stiff young man could be his own nephew.

He was puzzled by Stonor's arrival so soon after his message had been received. Had the boy been madly in love with Sophia, he could have understood it, but looking at that stony face, Edward Stonor could not believe that his nephew felt anything for Sophia. He had insisted on seeing her as soon as he arrived, it was true, but that pale countenance had revealed no emotion as it regarded the feverish girl on her pillow.

"My mother will be following here in a few days," Stonor informed him.

"There was no need for Maria to trouble herself, although it is very kind of her."

"She is fond of Sophia," Stonor said curtly.

Edward Stonor felt himself flushing at something in the tone. "I am glad to hear it," he said. "I'm sure my daughter is fond of Maria."

Stonor's grey eyes held a peculiar irony. He looked away. "When Sophia is well, I mean to marry her and take her to the South of France for a long honeymoon. After such an illness she should get away from the English winter. I will take her to find the sun."

Edward Stonor looked taken aback. "I hardly think there can be any suggestion of marriage at the moment."

"When she is better, I said," Stonor returned.

Edward Stonor looked mulishly at him. "Sophia should rest for a long time once she has recovered."

"She can rest in France," Stonor said, his chin and jaw rigid.

Edward opened his mouth to protest and met those grey eyes. He closed his mouth. The most gregarious of men, he found it hard to talk to his nephew. Stonor had a way of speaking that made him unanswerable. For such a young man he had a most unbending manner, Edward thought.

The doctor came at three that afternoon. He visited Sophia and came down to join Edward and Stonor in the library. Edward introduced his nephew with a brusque air that told Ben West that his friend did not much care for the young man.

"Has your uncle warned you of the state of Sophia's health?" the doctor asked Stonor as he shook hands.

"I know that she's been dangerously ill and is not yet out of danger," Stonor said coolly. "What else is there to know?"

The doctor glanced at Edward. "Quite a good deal, I'm afraid," he said. "It begins to look to me as though, for Sophia, marriage is out of the question."

Stonor stiffened. "Why?" he asked in level tones.

"Her heart has been weakened. If she lives it would be dangerous for her to marry. There is the strong probability that childbed would be fatal for her."

There was a long silence. Stonor turned away and walked to the window. With his back to the other two, he asked quietly, "Are you guessing or is that certain?"

"In medicine we are always guessing," Ben West said drily. "I've seen this sort of fever before, though. I know what it does to the heart. She is fighting for her life, and the strain is slowly weakening her."

"But if she recovers, surely her heart will strengthen?"

The doctor smiled wryly. "My dear young man, let us hope so, but imagine if you will that the heart is an engine. If you overwork it it is never as strong again."

Stonor stared out again, his eyes on the trees moving lazily in the wind.

Edward Stonor had his hand to his eyes. Roughly he muttered, "She must never marry."

Stonor turned, very upright. "This changes nothing. We will still be married."

"God help you, man," the doctor broke out, staring. "Don't you understand? You'll risk her life. If you made her pregnant, she could die in childbirth."

"I understand perfectly," Stonor said expressionlessly. "I won't make her pregnant."

The doctor's brows drew together. "You're either a fool or a saint," he said with a twist of his lips. "If you hope to avoid pregnancy in some way while still enjoying your marital rights, I must tell you that it is impossible. If there were some way of doing so, I'd be the first to use it. None of the methods works, believe me. I've five children to prove it." He surveyed Stonor. "And if you mean that you will not consummate the marriage—well, that's outside my province, but I advise you to consider very carefully. Such a marriage could be bitter."

Edward Stonor broke in huskily. "It's out of the question. I won't risk her life for anything."

"Neither will I," Stonor said. "But I will marry her."

He walked out and closed the door, leaving them staring at each other.

"He's a damned cold fish," the doctor said.

"I won't have him marry my little Sophia!" Edward said furiously. "There's no blood in his veins."

"In Sophia's condition that may well be an advantage," said the doctor with a sigh. "It would be far worse if he were wildly in love with her."

Edward Stonor dropped his head into his hands.

Stonor walked into Sophia's bedroom and glanced at the nurse, his eyes hooded by their heavy lids. "I will watch with her for an hour. You must need the rest."

The nurse curtsied and went out. As soon as she had gone, Stonor sat down on the edge of the bed and lifted Sophia carefully into his arms as though she were a child. He settled her against him, her head on his shoulder, staring into her flushed face and pushing back her tangled hair. Seeing a brush upon the table, he reached over and picked it up. He began to brush her hair, and the soft movements of the brush seemed to soothe her. She lay peacefully against him, her restless twisting still. Stonor dipped his handkerchief in the cold water standing in a jug beside the bed. Gently he wiped her hot face, and she gasped with pleasurable relief, her eyes still shut.

She slept, resting on him, as though the feel of the hard body comforted her. Stonor's fingers tentatively moved over her face, the tips caressing, feeling the hollows in her cheeks, the curve of the passionate mouth, the shape of the nose. Her lids fluttered as his cold fingertips brushed them. "Wolfe," she whispered threadily.

Stonor's body hardened. He stared at her, eyes narrowed, then he laid her down on the bed, arranged the linen with great precision around her and went out without a backwards glance.

That night her temperature broke. Sweat poured over her body in running rivulets. The nurse sponged her dry again and again, changing her nightclothes carefully each time, stripping her bed and remaking it with dry linen. The doctor remained at the bedside, his face concerned.

Stonor heard the running footsteps of the servants and was aroused. He came into the room and stood at the foot of the bed, staring as Sophia tossed and muttered, her face shining with perspiration.

The doctor looked around. "Her temperature is breaking," he said. "It's the testing time, the crisis point. If her heart can take this, she will live."

Stonor stayed there for several hours. When he went to bed again, Sophia was sleeping and the crisis was past. He ordered that his presence in the house should be kept from her. "I don't want her disturbed," he told her father. "When she is safely out of danger, I'll see her."

Sophia recovered slowly. For a few days she was aware of nothing but her own bodily weakness, submitting like a weary child to being washed and cared for by the nurse. It was a week before she thought of Wolfe. What must he be thinking? Would he have got news of her illness? What was happening? She had to know. Worry made her ill again, keeping her

awake. At last she begged the nurse to let her write a few lines
to a friend. The woman good-naturedly agreed and provided
writing materials, and Sophia scribbled a few uneven lines to
Wolfe. She gave the note to the nurse, saying, "Please see that
it goes at once." She gave the woman a nervous look. "And
do not give it to my father. Send it yourself."

The nurse read the name on the envelope as she carried it
from the room and smiled to herself.

Stonor sat in the library with the estate account books,
frowning over them. Many tenants were behind with their
rents, and most of the properties were badly in need of repair.
Stonor foresaw that he would need to devote a good deal of
time to bringing the estate back to life.

The nurse knocked and entered, curtsying. Stonor looked
up, his face tightened. "What's wrong?"

"Miss Sophia asked me to give you this, sir," the nurse
said, a coy smile on her face.

He looked at the note, frowning darkly. "You told her I
was here? I thought I ordered you to say nothing of my
presence?"

"She doesn't know," the nurse retorted tartly. "She asked
me to send the letter to you at Bristol."

Stonor sat very still. He took the note abruptly. "Very well,
you may go."

Alone, he looked at the address, then ripped open the envelope. His eye scanned the uneven words rapidly. His hand
clenched on the paper, screwing it into a ball. For a few moments he did not move. Then he carefully smoothed out the
paper and read it again.

Sophia lay on her pillows, her eyes closed. She felt weak
and languid, unable to think clearly. A movement in the room
attracted her attention. She opened her eyes slowly and
glanced towards the door, stricken as she caught sight of
Stonor.

He walked across the room, staring at her. She shrank
against her pillows, silent and trembling. Stonor took the letter from his jacket and laid it on her quilt, smoothing it out.
Sophia glanced down and her breath caught.

"So, he's alive," Stonor said between his tight, pale lips.
"And you have been meeting him. I suppose I may guess at
the nature of those meetings."

Sophia's eyes met his. She did not answer, biting her lips.
Stonor seemed to wait for an expected reply. When it did not

come, he said coldly, "Well, it is over now. You'll marry me as soon as you are well enough."

"No!" Sophia burst out. "I shall marry Wolfe."

Stonor's mouth had an icy amusement. "Do you think he will want a wife he may never touch?"

She stared, bewildered.

Softly, Stonor told her. "Your illness has left you with a weak heart. Any man who marries you must choose between killing you by making you pregnant, or living with a wife he cannot have."

The shock left her silent for a moment. Her eyes grew brilliant with pain, and her skin shone with a white intensity. "You're lying!"

"Ask your doctor. He's warned me of the consequences should we marry."

"No!" she moaned.

"Yes," Stonor said, almost as though delighting in bearing this news to her.

She stared at him, her face distraught.

"You know my half-brother," Stonor said. "Do you imagine he could be happy married to you under such conditions? Could you live, Sophia, watching him finding his relief in other women's arms? He would, and you know it. He has never found celibacy attractive. He may love you now, but he would grow to hate you, tied to a woman he can't have, unable to have children, unable to lay a hand on you."

"Be quiet!"

"How would you feel, Sophia, aware of his nightly pleasures elsewhere? You'd be consumed with jealousy, tortured night and day."

She turned away from his remorseless voice, burying herself in her pillow, the thin fingers twisting in the linen, tears soaking the pillow beneath her face.

Stonor watched her, his face expressionless. After a few minutes he sat beside her on the bed and took her thin shoulders, turning her to face him. Her tear-stained face stared at him. He carefully wiped her wet cheeks, his touch delicate.

"We'll be married as soon as you're fit to travel," he said. "I shall take you to France. You'll begin to recover your health there."

"Why do you insist on marrying me?" she demanded wildly. "I don't understand."

"There is nothing to understand," Stonor told her coolly.

"I made up my mind that you would be my wife, and I don't intend to change it."

Her eyes spat fire at him. "Are you hoping to make me pregnant and kill me?"

His mouth closed tightly. After a pause he said in icy tones, "Don't be childish, Sophia."

"Then you'll have to find your pleasure outside the marriage bed," she flung.

"Does that concern you?" His voice was ironic. "If I were my half-brother, it would drive you mad with jealousy, but I could keep a dozen mistresses and you wouldn't turn a hair."

She surveyed him, a funny little sob coming from her now and then. After a long silence she said, "You are as stubborn as a mule, Stonor. I shall never understand you."

His face held a peculiar pale irony. "No," he agreed. "I doubt if you ever will."

Unsteadily she sighed. "How can you bear to have me as your wife? You know I love Wolfe. Every time you look at me you will remember that Wolfe was my lover."

Stonor's cheek muscles flickered briefly. His eyes moved away from her and came back. "After today we'll never mention his name again."

She moved restlessly. "But children, Stonor! You realize I can give you no children, and you'll need an heir."

"I've a brother and a sister. In time they'll give us an heir, I imagine. I shall accept our childless state." His mouth twisted. "I do face facts, Sophia. I recommend you to do the same."

She gave him a bewildered, miserable look and a long sigh wrenched from her.

"I'm tied hand and foot, aren't I, Stonor? I have no choice."

"None," he said curtly.

"What sort of marriage will we have?" she asked helplessly. "What sort of life can we ever make together?"

He was silent, staring into her wet blue eyes. His face was quite calm, quite expressionless. "You will have to learn to live with it," he said, turning to walk out of the room.

# CHAPTER NINE

Wolfe sat on his horse among the closely clustered trees in the park, watching the house but keeping carefully out of sight. He managed to pick up news of Sophia's illness in the village, hiding his shock as he listened. In such a small place everyone knew the smallest details of what was afoot in the big house. Sophia's weakened heart and Stonor's insistence on proceeding with the marriage were both known and discussed openly in the village inn. Wolfe brooded over both facts as he watched the house. He had to see her. If he had to fight his way into the house, he would see her. A savage stab of anger made him bend over his horse's neck, gasping. If only he had not coaxed her to meet him that night! None of this would have happened.

A distant sound made him sit upright again, alert, sharp-eyed. The clatter of horses' hooves on cobbles grew louder. Two men rode out of the stable yard and turned into the green distances of the park, their mounts quickening their speed as they felt grass under their feet.

Stonor, thought Wolfe, a tight smile on his mouth. He could not at this distance see his half-brother's face, but he knew that tall, thin figure.

Waiting until the two men had disappeared among the far-off trees, Wolfe glanced at the house. He slipped through to the winding drive and rode casually towards the front door, taking his time, clamping a polite mask over the strained excitement he was feeling.

The maid who opened the door curtsied, giving him a quick, interested look. "Good morning, sir."

Wolfe strolled calmly past her. "I've come to see Miss Stonor," he drawled in the confident tone of one who is expected. "My name is Whitley. Is my brother still here?"

The girl looked surprised, but smiled. "He is, sir, but he has ridden out just this moment. He shouldn't be out long. Will you wait for him in the library?"

Wolfe slid out of his cloak and the girl took it over one arm.

"While I wait I might as well see Miss Sophia," he murmured coolly.

"I do not know if she is having visitors yet, sir," said the girl, frowning.

"Ask her if she will see me." Wolfe smiled at her, using all his charm, his eyes flattering her.

For a moment the girl hesitated, then she curtsied. "Yes, sir."

"I'll wait here," Wolfe said quickly, seeing her turn to move down the hall. He did not want her to go in search of some more senior member of the staff for instructions. Under his calm smile he was possessed with impatience and urgency.

The girl carefully hung his cloak on the hall stand while he watched her, grinding his teeth at her slowness. She went up the stairs, her white cap tails fluttering, her skirts rustling. Wolfe stared after her. His mouth was dry. Inwardly he urged her on, wishing that she would walk faster. He had no time to lose. Stonor might come back at any moment. He moved to the stairs, his foot on the lowest tread, staring up into the empty shadows.

The girl seemed to be taking centuries. What was she doing? Wolfe clenched his hand on the polished banister rail. He took a few steps and listened. Sophia, he thought urgently, hurry! Why isn't that girl coming back?

In the bedroom the maid was looking uncertainly at the flushed, sleeping face on the pillow. Sophia's hand was curled under her cheek and she looked so peaceful that the girl hesitated to wake her. Wolfe's charming smile had made such an impression on her, though, that she still hovered, half-hoping that Sophia would wake up of her own accord.

Sophia did not stir. The girl sighed and went out. As soon as she appeared at the top of the stairs, Wolfe began to climb them eagerly.

"Oh, sir, she is asleep," the maid said regretfully, blocking his ascent.

Wolfe almost broke out into rage. His eyes flashed, and the girl looked startled.

Before Wolfe could say anything another voice spoke from below in the hall, a voice which made him swing instinctively and look down.

"I'll deal with this, Betty."

The maid, very flushed and eaten with curiosity, slipped

around Wolfe's tall figure and vanished. The two young men stared at each other. Wolfe's brain revolved rapidly. His eyes flickered in thought. Stonor read his mind, and a cold smile touched his lips.

"It would do you no good to go up there. I wouldn't let you reach the door."

"How would you stop me?" Wolfe sneered, an angry smile on his lips.

Stonor softly brought his hand out of his pocket. The light from the high hall windows suddenly held a metallic glimmer. "I've been waiting for you," Stonor said in a quiet, calm voice. "I knew you would come."

"You wouldn't use that." Wolfe tilted his head with an arrogant, contemptuous amusement.

Stonor smiled. "Oh, but I would." His finger moved. Wolfe heard the click as the catch engaged. Stonor surveyed him with icy grey eyes. "You have one minute to get out of that door."

Staring at the pistol barrel, his face expressionless, Wolfe calculated the odds. He looked up and met Stonor's level, unblinking eyes.

"I'll be back," Wolfe said with a snarl. "You can't keep me away from her forever."

"We'll see about that." Stonor's voice held iron determination.

Wolfe began to walk down the stairs, taking his time. "She can't share your bed, can she, Stonor? They told me in the village. You'll never be able to have her. That must be a great relief to her. She'll be spared having to put up with your...."

His words broke off as Stonor whipped the pistol barrel around his face. Wolfe reeled, choking, a long bloody graze across his cheek. His eyes blazed and for a second he almost came back at Stonor, his hands clenched into claws. Stonor's hand lifted the pistol. Wolfe sucked in a harsh breath. Stonor opened the door.

"Do I have to kick you out of the house?"

Slowly, wiping the blood from his jaw, Wolfe walked out into the sunshine.

"If you come back you'll be shot on sight," Stonor promised softly. "I'll give instructions to every groom, every footman, that you are a dangerous criminal who must be killed without compunction."

"Damn you to hell," Wolfe said, then he climbed onto his

horse and rode down the drive while Stonor stood and watched.

Lucy was shaken when Wolfe told her of his imminent departure to America. "You can't leave me here," she pleaded, clutching his arm.

"Luther will look after you." Wolfe's face had a harsh frown, and her eyes lingered on the strange darkened mark on his face. He had not told her how he had got it, but his manner since he returned had been sufficient to warn his mother that something was very wrong.

"Wolfe, don't go! America is so far away. I'll never see you again, I know it."

"I'll be back," he said grimly, as though it was not she he was speaking to at all, his eyes set on something only he could see.

"They die like flies on these boats," Lucy said anxiously. "You could get a job here in England, Wolfe. Why go so far?"

"We've talked it over again and again. I am sick of England. I'm sick of poverty and petty, narrow-minded little people who want to screw every farthing they can out of you." He looked at her and his eyes held a brief gentleness. "Oh, don't fret, Mother. I'll be back. I promise I'll be back."

# CHAPTER TEN

Once in France it might have been expected that Sophia would slowly thaw and relax in Stonor's company, but as day followed day she grew quieter and more withdrawn. Stonor said nothing, but he watched her, his eyes that ironic grey.

She began to learn French so that she could talk to the servants. It gave her an excuse for concentrating on a book and ignoring Stonor. He worked on the papers his brother sent him from England. Although Grey was nominally in charge, Stonor was relying on their chief clerk to steer the firm while he was away.

Two months after their arrival in France, he and Sophia sat after dinner talking when without warning Sophia fainted. Stonor leaped to catch her, his face stupefied.

He lifted her into his arms and rang for a servant. "Fetch the doctor," he ordered. The servant stared without apparent understanding. "The doctor," Stonor raged, glaring. *"Docteur..."*

The man set off at a run, and Stonor carried Sophia to her chamber, laid her on the bed. She began to stir, her lashes fluttering, and he bent over her, chafing her fingers.

She looked at him blankly.

"Are you in pain?" His voice was anxious, his face very pale.

Her face was colourless, her eyes shocked, and she did not answer him, her lips trembling.

"Sophia, have you any pain?" he repeated urgently, staring at her.

The doctor hurried into the room and pushed Stonor aside. A small, pompous Frenchman in a stiff collar and black suit, his manner self-important, he waved Stonor from the room. *"M'sieur, s'il vous plaît!"*

Reluctantly Stonor obeyed. He paced up and down outside, his hands behind his back, so tense that when the doctor emerged some time later, Stonor stared at him without speaking.

The doctor, however, had no such inhibitions. A frown on his face, he looked at Stonor with distaste. The flood of French which came from him meant nothing to Stonor. He held up a hand urgently and called for the French majordomo of the household who spoke English and ordered him to translate. The doctor repeated himself, and the servant looked at Stonor in wooden calm. Coughing, he said, "*M'sieur le docteur* is distressed, sir. It appears that madame is *enceinte*."

Stonor's lips went white. "What?"

"The doctor understood that you were aware of the danger of such a possibility," the servant went on, eyeing Stonor.

The doctor burst out again, his arms waving like windmills. Stonor did not need to understand French to know that he was being accused with angry contempt of having endangered Sophia's life, but the servant immediately translated the words all the same. "*M'sieur le docteur* cannot give you any hope that madame will survive the length of the pregnancy, let alone give birth to a live child."

Stonor's face was so still that it might have been carved from the granite of the cliffs near the house. He turned and stiffly walked into his own room.

The servant stared after him and shrugged. "Well, he is a man!" he said to the doctor. "What else could you expect? She's a very beautiful woman."

Distastefully the doctor grimaced. "But he was warned. It could kill her. She's in no condition to give birth."

He went back to Sophia, who glanced past him nervously as though expecting to see Stonor's tall figure. "I have informed your husband, madame," the doctor said gently. "He was disturbed by the news, but he will visit you in a little while."

Sophia swallowed. "What did he say?" She was terrified of Stonor's reaction to the news that she was carrying Wolfe's child. She had known for some time that she was pregnant, and the terror of it had made her tense and disturbed for weeks.

The doctor shrugged. "He said nothing." His full red mouth formed a moue of repulsion. He did not understand a man of Stonor's temperament. Himself, he reacted violently to everything that happened to him. He looked at the girl's beautiful white face with compassion.

"Poor child," he said in French, taking her wrist between finger and thumb. He frowned over her rapid pulse. "Now I am going to give you some serious instructions. From today

you will stay in bed; rest constantly. Under no circumstances
will your marital relations with your husband continue." He
caught her round, startled eyes. "You understand me,
madame? If you wish to deliver your child safely, you will do
as I order. Your husband is not to touch you again."

He misunderstood her worried frown. "Now I shall speak
to your husband myself about this, so there will be no further
mistake. I shall make up a tonic for you, and you will eat exactly as I prescribe. Cheese, meat, eggs, fruit. No sweetmeats,
no fat. You will drink milk and a little wine."

He patted her cheek. "The maid shall stay with you from
now on. You are not to be left alone." And let that dog of a
husband come near you again, he thought wrathfully.

He left her and Sophia stared out the window, shivering.
Poor Stonor, she thought. To be blamed for something of
which he wasn't guilty: It must be driving him mad. Her fingers twisted. What would he do? What would he say? The
doctor's description had been uninformative. Stonor had been
"disturbed," he had said. Had he been so blindly angry that
he had raged? Or had he hidden his reaction from them? She
could believe either of him.

She had expected a violent reaction when at last he discovered her condition, and she had been afraid. Not for herself.
She had lived with the idea of death since she first knew of her
heart condition, and she had half-welcomed the idea. But now
she wanted to live for the sake of her baby, Wolfe's baby. She
wanted to carry the child, see him open his eyes. She was sure
it would be a boy, Wolfe's son.

The maid came to the bed with a cup of milk, and Sophia
turned in surprise. Smiling gently, the woman held it to her
lips.

"Come, madame, drink for the baby's sake," she said indulgently.

Sophia smiled, suddenly alight, and the maid looked at her
with pity. She looked so young to be bearing a child, her face
so pale and delicate, her black curls framing features stamped
with pain. She was only a child herself, the woman thought,
grimacing.

Stonor came into the room a short time later, and the maid
gave him a fierce, angry look. He ignored her, coming to the
bed, looking down into Sophia's white face, his own impassive.

Whatever his reactions to her pregnancy, they did not show

on him now. Sophia met his eyes with an effort. A veil was drawn over their expression, the slate grey of them opaque. The regular, handsome coldness of the features gave her no clue as to his thoughts. She trembled, her hands twisting faster.

Stonor looked down at them and put his own over them, stilling their agitated movements.

"Don't be afraid, Sophia," he said calmly.

She swallowed. "The child," she whispered. "It is Wolfe's..."

Stonor's face quivered in a muscular spasm. His lips shaped icy words. "Do you think I don't know that?"

She looked away, trembling.

There was a silence, then Stonor said in level tones, "But never again will we refer to it as his. From today it is my child. I will accept it, rear it, treat it as my own if you swear to me now to put all thought of Wolfe Whitley from your head."

Her head swung around. Her blue eyes, worried and incredulous, were so wide they stretched the white skin of her face into a mask.

His mouth twisted sardonically. "Remember what I offer you, Sophia. Wolfe Whitley's son will be heir to Queen's Stonor, and I will do nothing to deny him his right. But only if you give me your word that you will never think of my half-brother again. He will be forgotten from today. You will never tell anyone that this is not my child." He drew a harsh breath. "And particularly not Wolfe. You will never tell him that the child is his."

Sophia stared, trying to read his face. His offer amazed her, bewildered her. Why was he doing it?

Her silence made Stonor stiffen. "Well?" he asked. "Is it a bargain?"

"I don't understand," she said faintly. Would she never penetrate that cold mask of a face? She stared into his grey eyes and saw nothing but remorseless determination.

"You don't have to understand," Stonor said in sudden irritation. "All you have to do is agree. Give me your word now, Sophia. The child is mine, not Wolfe's." He leaned over and put his hand flat on the slight swell of her body. Sophia jerked as if stung, and he looked at her with narrowed eyes.

"It is mine," he said through his teeth.

She could not drag her eyes away from his face. As if he were making her say it, she found herself whispering, "Yes. It is yours."

Stonor's eyes moved back to where his hand lay, then he got up and moved from the room without a backward look, leaving her lying there in stunned silence.

The months of Sophia's pregnancy seemed long and wearisome. As her frail body grew swollen, Stonor spent more and more time with her, under the watchful, hostile gaze of the French servants. He sat beside her bed, reading to her from English newspapers or novels sent out from England, or telling her of the places he had visited the previous day. Each day he went out alone, on a horse, riding around the district, bringing her back spring and later summer flowers, sketches of old stone churches, tales of local folklore.

The peasants talked of their ancient tongue, the *langue d'Oc*, which they rarely spoke now that French was dominant. Stonor told her of their fierce pride in their past and the grinding poverty of their lives.

"When I was a boy, I remember the onion seller coming to our house each year. He looked so strange, with strings of golden onions hanging around his neck. I used to wonder what sort of country he came from." Stonor smiled at her as he spoke.

She remembered Wolfe laughing as he spoke of Stonor's jealousy as their shared father took Wolfe with him to watch cricket, leaving Stonor behind. What had that childhood done to him?

He read her letters from Aunt Maria, filled with small details of London life, complaints about the servants, news of Elizabeth's marriage to Tom. Stonor's face held dry irony as he read a list of the wedding presents Elizabeth had received. His sister had complained when Stonor had made it clear that he and Sophia were not coming back to England for the wedding, but her irritation had gone when she got Stonor's generous wedding gift.

"Tom's a fool," Stonor said, folding the letter. "My sister is too much like my mother to make him happy."

Sophia agreed, but she said, "Aunt Maria might have been happier with another man. You cannot pretend that she has been a bad mother to you, Stonor."

His mouth twisted. "No," he agreed.

"And I am fond of your mother! I prefer her to your sister. There's a hardness about Elizabeth that I find unpleasant."

"She's a little bitch," Stonor nodded.

Sophia laughed and his eyes flashed to her face, watching her with unreadable intensity.

"If you plant a tree among stones, you must not be surprised if it does not grow straight," Stonor said abruptly. "Elizabeth and Grey have been warped by the atmosphere in which they grew up."

She lowered her eyes. "You grew up with them, Stonor."

His voice held dry understanding. "And I'm warped, too, you mean?"

Her hands moved uneasily on the covers. "I am not sure what I mean."

"Your father loves you," he said coolly. "He shows it every time you are together. Even though he wanted you to marry me, once he knew how ill you were, everything else went from his head. I doubt if you can understand how it feels to have a father who never even sees you, who walks past you as if you were not there and goes instead to another child." His voice hardened and grew harsh. "I would be less than human if I did not resent that."

She was moved. Her small hand reached out to touch his. "Poor Stonor."

He looked startled, then his hand closed over her own. "Once when I was five, I got a hobby horse for my birthday. It had scarlet ribbons and bells and when I rode it, the bells jingled like music. For a few weeks I played with it every day, then one day I left it in the hall while I had my tea, and when I went out there it was broken. Wolfe had borrowed it, ridden it down the street and a cart had run over it."

Sophia watched his cold face. So many years had passed since that hobby horse was broken, yet she felt the bitter anger in his voice even now.

He looked at her. "I could tell you a dozen different tales, all with the same ending. Everything I had, Wolfe took. Everything I loved, he stole. He did it deliberately."

"No," she protested.

Stonor's features had a sharp irony. "He destroys, he steals, he covets everything of mine. There was war between us from the day my father brought him and his mother to the house. God knows, Grey resents my being the elder, but he does not hate me. My God, though, Wolfe hates me!" He shot her a quick look, then lowered his eyes. "He watches me to see where he may plant his darts with most effect."

Her brow was creased, her eyes disturbed. "I think you misunderstand him, Stonor." She remembered Wolfe saying that Stonor hated him, that hatred can be a bond as strong as love, and then that he and Stonor had made a special study of each other. Much as she wished to deny it, what Stonor had just said was true of Wolfe.

Stonor's mouth moved wryly. "No, I don't misunderstand him, Sophia, you do."

Her distressed look brought a shrug from him. "Well, let us change the subject. We'll never agree about him." His grey eyes moved to the rounded swell of her body. "All that can ever be done against Wolfe is to try to blunt his arrows."

The phrase bothered her, puzzled her, and later when she was alone, she thought about it, about the hard glint in the grey eyes as Stonor looked at her. What had he meant?

It occurred to her that in insisting on marrying her, in claiming her unborn child as his own, Stonor was in some sense still fighting Wolfe. Was that the reason for his otherwise inexplicable behaviour? Looked at in one light, Wolfe had won the battle between himself and Stonor over her. He had made love to her, he had left his seed inside her. Most men, when they discovered that, would have repudiated her with bitter anger, but Stonor had acted so oddly. Had his generosity been fuelled by a desire to reverse Wolfe's victory and turn it into defeat? Wolfe might well see it as defeat once he knew she had married Stonor after all, once he heard that she had borne a child apparently to Stonor. Stonor's insistence that she must never tell Wolfe that the child was his might well mean that he wished Wolfe to believe that Sophia had accepted him in every sense of the word.

Sophia was disturbed by this thought. Stonor, if she was right, would be using her as a weapon in his duel with his half-brother. She did not wish to be used against Wolfe. It made her feel disloyal.

She could not fault Stonor's treatment of her, however. He was the most indulgent of husbands. If she professed a desire for fruit, he would go out of his way to bring her the best in season. He brought her flowers, which he picked in the meadows himself. He discovered her favourite foods and made sure the cook provided them at mealtimes. One of the surprise gifts he brought her was an old mandolin, which Sophia plucked at desultorily, learning to play it by ear. Stonor liked to sit and listen while she played old French airs that the servants hummed for her until she picked them up.

These long hours together began a very gradual alteration in their relationship. At first she was stiff and shy with him, but soon when he came into her room, Sophia gave him her brilliant, dancing smile and got back Stonor's hesitant smile in return.

"Oh, I'm so bored, Stonor," she would cry. "Read me some Dickens."

He would fetch one of the novels and read it in his cool, quiet voice while she fidgeted on her bed, weary of her long idleness, conscious of the brilliance of the summer sun outside.

Stonor got up very early and went out alone on foot, walking across the open fields, his pale face set in a mask of silent thought. One day he fell into talk with a local shepherd, watching fascinated as the man delivered twin lambs to a struggling ewe, his horny hands gentle as he delved into the animal's body to assist the birth. Stonor winced yet could not help watching.

Abruptly, he said: "My wife expects a child."

The shepherd, a grizzled man in his sixties, grinned. "I've delivered eight living children to my own wife, sir, in my time."

Stonor stared, not believing what he heard. "You have?"

The shepherd laughed. "Aye, we live too far from the village to fetch the midwife in time, and she's a drunken old hag, anyway. I've rarely seen her sober." He eyed Stonor. "Don't let her meddle with your wife, m'sieur. She'd kill her or the babe. Many a wife has gone to her maker with that old crone's help."

Stonor looked at him grimly. "We shall have the doctor."

The shepherd nodded. "He's a good man. You may trust him. But for myself, sir, I trust my own two hands. A sheep or a woman—what's the odds? I've helped so many lambs into the world I know what to do."

Stonor came into the habit of walking that way in the bright dawn light to talk to the old man. He once helped the shepherd hold a ewe as she panted to escape, heavy with lamb. As the old man deftly pulled the wet body of the newborn creature forth, blood spurted over Stonor's shoes and trousers. Curiously he looked on, seeing the weary ewe lick her offspring. Stonor questioned the shepherd closely about birth.

"I tell you, sir, if she trusts you, all will be well. She must not fight the pain. Let her ride with it. I've seen my wife, as if she were caught in the undertow of a swift river, rolling with it, letting it carry her. They use less energy that way. If she struggles her heart won't take the strain. The first time, fear is the worst enemy. They go blind into it, you see, not knowing what will come. Conquer fear and you've a good chance."

Stonor listened soberly. He came again and again, surpris-

ing and amusing the old man, always eager to talk of the same
subject.

"You will be a midwife, I think, *m'sieur*," he teased.

"My wife is delicate," Stonor said. "She will need all the
help she can get."

Stonor leaned back against the hedge, the sun warm on his
face. The anxiety of the past months had etched itself into the
lines around eyes and mouth, and in that glare of southern light
they showed cruelly, arousing the old man's pity, and giving
Stonor a look of vulnerability that betrayed him at times.

His whole mind was now focused on the coming event. It
loomed before him like a dark fence he must take. Lack of
sleep made his eyes bloodshot as if they burned ceaselessly,
although when he was alone with Sophia as the summer wore
on, he carefully avoided looking at her, as if the very sight of
the swollen, slight body made him wince.

She had grown heavy now, not merely in body but in mind.
Her personality seemed to have undergone a sea change. The
child she carried seemed to have slowed her thoughts. She lay
contentedly, watching the seasons through her window, barely seeming to stir from her pillows, her small hands constantly
wrapped protectively over her burden as if she comforted the
child and kept it safe.

Stonor sensed that she, too, awaited the birth with a feeling
of approaching climax. Did she fear the birth? he wondered.
Or was she merely awaiting it fatalistically, believing she
would die yet hoping to deliver her child safely before she did?
He did not question her, afraid of the answer.

The southern spring warmed rapidly into summer. The
afternoons were heavy with heat. The drawn shutters gave the
rooms some coolness, but a languid warmth penetrated everywhere, sapping Sophia's strength, giving Stonor a new healthy
bronze face and body that deceived those around him into
imagining that he was calm and assured about the birth. His
long walks across the fields and his constant rides around the
district turned his pale features into the dark, weather-lined
mask as if they were carved from wood, and his thin body
grew daily more muscular; his shoulders broadening, his chest
expanding, his thighs and calves growing stronger.

The maids, who used to spit aside as they spoke of him,
began secretly to eye him with interest. The regular, handsome features were improved by his tan. The city pallor had
gone, the thin body and limbs had acquired a lithe power,

which gave him a new sexual promise. It was not long before Stonor grew aware of their new interest in him, but he gave them no gleam of encouragement.

He had not touched a woman for more than a year, and he was aware that this celibacy prickled under his conscious mind irritatingly, but he had no flicker of interest in relieving his needs with one of the servants.

He and Sophia had agreed that they would not mention her pregnancy to her father. News of it would merely alarm him.

"We will write to him when the child has been born," Stonor told her, not adding the obvious rider that he would wait to see if Sophia survived the birth before telling her father.

Sophia looked away, hesitating. "If...if I do not live, Stonor, promise you will look after my baby."

Stonor's face was cold. "I promise."

The words did not reassure her. She looked ahead into a time when she was not here and Stonor had possession of Wolfe's son, and she shivered. He would inflict a life of misery upon the child, she thought. She did not understand Stonor, but she was aware that he had a depth of determination that was chilling in its inexorability.

Wishing to coax him, she took his hand suddenly, the movement surprising him into a sharp glance. Sophia placed it on her swollen body. "Feel him kick, Stonor."

Stonor's hand pressed down on her and the little fluttering grew beneath his touch. Stonor smiled suddenly, his face altering.

"He is lively," he agreed. "Does it hurt you, Sophia?"

"Oh, no, but it is a strange feeling."

Stonor's fingers moved, splayed against her. He did not look at her. "You must not think of dying, Sophia. You must plan to live." He paused, his face impossible to read. "For the child's sake, if not your own."

Sophia said huskily, "You had a sad childhood, Stonor. Do not give my child one."

"You will be here to see I do not," he insisted. "You will live, Sophia." His hand moved to touch her face briefly. "You will live."

Sophia sighed. She had hoped to get from him a promise that would relieve her weary mind of the necessity to fight, and Stonor was refusing point-blank to give that promise.

One June evening Stonor lay on his bed with the shutters open to admit a cooling southern wind, his body tormented by emotions he could not suppress, when he heard from Sophia's room next door a smothered cry of pain.

Stonor leapt from his bed and ran into her room. The maid was asleep in her chair, her head fallen to one side, her snoring making a whistling sound. The room was dark. The shutters were closed and a stuffy heat filled it.

He moved to the bed. Sophia lay with her eyes closed, her black hair in wild disorder on the pillows, both her hands clasped at her back, the rise of her stomach visible beneath the thin sheet covering her.

Stonor stared at her, wondering if she had had a nightmare. As he watched her, she arched, another deep, choking cry on her lips. Stonor sprang to the maid, shaking her angrily awake. She stared at him, wide-eyed.

"Run and fetch the doctor. I think your mistress is in labour," he said hoarsely.

The girl took a look at Sophia, who had now opened her eyes at the sound of Stonor's voice. She was staring at them, her face totally white, her lower lip bitten with blood where she had sunk her teeth into it in her pain.

The maid ran from the room. Stonor sat down on the edge of the bed, lifting Sophia. She began to groan, tensing as another contraction came, and he laid her head on his shoulder, supporting her, his hands moving over her slender back, gently massaging her.

"Listen, Sophia," he said calmly. "You must breathe as I do, deeply and quietly."

Puzzled and frightened, she stared at him. The pain came again, shooting from her back, wrenching at her, and she fought against it wildly, her breathing fast and shallow.

"Not like that," Stonor whispered. "Slowly, Sophia; breathe slowly." He held her eyes, breathing in a regular fashion, and Sophia relaxed and began breathing with him. Stonor laid her down and moved to the windows, throwing open the shutters. A cool breeze blew in onto Sophia's perspiring white face. Stonor bathed her forehead and cheeks with cool water, whispering to her as he softly drew the cloth over her skin.

"Relax; do not fight the pain. You must roll with it, let it carry you. Do not fight it. Breathe deeply and calmly, as though you were yawning. Let your body open to the pain, Sophia."

Sophia held her breath a second, staring at his face. Then with her eyes fixed on him she began to obey him. He felt her make an effort to relax as her body went limp in his hold. Then the contraction came again. Stonor held her gaze, talking, calming her, ordering her to do as he commanded.

The maid dashed in, panting. "Oh, *m'sieur*, the doctor is two miles away at a farm. I've sent for him, but until he comes, here is the midwife."

Stonor, white under his bronze, turned and stared in bitter fury at the fat, shambling creature who scurried into the room. He did not need to have her approach nearer to smell the wine on her breath. She stumbled as she came and only just managed to curtsy to him.

Stonor's body shook with terror and rage. "Get that drunken old hag out of here," he hissed. "Get her out!"

The maid stared in disbelief. "But, *m'sieur*, madame must have someone to deliver the child."

Stonor rose in fury and pushed both women out of the room. He shut and bolted the door and turned to find Sophia distraught, heaving in agony, the sweat rolling down her white face.

"You are going to kill me, kill the child," she screamed.

Stonor flung himself across the room, catching her ungainly body as she struggled to get off the bed.

"Lie still," he said hoarsely. "Don't be afraid, Sophia. I will not let you die."

She struggled in his hands, staring at him hopelessly. Outside, the servants clustered, muttering. One of them had ridden to fetch the doctor. The others argued, some for breaking down the door, others for leaving the dangerous Englishman to do as he pleased.

Stonor pressed Sophia down on the bed and removed her pillows. "Now you must save your energy for later, so you must learn to ride the pain, Sophia. Lean on me, hold my hands, I will take the pain for you as much as I can."

Sophia sobbed, staring into the grey eyes, and felt a hypnotic sense of security invading her. Stonor's unbreakable will, hard as iron, cold as forged steel, was bending her to his mind. She began to breathe slower, more heavily and relaxed, as her hands gripped tightly in his, her eyes held by his determined stare.

"Hold me," he whispered. "I will bear the pain for you. Feel it going through your hands into me. Look at me all the time, Sophia. Believe that I will not let it hurt you."

She did believe. She began to feel a strange, rhythmic pulsing in her body where pain had been all she knew before. Stonor talked softly to her all the the time, soothing, calming, reassuring her. The clock on the mantelpiece ticked slowly, and the ticking of the clock and Stonor's soft voice seemed to merge into one sound. Sophia listened to both and the pain faded, becoming a recurrent pattern with which she rode without resistance.

Suddenly she jerked, staring helplessly at Stonor. "Oh. . ."

"What is it?" he asked urgently.

Suddenly they heard the doctor run up the stairs. He found the landing cluttered with servants listening with tense, excited faces at the bolted door.

"Open it," the doctor commanded.

"It is locked," they told him. "The Englishman locked us all out and he is killing the child."

The doctor hammered at the door, shouting, "Let me in, *m'sieur*. Do you want to kill them both?"

Stonor was deaf to his angry shouting. "Harder, Sophia!" he was saying. "One more push. His head is there, I can see it. I know it is tiring, but you must give one more push."

"I can't," Sophia groaned. She was damp with perspiration, her fading store of energy almost done. Stonor held her slight legs bent back, the nightshirt clinging damply to his back where he was sweating violently.

Stonor's face tautened. "You must," he groaned. "One more push, Sophia."

She drew a shaky breath. He heard the agony in her effort to push the child out of her body and he winced, but his hands were suddenly grabbing the baby, feeling the wet, slippery little body come convulsively out into his palms as he helped it from Sophia's exhausted body.

Sophia gave a long sigh, her lids closing. Stonor looked at her, terrified by the deathly colour of her face. Behind him he heard the crash of a crowbar and the splintering of wood as the servants broke into the room.

"Get out of here," he ordered fiercely, swinging towards them with the baby in his hands. The doctor stared in astonishment; then he waved all the servants out of the room and shut the broken door on their gaping faces. Stonor bent over Sophia's limp body. Her lips seemed to him scarcely to move. The doctor came swiftly to take over the rest of the birth. As he cut the cord and tied it, blood spurted over Stonor's nightshirt and bent face. Stonor did not seem to notice. He was holding the naked, wailing baby against Sophia's almost immobile breast.

"Sophia! Open your eyes."

She was as white as her gown and she did not move or show any sign of having heard.

Stonor's pale lips barely parted. He whispered into her ear, "Wolfe's baby, Sophia. You can't die and leave Wolfe's baby."

Sophia's eyes fluttered slowly open, like stains between the crumpled lids, a deep weariness in them. She looked at Stonor's bent, insistent face. "Look at your son, Sophia," he said with a long sigh. "Don't you want to hold him?" His face held a peculiar bitter irony. "Look at that black hair—Wolfe's hair."

She looked down then and her hands caught at the naked wet body, holding it possessively against her. The doctor watched. Stonor's hands hung stiffly at his sides. They were stained with blood from the body of the child. Sophia's face softened into life as a faint colour came back into her cheeks. A tired smile touched her lips. The baby squirmed weakly, a choked cry like the wail of a kitten on its lips.

"I shall call him Daniel," Sophia said.

"Daniel," Stonor echoed, and seemed to give before the bitter, urgent tension which had held him all this time as he fought for her life. His body sagged. The doctor looked at him with twisted lips.

"You have done wonders, *m'sieur*, but you should go and rest now. Send the women in here to look after your wife. For you, I prescribe a bottle of brandy and some sleep."

Stonor gave Sophia a last look and walked slowly from the room. The maids backed away, staring at his blood-stained, dishevelled figure. "Go and help the doctor," he said. "And fetch me a decanter of brandy and a glass."

He walked into his own room and closed the door. Collapsing on the bed, he put his shaking hands over his eyes. From Sophia's room came the thin wail of the child. Stonor turned his head to listen to it, and he gave a deep, wrenched sigh.

# CHAPTER ELEVEN

In the pale light of dawn, Stonor crept into Sophia's room. He stood beside the bed watching her. She had flushed cheeks this morning. A deep sleep engulfed her after her exertions of the day before. Anxiously picking up her wrist, he felt for the pulse of her life, afraid of a recurrence of fever, but the beat was slow and strong. He raised it to his lips, his kiss brushing the throbbing little blue vein, and Sophia slowly opened her eyes to look and see him.

Stonor was unaware that she had woken. Hurriedly Sophia shut her eyes again, oddly embarrassed. The intimacy into which they had moved during her hours of labour made her feel nervous and overconscious of him. Stonor gently laid her hand down again and turned towards the wicker cradle beside the bed.

Sophia's heart tautened. She watched through lowered lashes as he bent. His face, visible in the dawn light, was a cold mask, expressionless and grim. He lifted the sleeping baby from its covers, his hands seeming to her menacing as they held the child.

Heavily swaddled, the baby fretfully turned his head, his small mouth pouting. Sophia put a long finger against the crumpled cheek. The pink little mouth turned avidly, seeking it instinctively, making little sounds of hunger. Sophia suddenly saw Stonor's face blaze as the baby fastened his mouth around his fingertip, sucking at it greedily. A smile touched the cold, straight lips. She heard him whisper huskily, "Hallo, Daniel."

All her woman's instincts told her then that Stonor was no threat to her baby. She caught the note of tenderness, of possession, in his voice, and remembered with a quiver how he had held the child between his bloody hands last night, bidding her to live for the child's sake. Stonor had insisted that the child was his, and yet, to save her life, he had deliberately invoked Wolfe's name. Had she been wrong about Stonor? Last night she had leaned on him in hours of agony, and he had dragged her through it safely. What sort of man was he? Wolfe's deadly enemy, but to her? And to her child. Wolfe's child? Could she trust him after all?

Stonor turned and caught her blue eyes wide open and fixed on him. A flush rose into his face as if he were embarrassed by being seen in an attitude of tenderness towards the child. He moved towards the bed, still carrying Daniel, and laid him in her outstretched arms. Sophia looked down at the fine, ruffled black hair on that small head. Black, she thought. Wolfe's hair. The little eyes staring at her blankly were as blue as her own, a deep dark blue like the purple of pansies.

"He has your hair and eyes," Stonor said, as if last night he had never mentioned Wolfe's name. "He is your image."

Was he burying the memory of having ever seen anything of Wolfe in the boy?

The baby's mouth sought avidly, the head turning to her. "He is hungry," she laughed.

"We must get a wet nurse for him." Stonor sat on the bed to watch them both.

"I will feed him myself."

"You are not strong enough," Stonor argued, frowning. "It will sap your strength."

"Of course not, Stonor," she said lightly, smiling up at him. The baby gave a fretful wail, the pink rosebud mouth still searching, and Sophia looked down, smiling.

She began to undo the buttons on her nightdress. Stonor stiffened, staring. Sophia's smooth, white-skinned breasts were much enlarged, their veins taut, the nipples dark and surrounded by the altered pigment of pregnancy. Without even thinking of Stonor, she took the baby's small head and lifted it into position. Taking one hard pink nipple between finger and thumb, she squeezed it, pushing it into the open, seeking mouth.

Stonor's breath came thickly. He watched, his hand tight on the bed curtains as the child began to suck convulsively, his eyes closing in greed, his little hand beginning to pat and stroke the warm white flesh against his face.

Sophia laughed and looked up at Stonor, flushing as she suddenly took in the way he was staring at her exposed breasts. He met her eyes and his face became blank.

"When you are both well enough to travel, we will take Daniel back to Queen's Stonor," he said in a cool, steady voice. "It will be a shock for your father, so I think we will keep his birth a secret until we get back. We will say he was born before his time. He is very small. They will believe us.''

Her colour deepened. ''You're so kind, Stonor,'' she said on impulse.

He half-moved as if to rise, and she put her hand over his arm, holding him there. ''Let me thank you, Stonor. I realize I owe my life to you. I was frightened last night. You were a tower of strength to me.''

He kept his eyes down. ''I couldn't let you die in the hands of a drunken old hag.''

''All the same, you worked a miracle for me and Daniel, and I want to thank you.''

She leaned forwards to touch her lips against his softly, and Stonor's hand came up in an abrupt movement to catch the back of her neck, pulling her towards him. His mouth moved in a searching warmth, opening her lips, penetrating them deeply. She stared as she yielded, seeing his lids drawn down over his eyes, giving him the blind look of a statue.

She did not move away or flinch, remembering his hard, comforting strength the night before.

He drew back suddenly, pulling his mouth away from hers as if he had to force himself to do it, and looked down at the baby still feeding at her breast. Stonor's flushed face broke into a smile.

''Is he getting any milk from you so soon, Sophia?''

She was as flushed and shaken as he was. Huskily she said, ''I don't think so, but he seems to be enjoying it.''

''Yes,'' Stonor said, the thickness of his voice deepening her embarrassed awareness of him. He put his long index finger to the damp, perspiring head of the baby. ''When I look at him, I shall never forget for the rest of my life that it was my hands that lifted him into the world. It was an experience I shall never forget. I hadn't realized what an extraordinary event birth is! I feel as if I had given him life myself.''

''In a way, you did. I'd have died without you, Stonor. I thought I was going to die, but you made me live. Daniel is as much your son as mine.''

Stonor looked up and their eyes met. His had a pale light in them. ''I told you that he would be. I meant every word. Daniel is our son.'' He repeated the words deeply. ''Ours.''

Her hand groped for his, her emotions shaken. Stonor caught it, and held it between both his own. ''And you will love him, Stonor?'' she pleaded with her blue eyes on his face.

"As I would my own," he promised.

There was a prickling silence between them. Sophia said brightly, "But how did you know what to do? You were so certain, so confident! Yet you cannot ever have done such a thing before."

He grinned as though relieved by her change of subject. "I met a shepherd," he said.

"A shepherd?" Sophia stared incredulously.

"I watched him delivering lambs and talked to him about birth. He had delivered all his own children. I thought I might be of help to you during the birth and meant to make the doctor let me stay." His eyes held amusement. "But in the event, I did it all myself."

"Stonor, you are amazing," she gasped, laughing, and for the first time felt a little tingle of warmth towards him. "You mean you did all that merely from having watched a shepherd deliver lambs?"

He laughed back. "I learn quickly."

"How lucky for me that you do," she told him, watching the first rays of the sun shoot through the blinds and turn his hair into a gleaming cap of gold.

His eyes held mockery. "The shepherd told me there was no difference between a woman and a sheep."

Sophia's laughter rose again. "How charming!"

The baby's head fell away from her, a wail of irritation on his tongue. She gently switched him to the other breast and Stonor's eyes followed the hungry, sucking motion of the small, dark head in open fascination. Sophia caught his expression and gave him a nervous smile.

"We must never let your mother know you delivered my child. How shocked she would be!"

His face hardened. "My mother is a narrow-minded, puritanical fool! Don't let her attitude sway you."

Sophia had a flashing vision of the night before, remembering the moments of agony when Stonor bent back her sprawled thighs, his thin hands moving between them, deftly pulling Daniel into the world. Hot colour rose into her face. She could imagine Aunt Maria's look of horror and disgust. Sophia herself found it hard to believe that it had all happened. She had always seen Stonor as so cold and formal, more of a statue than a man, yet even Wolfe had never known her in such intimacy. Last night she had been a creature in the grip of a violent, natural process, and Stonor had been cool, confident and determined, as he pulled her through it. She looked at him through her lashes. Neither of them would ever be able to forget those hours in this room. A bond had been forged between them. They had faced and defeated death together. Few husbands and wives could ever have known such moments of intimacy.

The maid came into the room, halting as she saw them. Stonor gave her a curt nod. "Your mistress is hungry. Bring our breakfast here. We will eat together."

The maid curtsied. After what had happened the night before, the whole household was revising its opinion of Stonor. The doctor had been unstinting in his praise of him. Sophia had come through the birth with a live, strong child, and the doctor said that he could not have done better himself. Seeing the Englishman with the blood-stained child in his hands, forcing his weary wife back to awareness and life by laying it on her breast, the doctor had begun to admire him, and he had given the servants a new view of Stonor.

They ate croissants and milky coffee after the baby was laid again in his crib. Sophia bent over the food hungrily, her thick black hair tumbling over her slender shoulders, her body now free of its huge swollen burden, yet with a new rounded warmth that added to her delicate femininity, the fullness of her breasts shaping her white nightgown.

Stonor laughed as he watched her. "Are you ravenous?"

"Oh, starving," she sighed. "I could eat a horse."

The doctor arrived and congratulated them both on their son. "But you must get a wet nurse," he told them. "Your wife should not feed the child herself."

Stonor glanced at Sophia, his grey eyes calm. "The doctor is right. It will be tiring for you."

She opened her blue eyes at him, deliberately appealing. "I want to feed him, Stonor!"

His grey eyes held a smile. "You stubborn creature! Well, we will see. If you lose ground, promise to stop and let a nurse take over."

"I promise," she said, smiling at him.

When the doctor had gone, shrugging, Sophia lay back on her pillows and Stonor read a batch of English letters to her. She lost interest halfway through one from Elizabeth cataloguing the furniture she had bought for her new home. Stonor stopped reading, aware that she was not listening, and caught her making faces at the baby, who watched her with blinking blue eyes.

Sophia looked around, a mischievous smile on her lips. "I'm sorry. Elizabeth is so boring about her possessions."

"She always was," he agreed. "She was a very possessive child. She had to have the prettiest dolls, the most luxurious doll clothes."

"And now she has poor Tom in her doll house!"

"God help him." Stonor's mouth was grim. Sophia looked down at the baby, chuckling at him. Stonor stopped and picked Daniel up, then laid him in her arms. "Go on," he said with amusement. "Play with him if you must."

She dimpled. "Am I boring you?"

"No," he said, looking into her eyes. "I like to see you with him in your arms. My mother was never demonstrative. I always felt that she disliked to be touched. She almost flinched if one kissed her cheek."

Sophia's smile died. She gave him a long, grave look. "Were you very unhappy as a child, Stonor?"

"It was hardly paradise," he said wryly.

She looked at Daniel, touched his hair lightly. "A mother who flinched if you kissed her and a father who ignored you. No wonder you grew up as you did."

"Daniel shall not suffer like that," Stonor said in level tones.

Sophia smiled at him. "No, we will both love him." She held the baby out to him. "Show him that you love him, Stonor."

He looked almost alarmed, then he held the baby close to his shoulder, kissing the crumpled pink face, and Sophia laughed at his nervous handling of the fragile, vulnerable little body.

A fortnight later Sophia was allowed to come downstairs into the warm summer air. She wore a loose, silken wrap which flattered the curves her body had so recently acquired. Lying on a chaise longue in the open window, she watched the birds flying from the old stone walls of the garden to the fruit trees, their dark wings making patterns on the sky. She was content, listening to the languors of the southern summer, the endless chirp of the cicadas, the rustle of the sea breeze, the creak of the orchard trees against the walls. Stonor sat beside her, reading an English newspaper. He looked up and saw the relaxed, happy look on her face. She had just fed Daniel upstairs, and her face was soft with physical pleasure.

Stonor reached to a bowl of fruit and offered her a golden-skinned peach. She turned, smiling, to take it.

"Shall I peel it for you?"

"I like the skin," she said impishly. "It is like eating a furry mouse."

Stonor laughed. "You horrible creature! What a picture that conjures up."

She bit into the peach with relish, and he watched, smiling. "You do everything with such pleasure," he told her. "I never knew anyone with so much life." His eyes wandered. "Your skin has a peachlike quality now. You're beginning to gain colour and weight. You look quite well."

"I'm getting fat," she said cheerfully, and his grey eyes moved over her relaxed body, tracing the fullness of her breasts under the loose silk.

At that moment one of the young maids came into the room with a message. The doctor was sorry he would be delayed on his daily visit because another patient had summoned him. The girl curtsied before withdrawing, but Sophia suddenly caught her glance at Stonor. There was a look of eager admiration in her dark eyes, a provocative invitation in the curve of the red mouth. Stonor's cool, handsome face showed nothing. The girl swayed out, her body sensual.

Sophia lowered her eyes, watching Stonor, eating her peach, her small white teeth biting into the juicy, golden interior. She knew she had not imagined the girl's silent invitation to him. For the first time Sophia wondered if he had been satisfying himself with any of the maids in the house during the last months. There were several pretty girls among them.

Her blue eyes began to study his appearance with new interest. His looks had changed a great deal, she realized. His skin had a smooth, bronze sheen. His shoulders had filled out, his chest deepened, making his lean-hipped body distinctly attractive. Even his hard, cold features would not deter women from desiring him, Sophia thought. Possibly it might even fascinate them. They would long to light a fire within those cold grey eyes, to see his icy reserve melt for them.

Had any of them succeeded? Remembering how Stonor had forced her to do as he wished during Daniel's birth, she could believe that he might make a very dominant lover.

She concentrated on her peach. It was no business of hers, she hurriedly reminded herself. Stonor had every right to take any woman he chose, and she had no interest in his love life.

Yet from that moment she could not help but notice the way the maids eyed him and their eager smiles if he spoke to them.

Sophia herself began to notice the powerful movements of his lean, hard body as he moved around the rooms.

Her new awareness of him began to alter their relationship. She had grown used to feeding Daniel in front of him without thinking about it, but a few days later when Stonor came into the room when the baby was at her breast, she blushed, looking startled.

Stonor frowned. "What is it?"

"Nothing," she muttered, her eyes down.

Stonor sat on the bed and lifted her chin to make her look at him. "Don't lie to me, Sophia."

"It is just that..." Her voice broke off, her cheeks flushed. "Well, we will be going home soon, and perhaps it would be best if you did not enter my room while I was feeding Daniel."

He swore under his breath, and her eyes rose in a startled movement. Stonor's fingers tightened on her chin. "You're not shutting me out, Sophia," he said tersely. "I thought we had a bargain. I delivered the boy. Have you already forgotten that? I want no secrets between us. I've seen him at your breast dozens of times. I don't give a fig for the puritanical horror of women like my mother. We'll lead our lives in our own way. Forget the straightjacket code of so-called decent women. I like to see the boy at your breast." His hand shook her chin. "Do you understand?"

She silently nodded, astonished by his anger. His fingers softened, moved up her hot cheek, caressed the tender line of her mouth.

"It gives me great pleasure to watch Daniel drawing nourishment from your body," he whispered. While he held her cheek with one hand, the other moved to detach Daniel from her. She looked down in bewildered surprise, not protesting because she did not know what he meant to do. Stonor stared at her breasts as he moved the small, dark head from one to the other. His fingers left her face. He sensitively touched the nipple. Stroking the hard, dark pink flesh, he pursed it until it was shaped to slide into Daniel's eager mouth.

Sophia grew conscious of a flushed awareness of Stonor. She couldn't look at him. While the baby hungrily attacked her breast, Stonor touched it, his fingers stroking the warm white curve, sensuous, caressing, as if desiring to share the child's enjoyment of her.

She felt a queer, melting warmth in the centre of her body

and was shaken and shocked to realize that Stonor had aroused new instincts in her.

"I had a wet nurse when I was a baby," Stonor said drily. "My mother would have found the process of feeding a child too disgusting to bear."

Sophia could not speak. Daniel's little mouth sucked ravenously and Stonor's long hands slowly, pleasurably fondled her breast.

"I envy him," he murmured huskily. "He looks so content lying there with his mouth around your breast."

He looked up at her, and her wide, startled eyes met his. Stonor bent forward and his mouth slowly closed over her own. Helplessly her lips parted, yielded to his deeper and deeper exploration. He had both hands on her breasts now, stroking them as he kissed her, and Sophia trembled, closing her eyes, astonished by the pleasure she was feeling.

There was a tap at the door. Stonor jumped away. His face darkly flushed, he went to the door, breathing in shallow, erratic gasps, and she heard him speak to the servant who stood there.

Stonor went out, closing the door, and Sophia sat against her pillows with her heart beating far too fast and total incredulity in her face.

Although her relationship with Stonor had been softening, and becoming closer, she had never imagined herself responding to him in the way she just had. She had begun to think that they might find a quiet companionship in marriage, but it had not entered her head to consider any more intimate relationship. She had not conceived that Stonor would desire it. His attitude to her had been brotherly at times, at times it had been cold, but it had never been sensuous before.

Then she remembered his hot lovemaking on the night he had first proposed to her in the conservatory. The memory of that had faded until now. She had found herself growing more and more used to Stonor's presence in her life, in her bedroom. Now she was thrown into blushing confusion.

How could she have forgotten the sensuality Stonor had shown her long ago? The events of her pregnancy had buried the memory of it, supplanting it with other images of Stonor: Stonor reading newspapers to her, speaking crisply to the servants, laughing as she played false notes while she learned the mandolin. He had become so much a part of her life.

The doctor persuaded Sophia the next day to let the wet nurse feed Daniel at night so that she could have an unbroken night's rest. "Soon he will wake less and less often for these feeds, but for the moment, madame, I beg you, take what rest you can."

Sophia reluctantly agreed, and that night for the first time Daniel's crib was removed to another room where he could be attended by the wet nurse. Stonor came in to say good night to Sophia after the maid had gone, leaving her ready for sleep. She was curled round on her side, her black hair loose about her shoulders, a droop to her lips.

"What's wrong?" he said, sitting down on the bed beside her.

"I wish I had not agreed to let that woman feed Daniel!" she burst out.

"It was the most sensible decision," Stonor assured her, his hands beginning to play with her curls, brushing them back from her cross face.

"My breasts ache with milk," she said petulantly.

There was a curious little silence. Stonor's hand slid around her neck under her hair, stroking her nape. "That will pass," he said.

She put a hand to the hot stiff breasts, sighing. "I suppose it will."

Lying on her back, she closed her eyes. "Good night, Stonor."

He did not move. The hand at her neck moved down to flatten the small, round collar of her nightgown. The fingers trailed down slowly. She felt a button sliding out of a buttonhole and her eyes opened.

"Stonor!" She whispered his name in husky protest, but he seemed unaware of her now.

He had opened the nightgown and was pushing the material away from her body. His eyes moved over her full, aching breasts. The nipples hardened under his stare and Sophia's heart began beating violently. She couldn't move or speak, staring at him.

Slowly Stonor bent his head. One of his hands lightly cupped a breast, turning it upwards. His fingers stroked over the brown-pigmented circle surrounding the nipple. His face had a taut, intent hunger in it. She heard a hoarse sigh from him, then his mouth opened around her nipple and she was seized by a dizzy sense of sensual pleasure. Her head fell back on the pillow; she breathed rapidly. Stonor's head lay against her white breast as if he were Daniel, his tongue inciting her milk, hard and demanding, his lips sucking hungrily. She felt the milk flowing into his receptive mouth. Her hand came up on instinct to his head, stroking his hair, holding him against her. She ceased to think. She merely abandoned herself to the intense sexual pleasure of what he was doing to her.

Stonor's hands moved over her body, caressing her warm, relaxed limbs, finding her waist, her rounded hips, the pale thighs. He pushed her nightgown upwards and the fingers stroked her bare skin.

Her other breast was aching heavily, the pressure of milk growing as Stonor drained the first. Sophia put her hand against his neck and pulled at his hair, dragging him away from her.

He looked at her, his eyes burning, flecks of milk pale on his parted lips. Her eyes were half-closed, dazed. She silently pushed his head towards her other breast and with a groan he took the nipple.

Sophia's eyes closed entirely. She began to moan in pleasure, her body moving against him, one hand on his head, the other stroking his shoulders, his back. Stonor touched her restlessly, his pale golden head fixed to her breast. Heat burned all over her. She pressed herself against him, the long needles of sexual pleasure now piercing.

"Stonor," she moaned, twisting closer to him.

He pulled away from her and sat up, breathing so fiercely that he sounded as if he were struggling for breath. Their eyes met and she did not recognize him for a moment. His face was transformed, the grey eyes brilliant, feverish, all the coldness gone and a deep passion in his features.

"Good night, Sophia," he muttered, rising.

She caught at his hand and he turned to look at her with triumph and desire in his face.

"Stay," she whispered shakily.

His eyes leaped with fire. "Oh, God, if I dared!" He drew a long, shuddering breath. "But I can't. You know that. It would cost you your life if I made you pregnant again."

He walked out of the room very fast, and she lay sobbing, suffering intensely from a frustrated desire she could not appease. It had been totally outside her experience, that strange, secret lovemaking. She was too innocent to have considered the hidden paths of sensuality. Stonor's use of her body had left her nervously excited, aware that she would have given anything to have him stay, to have their lovemaking continue to a natural climax.

She fell asleep with difficulty and woke to find the image of Stonor's head at her breast at once in her mind. Her face burned.

He came into the bedroom while she was feeding Daniel. She could not meet his eyes. Her face was flushed and uneasy, her fingers trembling as she stroked the damp, dark hair on the baby's head.

Stonor sat down on the edge of the bed, watching her, and she tried vainly to think of something to say. When at last she did steal a glance at him, she found his face sardonic.

His grey eyes held hers, cold humour in them. "There is no need to look at me like that, Sophia. I've no intention of succeeding Daniel at your breasts this morning."

"Oh!" The angry little cry broke out of her. Her colour flared angrily, the blue eyes flashing.

"I must have been slightly drunk," he said, his mouth a hard, cold line in his handsome face. "It won't happen again."

She was conscious of a queer, chill sensation at the words. Looking down, she said tartly, "I'm sure one of the maids will oblige you."

Stonor's eyes narrowed in sudden speculation on her face. "Do you give me leave to find out?"

She flushed and bit her lip. "Would you ask my permission? Do you think I haven't seen the way they look at you?"

His fingers fastened on her chin, tilting her head. "How do they look at me?" he asked softly.

"You know very well!"

"Show me," he whispered, his eyes delving into hers, sending a long, dizzy awareness to the core of her body.

Her heart was beating so fast she could scarcely breathe. She turned her face away so that he could only see the pure profile, her rich black hair in soft disorder around her throat.

"Don't tell me that all these months you've slept alone!" What is the matter with me, she asked herself in disbelief. Am I jealous? Why am I talking to him like this?

"Would you mind if I had not?" Stonor asked softly, watching the long white throat, his eyes on the beating pulse at the base of it.

"I don't care what you do!" Sophia muttered, knowing she lied.

His face froze into that cold mask. He released her and stood up, bowing. "Thank you for your kind permission. Which of them would you recommend?"

"How dare you speak to me like that?" she gasped furiously. "I do not care what you do so long as you don't come to me to amuse yourself."

His eyes were ice floes. "I had the strangest impression last night that you were quite amused yourself," he drawled unpleasantly.

Her face had a hot, shamed look. "Get out of my room!"

"Are you keeping yourself for my dear half-brother, Sophia?" he asked in sudden savagery. "Is that it? Last night you begged me to stay with you, but afterwards you had time to think, didn't you? Do you feel you've betrayed the pure, noble love you have for him? Hasn't it entered that stupid little head of yours that Wolfe Whitley will have spent the last year in a score of different beds without thinking of you once?"

Her colour ebbed away. She looked at him with hatred. "Go away, Stonor. I hate to hear you mention his name."

He looked at her as if he would like to kill her, then he turned on his heel and walked rapidly out of the room.

For a day and a night she did not set eyes on him. The amused, secretive glances of the servants suggested to her that Stonor had gone off in search of a woman, and she was angry with herself because she could not deny that that thought made her jealous. She tried to concentrate on Daniel, but her mind was busy with pictures of Stonor making love to another woman and she could not chase them away.

He came back as she sat down to dinner the next night. She was seated alone, the candles shedding a soft light around her, the servants moving behind her chair. She looked up as Stonor entered, and her hand trembled on her cutlery.

He gave her a curt bow and sat down opposite. The servants hurried to serve him, and Sophia pretended to be absorbed in her own meal, but she stole little glances across the table at him when his head was bent. He was wearing an elegant dark suit, his broad shoulders filling it smoothly, the regular, handsome features set in their old mask.

The tough, bronzed face wore no expression she could read, but her traitorous senses quickened as she watched him bite into his roll, his white teeth even and efficient, the movements of his mouth sending a quiver to the ends of her nerves.

Had he been with a woman? She tried to guess from his appearance and got nowhere.

Later they retired to the drawing room and sat politely on the cushion-lined sofa. Stonor gave her a dry glance. "Since you are determined not to ask the reason for my absence, I suppose I must tell you."

"I don't want to know!" she cried angrily.

His mouth curved into a mocking smile. "Why are you so angry, Sophia?"

"I'm not," she lied.

Stonor straightened, his face becoming sombre. "Are we to live like this for the rest of our lives? I thought we were reaching an understanding. You have been different since Daniel was born."

She was filled with self-reproach; her eyes softened.

"Oh, I'm sorry, Stonor!" He had saved her life and this was how she repaid him!

He stared at her. "I lost my head," he said bitterly. "Do you think I find celibacy easy? You're a very desirable girl, Sophia, and I'd be less than human if I were unaware of it."

She held out her hands impulsively. "I am sorry, Stonor! Do let us forget it! I was as much to blame as you."

He took her hands and held them, looking at her levelly. "I should never have touched you. I realize that. It can lead to nothing but tension between us. That isn't what I want."

"Nor I," she protested.

"We can be happy, Sophia," he said in quiet tones.

"Yes," she said gently. She leaned across and kissed his cheek. "Shall we start again, Stonor?"

He nodded. "We know now what to avoid," he said drily. "Perhaps you were right. Perhaps I should not come to your room when you are feeding Daniel."

She looked away. "Where did you go while you were away?"

"I've been making arrangements for our journey back to England," Stonor said. "I've spent too long abroad. I must get back to work. Grey is hopeless. God knows what sort of mess I'll find when I get home."

Although Sophia longed to see Queen's Stonor and England once again, she felt sad at the ending of their quiet months in France. She had come to love the secluded little district in which they had been living, and she knew she would always remember it, both for its own sake and because Daniel had been born there.

# CHAPTER TWELVE

The summer had ripened to a fertile brilliance when they arrived at Queen's Stonor at last. It was a day of burning heat and lazy somnolence. The park grass, bleached white by long days of sun, shimmered under the dark oak-tree shadows. Buttercups sprang wildly here and there, the golden gleam of their lustred petals showing through the pale grass in metallic flashes. Poppies, red as blood, fragile, trembling, moved with the grass in the wind's path. Windows glittering, roofs and chimneys cutting the blue sky, the house seemed to welcome them as their carriage bowled up the drive.

Sophia hung out of the lowered window, gazing at her home. Stonor leaned on the seat opposite, his grey eyes glinting through his lids as he watched her body moving to the sway of the carriage. Sophia was aware of his gaze. She had often wished she were not so aware of Stonor, but in the past weeks she had become more and more conscious of the sensual promise implicit in his hard mouth and strong body. Since their quarrel he had rarely given any sign of interest in her. Polite, restrained, aloof, he moved through her life at a distance, and she hated herself for being so deeply aware of him whenever he came within reach of her eyes.

She had thought about him when he was not present, and in those long hours of thought had come to the conclusion that he had married her out of obstinacy. She had begun to know his character. Stonor had a tenacious, unyielding sense of his own will. Having once decided to marry her, he would permit nothing to interfere with his plans—neither Wolfe Whitley nor death itself. Stonor's will was unbending, iron, frozen. He had used it to defeat death on her behalf, and for that Sophia was grateful. During her pregnancy she had become so used to the idea that she would die that she had been resigned to it. Her weeks of total indolence had made her faintly depressed, deprived her of any wish to live. But once she had held Wolfe's son in her arms, she had become conscious of a

great thirst for life, and she had been very aware that she had
Stonor to thank that she was alive.

His willpower awed and alarmed her. When that hard
mouth set, she knew nothing would bend him. Confronted
with the fact that she could never be a real wife to him, he had
brushed aside common-sense solutions, insisting on going on
with the marriage, refusing to alter his plans by a hair's
breadth. He had even accepted her pregnancy by Wolfe because his will would not permit him to allow fate or circumstance to cross it. Death, when it challenged Stonor, had
merely provided him with a foe to meet in battle and defeat.

He is a terrifying man, Sophia thought, and had a queer
flicker of excitement as she thought: what would it be like to
have such a man in one's power? Watching other women in
his presence, she knew that she was not the only one to have
such a thought. Women assessed him with sidelong glances,
read his coldly formal good looks and speculated on their
chances of cracking the ice that surrounded him.

Sophia was beginning to understand the deep-seated causes
for his icy self-control. He had learned in childhood to hide
his feelings, to exist alone, to resist pain. The lessons had built
this wall of ice around him, but Sophia knew that underneath
there was quite a different man.

The revelation of his sensuality had been a shock, tearing
away one veil that hid his secret personality. Of course he had
given her hints of it before—his brutal lovemaking the night
he first proposed, his coaxing kisses at Kew—but she had been
repelled and horrified then. What change had been wrought in
her over these months to make his advances not repellent but
attractive?

In their daily lives they had begun to exchange pleasant,
comfortable feelings. Sophia found him easy to live with, but
that did not fully explain her new and growing attraction to
him.

The carriage came to a rest beside the front door. Sophia
leaped up and Stonor caught her arm, making her wait while
the steps were lowered. He descended first, turning with prof-
fered hand to help her down. Sophia gave him a frustrated,
impatient look, her blue eyes burning in her golden-skinned
face. Stonor's mouth twitched in amusement, reading that
look, seeing her childlike eagerness to reach her home.

Since Daniel's birth her skin had taken on a warm, southern
hue. Stonor had seen to it that she spent hours out in the

French sunshine, sitting in the garden, the sun soaking into her pale skin. The healthy tan she had achieved had delighted him, although the servants had shaken their heads in disbelief. Fashionable women wore hats and carried parasols in the sun to keep their complexions the pallid colour presently admired. Stonor had insisted, on the contrary, that Sophia should be as brown as a gypsy, and his cold eyes approved the contrast between silken black hair and peachlike golden skin.

During their absence Stonor's agents had been busy on the estate. He had given instructions that all the structural repairs should be completed; had ordered the repair of walls, fences, roofs; had ordered new carpets, curtains and furniture; had seen to it that the decor was renewed to his taste. New servants had been engaged in London to flesh out the local staff, and a neat, dark livery had been obtained for them.

Stonor's cool eyes lifted to survey the façade of the house, noting with satisfaction the changes that were visible from outside. The work had been done well. He was satisfied.

Edward Stonor came running down the steps, his arms outstretched, a smile of joy and relief on his face as he again held the slender body of his daughter in his embrace.

He looked down into her eyes. The wan, weak frailty he had last seen had gone. Sophia was a golden gypsy, blue eyes blindingly bright, and her father smiled with delight. Her body was far more rounded and feminine, her waist tiny, her hips smoothly curved, the full thrust of her breasts pushing against her dress. The wild young girl had become a woman.

"Welcome home, both of you!" Edward Stonor turned to shake hands with his son-in-law. "I thought you were never coming back! Was France so spell-binding?"

"Oh, Papa, it was beautiful!" Sophia said eagerly.

"It seems to have worked wonders for you."

"She looks well, doesn't she?" Stonor's lips had a satisfied set to them. Both men contemplated her, smiling. She twirled like a child with her full skirts floating.

"Do I?"

Her father's scrutiny was smiling. "Marriage suits you, I see."

Stonor looked at her, and Sophia felt her colour rise. She laughed, though, but just then Dorcas, the nurse, emerged from the carriage slowly, getting down the steps one at a time, with Daniel in her arms.

Edward Stonor's head swung in disbelief. The baby wailed

crossly at the disturbance of his sleep. Stonor, watching his
father-in-law, saw his face register first incredulity, then bewilderment and then a flash of bitter anger. Sophia saw it,
too, and felt a qualm as her papa turned to face Stonor, the
hostile accusation of his eyes making her wince.

"A child?" His voice shook. "It is not Sophia's child?
After what the doctor told you?"

She clasped at his arm, tugging like a child for attention.
"Papa, oh, Papa darling, do not be cross with Stonor. It is
/not his fault. It is mine."

Her father's eyes dropped to her pleading upturned face, a
look of pity, affront and disbelief in them. Stonor suppressed
a wry smile. He knew as well as his father-in-law that a child
could only be conceived by the weakness of a man. He had
sworn he would not get Sophia pregnant, and she could never
hope to convince her father that she was guilty of anything
other than a loving submission.

"I've no excuse, sir," Stonor said calmly, his grey eyes on
Sophia's face, warning her to say no more. "I regret it, but
the boy is alive, and so is Sophia, and there will never be another child, I promise you."

"You risked her life, damn you!" Edward Stonor's
savagery burst out, forgetting the listening ears of servants,
forgetting his pleasure in their safe return, forgetting everything but a buried dislike of Stonor that had been growing in
him since their first meeting.

"Believe me, sir, if it could have been otherwise, I would
have been very happy," Stonor said drily, and Sophia glanced
at him unhappily, noting the hidden irony in his eyes.

Edward Stonor was darkly flushed. "You gave me your
word, you scoundrel!"

"Oh, Papa! Don't!" Sophia tried to stand between them,
trembling, holding her father's arm.

"She could have died!" Her father spat over her head.

Filled with the knowledge that she might well have done if
Stonor had not saved her, Sophia looked anxiously, pleadingly at her father.

"Please, don't quarrel with Stonor, Papa. Oh, don't. You
are ruining my first day home." Her hand sought sideways
for Stonor's and held it, bringing it towards her father.
"Please, say you forgive us!"

Edward Stonor looked down at her flushed, unhappy face
and sighed, his shoulders slumping, too easy-going to keep a

quarrel alive for long. "Well; thank God you came through it." He gave Stonor a fierce look. "It must never happen again."

"Do you think I don't know that?" Stonor's voice was abruptly harsh, breaking hoarsely on the final word.

Sophia looked anxiously at him. He caught her glance and turned away, his body stiff and erect, and moved into the house.

Dorcas had come up, curious and wide-eyed, and Sophia turned to take the baby from her. Smothered in lace and frills, he looked hot and cross, his blue eyes open in a squinting scowl. Edward's face softened.

"A boy, Stonor said?"

"Daniel," Sophia told him.

They both regarded the baby, who gave a great, red-faced yawn and then wailed irritably. Edward Stonor took him into his arms, one hand at the back of his flopping head, and lifted him up to the blue summer sky, laughing now, his eyes brimful of delight which was unshadowed by fear.

"Daniel," he said. "Daniel! Well, life's full of surprises, but this one I had not hoped for. He's a fine-looking boy, Sophia. Why did you call him Daniel? That's not a family name."

"I like it," she said, and watching Stonor's departing back, she said softly, "He is Daniel Stonor Whitley."

Stonor halted on the threshold as though she had shot him. She saw him slowly turn to look back at her, and her eyes submissively, gently, met his with a smile. His grey glance had a fierce, brilliant light. He did not smile back but merely sent that penetrating look towards her as though trying to read her mind, and under his hard stare she felt a strange trembling along her limbs. She had added his name on impulse, never having thought of it before, driven by a sense of guilt because Stonor had borne that blame for Daniel's birth while being totally blameless. Instinct had shown her a way to please him, to thank him for bearing the blame that her father had flung at him so angrily.

She owed him so much, and she could give him so little. Although she had hated Stonor before their marriage, she had come to rely on him. He had brought Daniel into the world with his own willpower. She would never have stood up to that prolonged and painful birth without him. Stonor had never reproached her for Daniel's conception. He had turned their grim mockery of a marriage into a family—as doting a father towards Daniel as if he had really been his father, as indulgent a husband to her as she could hope. It seemed little enough to give Daniel his name and so cement the relationship.

Her father smiled and sighed. "Well, as heir to Queen's Stonor, I'm glad he carries the name." His eyes brightened. "He could add a hyphen later; many families do. Stonor-Whitley, that's got a ring to it."

Sophia laughed. "Does it matter what his surname is, Papa? He is my son."

"True," Edward Stonor nodded. His face roughened. "I'm surprised Stonor risked it, but I'm glad to have the boy." His eyes travelled around the park and up to the house. "Oh, yes, I'm glad to have him."

Only in her bedroom later did it occur to Sophia that by giving Daniel the second name of Stonor, she was finally erasing all Wolfe's share in him and transferring it to Stonor.

Was that the meaning of Stonor's hard, probing look? Did he see it in that light?

Wolfe's seed had sown Daniel in her body, yet ever since that night it had been Stonor who had fathered him—nursing her doggedly through her difficult pregnancy, accepting the fathership of the child, stubbornly forcing her to deliver Daniel and go on living.

Daniel was Stonor's son in everything but that one vital factor, the act of conception, and giving him Stonor's name had put a new stamp on the relationship between them. Considering that, Sophia was glad that she had spoken so impulsively. Stonor had been so good until now. Many men finding themselves in his position might well have flung her out of doors, turned her off to fend for herself, a ruined woman. Stonor had acted so differently.

She looked around her bedroom. Stonor had spent much time and thought in ordering the decoration of it, having it delicately, expensively furnished in the most exquisite materials. Fine blue silk brocades, blue-sprigged wallpaper, a silk quilted bedcover—he had turned the shabby girl's bedroom of her childhood into an elegant boudoir, all gilded mirrors, fine ornaments, deep carpets.

She wandered around, touching things curiously. Stonor had made her a beautiful setting. In her soft, flowing wrap, her black hair loose around her golden-skinned face, she bent with pleasure to inhale the perfume of a vase of summer flowers that flooded the air with their heavy scent.

Pulling a red rose from the vase, she wove the stem into her black hair, laughing at herself in the mirror. The crimson petals gave a touch of the exotic to her face, as the pearl-glass lamps shimmered around her, their delicate light flattering her smooth skin.

She had left Stonor downstairs with her father, passing the port and nuts across the dinner table. Although her father was now making an effort to be pleasant, he was still inclined to sulk about the changes Stonor had made in the house. He was happy to see the place return to its former glory, yet he wished it to happen later, so that he might keep it as it was the shabby, lovely, decaying house as he had known it all his life. Sophia had left them to their barbed discussion, knowing who would win. She had not lived with Stonor for so long without knowing that in an argument he would emerge the victor.

Closing her eyes, she whirled around the room, swaying, humming softly to herself; a gay waltz tune they had picked up in France, a lilting melody full of laughter and romance. Her return home had brought a flush of happiness to her face and a curve to her lips. Her skirts flared out, the fine lawn and lace of her nightgown showing beneath her loose silk wrap, her black hair flying wildly as she waltzed.

She did not hear the door open nor realize she was being watched. Eyes shut, she spun around dizzily, laughing. She was suddenly caught in hard arms and whirled onwards, finding herself in Stonor's arms.

It was months since she had danced. She laughed up at him, her feet eager to continue, and her slender, rounded body swaying in his arms, she followed his lead.

As he spun her, she felt his thigh against her own, the tense pressure of hard muscles, and to her shamed dismay she felt her pulses begin to clamour.

Stonor halted, looking at her hard, and her blue eyes looked up submissively, a shy expression in her face. Stonor bent her backwards in his arms, her black hair falling loosely over his hand.

His mouth was on her own before she had time to think. At the first touch Sophia felt herself flame into reaction; unbidden, unconscious reaction she could neither halt nor define. Her lips parted hungrily, her arms slid around his neck, and Stonor kissed her deeply, his arms holding her fiercely, one hand caressing her body.

His mouth was hard, hot, parting hers in a passionate exploration, tasting her inner moisture with his tongue. She did not recoil from the intimacy of the kiss. Her body moved invitingly against him, pressing towards him as if she deliberately tried to provoke him. Drowning in sensual awareness, she was unconscious of everything now but the needs of her body, needing that hard male pressure, her heart thudding against her breastbone.

Stonor suddenly broke off, pulling his head back. His face was darkly flushed and his grey eyes ate her. "No, Sophia," he muttered. "We can't."

His hands went to her wrists, unlocking them from around his neck, pushing her away, but the glittering of his eyes told her that Stonor was deeply tempted.

He moved away while she watched him. With his back to her he said huskily, "I shall have to go to London tomorrow. I don't know how long I shall be there, but you will be happy here at Queen's Stonor, won't you?"

"I shall miss you," Sophia said softly.

Stonor did not turn around. There was a long silence. Then he said brusquely, "Is there anything I can get you in London? Anything you need?"

You, Sophia thought suddenly. I need you. But Stonor was right. They dared not let the new feelings between them flower into real lovemaking. She bit down on her lower lip, struggling with sensations that disturbed and worried her.

"I have all I need, thank you, Stonor." The polite little sentence veiled her thoughts, and Stonor nodded, turning then, his face in its accustomed mask.

"Good night, Sophia," he said, moving to the door.

She heard it close with regret.

# CHAPTER THIRTEEN

Maria Whitley sat at her luncheon table contemplating her own shadow as it fell across the damask cloth. The servants moved behind her chair on hushed feet, obsequiously attending to her, although behind her back they exchanged wry looks as she nibbled at her meal.

"Some more asparagus, madam?" enquired the maid, her long white streamers floating down her back as she bent to offer the silver dish.

Maria shook her head, pushing the food around her plate. She had no appetite these days. The large town house was like a shell filled with the sound of other times, whispering with melancholy echoes. She had never imagined she would miss James Whitley. His death had left her raging against him, but now her anger had drained into the sand of her daily life and she found herself listening for his step on the stair, standing by the dressing table with his silver hairbrush in her hand, staring like a fool at the few pale hairs still caught among the bristles.

Where had life gone? The years of estrangement, the years while their children grew up in this embattled house, had been so busy. Once the house had been filled to overflowing with people. She had once wished for a little peace and solitude. Now she had it in abundance, and it weighed on her spirits like lead.

Her plate was removed and a rainbow jelly placed before her. She touched it with her spoon and saw it quiver, flashing light. Vacantly she contemplated it while the servants watched, their faces bored.

Everything had ended so suddenly. James's death had begun a landslide that had swept the family away, leaving her alone in this house. Stonor had gone abroad with Sophia and God knew when he was coming back. Elizabeth had married and become too preoccupied with her own life to spare time for her mother. A few weeks ago Elizabeth had told her petulantly that she was expecting a child. Maria had been delighted, eager to discuss it with her, but Elizabeth had brushed aside her mother's pleasure.

"It is too bad of Tom. I did not want to have a child so soon. I've more than enough to do without swelling like a pumpkin."

Maria had been shocked, horrified, but she had come to realize that her pretty, blue-eyed daughter was far from the sweet child she had always supposed her to be. She would not have with Elizabeth the cozy, intimate talks she had imagined they would one day be able to share.

Grey had moved into the apartment once occupied by that woman. While he was out Maria took to creeping secretly up there, standing staring in the rooms that had once held her husband's mistress. All the furniture had gone, been burned as she had insisted, but the rooms still held the ghosts of memory. At first she had found it bitter, a gall that burned like acid in her throat, but gradually she saw the past in a strange, bewildering light, as though that woman had been a persona of her own, a hidden dream, so that she almost came to feel that that secret world had been her own. She walked the rooms softly, smiling, seeing James as he had once been with her, his eyes watching her hungrily, and now she was responding, giving what she had never given, smiling back at him over her shoulder.

To and fro she walked, her skirts brushing the floor, moving her body consciously, smiling.

There was no one to see, no one to laugh with, but they might not have laughed if they had seen the thin, severe old woman in her lace-trimmed gown smiling at invisible shadows in the silent rooms.

When she went to bed, there was a decanter of port in a cupboard, a glass and the endless silence for company. Maria could no longer sleep without a few glasses of port to help her. If she went to bed sober, she tossed all night and saw things she did not wish to see. Flushed with the heavy wine, she was able to slide quietly and comfortably into her dream world where James looked at her as he once had, and she was freed of fear and guilt and self-reproach, looking back at James invitingly.

The rainbow jelly, untouched, was removed without comment. A tiny cup of coffee was placed before her. Maria vaguely spooned sugar into it and left it to cool in front of her while the servants shuffled their feet and sighed.

The doorbell rang. Maria looked up, surprised. She heard voices, and then the dining-room door opened and Stonor strode into the room.

For a moment Maria did not know him. She stared with jaw dropped. Stonor laughed at her expression and came around to kiss her.

"No welcome, Mama?"

He was surprised and taken aback by her cry of joy, the clinging clasp of the thin arms around his neck.

"Stonor, my dear boy! Is it really you? But how you've changed! I did not know you!"

Stonor could not remember her ever having given him such a show of affection before. He looked down at her probingly, seeing the sunken white cheeks, the lacklustre eyes. She did not look well.

"How are you, Mama?" he asked, taking the chair beside her. He glanced over his shoulder. "Is that coffee fresh, Robbins? I'll take a cup." He looked at Maria. "Drink yours, Mama. It is getting cold."

Maria could not take her eyes from him. She was incredulous at the gleam of his brown skin, his healthy strength of body. "You look so different! So well! France obviously agreed with you. Why didn't you let us know you were coming home?" Then, surprised, "Where is Sophia?"

"It seemed best to leave her at Queen's Stonor," he said.

"Is she well?" Maria looked anxiously at him. "Never say she is worse?"

"No, no," he reassured. "She had already travelled all the way across France. I wanted her to have a long rest." His grey eyes slid sideways to observe her, amusement in the curl of his mouth. "I've news that will surprise you, Mama. We did not write to tell you before because it might have worried you all, but now all is over and it is safe to tell you." He paused, smiling. "You are a grandmother. Sophia has a son."

Maria's face reflected her incredulity. "But the doctors. . ."

Stonor shrugged. "I know, and it was touch and go, but she came through it and we have our son."

"A son." Maria repeated the words heavily, her hands at her breast. "Oh, Stonor."

Behind their backs the servants were exchanging long, fascinated looks. They all knew of the warning given to Stonor. Maria and Elizabeth had talked of it in front of them.

The well-trained faces shone with excited curiosity. Later in the kitchen as they talked of it, one of them would say, as she thought now: "Trust him to do as he pleased and damn everyone." Stonor was something of an ogre to them. He used his cold tongue like a flail and he saw everything, especially when the servants wished he were blind.

"We call him Daniel," Stonor said, and his mother murmured the name, smiling tearfully.

Her face sobered. "How did Sophia take the birth? I hope it did not further damage her heart?"

"I think not," Stonor said unrevealingly. "She is very well. When you see her, you'll see a great change in her. France worked wonders for her. We led a very quiet life—plenty of rest and sunshine for Sophia." His mouth straightened. "If she was beautiful before, she's ten times more so now."

Maria looked at him uneasily. "It was a risk, Stonor. I realize how you felt, but it was a risk to the child." She shivered as she remembered Sophia's wild tears the night Stonor had kissed her in the conservatory. What had the poor child been through?

Stonor's face was the usual cold, unreadable mask. "It is over now. We have our heir, and there will never be another child." He glanced at the servants. "Is that food still hot? I'll eat something before I go." Robbins served him hurriedly, and Stonor glanced at his mother. "I have to get around to the office after this and find out just what Grey has been up to!" He turned to concentrate on his meal, relishing the smooth, earthy flavour of the asparagus, the thick creamed potato, the lean pink beef.

"This is very good," he congratulated Robbins as he cleared his plate.

"Yes, it does look nice," Maria said in surprise, suddenly realizing that she had barely touched her own meal.

"Tell me more about Daniel," Maria invited. "Robbins, I think Master Stonor could eat some of that jelly. Get some fresh coffee, too."

"I could eat some cheese," Stonor observed, glancing at the untouched cheese platter. "And those biscuits, Robbins."

He cut himself a large slice of double Gloucester and took some biscuits. "Daniel has black hair, eats like a horse and cries if he does not get his own way," he told his mother. "In other words, he is a typical baby, I suppose."

"You have a wet nurse for him?"

"No," Stonor said rather shortly. "No, Sophia feeds him herself."

Maria looked shocked. "Oh, but Stonor, is that wise?" She lowered her voice as though afraid of horrifying the servants. "It is very bad for her figure, you know, and it will drain her strength."

Stonor gestured for more coffee, sipped it. "All the same, it is Sophia's wish and the child thrives on it."

Maria abandoned the argument. "What did her father say when he saw the child? Edward must have been so pleased and relieved!"

"He was surprised," Stonor said with conscious irony.

Maria was flushed and excited. "Wait until Elizabeth hears! She is expecting, you know."

"Really?" Stonor was indifferent. "How's Tom these days?"

"I rarely see him." Maria paused. "Or Elizabeth, come to that. She is too busy."

Stonor gave her a comprehending look. "Why don't you go down to Queen's Stonor, Mama? Sophia would like it."

The pink in Maria's cheeks deepened. "Do you think she would? She might feel I was intruding."

"It's your home," Stonor said flatly. "And anyway, Sophia is very fond of you. She has told me so herself many times."

"I'll think about it," Maria said, already trembling with eager expectation.

Stonor pushed away his coffee cup and stood up. "I must get off to the office. I want to take Grey by surprise."

Maria looked worried. "I see so little of him. Has he been slacking, Stonor?"

He eyed her, his mouth grim. "I shan't know what he's been up to until I've seen the books."

"The books?" Maria paled.

"Don't worry about it, Mama, I'll sort it out," Stonor said with a metallic ring to his voice.

It had seemed strange to him to come back to the familiar house and find its familiarity reduced, made novel by the year away. He paused on the pavement on his way out, glancing up at the windows from which he had once watched his father and Wolfe Whitley as they went off together on one of their weekend expeditions.

Stonor's eyes held a grim amusement. He looked up further

at the windows that had once sheltered Wolfe and his mother. Grey occupied those rooms now. Once Stonor had watched them with a silent hatred. Now he grinned at them as though Wolfe still stood there, watching him.

"He who laugh last," he murmured softly and turned away.

At the offices of the Whitley firm, Stonor sat behind his father's desk and looked up from a long search through the account books. Grey lounged in a chair in front of him, defiant, pale, and rebellious.

"What have you done with it all?" Stonor asked curtly.

Grey shrugged, giving no answer.

Stonor's hand hit the desk palm down. The crack of it made Grey jump.

"I want an answer. Do I have to call in the police?"

Grey hunched his body, glaring at him. "Do as you damned well please! It'll look well, won't it? The city will laugh itself sick. Is it my fault if I've no head for business? You went off to France without caring what a load you'd left for me to carry."

"I don't read inefficiency in these figures," Stonor said with cold contempt. "I read embezzlement."

Grey whitened, the scar on his face a livid flash. "What are you saying? That I stole it? Of course I didn't."

Stonor's long fingers peeled the pages back, his eyes on his brother's face. "In the beginning it was a little here, a little there but then you got careless and greedy, Grey. Now tell me—what have you done with it? What has it gone on? Horses? Gambling? Women?"

Grey did not answer, staring at him, his scar twitching. A year ago they had been strangely alike—two thin, pale young men with soft, gold-brown hair. Now Stonor looked far older than Grey. His body had a formidable maturity, his face a presence that left Grey speechless with anger and fear. The bronzed skin and light eyes made his features into a taut, cold mask.

"I'll have the truth, damn you!" Stonor said through his teeth.

"There's barely a year between us," Grey muttered. "Why should you have it all?"

"We've been over this before. It makes no odds. This is my firm and I ask you again, Grey—where is the money you've stolen from it?"

Grey shot to his feet. "Are you calling me a thief?"

"That's exactly what I'm calling you!"

"I ought to thrash you!"

Stonor rose slowly, dwarfing Grey, his eyes steady. "Yes?" he asked with soft menace.

Grey's hands shook at his sides, angry defiance in his face. "I'm not afraid of you!"

Stonor laughed, his white teeth even as his lips parted.

The laughter enraged Grey, and even more did he resent the fact that Stonor had laughed deliberately, knowing what it would do to his brother. There had always been this distance between them. Stonor had always had an invisible advantage over him, one of which Grey was furiously aware but that he could not quite place. It lay in Stonor's ability to control himself, to act and speak consciously, with deliberation. Grey's temper rose without his being able to stop it. He stuttered in his rage, hating himself because of his weakness, hating Stonor because he was stronger.

"It should have been equally divided between the two of us. I've as much right to it as you have."

Stonor stood staring at him, his long hands holding his lapels, the black jacket exposing a figure that made Grey more than ever aware of his own puny height and body.

"I was going to leave you in charge here in London while I moved down west." He shrugged. "That's out. I couldn't trust you."

Grey swallowed, struggling with his temper, then it burst out rawly in a spiteful sneer. "Daren't leave, Sophia, eh? Afraid Wolfe will sneak into your bed?"

The whole weight of Stonor's body was behind the blow that sent Grey crashing across the office. Blood gushed from Grey's nose and ran down his jaw. He put a hand to his face, smearing blood across his skin, and looked at Stonor with hatred. He had always been resentful of his elder brother's strength of character, his secrecy, his icy control, and now the inner core of Stonor was made visible in his body. Grey was humiliated and bitter. He would have liked to get up and beat Stonor into a pulp but he knew he couldn't, and that made him hate him more.

Stonor looked down at his brother, the white rage fading from his eyes, and sighed heavily. "Grey, don't be a fool. Why the hell did you provoke me? You're in enough trouble as it is. You haven't even expressed any regret for what you've done."

"Why should I?" Grey muttered sullenly.

"Get up," Stonor said, turning away.

Grey watched the long, lean back as his mouth worked viciously. He wanted to send Stonor into a rage as terrible as he felt himself. He wanted to bring his brother down from the cool heights on which he walked, to reduce him to Grey's own level. Softly he said, "Maybe Mama believed that cock-and-bull story about Wolfe breaking in to rape Sophia that night, but we know better, don't we?"

"Shut up," Stonor said, whirling around, his face dangerous.

Grey grinned at him, watching him. "Too bad Mama caught them that time, but I've no doubt Wolfe had already had her often enough."

Stonor bent and yanked Grey to his feet, gathering his jacket as a purchase. He shook him violently, his white face bent to glare at him. "Say one more word and I'll kill you." His thick breathing told Grey that he had broken through Stonor's control and he was fiercely glad for a moment, but the look in his brother's eyes made his courage sink. Even to have the satisfaction of seeing Stonor snap, he dared not say any more. He was too scared.

Grey was silent, and Stonor slowly released him. "I shan't call the police," he said at last. "Not for your sake, but for Mama's. But I don't want you on these premises again. I'll fund you to go abroad. Try the colonies—Australia or Africa."

Grey's features twitched violently. "I don't want to go to the damned colonies."

"Too bad. You either go or you make your own life here without any help from me." Stonor's voice was cool and firm, his breathing restored to normal. "You've had a thousand from the firm, I calculate. I'll give you another thousand to start again abroad. After that you're on your own."

Grey thought of the London streets he prowled each night, the smiles of pretty women, the jokes, the cigars and brandy with his friends. "I'm damned if I'll go," he said, his face reddening. Everything he enjoyed was here in London. While Stonor had been away, Grey had been master here and in his home. He had sauntered through the days and nights, for the first time having plenty of money in his pockets, playing the part of a wealthy young man to impress the dancers and actresses he chased, doing as little as possible at the office. He shuddered at the thought of the life he could look forward to now.

"You should have thought of the consequences before you dipped your hand into the till." Stonor looked at him levelly, half-sorry for him, half-contemptuous. He had never felt the urge to kick over the traces as Grey had done. He was irritable as he faced the fact that Grey's failure meant that now he could not leave the firm in Grey's charge while he lived at Queen's Stonor with Sophia and worked in Bristol, building a new business down there. It would all have been so simple. He had given Grey a chance, and Grey had thrown it away for a few hours of pleasure.

"What's a few pounds to you? You've plenty, God knows."

"I could prosecute. You realize that?"

"Go to hell," Grey muttered.

"I'll leave that to you," Stonor said drily.

Grey pushed his pale hair back from his sweating forehead. "My God, you've no blood in your veins. No wonder Sophia preferred Wolfe."

Stonor stiffened. "That's enough." The snap of his tone curled like a whip. "I'll arrange a passage for you wherever you want to go. When you get there, you'll find I've opened an account for you at a bank. You can draw money as and when you please, but if you're wise you'll try to use it carefully. There will be no more when it's gone."

Grey breathed feverishly, wiping the trickling blood from his mouth. His eyes hated Stonor. "Wolfe always did have a way with whores," he said, and then the savage white mask of Stonor's face terrified him. Grey bolted like a rabbit, pulling open the office door and running down the corridor. Stonor came after him, stopped short and stood there, his hands clenched at his sides, fighting for control. Grey vanished, and Stonor slowly walked back into his office, slammed the door and stood there, swearing softly under his breath.

He knew that Grey had been deliberately trying to provoke him again, but the taunts had slid home like knives. Mention of Wolfe had always pricked Stonor's calm. The good-humoured cheerfulness he had felt that morning as he walked into his home and kissed his mother had gone, shattered. Stonor knew that Grey had to leave England. There was a wildness, an instability in Grey that nothing could erase. If he stayed, Stonor guessed he would always have trouble with him. He had hoped that by giving his brother some responsibility and freedom, he would persuade him to grow up, but Grey had misused that trust. He was hopeless.

The chief clerk came quietly into the room, and Stonor surveyed him ruefully.

"A difficult interview, sir?" Walters knew all about it. He knew about everything that happened at the firm. He was a quiet, discreet and efficient man whose integrity was above reproach.

Stonor shrugged. "Well, it's over now." He was not going to discuss his brother with an employee. It was bad enough that anyone should know what Grey had done.

The man took the hint. He smoothly slid into a discussion about the problem of pilfering at the warehouses and the means for catching those responsible. The dockers who manhandled the cargo to and from the ships were prone to let a case fall by the wayside. They needed constant supervision. Stonor listened, nodding, and put in a crisp word here and there. The chief clerk watched him, thinking of the gulf between one brother and the other. Stonor from his first days at the firm had taken to the business. He was level-headed, hardworking and clear-minded. The chief clerk was relieved to think that it would be Stonor, not Grey, who would control the business. His own life was so closely bound up with the firm. He was too old now to get another job at the same salary. God knows how long the business would have lasted if Grey Whitley had controlled it, he thought.

Stonor had wiped from his face all traces of the rage that Grey had awakened in him. He talked softly and coolly, and the chief clerk could not guess at anything below that bland surface.

"I trust Miss Elizabeth is well, sir?" he asked. He admired the pretty blonde girl who had sometimes visited the office.

Stonor regarded him wryly. "Very well, thank you," he said, aware that the man had no conception of his sister's true character. Elizabeth played her kittenish tricks on every man she met, but Stonor knew her too well to be fooled.

Later that evening he sat in Elizabeth's drawing room while she complained about Tom's income. Marriage had altered her ideas of the amount she needed for herself. Stonor's indifference annoyed her. He might show some sympathy, she thought, pursing her lips. He had enough, God knew. Papa had left most of the money to him. She eyed his grave face and put out her sharp little claws, smiling sweetly.

"I'm surprised at you, Stonor, for forcing Sophia to bear a child, though. Mama told me Sophia was strictly forbidden to have one." She fanned herself, watching him with sweet blue eyes. "But there! Men are such brutes! Poor Sophia, how I feel for her! How unfeeling of you."

Stonor's eyes flickered, and a restless movement around his controlled mouth told Elizabeth that her words were getting home.

"But then I never did think Sophia was as ladylike as she might have been," Elizabeth went on softly. "That night Papa died..."

Stonor leapt to his feet. "Christ, you bitch, shut up," he said hoarsely as he strode to the door.

It slammed behind him, and Elizabeth leaned back on her silken sofa, smiling. A greedy twist pulled at her mouth as she thought of the necklace that Stonor had shown her earlier, a gift for Sophia, the prettiest thing imaginable—a gold setting with sapphires and diamonds designed as small flowers. Elizabeth had coveted it on sight. It would have looked very well on her new ball-gown.

Tom never bought her such pretty things. He was always more concerned with his business, always talking of economy and care. Elizabeth was sick of it. Her eyes slanted as she enviously considered the very different life Sophia would lead as mistress of that fine house, with Stonor showering jewels and clothes on her. Sophia would want for nothing.

Elizabeth remembered the night she had stood in the door of Sophia's room and seen her flushed face and hectic eyes, seen Wolfe Whitley's handsome dark face at her shoulder, known in a flash that the two of them were sensually involved. Elizabeth had a nose for such things. She wondered that she had not seen it before, but then she'd had no chance to notice it. They'd been very sly. Meeting secretly, no doubt. She laughed. No wonder Stonor had flown off in a temper. He knew, of course. He'd seen it that night, too, seen the awareness between the two of them. It was as plain as a pikestaff when one saw them together. That sort of passion couldn't be hidden.

She moved to a wall mirror, watching the alluring sweetness of her own body as it swayed. She'd made a poor bargain in Tom. She could have made a better if she hadn't been in such a hurry. She made a face at herself. Her first avid enjoyment of Tom's lovemaking had faded. He bored her now. She'd eaten him up and now she wanted to spit out the pips, but she was married, shackled to him. She wanted more, much more than Tom could give her. Domestic life palled. If only she had the chance, she would look for a man whose money could cushion life far more pleasantly than Tom could do—carriages, jewels, clothes, smart parties.

At the moment her sense of power was fed only by achieving pain, seeing her malice prick other people's skins, as it just had Stonor's. She laughed, her eyes catlike. He'd looked like someone in hell as he left the room. She'd hit a vulnerable spot there. She must remember that. Stonor for so long had been invulnerable, above her spiteful digs. It was interesting to discover that at last he had an Achilles' heel.

She had despised Sophia, seeing her as a ninny, but now she thought of her with amusement. Clever Sophia, having her fun with Wolfe and marrying Stonor into the bargain, having her cake and eating it. Sophia must be shrewder than she looked if she had managed to get her hooks so deeply into Stonor that she could make him look like that.

In the quiet Spitalfields house Stonor sat at his writing desk struggling with a letter to Sophia. He had already torn up several attempts. For once his hand kept disobeying him, writing things he would not permit himself to say. On the fourth attempt he managed a brief, polite letter and sealed it with a sigh of relief.

He would be here in London for weeks, he saw. He had much to do at the firm. Grey had left the business in an appalling state. Stonor put his head in his hands, and sighed.

In her bedroom Maria Whitley finished her third glass of port and lay back on her pillows, smiling into the darkness. All thought of Stonor had gone. She relaxed under the sheets, and the dream world she had come to prefer engulfed her.

# CHAPTER FOURTEEN

Wolfe Whitley left the ship in New Orleans. He was not sorry. The deep, heaving waters over which they had sailed had received more than one of his fellow travellers. Wolfe's body was hardened by the long rigours of the voyage. His face was tanned and weathered by the fierce winds, his eyes those of a wary animal. He had had to fight for food among a ravening horde of other men. His years of adventure along the Ratcliffe Highway had taught him a good deal, but the voyage to America had shown him just how strong was his capacity to survive. On an immigrant ship life was cheap. Poor, scanty food; bad odours; overcrowding; weakened men who were unfit to start with; weeping women who were the prey of the unscrupulous among the men—conditions had been intolerable. Only the strong, the savage, could survive. Wolfe had meant to arrive in the New World alive. He had sewn his money into the soles of his shoes before the voyage began, taking care never to remove the shoes.

He had learned to prey on his shipmates with the other scavengers. Wolfe felt no regret for that. It had been necessary. Wolfe saw only one law in life—the survival of those who refused to go under.

His brown face had a neat black beard, to remove the necessity of shaving on board, and his first object on leaving the ship was to find somewhere where he could shave, wash and have his clothes pressed. During the voyage his baggage had vanished. All he had was what he stood up in.

He found a narrow shop in a back street that advertised cleaning of clothes. A Chinese woman in black tunic and trousers squinted at him doubtfully but agreed to press his clothes while he waited in her tiny lean-to shack behind the shop. Wolfe stripped and sat on her low cot while she went away with the clothes. Her daughter slipped into the room. "Shave, sir?" she lisped in her soft high voice.

Wolfe nodded and the girl methodically shaved him, her

small hands neat and deft. Small and slender, she moved with such grace that Wolfe watched her pleasurably.

When she had finished, she knelt at his feet, her silky black head bent submissively. "You want me, sir?" She asked it without shame or embarrassment, without coyness or crudity. It was a gentle question asked directly.

Wolfe's fingers lifted her chin. The smooth-skinned olive face, bland and empty, the slanting black eyes like bottomless wells from which he could retrieve no thought, were offered without protest to his stare.

Wolfe caressed her cheek with one finger. "How much?"

She looked at him, a flicker of speculation in her black eyes, assessing how much he might pay. His presence in the poor quarter of the city indicated that he had little money, but his arrogant, confident manner puzzled the girl.

"Five dollar," she said.

Wolfe laughed, shaking his head. She at once said, "Three dollar."

Wolfe lifted her thin body into his arms, settling her on the blanket. He surveyed her for a moment. She waited patiently.

He moved abruptly and caught the merest hint of a flinch from her. Wolfe's eyes narrowed. He lifted her and gently slid her tunic over her head. His quick eyes saw the marks at once, but he said nothing. He removed her trousers and the whole story lay bare to him. He saw the bruises all over her body, some new, some fading. Her back, arms, thighs, and breasts wore tangible evidence.

Lowering his head, Wolfe kissed her throat softly, his mouth brushing her skin seductively. The girl lay there, and gradually her black eyes took on a startled look.

Wolfe could guess from the slow, bewildered response that he began to get that, like most whores, she had had little tenderness shown to her before. Wolfe had plenty of time. He had nothing better to do, and it was a long time since he had had a woman who did not nauseate him. On board he had taken one now and then from mere physical need but never enjoyed it except as a temporary relief. The women who were eager for it made his stomach turn. Those he had to force gave him no pleasure.

Now the long black hair excited him, although he refused to admit to himself the reason for it, and the slight, delicate body trembling in his arms made his heart beat faster.

Between the pale golden thighs his body twisted, driving her into gradual frenzy, using all the tricks he had learned from forgotten women in the dark streets of London.

"Who beats you? Your mother?" he asked.

"Oh no," she said, shocked. "My man."

He nodded. It was not an unusual story. "Why not get rid of him?" Wolfe asked.

The girl shrugged. "He would not go."

Wolfe's hands played with her thighs. "I could make him."

The girl looked hard. "You?"

Wolfe smiled at her, a hard, rakish, charming smile. Without answering, he bent himself to pleasing her. His mind slid away as his body went through automatic motions. He had had to go, to leave her behind, but in abandoning her to Stonor, he knew he had killed half of himself. What else could he have done? How could he risk her life by carrying her off to a country like this one, miles from her home, when he had no money, no home? God knew what unknown fate awaited him, but Sophia could not have lived from hand to mouth with him. The news of her weakened heart had been the death knell of his hopes. At least Stonor would take care of her. Wolfe smiled savagely, gritting his teeth. Oh, yes, Stonor would do that. He wondered if Stonor had yet discovered that Sophia was no longer a virgin. A cruel smile touched his mouth and he gently incited the Chinese girl to a sobbing climax, her nails digging into his back.

Wolfe couldn't make up his mind which he preferred—the thought that Stonor knew he had had Sophia, or that he was ignorant of it but suspected. Wolfe would have liked to have been present when Stonor found out. He would have liked watching Stonor's face.

The Chinese girl lay limply under him, worn out by ecstasy, her lids fluttering. Wolfe caressed her black hair, and she kissed his hand timidly like a grateful animal.

The mother came back, chuckling softly as Wolfe rolled off her daughter. The girl spoke to her in their native tongue, and they both stared at Wolfe. He dressed in his neatly pressed clothes and paid the mother. She ducked her head politely, then said, "You stay? Make other go away?"

Wolfe shrugged. "I'll see."

The other turned out to be a brutal Irishman with broad shoulders and a heavy, sullen face. Wolfe and he faced each other in the small room and the Irishman snarled, showing his teeth. "Well, me bucko?" He swung his great fists. "You want to make trouble, do you?"

Wolfe had not undergone the rigours of that long voyage for nothing. Ten minutes later, his own broad back smarting from the whip he had used on the Chinese girl, the other man stumbled away, swearing revenge.

Wolfe stayed with the Chinese girl for a month. She was a quiet, gentle, colourless girl. For a long time her black hair and slender body were sufficient to feed Wolfe's appetite, but he grew bored. She had given him what he needed—a base from which to launch himself in this new country. Twice her previous lover had tried to get her back. He came alone. He came with two friends. Each time he failed. Wolfe was able to deal with him without any effort. Large though he was, the man had no brains. Wolfe might well have gone earlier if he had not wished to protect the girl from all possible vengeance.

He found the girl a Chinese man with a thin, lined face and a soft voice who was ready to take on the role of her protector. Chi Lo was not happy about it. She wept, winding her arms and legs around Wolfe's calf, kneeling, begging.

Wolfe had not done badly on the deal. Her new man had paid him a respectable price, and he had had fifty per cent of all her earnings for the previous month. He patted her black hair, whispering gently. "Sorry, Chi Lo. That's life."

Within a day of leaving her behind, he had forgotten her name. As Wolfe saw it, she had gained on the deal. Her new man would not beat hr. Wolfe had seen to it that he picked someone of a kind, even temper, and the Chinese man had betrayed eagerness as he looked at the girl's slender body. He might even marry her one day if she played her cards right.

Wolfe had already picked out his new berth. In his strolls around the streets of the city, he had naturally been drawn to the elegant, shabby eighteenth-century houses, with their ironwork balconies on which girls lounged in carefully arranged dishabille of black lace petticoats, half-naked thighs, white bosoms nestling beneath excitingly revealing bodices. Unlike the ugly parts of the Ratcliffe Highway, with its dark alleys and sinister narrow lanes that tumbled criss-cross down to the river, New Orleans housed its brothels in exquisite buildings.

He had been astonished to discover the city to be so beautiful. The French architecture still dominated the streets despite the rapid expansion that trade had brought in the last century. Somehow Wolfe had imagined America to be a raw, new land of shack towns. New Orleans opened his eyes. The air seemed to him to smell of money. There was a fortune to be made here if one had a good brain and sufficient luck.

Wolfe did not have enough capital to start in business for himself. He had no intention of becoming a low-paid clerk. He turned naturally to making money as he had learned to do it. It had been his experience that a young man with his face and body could always charm money out of women.

Ada was his second woman in America. He had met her when he wandered into a saloon one night. Wolfe had soon observed her leaving the bar with men, and returning half an hour later to sit and drink at a little table. She was a magnificent woman in her forties, her hair piled high on her strong face, her eyes sleepy and amused. The blonde curls had a slightly synthetic look, but there was nothing false about the white bosom that rose like a panting edifice out of her gown.

The second night he had come Ada beckoned him over. "Like to buy me a drink, fella?"

"Love to," Wolfe had replied, grinning, using all his charm. "If I had the money."

Ada's sleepy eyes had sharpened. "Broke?"

Wolfe had shrugged. Ada had run her eyes over him, brought them back to his handsome face.

"A fella with a face like yours doesn't need to go short of money."

A week later Wolfe had left the Chinese girl and moved into Ada's comfortable hotel bedroom. He found it no hardship to accommodate Ada in her thirst for pleasure. Wolfe liked making love, and Ada, even in her forties, was an exciting woman. She found Wolfe satisfactory in every sense of the word. He strong-armed for her, being ruthless when it came to dealing with troublemakers. He kept her happy in bed. He was a lively, amusing companion.

Wolfe had been with Ada for several months before he began to get tired of the life. One night he pushed his way through the doors of a gambling den after being briefly inspected by the Negro who guarded them, and made his way to a long bar that curved around the wall. As he drank, Wolfe surveyed the plush and gilt room. Scantily clad girls bent over the tables, encouraging the gamblers. A pianist played bright melodies. Glass glittered overhead and on the wall behind the bar.

"Buy me a drink?"

Wolfe turned to look at the girl who had approached him. She was barely older than himself, he saw. The blaze of her natural red-gold curls gave her oval features a gentle pallor that was obscured by the heavy cosmetics she wore.

"Why not?" Wolfe had already learned to mimic the American drawl. He knew the advantage of the chameleon, taking on the colour of his surroundings, merging into the background.

She got her drink and played with it, her eyes inviting. "Want to come upstairs? Or would you rather play at the tables?"

"Maybe both," Wolfe said.

She smiled artificially, her even white teeth displayed. "I'd like that."

"You will," Wolfe said, his eyes filled with amusement. "Although you think you won't."

She froze, her eyes widened in surprise. He gave her another smile; his hard, handsome face was charming. "Let's see what fish we can find in the sea, shall we? Tell me something about the other players."

"You a sharp?" Her voice hardened.

"Do I look like one?"

"You look like a snake." She sounded hostile now; her face became cold.

Wolfe's eyes lit with mockery. "Careful lady. Snakes have poison fangs."

"I believe you!"

Her aggression was unusual in women of her profession, and he considered her lazily. She had a smooth, swaying body that he found attractive. The intelligence of her green eyes interested him. He found women easy to conquer. This girl, he thought suddenly, might be different. It would be amusing to find out.

"What's your name?"

"Eleanor," she said reluctantly, as if like a savage she disliked admitting to her name, thinking it gave power over her to the one who heard it.

"I'm Wolfe," he said softly. "And no wisecracks. They've all been made before."

"I wouldn't want to bore you."

"I've a feeling you won't," Wolfe said, grinning.

She moved restlessly, almost as though tempted to walk away. Wolfe watched her, still amused, reading her mind without difficulty. He sensed that she was resisting his charm, determined to dislike him, and that made him all the more determined.

"Introduce me to that game over there," Wolfe said. He had been observing these particular players for some time, and he had their number. Their faces were easy to read. Wolfe had learned to gamble as a very young boy. He could make his face as empty as a dead bottle.

He made no effort to win a hand for some time, playing with his eyes on Eleanor as though fascinated by her. Among the group was a fat, untidy newspaper owner from a small town in Illinois. Eleanor knew him because she had a farmer brother in that state, and the newspaper man had made the fact a contact between them. Eleanor's red hair and lovely body fascinated the man. He could not keep his mind on the cards. He kept glancing at the girl's white shoulders and plunging neckline.

Wolfe had noted it early on, and he was deliberately playing on the man's jealousy. He kept him distracted, touching Eleanor's neck, putting his arm around her waist. The man sweated and stared and asked angrily: "Are you playing cards or not?"

Wolfe began to play hard. The cards fell exactly as he wished. Soon a scuffled pile of notes, coins and pieces of paper lay in front of him.

The newspaper owner woke up to heavy losses. He pushed his chair back with a scowl. "I'm cleaned out."

"Running away so soon?" Wolfe lit a cigar, his handsome face grinning through the cloud of blue smoke. He openly fondled Eleanor's half-exposed white breasts, sliding his hand between them, smiling at her. "Let's you and I go upstairs, darling."

The other man sat abruptly, swallowing. Wolfe read his face, saw him thinking that Wolfe's run of luck couldn't hold. The wet eyes slid over Eleanor's lovely body. "Will you take my note of hand?"

"Why not?" Wolfe took the cigar out and looked at the glowing tip. "Winner gets the lady for the night."

Under the table his hand pinched Eleanor's knee in the silk dress. His eyes caught her angry look. Wolfe mockingly winked at her.

"Which of us would you prefer, darling? Who are you hoping for?"

Eleanor gave no sign of having heard at first, then, angry and tight-lipped, she turned from him to the fat newspaper man. She put her smooth hand against his cheek, smiling at him sweetly.

"I've got my fingers crossed for you, Nat."

The man swallowed, his forehead wet with sweat. He had been to her room twice, paying through the nose for the privilege, and he was infatuated with her. He wasn't the first. Although most men came, took what they wanted and left, there were always some men looking for something more than a few moments of bodily relief in her bed. Eleanor would have been sorry for the fat little man with his lonely, lusting eyes if she had not disliked his touch to the point of disgust.

She had intended to show Wolfe that she despised him by turning with a smile to the other man. His arrogant confidence maddened her. She glanced at him through half-closed eyes to see what effect her deliberate snub had had and was surprised and discomforted to see his careless, amused grin.

Two hours later the newspaper man leaned his head in his hands, groaning, while Wolfe pushed the money and notes into his pocket, eyeing the bent head with wry compassion. Poor silly fool, he thought. The little crowd that had gathered to watch moved away. Wolfe stood up and took Eleanor's slim waist, grinning at her. "And now for you, darling," he said softly.

It was Eleanor who saw the pistol come from the newspaper man's pocket.

"Wolfe! Look out!" she screamed.

Spinning, Wolfe saw the pistol. He leaped, pushing the other man's arm towards the ceiling. The shot went harmlessly into the plaster. A shower of white flakes drifted onto the newspaper man's sweating head.

Two large Negro bouncers came at a run, seized the older man and carried him struggling to the door. There was a scuffle. The man broke free. Another shot exploded. The Negroes caught the sagging body.

"Oh, God," Eleanor moaned.

Wolfe watched, and she wondered what lay behind the cold, brilliant eyes. The incisive edge of his profile was unrevealing.

"Upstairs," he said curtly, turning.

Her face showed disbelief. "Now?" After that? she thought.

"Now," Wolfe said, moving to the stairs.

"What will happen now?" he asked as he walked into her room and looked around it. "What will they do about the body?"

"It happens all the time," Eleanor said. "The management disposes of everything very quietly. No need for you to get involved."

She stared at him as he flung himself onto her silk-covered bed. He put his hands behind the black head, a curious look in his glittering eyes. Suddenly he felt oddly unwilling to touch her. Redheaded women left him cold. When the woman in his arms had black hair, he could weave a web of pretence that lured him into bodily relief, but a redhead did nothing to him.

Curtly he said, "Get your clothes off."

Eleanor's furious look left him unworried. Her lips tight, she began to remove her clothes, and he lounged back watching her. When she was naked, she came towards the bed, and Wolfe did not move.

"Well, don't you want me?" There was pique in her tone, a thread of irritated resentment.

"Undo my shirt," he said lazily. The girl's spirit flicked him. He wanted to make her behave as submissively as Chi Lo had done, to kneel at his feet and beg as meekly and pleadingly, not to offer her body so indifferently.

She eyed him, her mouth twitching angrily. He didn't move. Naked she bent to undress him, and he watched the slow rise of dark colour in her face. She knew he was deliberately taunting her. In the past Wolfe had amused himself by treating whores as though they were ladies, seducing them, using gentle lures instead of hard brutality. Something in Eleanor made him want to hurt instead of please. He was enjoying her irritated resistance to his will, enjoying the look of humiliation in her green eyes, enjoying the fact that he could force her to do as he pleased.

He stretched out one foot. "Take off my shoes."

She straightened, eyes flashing. Wolfe leaned forwards, and his hands took hold of her naked shoulders, forcing her to her knees. "Now pull my shoes off," he said between smiling, hard lips.

"I'm damned if I will," Eleanor hissed.

He held her down as she tried to rise. "Do as I tell you, or I'll make you crawl and beg to do it."

Her face flooded with hot colour. "You bastard! You low-down, rotten swine."

"Do it," Wolfe said in those lazy tones, smiling.

She fumbled with his shoes, her hands shaking. Wolfe watched her, a glint in his eyes.

"How long have you been a whore?"

"Long enough to cut your throat if you annoy me," she said tightly. "As I said, the management is good at disposing of unwanted bodies."

"You think you could move faster than me? Try it, lady," Wolfe said softly.

She looked at him in frustration, reading the impervious brightness of the strange eyes. She had never seen eyes of such a colour, neither blue nor green, but partly both, their size and shape almost feminine in beauty. She did not want to see the incredible good looks, the charm, the sexy arrogance. She wanted to hate and despise him.

He pulled her onto the bed, a hand buried in her rich red hair, curling his fingers around the silken strands. Eleanor angrily hit out at him, her arm swinging violently. He forced her down onto the pillows, holding her there, his hard thigh pressed over hers, his hands biting into her naked flesh.

"Get off me," she gasped. "I don't want your dirty money."

As she spoke he took her mouth so violently that she was unable to breathe, suffocating under the relentless pressure, his tongue meltingly caressing hers, his lips coaxing, bruising, stroking in turn.

Many men had used Eleanor Davis's body in the past two years. None of them had touched her heart. She had coldly, scornfully submitted to depraved practices without losing any of her own self-respect by enjoying it.

Now she fought, sensing with fear and misery that this man was dangerous to her. His body had a smooth, golden power that she found far too attractive. She resisted Wolfe, she resisted her own feelings. She felt like a straw swirling around and around in a maelstrom that might suck her down to oblivion. If this man chose he could destroy her, she suspected.

Left an orphan during the Civil War, Eleanor had been made more or less a servant on her brother's farm in Illinois. She had run away and got work in an elegant, respectable house in New Orleans. A month later the master caught her on the stairs, dragged her into a bedroom and raped her forcibly, leaving her bleeding and weeping on the bed, where the mistress later discovered her and threw her angrily out of the house.

Her mind hard with despair and resentment, Eleanor had made her choice between a life of grinding servitude where she might be forced to accept the unwanted attentions of her employer, and the free, well-paid life of a whore. She had never regretted the choice. She had learned to separate her mind from her body, never caring about the use made of it by her clients, submitting icily to whatever was done to her except actual brutality. Outside the room she had at the house, she ate well, wore fine clothes and was protected by the Negroes downstairs. Half her earnings went to the owner of the house, but Eleanor did not resent that.

None of the occasions when men used her body had ever stayed in her mind. She would not let them. The only time she ever found hard to forget was that first time—her own disbelief and fear as the red-faced, panting man with his flushed bald head forced her backwards into that room and fumbled at her clothes, silently mounting her on the bed. She had not expected it. She had been so terrified that she hadn't even cried out. In nightmares she still went through it all again, the violent destruction of her innocence under the thrusting, sweating old man. Every man who had been with her since had been a mere dream. That time had been the moment when Eleanor shut life out of her head.

And now she felt a rending fear as Wolfe Whitley lay above her. Although she fought it she found it harder and harder to separate mind and body. She was increasingly aware of little fiery sparks of pleasure he was igniting in her flesh, pleasure she had never felt before in her life, and that terrified her. She tried to force herself to blank him out, but Wolfe seemed to know what she was trying to do. His gleaming eyes watched her. He smiled that slow, mocking smile, and his hands smoothly touched her body, their exploration so soft, so caressing that she was choking.

His mouth came down again, hotly inciting her, parting her lips and probing within as if he loved the taste of her.

She began to breathe so fast her lungs hurt. Her heart was thudding against her breastbone. Every time Wolfe moved, she felt herself tremble with aroused sensuality. She wanted to touch him. Her hands were shaking, curling in on themselves in an attempt to stop themselves from reaching up to stroke his gleaming shoulders and broad back.

Wolfe looked down at her with narrowed, smiling eyes,

reading her condition accurately. Her hostile aggression had gone. She was heated, shaking.

His hands gently parted the white thighs. Eleanor shuddered. "Oh, no, please, no," she moaned, gazing at him with tears in her eyes. Suddenly the last two years were nothing. She was a trembling virgin, her body untouched, and Wolfe was the first man. Eleanor's tears ran down her face. "Don't, please," she begged.

Silkily he penetrated her, sliding like the snake she had called him deep into her body, and Eleanor was lost.

She gave a wild cry of pleasure, giving way entirely, twining her arms and legs around him, her hands grasping the smooth, strong muscles of his long back, her nails digging into his skin, high gasps of painful pleasure breaking from her throat.

She was not blind to the fact that Wolfe's arousal of her had been coolly deliberate. His strange eyes had watched her as if behind them the brain observed detachedly, extending its power over her while quite removed from pleasure itself. Eleanor despised herself and struggled to break free from the hold he had gained over her senses, but he had no intention of allowing her to escape. Holding her down, his lean body moved against her, teasing her, tantalizing her, while he watched her between half-lowered lids, a sense of wilful power tasting sweet in his throat, triumph in his hard face.

Eleanor had learned to excite men with her caresses, but none of them had ever turned that skill upon her. She had not believed herself capable of a desire so fierce, so consuming. Her own need grew and grew until she totally lost her head, pressing herself upwards to meet him, groaning, covering his bare chest and shoulders with frantic kisses.

The fierce erotic writhing of her body began to affect Wolfe at last. He felt tension coiling inside him. Unconsciously he moved faster, harder, driving up inside her. Eleanor quickened with him, moaning.

Never since the night he lay with Sophia in the park had Wolfe felt such an urgent need. Eleanor's slim, gasping body sent a wave of heat to his loins. He shuddered as the wild uncoiling of his tension reverberated through his body. Eleanor was sobbing fiercely, arching to receive him, her cries of pleasure muffled on his skin. He had meant to force her to that peak while staying in control himself. He had intended to humiliate her by making her reach a climax without showing any sign of pleasure himself. But now they reached the peak together, their bodies unified in pleasure.

Only as he sagged breathlessly onto her did Wolfe realize that, for the first time in months, he had enjoyed a woman without thinking of Sophia.

Eleanor's weeping afterwards brought a frown to his face. "What the hell's wrong now?" he asked, forcing her face out of hiding on his chest.

She looked at him, her green eyes wet, her lashes stuck together. "You swine," she hiccupped. "Oh, God, you swine."

Angrily Wolfe said, "You're a whore, aren't you? Was it so damned unpleasant?"

She went for his face with talonlike nails, and he wrenched her arms down, slapping her face.

"I hate you," she yelled, twisting under him.

Wolfe felt the warm, white body moving with a sensation of great enjoyment. His lazy eyes told her as much; and she heaved to displace him, snarling like a tiger.

"Keep still, you silly bitch," he laughed at her. "Anyone would think I'd forced you to go through some depraved game with me. You've done it before. Even that fat fool I was playing cards with has had you—don't tell me he hasn't. I saw the way he looked at you."

Eleanor fought for control and managed to lie still, staring at him with cold contempt. "If you've finished, get out, and don't forget to pay before you go."

Wolfe raised his eyebrows mockingly. "Pay? You? You should pay me, lady. You got more pleasure than I did."

Her indrawn gasp and whitening face made him wish he hadn't said it. He stared at her, his mouth compressed.

"I'm sorry. I shouldn't have said that." His hand gently slid along her taut cheekbone, stroking back the perspiration-darkened hair. "It was good for me too. Better than I remember for months."

Eleanor couldn't move her eyes away from him. "Why did you come here? Don't tell me you need to buy it," she said bitterly.

Wolfe shrugged. "I just wandered in off the street. I was bored."

Her eyes flinched. "I hope I eased your boredom." The tone was meant to sting, but Wolfe suddenly smiled, all his charm in his face.

"You were beautiful. Thank you."

Eleanor wanted to cry again. She couldn't hold his eyes because she was betraying herself with every look. Wolfe watched her lashes fall and smiled to himself.

She was fighting it all the way, but he knew he had her. He bent and touched his lips to her breast, feeling the small nipple harden and swell at his touch.

"Beautiful," he whispered softly. "I want to have you again—you know that, don't you?"

She swallowed, keeping her eyes shut. "This is a free house. Come whenever you like." She made her voice brittle and cold. "If I'm not free, there are plenty of others."

Wolfe's lips played with her breasts. "Now," he whispered. "I want you again now."

Her eyes flew open at that. There was despair in her face. "No," she said harshly. "No." She couldn't stand it if he made love to her again.

Wolfe smiled. The struggle this time was brief, and Eleanor went down under the flood of her passion with a strangled cry.

Afterwards she lay white and still, not looking at him. Wolfe fondled her smooth shoulders. "How much to buy you out of here?" he asked.

Eleanor turned her head incredulously. Wolfe kissed the tip of her nose. "How do you fancy going back to Illinois?"

# CHAPTER FIFTEEN

A week later Wolfe stretched out on the bed in a hotel room, his hands linked behind his black head, lazily watching Eleanor brush her red curls in front of the dressing table. There was a curious smile on his mouth. Suddenly he said, "Wear that green dress today. We're getting married."

Eleanor's hand froze. In the mirror her eyes sought his and red colour flooded into her face. "Very funny," she said savagely. "Quite a wit, aren't you?"

Without replying, Wolfe slid off the bed and began to dress. Eleanor put down the brush and turned to get down a dress from the wardrobe.

"The green one, I said," Wolfe interrupted.

She ignored him, stepping into a yellow dress. His hand fell on her shoulder and whirled her around to face him. She glared with angry, bitter eyes. "Get your hands off me, you swine."

"The green one," he said softly.

After a silent battle of eyes she turned, hitching her shoulder so that his hand dropped away, and pulled the green dress out with a fierce yank of the hand. Wolfe grinned.

"That's better." He moved behind her and his mouth sought the pale curve of her nape, his lips slowly tracing a path down from it to her spine. Eleanor closed her eyes, shivering.

She was still fighting the hold he had over her, but the struggles were weakening day by day. It had amazed her when Wolfe had insisted on removing her from the gambling house. Eleanor knew the price he had paid, and she would have been filled with triumph if she could have believed that he had paid so much because he was madly in love with her. Why he had done it she couldn't guess, but Eleanor's woman's instincts told her that it was not because Wolfe was crazy about her. He enjoyed making love to her. That was obvious. He had spent a good deal of the past week showing her that. But he was always too much in control for her to imagine that she had reached his heart. If he had one, she thought bitterly. He was a handsome, mocking, smiling snake, and there were times when she felt like sticking a knife in his back.

When they were not making love, Wolfe got her to talk about her life before he met her. He listened intently, showing real interest, asking her about Illinois, the farm, her brother, her dead parents.

"Does your brother know how you've lived in New Orleans?" he had asked.

"Are you kidding?" She had laughed coldly. "He would never speak to me again. Jake's a religious man."

"Oh, God, one of those." Wolfe had given a contemptuous smile.

"What's wrong with that?" She had flared at once, turning on him. "Jake's a good man."

"I can imagine," Wolfe drawled, smiling his mocking little smile. "I have met them before. Church on Sunday, whoring on Monday. Full of pious speeches and secret lust. We have them in England too."

"Who are you to sneer at men who visit whores?" Eleanor had given him a scornful look. "You're no saint."

"No, thank God," he had said, smiling, touching his mouth to the warm skin of her arm. "How did you get into the game?"

She had stiffened. "What's that to you?"

"I'm curious," he had told her. "Did you choose the life or have it forced on you?"

She had told him then about being raped by her employer, thrown out of the house by his wife and deciding to become a whore. Eleanor had given him the story in cold, succinct little sentences, her face sick with disgust.

That had been yesterday, and she had realized as she told him that it was the first time she had ever spoken about it to anyone. Wolfe had gone on drawing it out of her, making her talk until all the horror and shame and fear had come out of her, and Wolfe had watched with those strange, changeable eyes, his face impassive.

Now he hunted in his inner pocket with a little grin and said, "We'd better try the ring, I guess."

Eleanor had her hands to her neckline, smoothing it down. Wolfe took her left hand while she stared incredulously. She looked at the broad gold band as if it were a mirage, then she looked up into his amused face.

"Hurry up or we'll be late," Wolfe said. "You don't want to be late for your wedding, do you?"

Hoarsely she said, "You're not serious."

"Get your bonnet on," Wolfe said. He slid the ring off. "A good fit, isn't it? I guessed the size."

She caught his lapels, staring at him. "Wolfe, are you playing a game with me? I'll kill you."

He laughed. "How like a woman. Ask her to marry you and she offers to kill you."

She shook him, her teeth bared. "Are you serious?"

His face sobered. His blue-green eyes looked at her levelly. "Yes."

"Why?" she asked unevenly. "Why?"

"I want you as my wife," Wolfe said, turning way. Eleanor stared at the black head as he walked towards the door. With automatic gestures she tied on her bonnet and followed him. All the way to church she suspected it was a cruel joke. Even as she nervously repeated the responses, she stared at Wolfe's handsome face and waited for him to puncture the balloon of this growing happiness. His words echoed in her ear. He wanted her as his wife. He wanted her. When he bent to kiss her, her lips clung feverishly. She felt like someone standing on a beach and feeling the slow slide of the wet pebbles under her feet, a wild instability inside her, a dizziness. If she did not stop it soon, she knew then, she would be helplessly, hopelessly in love with him.

Shortly after their marriage they left New Orleans to make their way to Illinois to claim the newspaper Wolfe had won in the gambling game. Before leaving the city Wolfe took the precaution of having legal documents drawn up, at a fat fee, by a smooth and cunning lawyer. After that Wolfe took Eleanor to a dressmaker and ordered a new wardrobe for her. The clothes were quite different from the ones she had worn in the gambling house—they were pretty, respectable clothes of a wife.

Wolfe had chosen muted, pale colours deliberately. "That red hair is a giveaway," he had grinned. "You don't need colour with that. We must try to make you look demure and modest." His rakish amusement mocked her. "If we can."

Eleanor had been annoyed at that, but she had begun to learn to hide her feelings from Wolfe. He was too quick. He used her emotions as weapons against her.

Wolfe was warily conscious of the fact that he found

Eleanor's presence in his life distinctly seductive. He did not couple how he felt with the word love, but he knew he wanted her around all the time. Sophia would be married by now. She was out of his reach. Wolfe had never intended to marry anyone else, but he could not bring himself to let Eleanor go just now, and he knew that it might mean trouble if he took her back to Illinois with him as his mistress. An illicit liaison of that sort would only stir up gossip and trouble. Wolfe did not want any trouble. He would have enough of that anyway. Also his cool brain pointed out that to arrive with a young wife who had a respectable connection with the state could do him no harm. Eleanor could be useful to him. She would establish his credit.

In order to make her respectable, all hints of her years in the gambling house must be expunged. Wolfe wanted no scandal.

He gave Eleanor none of his reasons for marrying her. He knew from her stunned amazement, her softened manner, that she was overwhelmed and puzzled. Wolfe meant to keep her that way. He had conquered her first resistance to him physically and now he had a strange desire to have Eleanor look at him with love as well as passion. He told himself that his desire to make her love him was based on a love of challenge, but he had somehow stopped visiting other women since he met her. Eleanor engrossed all his attention. Their hours in bed gave Wolfe more pleasure than he had expected he would ever get from anyone but Sophia.

Wolfe always put first things first. When they arrived at the little town in Illinois that housed his newspaper, he devoted himself to securing possession of it. It was still being brought out by a tiny staff of two—a bespectacled old man with white hair and a thin boy whose eager face clouded when he heard of the ex-proprietor's death.

Wolfe's legal documents were scrutinized by the local lawyer, who eyed him wryly but said, "He's right. The whole place is his."

Wolfe stood in the dusty little office and studied the two employees. "Right," he said, taking off his jacket. "Show me around and tell me everything."

He inspected the machinery, glanced through the columns of the tightly printed sheets, looked through the account books. The old man shuffled his feet.

"We going on as before?" he asked.

"I tell you what, Fred," Wolfe murmured. "You carry on until I know my way around. I don't know the town. You do. Give me a few weeks to find my feet. But this stuff is as dull as ditchwater. When I'm ready, we'll start to liven it up a little."

"Folks don't want lively stuff. They want what they've always had." Fred's pale eyes blinked over his glasses.

Wolfe grinned. "We'll see."

The rooms above the newspaper office were a shabby collection, but Wolfe could not afford to live anywhere else. He was not going to rent or buy a house while he had free accommodation available. Eleanor set to work in her demure grey dress and a voluminous white apron, sweeping, scrubbing, dusting, polishing. Wolfe told her to buy a few sticks of furniture to give the place a little more of an air.

There wasn't much choice in the town, but somehow Eleanor contrived to make the rooms look less like a deserted wasteland. It was the first time since childhood that she had had a home. She felt nervous and anxious as she looked around the rooms. Wolfe was binding her to him day by day. He was becoming a necessity to her. She had once been free. From the moment she met Wolfe, she had known he was a threat to her freedom, and so it had proved. The ring she wore was merely the outward sign of her inward dependence.

She had sworn that she would never need a human being, that she would exist and survive alone. Now her heart leaped when she heard his step on the stair, when she heard his voice down below giving orders to old Fred or young Chris.

Their arrival had caused something of a stir, of course. They had been met with hostility, suspicion and dislike, but within two weeks Wolfe had altered all that. He went around the town freely, smiling, talking, buying drinks at the saloon. Eleanor walked to church with him on Sunday in her neat, demure gown and bonnet, keeping her eyes down, her red hair hidden. Wolfe had laughed in their bed afterwards, biting her white throat softly. "You beautiful hypocrite. You looked like a dove."

"Isn't that how you wanted me to look?" she had flared.

His wicked eyes mocked her. "Of course it is, my love." His long lashes swept down to hide his expression. "I don't want every man in the place lusting after you."

She had quivered. Was he hinting at jealousy? But she hadn't dared to ask in case he merely laughed at her.

Soon when they walked the sidewalk, people greeted them cheerfully, their faces lighting up at Wolfe's charming smile. Eleanor with her eyes down knew when women fluttered at her husband's approach, knew that the charm she could not resist was irresistible to others, too, and resented it.

"Time I met your brother," Wolfe told her suddenly.

Jake Davis lived twenty miles from the town. When Wolfe and Eleanor drove up in a hired carriage, the dogs ran out barking and snarling, the chickens in the yard flew up squawking and children stood in corners, staring at them. Eleanor trembled as she got down on Wolfe's arm.

Jake came out in open shirt and dusty trousers. "Eleanor?" he said slowly, staring. "Nell, is it you?"

She had left the farm to get away from the endless work, the cleaning and cooking, the children wailing, the silence that lay all around the place.. Now she burst into childish tears and Jake kissed her cheek with a puzzled, embarrassed look. He was a tall, gaunt man with rawboned cheeks and hair of her own colour, darker on him, turning grey in places.

He was staring at Wolfe with suspicion. Wolfe gave him a smile which always conquered strangers, holding out his hand. "Hallo, Jake. I'm your brother-in-law."

Jake wrung his hand, smiling back now. "Married, eh? Well, now. That's something."

His wife Sarah came out, brushing wet hands down her print dress. Shyly she shook hands too, ducking her head in surprise at Wolfe's good looks and handsome clothes.

"Come into the house. You'll need a drink after such a long drive," Jake said hospitably.

The farmhouse was small and cramped, plainly furnished, scrupulously clean but showing clear evidence of poverty. Wolfe lounged and drank beer, stared with narrowed eyes, saw everything there was to be seen and knew everything there was to know.

He talked to Jake, drawing out of him his situation. During the last year of the Civil War, Jake had borrowed a large sum of money to buy the farm. Food prices had been sky-high during that period. He had at first made a huge profit. But he had had an enormous loan to repay, and with the end of the war, food prices had dropped like stones. The dissolution of the two armies had left farmers with a shrinking market for their produce.

Jake was desperate for money. He poured it all out naively,

his eyes telling Wolfe that as he took stock of his new brother-in-law's well-dressed affluence and apparent wealth, he was hoping to get a loan with which to repay the next quarter's interest. Jake had ceased to pay off any of the original loan. All he could manage was the interest, and as long as he paid that, he could stop the forcible repossession of the farm by the bank. It would mean an endless debt, a millstone around his neck, but at least he was living from hand to mouth somehow, and he still had the farm.

Jake was so busy with his own story that it completely escaped his notice that he had learned nothing of Wolfe beyond the fact that he owned a newspaper and was married to Eleanor.

Sarah and Eleanor laid the table for dinner, placing bowls of vegetables and a dish of salt pork in the centre. The children were roughly washed under the pump and sat silently, staring at their visitors. They waited until their plates were filled, then ate with ducked heads and absorbed interest.

Jake spoke bitterly about the bank, the railroad's high charges for its warehouses, the grinding poverty that was holding him and his family in the grip of these money men.

"Are other farmers in the same state?" Wolfe asked, frowning.

"Too damned many," Jake spat.

"Jake!" Sarah looked shocked, her round, weather-lined face very reproving. "Language."

"I can't help it," Jake said heavily. "When I think of what I have to do to make a few bucks, and those fat money men in their offices taking it all away from me."

"Prices may rise," Wolfe said.

"And if they do the railroad will charge more, and my interest will go up," Jake laughed harshly. "They got us coming and going."

They drank strong black coffee while the children escaped from the room under Sarah's watchful eye. Jake told them of a long string of farmers who had sold their land to get out of the endless circle of debt.

"Pittances they got, that's all. And what can they do then? Hire themselves out as hands for a few dollars and scrape and grind for the rest of their lives. How does a man make a living in this country?"

Wolfe was frowning, looking thoughtful. "There's nothing much about all this in my paper's back sheets."

Jake laughed. "You think there would be? They know which side their bread is buttered. Old Schultz wouldn't have them print any of the truth."

Wolfe eyed him. "Schultz. I've heard of him."

"Who hasn't? Mr. Money Man himself. He was an immigrant from Germany thirty years back. Now he has a fine big house in Chicago and a lot of money in the railroads. How do you think they make money? It isn't the passengers. No, they make it by charging the earth for storage and transport. That's what cripples the farmer. Our costs soar, and men like Schultz make money in buckets."

"If he lives in Chicago, I doubt if he's ever heard of our little newspaper."

"He has a big farm to the west of the town. Comes there in the spring. Schultz has his claws into all manner of things. Spreads his risks and doubles his profits that way."

Wolfe glanced at his gold watch. "Time to be off," he said with every appearance of regret. "We've got a long ride ahead of us."

"Come again, soon," Sarah said, kissing Eleanor. She whispered to her, "What a fine man you've got, dear. You are a lucky girl."

She and Eleanor walked out of the house, and Wolfe lingered with Jake. Glancing back, Eleanor distinctly saw money passing from hand to hand. Jake was very red when he and Wolfe joined them. He wrung Wolfe's hand several times before he let it go.

In the carriage on the way back across the dusty, rutted roads, Eleanor said huskily, "You lent him money, didn't you?"

Wolfe shot her a sidelong look. "What makes you think that?"

"I saw you." She swallowed. "It was good of you, but it's like throwing money down a well. Jake can't survive on that farm for much longer. You could see that."

"I saw," Wolfe said shortly.

The stars pricked the dark, smooth sky as Eleanor stared up at them. Beside her Wolfe's broad shoulders were stiff, as though he were deep in thought. She looked at his long hands on the reins, never moving, sure, confident. Oh, God, she thought, I love him. She wanted to lean her tired head on those broad shoulders, sink into the security of his body, but she sat upright and watched the distant, unreachable stars and fought to keep back tears.

She did not understand Wolfe at all. She had seen him in gay moods, in cold moods, sometimes cruel, sometimes kind, and she did not know the first thing about him. Already she was beginning to recognize one particular expression on his face, a look she hated to see. She never knew what caused it, but she suspected, she guessed.

An hour later she saw that look again and felt the blood run coldly in her veins. Wolfe was staring up at the sky, a dreamy, absent look on his face, as if he were occupied with thoughts which pleased and yet hurt him. His hard mouth had a passionate curve to it. His eyes were restless and absorbed. He had never told her a thing about his past. If she asked him about England, he was curtly uninformative. He had said to her at the beginning that his life before he came to America was none of her business, but Eleanor had not taken long to realize that, although he had had many women, no doubt, there had been one somewhere who had meant more than all the rest put together. Wolfe's evasions, as much as what he said, told her that. She watched him dreaming silently as he stared at the sky and knew that there was a woman in his mind. Who? she wondered. Someone in England?

Over the next months she was to get clues about her unknown rival. Once, walking along the sidewalk, she felt him stiffen at her side, the arm she held growing tense.

Eleanor looked up at him quickly, then followed his eyes and saw a girl in crisp white, her black hair shining in the sun. Eleanor had never seen her before. She recognized the young man with her and remembered then that he had mentioned that he was expecting his fiancée to join him very soon. Wolfe was staring hungrily when the girl glanced back at him. Eleanor felt a chill around her heart. So, she thought, the woman has black hair, and she is young. Her intuitions were becoming very keen where Wolfe was concerned. She was learning to read his looks, his tones.

One evening they had several local men to dinner to talk about a campaign Wolfe had launched in the newspaper, an attack upon the financial stranglehold that the banks and railroads had upon the farmers.

One of them had leaned forwards, striking his fist on the table, making the glass ring and dance. "That's sheer sophistry," he had said violently.

Another of them scratched his chin. "Don't know what that means, Ben, but you may well be right," he said comically.

"Sophistry means a false argument intended to deceive," Wolfe drawled, laughing.

The other man said drily, "Knew a girl called Sophy once. A regular hellcat."

Wolfe looked at him oddly, his cheek muscles taut. Eleanor caught the expression in his eyes and felt herself tensing, felt a flicker of pain in her chest. Sophy. . . . was that the unknown girl's name?

Then the talk went on fiercely, and Wolfe's face relapsed into its usual control. Eleanor barely heard a word. She was watching Wolfe and burning with a jealousy that she couldn't ease away.

The newspaper occupied most of his time during that first year. He had become involved in local politics. Eleanor never knew why Wolfe did things. He often seemed to her cynical, self-seeking, unscrupulous, and then he would do something that completely baffled her, making her think she had maligned and misread his motives.

He was putting all his energy into supporting the farmers, although from the start he knew the risks he took. He was given warnings by the other side early on and ignored them. His editorials had a brilliant mix of simple facts strongly laid out and wicked humour that held the railroads and banks up to ridicule. The paper sold faster and faster. Wolfe's black wit became famous in the area.

He received anonymous letters warning him to stop his campaign. Wolfe ignored them. Some of the more wealthy local people spoke to him in veiled terms. Wolfe ignored them. At last the other side turned to more direct action. One night as Wolfe walked back home from the saloon, three men stepped out of an alley and muscled him hurriedly into the shadows.

"Time you learned not to annoy people, mister," one of them hissed as he grabbed Wolfe's arms and yanked them behind his back. "We gonna have to show you how to behave, I reckon."

A heavily built man came at Wolfe, with his fist driving towards his stomach. Wolfe arched his body lithely and kicked both feet up into the man's sagging belly. With a choked gasp the man doubled up. Twisting abruptly, Wolfe pulled free of the other man, sending a hard fist into his neck before he knew what was happening. The third man turned and ran.

Wolfe looked down at the man writhing on the ground. He

put his foot on his neck. "Tell your bosses I'm tougher than I look."

He wiped his hands derisively, laughed and went. The next edition carried the story, wickedly funny, making the attack the story of the week.

A week later Wolfe woke up at two in the morning to hear sounds below in the newspaper office. He slid out of bed, the movement waking Eleanor. She sat up, frowning, "What..."

Wolfe's hand clamped over her mouth. Silently he shook his head at her, pointing. She watched, pale, as he crept across the room. Her heart began to pound as Wolfe opened the door, and she saw a pistol in his hand.

He moved like a cat, soft and silent. Eleanor dared not move, knowing that he meant her to stay still. She listened, shaking, hearing the faint sounds that had woken Wolfe.

The sound of shots awoke the whole street. Dogs barked. Lights went on in bedroom windows. Voices cried out excitedly, and there was the sound of running feet.

Eleanor ran to the door and stood on the stairs, watching Wolfe. Smoke hung grey on the air. Pistol in hand, Wolfe turned a man over with his foot in a casual, indifferent fashion.

The intruders had destroyed the office, spattering ink everywhere, tearing paper, scattering documents and stamping on them. A can of paraffin indicated that they had intended to set fire to the place. The dead man was identified as a homeless drifter who had been around the town for a few days. He had no name that anyone knew. The sheriff shrugged over it, and the man was buried.

"Schultz really means to get me," Wolfe said to Eleanor. "They would have burned the place down. We could both have died."

"What are you going to do?" she asked unhappily.

Wolfe grinned that wicked grin. "Print it."

It made great reading in the paper. People laughed as they read the story aloud to each other. Wolfe was turning the struggle into a pantomime, with blown-up cardboard villains playing the fool.

"Laughter hurts more than guns," Wolfe said.

Eleanor was terrified. From the night after Wolfe's fight in the alley, she had become afraid that one day they would kill him.

A few days later Wolfe got a letter from England. He was

pouring coffee as he read it, and suddenly coffee spilled all over the table. "What is it?" Eleanor said in alarm.

He didn't answer. He got up, his chair falling over, and walked out of the room with a set, blind face. She heard him going down the stairs, heard the slam of the door.

Eleanor stared at the coffee stains. What had been in that letter? She waited for Wolfe to come back. He did not reappear for the rest of the day, and when he did come in that night, he was dead drunk, falling over heavily as he staggered into the room. Eleanor lay in bed, her heart beating painfully. He stumbled about as he undressed and crashed into the bed. Eleanor listened to his thick breathing as he settled on his face.

In the morning she looked at him carefully, trying to read the expression on his face. It was impossible. His features had a hard, cold set to them. Whatever had caused such a disturbance in him was hidden from her now.

"I'm going to Chicago," he told her the next day.

Eleanor's face whitened. "Why?" she asked huskily. Was he leaving her? Was he going to that other woman?

"Business," he said in a clipped voice.

"What sort of business?"

Wolfe gave her an irritable look. "That's none of your affair."

In Chicago Wolfe went to see Schultz. The hard-eyed, heavy man lounged in a chair, keeping Wolfe standing, his fat mouth chewing on a large cigar. "Well, what d'yer want?"

"Money," Wolfe said and sat down in a chair without waiting to be asked.

Schultz laughed raucously. "What makes you think I'd give you a bent pin?"

"You want to see my editorials stop. You won't frighten me into it. If you want me to shut up, you're going to have to pay."

Schultz grinned. "You garbage rat. I knew you were up to some fancy work over there. Well, how much to write what I want you to write?"

"No," Wolfe said. "I'm not writing for you. I'm selling you my newspaper, and the price has got to be right."

"What the hell do I want with a newspaper?"

Wolfe shrugged. "Clean your shoes with it, as far as I care. I want out. I'm going back to England, and I want money to take with me."

Schultz's eyes narrowed. "I get it. You need the money right away, do you?"

Wolfe gave him a lazy grin. "I don't need anything. I'm not bargaining, Mr. Schultz. There's one price. Mine. All you have to do is make up your mind whether you're going to pay or not. If you don't I'll go back to work here."

Schultz clamped his mouth around his cigar. After a long pause he nodded. "Okay. It's a deal."

# CHAPTER SIXTEEN

Leaving America, Eleanor felt despair. She sensed that for Wolfe they were returning to the unknown, ever-present girl he kept locked up behind his masked face. While she watched the skyline fade, Wolfe lounged on the rail beside her, a restless eagerness in every line of his body.

She had been shattered when he had told her that he had sold the paper to Schultz. "Why?" she had cried, imagining that the bitter feud had worn him down after all. It had occurred to her that Wolfe was more frightened than he had shown, and she would have been both disillusioned and sympathetic to hear that.

Wolfe had given her a hard stare. "He paid well," Wolfe had said, and Eleanor had grown white.

"You did it for money?"

Wolfe's lip curled cynically. "What did you whore for? Fun?"

The question had made her wince and grow angry. "I had little choice. You did. How could you? If you wanted to sell, why not to someone else? Why to Schultz? You're selling out, selling out my brother and all the others like him. You're a rat."

Wolfe had pushed his hands into his pockets, his face dark and unsmiling. "You don't have to come to England. You can stay here."

The words had thrust into her heart. After a pause she had said stiffly, "Is that what you want?"

"It's not what I want. It's what you want. You may not want to throw in your lot with a rat."

His face had given her no clue as to his wishes, his feelings. He had surveyed her with remorseless indifference, and Eleanor had struggled with a rending desire to cry.

Her self-respect fought with her love, and in the end her love had won. She bent her head. "I'll come," she said flatly.

Wolfe had said no more about it. She wondered miserably

if he had been hoping to leave her behind. Did he regret marrying her? She had thought that Wolfe would sneak out of town without anyone knowing what he had done, but on the contrary, he had coolly informed everyone that he had sold to Schultz. Eleanor had found herself being cut in the street, heard hissing as Wolfe walked beside her.

She had been glad when they left. Jake had written a bitter letter to Wolfe, and without a word Wolfe had handed it to her.

Now as the ship left America, he glanced at her and said calmly: "We couldn't win that struggle, you know. The weak always go to the wall. Only the strong survive."

Eleanor grasped the rail. "But you are strong, Wolfe," she said.

His eyes held hers. "Not strong enough to fight that kind of money and survive. And anyway, I have to get back to England."

"Why?" she dared to ask.

His eyes moved away, searching the seas ahead of them as if looking for land, for promised haven to which they moved. "I've got to get back," he said, and he sounded obsessed, a driven man.

Eleanor was violently ill during that voyage. She found herself to be a poor sailor when the seas were rough. Wolfe nursed her. She could not have had a kinder, more efficient nurse. He showed no hint of irritation or disgust. He was gentle, thoughtful. And she wept whenever she was alone. Because behind his calm face she could sense a growing urgency as they drew nearer to England and the girl whose name she did not even know.

They landed at Bristol on a cool summer morning. Eleanor was deeply grateful to stand on dry land again and feel the steady earth beneath her feet instead of the swaying, tilting deck. She breathed salt air and stared at the huddle of whitewashed little houses, the gulls swooping over narrow streets.

Wolfe guided her along the quayside, and they took a cab to the boarding house that his mother ran. Eleanor had not even known of that until Wolfe told her as they walked.

When the door opened, Eleanor was taken aback by the rich golden hair and the ripe full figure of the woman who stood staring at them.

"Wolfe," the woman gasped. She held out her arms, clasped him, caressed his black head and kissed him. "Oh,

Wolfe, why didn't you say you were coming back? Why didn't you write and let me know? Have you just landed? Oh, Wolfe, if I'd only known.''

Wolfe disentangled himself, smiling. ''It seemed better to surprise you, Mother. You would only have worried yourself sick in case the ship was lost.''

Lucy's tear-filled eyes slid to Eleanor and widened. Wolfe turned and looked at his wife. ''Mother, this is Eleanor,'' he said.

Not ''this is my wife,'' Eleanor thought, her heart aching. She met Lucy's eyes, a pale shame in her face, wondering what this beautiful, kind-faced woman would make of her if she knew her past life. How much had Wolfe told her? Did Lucy know?

Lucy smiled warmly at her, enveloped her in her arms. ''Welcome to England, Eleanor. Oh, I'm so happy to see you. I never thought Wolfe would come home. I'd grown resigned to never seeing him again.''

''I told you I'd be back,'' Wolfe said with a gritty sound.

''Come in, both of you,'' Lucy said hurriedly. ''We don't want to stand around on the doorstep.''

''I want you to look after Eleanor, Mother,'' Wolfe returned easily. ''I have business to see to. I'll be back later.''

Lucy grabbed his sleeve, her face pale suddenly. ''Wolfe! Wait a moment.'' She looked at Eleanor and tried to smile. ''Go on in, my dear. Make yourself at home. I'll just have a word with Wolfe.''

Eleanor reluctantly walked in, knowing that Wolfe's mother was aware of whatever the secret was that held Wolfe in such urgent eagerness. She walked into the little kitchen and looked around at pots of geraniums flowering on the sills, a steamy atmosphere from a kettle filled with clothes bubbling in soapy water. He was going to find that woman, she thought. How could she bear it?

But she had known all along what was bringing him back to England, and she had silently accepted it. Now she had to go on accepting it. What choice did she have?

On the doorstep Lucy looked up at Wolfe. ''Stonor and Sophia are in London,'' she said.

Wolfe's face tightened. ''You mean they live there now? I thought they were living at Queen's Stonor.''

''They are. Stonor's opened a branch of the firm down

here, but the London end is being managed by someone else and Stonor goes up there now and then to see how things are. He's there now.'' She paused. ''And she is with him.''

''And their son,'' Wolfe said with a twist of the lips. ''How old is he now?''

''Oh, Wolfe, don't think about her,'' Lucy burst out. ''Forget her. Eleanor is a beautiful girl. What good will it do you to go looking for trouble?''

''How old is he?'' Wolfe asked.

''How did you hear?''

''Luther mentioned it. He saw them with the baby in a park in Bristol, walking with it. A boy, he said.''

''I haven't seen them,'' Lucy said. ''But they have got a son. I suppose he is about two years old.''

''Stonor didn't waste any time.'' Wolfe's mouth writhed. ''Damn him to hell. She could have died. They said she wasn't to have children—it could kill her, they said.'' His voice rose sharply. ''Why do you think I left her? I thought...'' His words stopped, choked in his throat. His long hands clenched. ''And all this time Stonor has been...'' Again he stopped, biting down on his lower lip.

He had felt safe in leaving Sophia behind. Wolfe had guessed that Stonor would insist on going through with the marriage, but he had imagined that Sophia's health would prevent any consummation of the marriage. For months now he had cheerfully envisaged Stonor leading a bitter, celibate life with Sophia. Then the letter from Luther had come, so casually mentioning their names and then adding a line about their son. It had been a shock that had almost sent Wolfe crazy.

Doctors had been wrong before. He shouldn't have accepted their view so blithely. Stonor had clearly not accepted it. He had made his marriage a real one, and Sophia had borne a child and survived.

Wolfe stared at the blue Bristol sky, fighting to keep his face normal. They had been married nearly three years, and all that time Stonor had been sleeping with Sophia. He closed his eyes, and his mother anxiously watched his grim face.

He might not have known if Luther hadn't remembered that Stonor was his half-brother. He could have gone on for years in America, never discovering that Sophia's heart was not as weak as the doctors had prophesied.

Once he knew, though, he had to get back to her. That fact

had rushed into him like floodwater, drowning the importance of everything else in his life.

Sophia was capable of an ordinary life after all. The thought nagged at him day and night. She wasn't out of reach. She was in Stonor's arms, and Wolfe could not live with that thought. He could live with Stonor's celibate possession of her, but not with that.

"Do come in, Wolfe," Lucy said huskily, horrified at the look in his face. "Sit down and tell me all about America! I've hardly had a chance to see you. There's so much to tell you, so much to hear."

"Not now," he said abruptly. "I've got to see Luther. Where will I find him?"

"He may be at the new shop down on Pencester Road. Since his father died Luther's opened two new shops. He's very ambitious."

Wolfe grinned. "I remember. I'll find him. Pencester Road? How far is that?"

"About half a mile," she said. "The new suburb on the Avon road."

Wolfe nodded. "I'll walk it. Look after Eleanor, Mother. She was very ill on the ship."

He walked away without looking back, and Lucy slowly went into the house. Eleanor met the kind eyes and lowered her own gaze, trembling. Lucy patted her arm.

"Sit down, dear. What you need is a cup of tea."

Eleanor laughed shakily. "Wolfe told me those would be your first words!"

Lucy smiled. "Tell me about yourself. Wolfe isn't a great letter writer. He told me you had married, but he said very little about you. Is that an American accent?"

Eleanor smiled. "Yes." She was finding Lucy's soft, drawling voice hard to follow. Wolfe had acquired a distinct American clip to his voice, and she was not used to the slower English accent.

"Wolfe met you in New Orleans," Lucy said, spooning tea into a large-bellied pot.

Eleanor bit her lip. "Yes." Her voice was shaking. How much did Lucy know?

"Is that where your family live?"

Eleanor shook her head. She talked briefly about her brother in Illinois, the newspaper Wolfe had owned, the trouble which had come of it. "So Wolfe sold up and we came back to England."

"He hasn't done too badly, then," Lucy said, her eyes full of questions. "He did make some money."

Eleanor's mouth had a wry cynicism. "He never told me how much, but no, I guess he didn't do too badly out of it. I think he twisted Schultz's arm for a fat figure."

"You didn't approve?"

"He sold out," Eleanor said fiercely. "Suddenly, like that." She snapped her fingers. "I don't know why. I thought they couldn't scare him a fraction. I thought he was as brave as a goddamned lion. Then he suddenly sold us all out."

Lucy poured the pale, straw-coloured tea into cups, her face not showing anything. She knew, Eleanor thought. She knew what had brought Wolfe hurrying back to England. What was it? She would go mad if she didn't find out.

Huskily she said, "Tell me about yourself, about the family. Wolfe never talks about anything private."

Lucy looked at her compassionately. She sat down, pushing the cup towards Eleanor. "I'll get you some food in a minute," she said, and then she started to tell Eleanor the whole story of Wolfe's life. She left out all mention of Sophia, but she told the truth about her own relationship with James Whitley, Wolfe's illegitimacy, his upbringing in a hostile house, his hatred for his half-brothers.

"I married Jack Duffey a year ago," she said. "He's a good man when he isn't drinking, and I make sure he doesn't do that. Maveen has gone back to Ireland to marry her second cousin, so Jack and I are alone here now, but we see quite a bit of Luther, my nephew. That's where Wolfe has gone now. To see Luther."

Eleanor held her eyes, trying to guess if this was the truth. Was that really where Wolfe had gone? She had waited for the words that would enlighten her at last about the unknown girl in Wolfe's life, but they had not come.

She looked at Lucy, her rich red hair clustered around her white face. "I know she exists," she said point-blank. "But not her name. Who is she? I've got to know. I can't go on like this, guessing and not knowing."

Lucy looked shaken. "My dear, I . . ."

"Please, for God's sake, tell me," Eleanor cried fiercely.

"Wolfe has mentioned her?"

Eleanor smiled bitterly. "Not a word. But I know."

Lucy sighed. "I suppose you would. It's safe enough, I promise you. She's married and has a son of her own."

"Married," Eleanor breathed, relief in her voice.

"Forget her," Lucy advised. "Wolfe will. I'm sure of that."

Their eyes met and both knew the other did not believe it, but they smiled as though they did and turned to talk of other things.

"It's great to see you," Luther said heartily, shaking Wolfe's hand with vigour. "So you're back. I thought you were doing well in America."

"I've decided to start up over here," Wolfe said.

"Doing what?" Luther asked.

"Anything I can turn my hand to," Wolfe said lightly. "First of all, a newspaper. You said there was room in Bristol for another newspaper."

"A radical, crusading newspaper," Luther said at once, his face becoming excited. "That's what we need, Wolfe. Not another lackey of the business quarter and the aristocracy. We need a voice that speaks out for the truth."

Wolfe grinned. "At least I shan't have the sort of troubles over here that I had in the States."

Luther stared. Wolfe had not confided the story to him. "What are you talking about?"

Wolfe told him of the threats, the attacks, the hostility. Luther's eyes shone angrily.

"Typical tactics. I tell you, they may do it differently over here, but you may expect attempts to stop you if you print the truth."

"They can try to stop me." Wolfe sounded almost as though he welcomed that. "I must find premises right away. Hire printers and some journalists."

"That will take money," Luther warned.

"I've got money." Wolfe shrugged.

"Enough?"

"More than enough." Wolfe eyed him, and Luther gave him a little smile.

"If you're looking for an investment, Wolfe, I'm in need of a partner. I'm expanding fast but I need capital. Shops eat money until they start to give it back."

"Tell me the details," Wolfe said, settling down.

Later he said, "With your political view it seems odd to have dreams of wealth."

"Only from the inside can one successfully wage war. When I'm rich, I shall be in a position to strike the enemy."

"You'll be the enemy," Wolfe said.

"Nonsense," Luther said irritably, brushing that aside. "You said yourself that the little man can't win against big money."

"Using my newspaper as your mouthpiece?" Wolfe asked.

"A newspaper is a useful platform."

"It will be *my* platform," Wolfe returned coolly. "It will speak with my mouth and that of no other man. Over in America I learned a lot about free speech. It's only free if you are strong enough to refuse to be silenced."

"But you sold out," Luther pointed out.

Wolfe grinned. "Not because they frightened me. I came back here for my own reasons. What Schultz tried to do had nothing to do with it."

"Well, what do you say? Will you come in with me?" Luther asked him with his eyes on Wolfe's face.

"Why not? Money has to work for its keep. I don't believe in keeping it lying around idle in a bank."

"I'll see that it does," Luther promised, smiling. "Wolfe, are you sure you want to risk your money in the newspaper business? It is a risk, especially with the sort of paper you plan to publish. Why not put all your money with me?"

Wolfe grinned. "All my eggs in one basket? No, I think not, Luther. And anyway, I got a taste for the newspaper business over in the States. I enjoy it. I discovered quite a talent for writing editorials. In fact, I've done all the jobs there are on a newspaper. I've run off editions myself, set type, corrected galleys, sold advertising—the lot. I've even covered local events. I once wrote up the church bazaar, and that's a fate I wouldn't wish on anyone."

Luther laughed deeply. "You at a church bazaar? I don't believe it!"

Over the next few weeks Wolfe found the premises in which to produce his newspaper and took out a long lease on them, hired staff, bought second-hand machinery from a newspaper in Bath that had gone out of production and personally called on the more important business firms to try to drum up advertising. He found that a thankless task. They had been advertising with the other Bristol newspapers for years and were frankly dubious about his ability to sell another paper in the area.

It was through Luther that Wolfe met his first big client, Southerby, the wholesaler who supplied Luther's shops.

Luther introduced Wolfe to him as the man prepared to back Luther's credit. Southerby was as doubtful about Luther's rapid expansion as the other big firms had been about Wolfe's chances with a new newspaper, but something about Wolfe impressed the wholesaler.

A small, thin, ferret-faced man, he eyed Wolfe's breadth and height with admiration. "Been in the States, Mr. Hunt says."

"New Orleans, Chicago, Illinois," Wolfe rattled off, grinning. "I barely touched America—it's a big country." His eyes laughed at the man.

"New Orleans?" Southerby's tongue passed over his pallid lips. "I've read that that's a sinful city."

"Mr. Southerby is a deacon of the church," Luther said gravely.

Wolfe's eyes met his. Turning his smile on Southerby, Wolfe probed softly, "I'm afraid it is, sir. You would never see such places over here in Bristol."

He caught the faint dew of perspiration breaking out on the little man's forehead. The grey hair was slipping back off his head like a mat on a polished floor, receding inch by inch to leave his scalp gleaming pink.

"You don't tell me..." A pause. "You actually saw such things?"

Solemnly Wolfe said, "Gambling dens, whorehouses, districts where no gentleman could walk a yard without being accosted by a painted wanton."

Mr. Southerby swallowed. "Shameful." His eyes glistened. "You must dine with me, Mr. Whitley, indeed you must. I have had it in mind to write an article for the church magazine on the subject of Babylon. Your experiences in America would be of considerable help to me in pointing to a modern example."

"I should be honoured, sir," Wolfe said without a flicker of expression.

He dined with the Southerby family, met the timid, silent little wife, saw her dismissed with the port and spent the rest of the evening giving Mr. Southerby a highly coloured version of his experiences in America, making himself out to be the shocked, horrified victim of a succession of eager women.

A week later Mr. Southerby signed an agreement for heavy advertising in Wolfe's new paper. Wolfe cultivated him assiduously, introducing him at dinner to Eleanor, watching with lowered, cynical eyes as Mr. Southerby stared with bulging eyes at her vivid hair and warm, sensual curves.

"Vile little animal," Eleanor spat afterwards in the privacy of her bedroom. "How can you smile at such men?"

"We need him," Wolfe said, grinning.

She gave him a long, fixed look. "You want me to be nice to him?"

Wolfe came up behind her and his mouth moved persuasively over her white nape. "Polite, Eleanor. Nothing more."

Bitterness made her flare. "Sure you wouldn't like to lend me to him for a night?"

His hands tightened on her shoulders. "Another crack like that and I might just slap you senseless."

She wrenched away, tossing back the red cloud of her hair. "Don't forget, I'm used to selling myself. I just didn't think you were."

Wolfe's eyes narrowed into glittering slits. "Curb that vicious tongue of yours or I'll do it for you."

She had spent the last weeks anxiously wondering if Wolfe was seeing her unknown rival. Worry and tension had eaten into her nerves, made her volatile, liable to break out into bitter words. She knew it was madness. Wolfe was not the man to stand such treatment from his wife. Eleanor had always felt a deep, silent gratitude for the fact that he rarely even breathed a word about her past. Just once or twice since they married had Wolfe brought it up, but even then it had never been with harshness or accusation, merely as a fact that he accepted. Eleanor had been overwhelmed by his tolerance and what she saw as his kindness. Only lately had she found his lack of anger over her past a painful sign of his total indifference to her. It was not that Wolfe was forgiving or kind, she had realized, just that he didn't give a damn what she had done or how many men had had her.

Now she said thickly, "I said you were a rat, I'm only beginning to realize just how much of a rat you are."

For a moment he stared at her, his body taut, his hands clenched at his sides, and she thought he was going to go for her in rage. She saw the effort he made to unwind, watched his face deliberately relax, a cynical, hard glint coming into his eyes.

"It takes one to know one," he said softly. He walked towards her and his hands yanked down the shoulder of her gown, holding her helpless but struggling. Wolfe bent his black head and began to kiss her throat, her breasts, his mouth insulting, bruising. Eleanor writhed, hitting him, kicking him. She knew he was quite openly treating her as he had treated her the first night they met. She knew it for the studied insult it was.

"Unlike the unfortunate Southerby, I don't have to go to look for a whore, do I?" Wolfe asked silkily. "I've got one waiting whenever I'm in the mood."

Her breath rasped in her throat. "You swine, you bastard," she whispered, the words hurting as they came from her.

He laughed recklessly. "I seem to remember you saying that before. But I got what I wanted that time, too."

He got what he wanted only after a prolonged struggle, and Eleanor hated him for the first time in months as she silently submitted to his bruising lovemaking. Wolfe looked at her afterwards with a strange blankness. It was the first time that he had made love to her and received no response. Her body had been frozen underneath him, and Eleanor had withheld herself in bitter enmity.

He stood up and walked out of the room without another word. Eleanor lay on the bed shuddering, her gown torn and dishevelled, her skin dark with bruises where he had manhandled her. Tears ran slowly down her face.

They were renting a house in the same street as that in which Luther Hunt lived. The two cousins met almost daily and talked business together, shut up in Luther's little office. Eleanor was forced into constant company with Luther's dull, brown-haired wife Susan, whose only topic of conversation was her son, Thomas, a sturdy little baby with two teeth and little hair. Eleanor learned to coo over Thomas, smiling, listening with all the marks of fascination as his mother described his latest great stride in the world.

It was beginning to disturb her that she herself showed no signs of becoming pregnant. She badly wanted a child. She felt sure that it would bind Wolfe to her. He might not love her, but she suspected that he would love his children, and it would be a chain between them if she were their mother.

From the night when Wolfe had forced her and she had refused to respond, their marriage had changed. Eleanor bitterly regretted what she had done as night followed night and Wolfe never came near her. He slept in one of the other bedrooms. Some evenings he did not come home at all. She never knew where he went. She had too much pride to ask. Cool, distant and polite, they lived together, appeared at church or at dinner with friends, and when they were alone barely spoke.

Wolfe was widening his circle of business acquaintances through Southerby. He had been introduced to all the leading businessmen of the city now. He had opened an account at the local bank, into which he had deposited a large part of his money, but he had another account elsewhere, so that he might draw on that without diminishing his major account too much. Wolfe wanted to establish his credit. He did not believe in letting the right hand know what the left was doing.

Six weeks after their arrival in England he accidentally overheard someone mentioning Stonor and discovered at last that Stonor and Sophia had returned from London.

Wolfe possessed his soul in patience. He went on getting ready to launch his paper, working with Luther on the accounts of the shops, consolidating his position among the other businessmen.

He had become a favourite dinner guest with a certain set— his wicked jokes, his charm, his knowledge of the world gave him a cachet. Ruthlessly Wolfe used the friendships he made to extend his acquaintance even further. He found that his surname was not without its own charm. The Whitley family at Queen's Stonor were much respected. When it was found that Wolfe was a distant relation, his social standing rapidly rose. Wolfe did not enlighten questioners about the exact relationship, but his casual use of Stonor's name now and then reinforced the belief that he was a member of the family.

Eleanor, listening, wondered how he could so shamelessly use Stonor when he hated and detested him, but she was already beginning to know that Wolfe had neither scruples nor morals. He cared only for the end, not the means.

She was still unaware of the identity of her rival. Lucy, when Eleanor called on her, evaded all questions, and of course Eleanor did not dream of mentioning it to Wolfe.

Two months after their arrival in Bristol, they received an invitation to a supper dance at the home of their banker. Eleanor had a new gown for it, a soft green with full, frilled skirts that cascaded as she walked, clinging smoothly to her body from neckline to hip. It was only in their carriage on the way to the house that she realized the tension and excitement possessing Wolfe. She looked sideways at him, seeing the brilliance of his eyes, the way he held his mouth steady as if it might give him away at any second. Her heart stopped. She knew then that her unknown rival might be present tonight.

# CHAPTER SEVENTEEN

Sophia was as blissfully unaware of Wolfe's approaching presence as Eleanor had been of Sophia's. As Sophia descended the stairs at Queen's Stonor, she caught an odd, strained look on Stonor's face and looked at him in surprise. He was far paler than usual, his body held upright and stiff, the grey eyes skimming over her in a strange fashion. Sophia had decided to wear one of her favourite gowns, a low-cut blue one that clung softly to her slender body, leaving her shoulders and part of her breasts bare, white lace sagging in a tiered scallop across the full skirts. It suited her and she knew it, so she was surprised by Stonor's frown.

Stonor had heard of Wolfe's return from America as soon as he and Sophia had returned from London. Finding that Wolfe had married a beautiful American girl had given Stonor a few days of such deep relief that he had almost felt he might come to like Wolfe. He had made it his business to catch a glimpse of Eleanor and had admired the graceful, elegant sway of her slim body, her vivid red hair and beautiful face. Surely, he had thought, Wolfe must love her. He would not have married her otherwise. Eleanor was lovely, and Stonor guessed her capable of strong sensual response. His own sensuality read it in the movements of her body.

A few days ago Wright, the banker, had said jovially, "By the way, Whitley, there's a relative of yours in the city now, did ye know?"

Stonor's face had been politely blank. "So I believe."

The banker had eyed him, trying to decipher his expression. "You are related, then? A second cousin or something?"

"We are related," Stonor had agreed in a bland tone.

"He and his wife are joining us on Friday night, that's the point," Wright said. "I just thought I'd mention it. One never knows with families."

"One never does," Stonor murmured.

"You don't object to meeting him then?"

Stonor gave him a quiet little smile. "Why should I? We have not met for some years."

"Been in America, I gather."

"Yes," Stonor said. "I shall look forward to meeting his wife."

The banker had laughed. "Stunning creature, quite magnificent."

Thank God, Stonor had thought. I hope she can hold him. He had known that he had to allow Sophia and Wolfe to meet. He could not hope to stop such a meeting eventually. He had to control events by making sure that he was present to observe the reactions of both of them.

Stonor was in a state of turmoil and doubt as they set out in their carriage for the party. His brain had made the decision, but it was not his brain that was in control of him as he sat beside Sophia. What would happen when they were face to face again? He had hoped against hope that Wolfe would never come back. How would Sophia react to the sight of him?

It had occurred to Stonor that he might drop a quiet word here and there, and so freeze Wolfe out of polite society. It would not take much. He only had to mention Wolfe's illegitimacy and all social pretensions would be over for him.

It had been a temptation, but Stonor's cold brain had rejected it. Wolfe would know who was to blame and he would want revenge, for a start. He wouldn't have far to look to find Stonor's weak spot, either. Stonor couldn't risk egging Wolfe into tit for tat. Also, if Wolfe were happily married and on the verge of financial success, it would be arrant madness to change the situation. If Wolfe had a stake in society, he might leave Sophia alone. He would have too much to risk if he pursued her.

Stonor sat beside Sophia, his brain going over and over it, knowing that he had acted in the most rational fashion yet unable to halt the nervous tension that had hold of him now.

Sophia wondered if something were wrong at the office. She could feel Stonor's inner turmoil as he sat beside her. He hadn't spoken since they had left the house, which was unusual. Since their return from France they had achieved a quietly balanced marriage at Queen's Stonor. The only cloud on their calm sky had been the death last autumn of her father—thrown from his horse as he took a particularly high hedge. Stonor had been a tower of strength to her during the black weeks that had followed. She had relied on him instinctively, as she had when Daniel was born, and he had pulled her through the depression that her father's death had caused.

Her admiration for Stonor had gone on growing during their three years together. Watching him cope with the worry of Grey's embezzlement and dismissal to Africa, with Tom Lister who had taken to gambling on the stock exchange and losing, with the hectic difficulties of moving to Bristol and setting up a new branch there, she had been awed by his unshakable strength.

They lived calmly together, their manner quietly pleasant, never becoming any more intimate than a kiss on the cheek at bedtime, the brief touch of Stonor's hand on her own. It seemed to content Stonor. Sophia sometimes wondered if he had a mistress hidden away somewhere. She knew she would never guess at it if he did. Stonor was a past master at hiding things.

Which made it all the more odd that tonight she should feel the coiled tension inside him.

Wolfe and Eleanor had been at the supper dance for half an hour. Eleanor had watched anxiously as Wolfe shed his dazzling charm on those he met, exercising all his power to amuse, circling around, smiling on fluttering ladies, whispering jokes to men who roared and nudged each other.

Eleanor, in her exquisite green silk, dazzled the eyes of the men. The vibrant red head, the experienced green eyes, the alluring sway of her body made her a useful foil to Wolfe. He knew it and he grinned as he watched his business acquaintances staring at her.

All the time she was aware of his impatience, caught his restless glances towards the door, knew that her rival was not yet here but that Wolfe was on tenterhooks for her arrival.

She would know when the other arrived. Wolfe would give himself away. She had never been able to read him so clearly, but he was so absorbed in his own emotions that he had forgotten to mask them from her.

He was giving himself away now with every look at the door as they circled in a waltz. Consumed with eagerness, tense, excited, his eyes flickered back at every step to see each new arrival.

Eleanor was so bitterly angry, so jealous, that she could have hit him across the face. In their relationship Wolfe had always been so much in control, coolly the master between them. Now for the first time she saw inside his head and read the hunger consuming him with anguished despair.

Suddenly she felt his body contract as though someone had punched him in the stomach. She looked at him quickly, saw fire leaping in the depths of his eyes, a quiver running over his hard mouth.

Turning, she looked across the room and saw the couple who had just arrived. Eleanor took in everything with one glance. She knew herself to be an excitingly attractive woman. Many men had told her so, including Wolfe himself, but as she stared at this young woman, she felt her heart sink. Sophia's sweetness and delicacy, the heart-wrenching fragility of her face, the smile in her great blue eyes were like a knife into Eleanor's soul. If she had seen a woman of the world, experienced and seductive, Eleanor could have hoped to fight fire with fire, but she knew immediately that Sophia had qualities she could not hope to match.

The banker, Wright, was bowing over Sophia's hand, kissing it reverently. At Sophia's side her tall cold-faced husband stood in a possessive attitude, his hand under her elbow. A whisper was running around the room. People converged, smiling. Eleanor saw the warm smile Sophia was giving to those who spoke to her, saw her unconsciously assured manner, her frank and delightful glances.

She's been petted and indulged all her life, Eleanor thought bitterly. She watched Sophia extending her hand to a succession of bowing, smiling gentlemen, accepting their homage as her right so calmly and yet without hauteur or conceit. Her smile was direct and open, her eyes looking into theirs in such a friendly fashion that each one seemed to believe himself particularly welcome. Men had been watching Eleanor tonight, but with a different expression. Something in her face and body hinted at her past experiences, perhaps, made the men look at her obliquely in sexual recognition. There was nothing of that as they greeted Sophia. They flocked around her as they might around a queen, and their wives were eager to pay their respects, gain smiles and little comments, show themselves to be one of her elect circle. Eleanor had met little friendship from these women so far—her gaudy hair and sensual body made them stiffen as though she were somehow suspect in their respectable circle.

Glancing at Wolfe, Eleanor found him intent, absorbed, still. The waltz had ended. People were moving around the

room, laughing, talking. Eleanor glanced back at the little
group that was eddying around Sophia. Who was she? Her
eyes moved to the man at Sophia's elbow. Handsome, she
thought, with a faint flicker of hope. Was the woman in love
with him? Were they happy together? Somehow the icy regu-
larity of his features made her doubt it. She couldn't believe
that anyone could fail to prefer Wolfe. His dark good looks
and charm were like a battering ram—no woman could with-
stand them. Eleanor had tried. She knew only too well what
power Wolfe could bring to bear if he chose.

Stonor had seen Wolfe the moment they entered the room. He
had felt the shock of seeing him, realizing with a qualm that
his half-brother had improved out of all recognition in the
years in America. Wolfe looked older, more assured, with arrogance blazing in his dark face now. Stonor moved closer to
Sophia. She looked at him in puzzled enquiry, her own nerves
quivering at the chaotic emotions she could sense in him.
What was wrong? she thought. Stonor was white. Was he ill?

The music began again, a sweet, whirling waltz tune that
made Sophia long to dance.

Wolfe took a step forwards and Eleanor tensely put her
hand on his sleeve, falling in beside him. He glanced down at
her almost with a visible shock, as though he had forgotten
her very existence.

Eleanor looked at his surprised face and did not know
whether she hated him or loved him.

"I think it is time you met my half-brother," he said then
with a strange, overbright smile.

The shock she felt was like a slap across the face. His
brother? His brother? As Wolfe walked towards the group,
Eleanor felt that shock echoing through her. No wonder Lucy
had refused to tell her the name of the woman he loved. It was
his brother's wife.

Sophia was intent on listening to Luther Hunt's wife, her
dark head bent towards her, a polite little smile on her lips.

Stonor's eyes rose. His face was totally blank.

"Good evening, Stonor," Wolfe said softly.

But his eyes were on Sophia, and at the sound of his voice,
her head flew up and her blue eyes filled with an incredulous
light as they flashed to meet his.

Stonor moved very slightly, blocking her from Wolfe, his
long hand coldly extended. "I heard you were back," he said.

Wolfe smiled. Eleanor saw that smile and flinched. The two men looked at each other, their hands still touching, and their faces were courteous except that their eyes warred in icy enmity.

"May I present my wife," Wolfe said, turning to bring Eleanor forwards. "Eleanor, my dear, this is Stonor."

Eleanor gave her hand into Stonor's fingers. He looked into her face briefly. "I am delighted to meet you, Eleanor," he said, and both of them were aware of the hidden irony beneath that remark. Stonor lifted her hand and kissed it. She shivered at the brush of those cold lips, her eyes seeking in his grey ones some reaction to what she sensed he must be perfectly aware of—her husband's remorseless but silent attention to his wife.

Sophia had not moved. She stood there, her eyes fixed on Wolfe, and he looked back at her.

Slowly Wolfe bowed, extending his hand. "May I have this dance, Mrs. Whitley?"

Sophia did not even look at Stonor. She moved forwards and Eleanor and Stonor watched the way Wolfe's arm closed around her waist in a movement of possession.

They moved into the press of dancers. Her small white hand lay on his shoulder. Her skirts flew around his legs as they whirled. Wolfe's hand had tightened on her tiny waist, and she had swayed so close that not a sheet of paper could have slid between them.

Sophia was in a state of shock. She danced mechanically, barely aware of what her body was doing, not looking at Wolfe because she was struggling to regain her lost control.

He did not speak. They flowed around the room in perfect harmony, matching their steps so smoothly that they seemed to glide. Sophia's eyes were lowered. She stared at the broad, dark shoulder just within her angle of vision.

He was back from America. He was in England. She seemed to be forcing her way through a jungle of thoughts that resisted all her attempts to make sense of them.

She suddenly remembered Stonor's coiled tension ever since they had left Queen's Stonor and realized what he had said to Wolfe just now. Stonor had known. He had known that Wolfe was back, that he would be here tonight.

Why hadn't he told her? Having asked herself that, she admitted that she knew the answer to the question. Stonor had not told her because he wanted her to have this shock—he wanted her surprised, shaken by Wolfe's presence. Why? Again even as she asked herself, the answer was in her mind. Stonor had wanted to watch her reaction.

His back to Stonor, Wolfe suddenly whispered through barely parted lips, "I must see you alone."

Sophia's long, dark lashes stirred against her cheeks and lifted to his face. A heated colour crept into her face. Her blue eyes were overbright and feverish.

She was aware of Stonor watching her. He stood beside Wolfe's wife with his face totally blank, icy, and his grey eyes never moved from Sophia's face.

Sophia caught a glimpse of him in one of the gilt-framed mirrors, seeing his face oddly like a mirage, coming and going as dancers whirled in front of him and then disappeared. He stood very straight, his body held stiffly in a way Sophia recognized. Stonor was using all his willpower to keep expression off his face.

"Answer me," Wolfe breathed in a voice which wasn't steady.

She looked at him, and he whirled her around so that her back was to Stonor, making it impossible for Stonor to lip read what she said. "Answer me, my darling," Wolfe whispered pleadingly.

The sound of his tender voice made her limbs melt. They had not met for three years, yet their bodies were swaying together, brushing, touching deliberately, as if each step were an act of love. The melodic gaiety of the music gave them a chance to express their emotions in movement. Sophia became aware of it for the first time, realizing how closely they were dancing. She had not known that Wolfe was holding her so tightly or that she was moving against him with an unconscious sensuality that her mind had not dictated.

"It's impossible," she sighed, looking into Wolfe's eyes.

"Why?" he demanded, still keeping his voice very low.

"Stonor," she reminded.

Wolfe had a reckless darkness in his face. "Damn Stonor. Why did you marry him? How could you? You've given him a son, too. My God, do you realize what that did to me when I heard?"

His voice was rising as he went on, and she gave an alarmed glance around, caught curious faces glancing at them, felt Stonor's intent, cold eyes narrowing.

"Don't quarrel, Wolfe, not tonight!" she pleaded, her blue eyes fixed on his face.

The anger went out of his hard features. His eyes filled with passion. "I'm sorry. No. Not tonight. It's been so long. I began to think I'd never hold you in my arms again."

She smiled, the sudden warm smile which had first made Wolfe love her. "Ssh . . ."

His arm tightened further, his eyes lingered on the curve of her pink lips.

"My God, Sophia," he said thickly, then his voice stopped as though what he had been about to say could not be said in a crowded room. "I've got to see you alone," he went on in those low, husky tones.

The music ended, and they parted. The reluctance with which Wolfe released her was almost visible, but he managed to give her a polite little smile and a jerky bow, offering her his arm so that he could escort her back to Stonor.

Stonor watched calmly as they approached. He had not spoken to Eleanor while her husband danced with his wife. They stood side by side, each absorbed in private thoughts. Suddenly Stonor glanced down at her. Eleanor drew a shaky breath, her eyes widening at what she read in his face. The glimpse he had given her of what lay beneath his surface coolness shocked her.

"Will you call at my office tomorrow morning, Mrs. Whitley?" Stonor murmured softly. "I think you and I should have a talk."

Eleanor's green eyes widened. She nodded.

Wolfe led Sophia back to them, and the little group flowed back around her. She flicked her fan, smiling, listening to Mr. Wright telling an anecdote about a recent visit to London, smiled at Mrs. Hunt when she talked eagerly of her little boy and said with coy emphasis, "How is your dear little man, Mrs. Whitley?"

Stonor turned his head, the light striking gold on his dusty pale hair. Sophia met his eyes. "Daniel is very well," she said to Mrs. Hunt.

"Our son grows more like his mother every day," Stonor said in cool tones. He smiled, a dry movement of his mouth. "Like you, Mrs. Hunt, Sophia dotes upon the boy. I think it would break her heart if they were ever parted."

Mrs. Hunt laughed breathily. "Oh, yes, indeed. I feel just the same about my Thomas."

Sophia's eyes were held by Stonor's level grey stare. She knew precisely what he was telling her, what gun he held at her head. Stonor intended her to know that Daniel was legally his child and that if she broke her word to him and turned to Wolfe, she would lose her son. Daniel was Stonor's ace. She could not fight that.

Wolfe was listening too. He heard the inexorable note in Stonor's voice. Eleanor felt his lean-hipped body beside her. She stared at Sophia's profile, read the passionate sensuality in the curve of her mouth. She did not doubt that Sophia Whitley loved Wolfe. She had seen the looks passing between them. Even now Sophia was turning her head and Wolfe was seeking her eyes. Eleanor watched the silent exchange, and it bit into her that they needed no clumsy instruments like words. Their eyes were talking. But what were they saying to each other?

Eleanor could have borne it if Wolfe had shown Sophia the cynical desire she had seen in his face as he looked at other women. She had caught him in the past eyeing pretty women across a room with a glint in his eye, a purely masculine gleam of appreciation and assessment.

As Eleanor looked back at him, though, she realized that the hard, ruthless man she knew had become a man possessed, his body taut with happiness merely to be in the same room as this woman. Sophia looked away and was drawn into talk again. Eleanor was addressed by Luther Hunt, and her attention was distracted, but as she talked, she was aware whenever Sophia turned her head and met Wolfe's eyes. It happened all the time. She lost count of the number of times the two of them looked at each other, and each time that subterranean contact was apparent.

The evening took on a nightmare quality for her. She danced with Luther, with Stonor Whitley, with Wolfe himself. Somehow she kept up a polite little stream of small talk. Wolfe never spoke to her. His eyes stayed on Sophia, who was dancing with Stonor. Eleanor wanted to hit him, make him look at her. Why had he ever married her? She had thought in the beginning that he needed her, wanted her; yet now he did not seem even conscious of her existence. His whole being was concentrated on the slender woman moving so quietly in Stonor Whitley's arms, and Eleanor could sense the intensity in him. Wolfe was jealous, she recognized. It disturbed her to know that. He had always been so self-possessed, so callously indifferent to others, ruthless in taking what he wanted, uncaring what other people thought or felt. Discovering that Wolfe could be jealous was like finding a flaw in metal, a weakness.

It was at that moment that Eleanor made up her mind to fight for him. The girl was his weakness. Why? She stared intently at Sophia, her eyes trying to pierce the girl's façade. What is it about her that holds Wolfe? If I knew that I would know how to fight it.

Have they been lovers? Or is it all in their heads? She couldn't guess at that. She had seen Wolfe grin rakishly at women before and known that he had been to bed with them. His eyes mocked, teased, invited, suggested. But when he looked at Sophia, there was a wordless intimacy between them, a feeling beyond sensuality. Eleanor could not decide whether he had ever made love to the girl. A trembling touched her throat. Was that it? Wolfe, the experienced seducer, held captive by the only girl he had never managed to get into his bed?

Yes, she thought eagerly. That's it. He has wanted her for a long time, and she has held him off.

If that was all, he would lose interest once he had had her. Eleanor glanced at his dark, tense face. Let him go to bed with her and get it over with, she thought. Then he would come back to her. She did not care if he took pleasure elsewhere if he only stayed with her.

After that dance Stonor abruptly took Sophia home. They drove without speaking, her eyes brilliant in the darkness of the carriage, her hands tightly linked in her lap.

Stonor assisted her to alight from the carriage, walked beside her into the dimly lit house. A sleepy-eyed maid curtsied, and took their outer clothes. Stonor glanced at Sophia courteously. "Will you take a glass of madeira before we go to bed?"

She guessed he was going to talk about Wolfe, and she was not ready to discuss him yet. She needed time to think, time to know what to do.

"I'm tired, Stonor. If you don't mind, I'll go straight to bed," she said quietly, half-turning to the stairs.

Stonor did not answer. She walked away, and he stood and watched her without moving. In her own room Sophia allowed her half-asleep maid to undress her and then bade her good night. Alone she sat and stared at herself in the mirror.

Long ago she had promised Stonor that she would forget Wolfe, but how could she forget him when he filled her mind like a dark shadow thrown across the ceiling by a fire? In the three years of her marriage to Stonor, she had never forgotten Wolfe. He had been always present in her mind, a lingering sadness, a sweet taste like honey whenever his name came into her mind. She had been a woman shut out from life, seeing it in mirrors, shadows of life passing on her horizon, but never coming near her. It was a wearying existence to be a wife but not a woman.

Stonor could have made their marriage real after Daniel's birth, but she knew he had turned away deliberately from the intimacy that had begun to grow between them. If she had been his wife in every sense, by now her love for Wolfe might have sunk into quiet ash, but the emptiness of her personal life had kept it alive. The night in the silent, moth-filled park when they had made love had remained at the back of her head all those years.

Stonor was a good husband. He petted and indulged her, was happy to spend his evenings alone with her at Queen's Stonor, watched with a smile as she played him waltz tunes and gay little songs on the piano, hovered beside her when they were in company, the perfect image of a devoted husband. Everyone commented on it. "You're so lucky, my dear. Such a handsome man and so devoted!" How many times had she heard a similar remark from envious women?

She had not been unhappy these three years. Indeed, she had been remarkably content, absorbed in the daily details of her life with Stonor and Daniel. They were a happy family, and she knew that the happiness was based on Stonor's determination that that was what they should be.

She looked at herself in the mirror, winding a black ringlet around her little finger thoughtfully. Not for the first time she asked herself what Stonor got out of it. What was his motive? At the beginning she had believed it to be an almost unbalanced hatred of Wolfe, a determination to snatch and keep what Stonor knew to be Wolfe's property. She had seen herself as his weapon in the war he fought against his half-brother, and she had resented it.

Her admiration for his character, his strength and kindness, had made her forget Stonor's reason for marrying her, for acting as father to her child, for moulding what might so easily have been a tragedy into some semblance of a happy life.

Stonor was far more difficult to read than Wolfe. He had many facets to his nature. On the surface he was a cold, sardonic man without feelings, but she had seen him at close quarters for a long time now, had relied again and again on his strength, and she could no longer see that hard exterior for anything but a mask.

What did it hide, though?

A flush came into her face as she remembered Wolfe's urgency, his whispered words during their dance. She knew what had brought him back across the Atlantic. Wolfe had not hidden it. He believed that Sophia was now capable of leading a full life. Daniel's birth had given him that idea. Wolfe had come back to claim her.

She walked up and down, biting her lip. Wolfe was married, though. Sophia had looked at his beautiful, redheaded wife and known that Eleanor was in love with him. The bitter look in the other woman's green eyes had told her much else. Sophia paced to and from the wall, wringing her hands. Why had he come back? Why had he married Eleanor and then come back here? He should have stayed in America.

She stood stock still, struggling with conflicting thoughts and emotions.

What was she to do?

In his own room Stonor sat listening as the soft footsteps moved up and down, up and down. As if he were present, he could read the thoughts and feelings fighting inside her. The only thing he could not guess was how she would resolve that conflict, and that was the one question that was eating him as he sat with bent head, listening.

When she got up to eat breakfast with Stonor, she was pale and calm, shadowed beneath the blue eyes, but she revealed nothing to his quick, probing look.

He went off to Bristol to his firm, and Sophia spent the day in the usual way at Queen's Stonor, playing with Daniel, seeing to the housekeeping, reading the menus that the cook sent up, ordering some new curtains for the nursery. While she went about her undemanding tasks, her head was still filled with unresolved questions.

Stonor received Eleanor in his office that morning. He seated her opposite him and offered her tea, which she politely refused. Stonor put his hands flat on his desk, studying her.

"May I be frank, Mrs. Whitley?"

"Please do be," she said with a rough note in her voice. "I'd be glad if someone would."

He inclined his head, a wry look on his face. "Your husband loves my wife." He watched her. "But you knew that, I think."

She smiled, a feverish movement of white lips. "Oh, yes, I knew. He makes no secret of it."

Stonor looked hard at her. "But you and he do live normally together?" The question came like a bullet, from his tight face.

It was a very personal question but she answered it, half-angrily, half-miserably. "Not for a while. Once." She shrugged, chewing her lower lip. "Since we came back to England, he has changed." She met his unrevealing eyes. "Since he came back to her."

The news came as a shock to Stonor. His eyes flickered. Eleanor's beauty had made him certain that Wolfe would not be able to resist her. He knew his half-brother's enjoyment of women, and this one was a very sensual creature.

"What has he said to you?" Stonor asked. "What are his plans? Has he mentioned Sophia? Told you what he means to do?"

Eleanor laughed wildly. "He's told me nothing. He has never even mentioned her name. He hasn't needed to—she has been in his head ever since I met him. I knew she existed before I set eyes on her. Now I've seen her, I know she is different." She looked at Stonor bitterly. "There've been others now and then. I always knew. It meant nothing. He likes women. He never looked at one of them the way he looks at her."

"No," Stonor said flatly. He had known that ever since Sophia and Wolfe had first met.

"I hate it when he goes to other women," Eleanor burst out. "It makes me sick. But if he'll get over her, I could bear it for a while."

Stonor did not need that explained. His grey eyes flashed at her, a sardonic coldness in them. "You are suggesting that we let them get it out of their systems?"

"Why not?" Eleanor said feverishly. "Oh, I realize it is a painful thing for both of us, but our marriages are at stake. I've never known Wolfe to stay faithful to anyone. He isn't the faithful type. If we could just close our eyes for a while, it might all blow over."

Stonor leaned back, playing with the arms of his chair, staring at her. "You imagine that they are frustrated lovers who might soon forget each other if they went to bed?"

Something in his voice made her stiffen. "Aren't they?" She whispered the question faintly.

Stonor shook his head.

"He's had her?" The question came out crudely, hoarsely. Eleanor was trembling. It was what she had been pinning her hopes on—the belief that Wolfe had never been able to make love to Sophia, and that that was the only magic the girl exerted over him.

Stonor's straight lips hardened. He looked at her with anger at the way the question had been phrased, but he nodded again.

She sagged, her head dropping into her hands. She lifted it again suddenly. "You're certain? I mean, how can you be sure?"

Stonor's brows rose. "I am totally certain. I don't know how often or for how long, but it went on long enough. I wish I could say that Wolfe didn't love her. I believed once that he did it to spite me, but he convinced me a long time ago that he really loves her."

Eleanor shivered, pain lancing her breast. "That's that, then." In harsh misery she cried, "Why did he ever marry me? Why bring me over here just to desert me for her? It was cruel. I wish I could hate him."

Stonor leaned forwards. "You have no child, have you? Maybe that would hold him. Is there no hope of that?"

She looked away, shaking her head.

Stonor sighed. "Then it all depends on Daniel."

She threw up her red head, gazing at him eagerly. "Your son! You think she wouldn't leave him?"

Stonor smiled briefly. "She adores him. We must hope her love for him outweighs her love for Wolfe."

Eleanor stared at him, curiosity coming into her face. "You love her?"

Stonor's face never moved. He looked at Eleanor levelly. "Why don't you ask Wolfe?"

The question puzzled her. She frowned, watching him. Stonor gave a hard little smile.

"Yes, ask Wolfe," he said. "Wolfe knows me better than anyone in the world. He ought to. We've hated each other since we were old enough to walk. You know the old saying—

know thy enemy? It's true. Wolfe and I know each other inside out. How else would we know where we could place our arrows to best advantage?''

Eleanor listened and stared, horrified. Lucy had said that the two half-brothers hated each other, but under Stonor's cool tones she heard a feeling that shook her to her marrow.

As she waited for Wolfe to come home that evening, Eleanor wondered suddenly if either of them loved Sophia at all. Was she merely the prize for which both men fought? A symbol to them of eventual victory? A laurel wreath that the winner of their long battle would wear?

She looked at the clock. Would he come? Was this to be her life from now on, watching the clock and waiting for a man who never came?

He walked into the room, tall, dark, hard-featured, and she gave him a careless, casual glance.

"You're early, Wolfe. Will you take a glass of sherry before dinner?''

He did not seem aware that she was acting. He nodded. "Thank you, Eleanor.''

She watched as he sank into a chair, relaxing easily. Her skirts rustling, she went to the decanter and poured his drink, carried it to him and watched as he sipped it. Her role in his life now, she thought, was to be an observer, to wait and watch. How could she bear it?

"I think we should have my dear half-brother and his wife to dinner soon,'' Wolfe said coolly, his eyes on the amber liquid in his glass.

Eleanor felt the stab of nerves around her body. Somehow she smiled. "Of course, Wolfe. I'll send an invitation.''

"Have Luther and his wife, too,'' Wolfe said. His eyes narrowed on the sherry. "Have Southerby, too. You know he likes to come and admire you, Eleanor.''

She swallowed. With an effort she said lightly, "Your half-brother seems quite devoted to his wife.''

Wolfe threw her a quick, shrewd look. His lips curved in a cold smile. "Doesn't he?''

What did that look mean? "She is very beautiful,'' Eleanor said, turning the point of the knife into her flesh.

Wolfe looked back at his glass. "Very.'' He might have been talking about someone he barely knew. His voice showed nothing.

"It is nice that they're so happy together." She knew she was talking too much. Wolfe would sense her feelings.

He laughed drily. "Delightful." The word came out with a bite.

"I hear they do not often appear in society. They are happiest in their own home."

Wolfe lifted his black head and his eyes met hers, a brilliant flaring in them. "Stonor would shut her in a harem if he dared."

Pain forced her into a mistake. She said pleadingly, "He loves her, Wolfe."

Wolfe's eyes narrowed speculatively. "You've been talking to him?" Their glance held, and Wolfe gave a sardonic smile. "I see you have. Did he tell you everything? Trying to queer my pitch, was he? Stonor's losing his touch. What did he think that would achieve? No, let me guess." His blue-green eyes mocked her. "Keep out of it, Eleanor. It is none of your business."

"I'm your wife, damn you," she burst out, her face filling with colour. She looked at him with anger and hurt. "Have you forgotten that? Why did you marry me? Why in God's name did you do it?"

He looked surprised, his eyes shifting. "Keep that red-rag temper of yours!"

"Why the hell should I?"

He stood up, putting down his glass, a sparkle in his eyes. "Because I say so."

She laughed angrily. "Why should I listen to you? Chasing your brother's wife right under my nose! How would you like it if I chased Stonor?"

Wolfe had an odd, puzzled look as he stared at her. "We won't discuss this any more," he said, moving towards the door.

As he left the room Eleanor swore viciously, words she had learned in her years in New Orleans, her hands clenched at her sides. She had meant to play it cool, to act wisely, and she had thrown all her calm aside like a fool. When would she learn?

# CHAPTER EIGHTEEN

The invitation to dinner with Wolfe and his wife threw Sophia into a state of nervous uncertainty. She placed it on the mantelpiece, as invitations were always placed, and watched with half-lowered eyes as Stonor stood and regarded it that evening.

His face told her nothing. He turned slowly and his eyes rested on her face. "I see we've had an invitation from Wolfe."

"Yes," she said. "Shall we go?"

"Are we doing anything else that night?"

"No."

Stonor shrugged his wide shoulders. "Then why not? His wife is very lovely. A spirited creature, and very much in love with Wolfe, I noticed."

Sophia lifted her eyes. Stonor looked into them probingly. She gave him a faint little smile, a wryness around her mouth. "I noticed that, too, Stonor."

He said nothing more. Sophia was cloaking her thoughts from him, and try as he would, he could not guess at them. That evening he came home early to attend Daniel's bath—the high point of the day for the boy and Sophia. She had him naked on her lap, laughing excitedly, having splashed walls and floor with water. A small wooden yacht sailed in the bath, bearing witness to the fun mother and child had been having.

Sophia had dried Daniel and now began pulling his nightshirt over his head. Emerging from the folds, he looked round and saw Stonor watching in the doorway.

"Papa!" The boy's small face shone with delight. He held out both arms. "You're early, Papa."

Stonor moved to lift him into his arms, kissing him. "Have you had a good bath?"

"We sailed his new boat," Sophia told him, indulgently watching as the boy wiggled one of Stonor's ears.

"Carry me to bed, Papa," Daniel begged. "A story. Tell a story."

The little procession went to the nursery. Tucked into bed, Daniel lay enraptured as Stonor told him the story of Jack the Giant Killer. When it was finished, both Stonor and Sophia kissed him, turned down the night light and went out leaving him half-drowsy, his nurse sitting at the table outside in the day nursery, one of Daniel's little shirts in her hands, mending a tear in the sleeve.

After dinner Sophia played a dashing mazurka for Stonor, her small fingers almost tripping over each other. It was a new piece she had learned, and he congratulated her when she sat still.

"Very accomplished, Sophia. You are improving a good deal."

"There is a letter from Elizabeth," she said, having forgotten it. She fetched it, and Stonor opened and read it, frowning. "What is it?" Sophia asked him anxiously.

"Tom," Stonor said shortly. "Elizabeth wants me to go up to London. Tom has apparently lost some more money. God in heaven, will he never learn? He has no head for gambling on the market. Why does he do it?"

"You know why he does it! He hopes to make a good deal of money for Elizabeth. She never stops complaining about his income, and poor Tom is at his wits' end."

Stonor folded the letter, his face pale. "I shall have to go." He stared at the carpet. "I've no choice." His eyes lifted and flicked to her face. She caught the hard expression in them. "It seems I won't be here for Wolfe's dinner party," he said. "You will have to go alone, Sophia."

In her bedroom Sophia lay in bed remembering the look on Stonor's face as he had said that. There had been something reckless in his eyes. In Wolfe, she would have put it down to some gamble he was taking, but Stonor was no gambler. She put her arms beneath her head. Or was he?

Stonor left for London the next day. Wolfe's dinner party was the following evening, and when Sophia drove up in her carriage alone to Wolfe's house, she had a feeling of nervous anxiety. Wolfe looked over her shoulder as he came forwards to take her hand. His blue-green eyes narrowed. "Where is Stonor?"

Eleanor, wearing a fixed bright smile, watched Sophia as she looked directly at Wolfe. "He has had to go up to London. I do apologize for his being absent."

Wolfe had a startled look. "He's gone away?"

He and Sophia stared at each other. "Yes," Sophia said.

A curious brightness grew in Wolfe's features. "Come and talk to my cousin and his wife," he said. "You must bear with her and her everlasting chat of her beloved infant."

Sophia smiled. "We have that, at least, in common," she murmured. "We both have beautiful sons."

His eyes searched hers. A pallor grew under his brown skin. "Is the boy like Stonor or like you?" He asked that harshly.

Sophia looked away. Daniel was Wolfe's image, but he must never know that. She hoped it would be a long time before he set eyes on Daniel. Once he saw him Wolfe would guess. Daniel's eyes were so much like his—of just such a shape, such a strange shifting colour, already holding that reckless gaiety, already bearing arrogance like a banner.

"Stonor says he is like me," she evaded, although it was true. Stonor had never admitted to recognizing Wolfe in the boy.

She moved past him to smile and shake hands with Mrs. Hunt, sank into a chair beside her, and listened while the other woman happily launched into talk of Thomas.

Luther and Wolfe talked to old Southerby, who kept glancing at Eleanor, fascinated by her. Revolting old brute, Eleanor thought. It disturbed her that Wolfe was not looking at Sophia. Stonor Whitley had gone to London. Why? She turned it over and over in her mind. Why had he gone suddenly, leaving the field clear for Wolfe? What was in his mind?

The evening was a crucifixion for her, watching Wolfe look across the table at Sophia with that strange eagerness, seeing Sophia glance away with a flushed face. Eleanor began to think that she could not stand much more of it. The pretence weighed on her like lead. They talked in such polite terms, smiled briefly at each other, convincing the Hunts and Southerby and his wife that they barely knew each other, yet all the time under their surfaces she could sense so much going on, a sensual urgency running between them like an invisible flame. As they all moved back to the drawing room, the women talked the usual small talk of such occasions, leaving the men to drink port and tell each other masculine jokes. Sophia glanced at Eleanor, and Eleanor looked at her with hard dislike, bringing a little frown between the younger woman's dark brows.

Mrs. Hunt made it easier by talking nonstop about the servant problem. "I am so sick of them all. They do as little as they can and want as much as they can get." She gave Sophia a sycophantic smile. "Of course you are so lucky at Queen's Stonor. Many of your servants have been with you for years, I believe."

"Most of them have always lived on the estate," Sophia agreed, a smile on her lips. "They are domestic tyrants, I'm afraid—they tend to like things done their own way and they will see me as a little girl still! But it is all done out of love. How can one complain?"

All done out of love, Eleanor thought, staring at her. No wonder she has that bright, uncomplicated sweetness. She's lapped in love. Stonor, Wolfe, the people at that house. Sophia Whitley has never known a moment's pain or unhappiness. Damn her. Why should she be so lucky?

The evening wore on far too slowly for her. She looked at the clock on the mantelpiece again and again, longing to have Sophia out of her house, out of Wolfe's eager stare.

It was Wolfe, of course, who put Sophia into her carriage. He wrapped the travelling-rug around her, tenderly pushed her small hands into the fur muff kept for her night drives. Bending down, he whispered, "I must see you."

"No, Wolfe," she whispered.

"I'll come to Queen's Stonor," he said and looked up, his eyes glinting in determination.

She paled. "You mustn't."

"He is away." Wolfe stared at her, his eyes narrowed. "Why has he gone? There can be only one reason."

"Business," she said at once. "Family business."

Wolfe shook his head, smiling drily. "You know that isn't the real answer. Stonor has gone knowing I will see you. He's given up." A strange sigh came from him. "Stonor has conceded."

Sophia stiffened, her hands tightened together inside the muff. "What do you mean?" But she knew what he meant, and Wolfe's reckless grin told her that he was not going to explain, that he was aware that she already knew.

"Tomorrow night," he said softly. The look he gave her was a caress in itself, passionate and tender. "Tomorrow, Sophia."

The drive home seemed very brief to her. She stared into the night and heard the clip of the hooves, the rattle of the wheels. She had known when Stonor went to London alone that he was leaving her quite deliberately. He had left the field to Wolfe.

He doesn't care, Sophia thought. The sensation inside her was strange and startling to her. The carriage arrived at the house, and she went inside with a thought-fixed expression. She had to make up her mind before tomorrow night. Wolfe would press her to come away with him. He would press for much more than that. There had been unmistakable urgency in his face as they parted.

She went to the night nursery to look at Daniel, and the nurse looked up at her, startled, her head wobbling up from her pillow, a trimmed nightcap covering her hair.

"Go back to sleep, Nurse," Sophia said softly. She bent over her son and pushed back an untidy lock of dark hair from his warm forehead. Wolfe's son, she thought. How angelic he looks asleep. Quite the opposite when he's awake. The darling, he has a scratch on his hand where the kitten was playing with him this morning. Stonor would never let him go. She kissed the little cheek, heard the deep sound of his breathing close to her, and knew she could not ever leave him.

"We are going to London tomorrow, Nurse," she murmured as she straightened. "We'll catch the eleven o'clock train from Bristol. See that Master Daniel is ready by nine, will you? We will stay with his grandmama for a few days to buy his winter clothing."

"Yes, Mrs. Whitley," the nurse said, looking delighted at the thought of a visit to London again so soon.

When Sophia arrived at the Spitalfields house, she found Maria alone. Fussing eagerly over Daniel, Maria welcomed them both. "Stonor didn't say you were coming up."

"I suddenly decided on it," Sophia said. She looked around the familiar drawing room. It had a grey, faded look now, as though life had seeped out of it. Maria looked like that, too. Her skin had a yellow tinge. "Why don't you come down to Queen's Stonor when we return, Aunt Maria? We love to have you, you know that. London is so dull for you."

Maria Whitley had a stubborn look. "Stonor wants me to sell this house. But I won't." It held her life. She could not leave it.

Sophia could not understand her. She had always talked of nothing but Queen's Stonor, yet now when she could spend the rest of her life there, she could rarely be persuaded to come.

"What do you find to do all day?"

Maria had a secretive look. "I have a good deal to do," she said flatly. Daniel was playing with the ivory bobbles on the end of the lace curtains, his small fingers pulling at them impatiently.

"Nurse, take Master Daniel to the nursery," Sophia ordered. "Daniel, you must not touch Grandmama's curtains like that."

"Leave him, leave him," Maria said. "He's doing no harm." She kissed his dark head as the nurse led him struggling past. "He is the image of James," she said.

Sophia could barely repress the stare of amazement she gave her. She had never once seen any likeness to James Whitley in the boy. Maria was becoming strange, she thought. Loneliness and sadness were making her odd.

"Is Stonor at the office?" she asked.

"At the moment, yes, but he is going to have dinner with Elizabeth and Tom tonight. We must send a message to tell him you are here."

"Don't bother," Sophia said. "We'll surprise him."

She dined with Maria alone, noting with concern how much wine Maria took with her meal. Did she always drink like that? Her worried eyes met those of Robbins, wooden behind Maria's chair. Robbins had a sardonic look, her face blank yet secretly derisive. The servants knew everything, of course. They always did. Something must be done, Sophia thought. Stonor must do something.

It was always to Stonor that they all turned. He was the necessary rock of their lives, the dependable element to them all. Did he guess at his mother's strange condition? He had seen her more often than Sophia had in the past year. What did he make of it?

When she had said good night to Maria, Sophia sat in the bedroom Stonor always used and waited for him to come back from Elizabeth's house. What sort of trouble had he found there? He would be tired, depressed, perhaps. Elizabeth did that to him. She was so discontented, so malicious, digging her little claws into him at every opportunity.

She heard a hansom cab draw up, heard the front door open and close, heard Stonor going into the drawing room. The servants were all in bed. A decanter of whisky had been left out for Stonor with a covered plate of sandwiches in case he felt hungry.

Sophia waited, seated in the cushioned bedroom chair, the lamp turned down beside her.

She heard Stonor stumble as he came up the stairs. Had he been drinking heavily?

A queer prickle ran down her back as the door opened. Stonor walked into the room heavily, closing the door. At first he did not see her. He stood with his back to the door, his eyes on the floor, his face white and dull. Suddenly he seemed to take in the light. He looked up. She saw his face before the reflex shutter came down hiding his expression.

Visibly he gathered himself together. The grey eyes regarded her coolly. "What are you doing here, Sophia?"

"Waiting for you," she said, smiling.

She watched him thinking it out. He was very tired, and the usual quick processes of his brain took longer. "Why?" he asked at last, as though he had given up trying to make sense of her presence.

Sophia stood up and came over to him. He wore dark evening dress. His broad shoulders sagged slightly beneath the smooth material, the weariness in him visible in every line of his tall, lithe body. She put her hands to his necktie, undoing it. "You look half-dead, Stonor. Was Elizabeth difficult?"

He looked down at her, his pale face immovable. "No more than usual."

Sophia began to unbutton his shirt. She heard the intake of breath. His hands came up to arrest the movements of hers, seizing her wrists.

Sophia looked at him through lowered lashes, a faint smile lingering on her lips.

"Why are you in London?" Stonor asked with flared nostrils. "Running away won't help."

"I'm not running away."

"No?" Stonor smiled grimly.

"It's you who are doing that," Sophia murmured.

The hands holding her wrists tightened. His breath rasped in his throat. "What?"

She moved closer. "Weren't you? Are you tired of me, Stonor? Is that why you fled to London, leaving me to Wolfe?"

His grey eyes flashed. He bent his head towards her, the lamplight turning his dusty hair gold as it always did, as she had seen so many times without thinking, as she thought now, how beautiful his hair looks. Stonor spoke so quietly that she had to watch his lips to be sure she heard him. "Do you think I'm inhuman? Do you think I was staying to watch, to hear you lying to me, to know you were seeing him in secret?"

Sophia looked gravely at him. "You think I would do that to you, Stonor?"

His pale mouth writhed. "You did before."

"That was before we were married," she defended herself. "Before I knew you, before I had a chance to find out what you were really like."

Stonor scarcely seemed to be listening to her. He was locked in a frozen wasteland, his eyes bitter. "How many times did he come to your room at night while the house was asleep? I knew you were seeing him secretly, but I never suspected then that it had gone so far so quickly."

Sophia burst out, "It hadn't! That night was the first time, and nothing happened even then!"

Stonor's laughter was derisive. "Why bother to lie to me now?"

"I'm not! We were not lovers while I was in your house. We met in the early mornings and walked around London. Wolfe showed me a part of London I would never otherwise have seen."

Taking flame, Stonor said furiously, "Damn him to hell, he had no right to take you to such places! I can guess the sort of street he would show you—you! A young girl, a child practically! He is unspeakable."

He was still holding her wrists, his fingers biting into them like cords. Sophia looked at him tenderly, her mouth gentle. "You know another side of me, Stonor. Wolfe did me no harm. There is a lot of Wolfe in me, I'm afraid." She laughed. "We're kindred spirits. It was all very innocent."

"Innocent!" Stonor's voice was hoarse. "He took you to the haunts of whores and thieves and you call it innocent!"

"It was," she said, remembering the delight and wonder of those mornings in the gold and rose of dawn, the empty London streets, the dark waters of the Thames.

Stonor watched, seeing the warm curve of her pink mouth, the smile in her blue eyes. "And when he seduced you, was that innocent?" he asked thickly.

Sophia thought of the moth-filled park, the silent watching house, the horse cropping near them, Wolfe's delicate fingers unlocking the secret of passion for her.

"Yes," she murmured. "Oh, yes, Stonor, that night above

all! You imagine Wolfe's motives to have been selfish and squalid—I know what you think—but you are wrong. He loved me. We loved each other. It was as innocent as the fall of snow.'' She lifted her blue eyes seriously to him. ''You lied to me when you told me he was dead. I was so miserable when I first got back to Queen's Stonor. Then Wolfe came and it was like the sun coming up. I met him that night in the park. One night. That is all we had.'' She paused, a sigh wrenching her. ''All we shall ever have.''

She caught the wary blaze of the grey eyes. Stonor bent down, speaking fast. ''You don't mean to go to him? You must not, Sophia. You have to look after your health, remember. You can't have another child. It would kill you.''

She lowered her eyes, her lashes flickering on her cheeks. ''Wolfe is a gambler. He would take the risk.''

Stonor drew a shaky breath. ''And you? Would you take it?''

''I'm sick of the shadows, Stonor, sick of being half-alive. I want to be a real woman. Oh, it is a risk, I admit, but it is one I'm now prepared to take.''

He watched her face, his breathing heavy. ''Have you forgotten Daniel? I won't let you take him away.''

''Did I say I wanted to?''

Stonor winced. ''You're leaving him too?'' He gripped her wrists for a second, then suddenly threw them down, turning away. ''Why did you come here? To tell me you were leaving me? Is he waiting for you somewhere in London?'' His voice broke off. He clenched his hands into fists. ''I'll kill him, Sophia. I warn you, if you go to him, I'll kill him.''

''Why?'' The question was very soft.

Lamplight glittered over his hair as he turned, his cold face brilliant with jealousy and passion, the ice in his grey eyes dissolved into fierce emotion. ''You cruel little bitch, what do you want from me? You want to see me grovel, beg like an abject fool? My God, you're right. There's more of Wolfe in you than I would admit to myself. What he could never do himself he's used you to achieve.''

''Tell me, Stonor,'' she whispered gently.

''So that you and Wolfe can laugh together afterwards? I'm damned if I will.'' He swivelled on his heel and strode to the door, a very tall, hard man with bitter eyes. ''Get out. Go to him if you're going. You won't have long. As soon as I find you, I'll kill him.''

She stared at him, her face blank, then she walked towards him.
He held the door, his face averted. As she reached him, she stood
on tiptoe, her arms going around his neck, and kissed him.

The door slammed shut. Stonor's arms clamped round her.
Pulling her fiercely towards him, his head came down blindly,
crushing her lips under his own, parting them, invading her
mouth with a force that did not care if it hurt her.

She lay against his body, hearing the accelerating beat of his
heart grow louder and louder, her fingers running through the
smooth, pale hair.

Stonor suddenly picked her up like a child, still kissing her,
and carried her to the bed. Pushing her down on it, he covered
her body with his own, forcing her down into the yielding
mattress, and his long hands found the warm swell of her
breasts and closed over them in savage possession.

His lips slid to her throat, his teeth grazing her skin, his
tongue warm. "That was a mistake, Sophia," he said thickly.
"You shouldn't have touched me. If you're going to risk your
life with him, you can risk it with me. God knows, I've wanted it long enough."

Sophia stretched sensuously, warm and yielding, her fingers
moving to undo his shirt.

Feeling their movement, Stonor lifted his head from her
and stared down at her. She met his eyes with a little smile.

"I began to think I'd have to seduce you, Stonor," she said
in wicked tones, her blue eyes teasing.

He stiffened. "What?"

"Did you think I could live with you for three years and not
learn to love you?"

"Don't lie to me," he ground out angrily.

"Why should I?"

"Wolfe—" he began, and she put her hand over his mouth.

"Wolfe was my first love, and I suppose a woman always
has a weakness for the first man in her life. He's hardly ad-
mirable. I know—he's unscrupulous, amoral and very charming. Wolfe has so many weaknesses, but you have very few."
She eyed him with a mocking, teasing smile. "I'm one of
them, aren't I, Stonor darling?"

"You're all of them," Stonor said thickly, staring at her
with restless, incredulous eyes.

She had finished undoing his shirt. Her fingers slid silkily
over the muscled chest to his shoulders, stole around his neck
and played with the warm strands of his hair.

"Tell me now, Stonor, tell me before we make love."

"Are we going to?" he asked unsteadily, still staring as though he did not believe it was happening.

Sophia eyed him impishly. "If I have anything to do with it, we are."

He gave a long groan. "It's too dangerous for you. It means risking your precious life, and I couldn't bear to live if anything happened to you. What we've had for the past three years is better than nothing at all."

She raised her head and drew her lips slowly down his body, hearing the gasp, the eager groan he gave. "Take a gamble, Stonor. I'm far stronger than I was three years ago. I survived Daniel's birth even though I'd been so ill not long before. I'm certain I could survive if I became pregnant again." She gave a soft, stifled laugh. "And I want to have your child, Stonor. Don't you understand? I want you and I want to bear you a child."

His hands framed her face, his palms on her dark hair. "My darling," he whispered. "Oh, God, I love you, Sophia. I've loved you since the day I saw you, the day you arrived in London. One look and I felt my heart turn over. You were so small and sweet, your smile was so warm. I'd been frozen in the ice of that house for years, and I had been expecting someone like my mother, some frigid little virgin with a cold face. Then you came into the room and you smiled, and I was incredulous at my luck. I felt like someone who has been locked in a tomb coming out into sunshine."

"My poor darling Stonor," she said gravely, looking at him with love and compassion. "I'm sorry for all the pain I've ever given you. I wish I could go back to that day and start again."

"I never blamed you," he said flatly. "I knew it was Wolfe. He guessed the minute he saw me with you. He pursued you deliberately. It was the same story all over again—Wolfe stealing what he knew I loved."

"Yes," she said, sighing. Wolfe had started out with a deliberate plan, but from the moment they actually met, things had changed for him. Their meeting had been like the collision of storm clouds, a natural explosion that had nothing to do with intention or thought. Wolfe had fallen in love as immediately as Stonor had done. It had been a strange twist of fate for all three of them.

Stonor read the thought in her face and his mouth twisted.

"Oh, yes, he loves you. I wish I could say he didn't. That came later, but he set out to seduce you, Sophia."

She nodded. "I know. But, Stonor, even if he hadn't, it would all have happened as it did because you can't legislate for feelings, you can't plan for love."

"You still love him," Stonor said, drawing back, his face chilling over. "I hear it when you say his name."

"Love can't be contained or buried, Stonor. Haven't you learned that yet? But there is love and love. The way I feel about Wolfe now is very close to the way I feel about Daniel. They are both of them wild and difficult children. Wolfe is a wicked, disgraceful darling and I love him. Maybe I always shall. But you are the man I want, Stonor. You are the husband I want." She laid her hand against his cheek, smiling, tenderness in her face. "I love you far more deeply than I even knew. When you went to London and left me alone, I was hurt and surprised. You've always fought for me before. Suddenly you walked away, and I felt you had abandoned me. I couldn't bear it. I had to come after you and get you back. I can't live without you, Stonor."

He was flushed and breathing hard, his face transfigured. Sophia smiled at him, invitingly. "Love me, Stonor. Have faith and risk it. We need each other."

He looked like a sleepwalker as he found her mouth, kissing her urgently, passionately, and getting a response that made him shake. It tore away the last of his restraint. The white-hot heat in Stonor was unleashed at last, burning in him as he touched her with trembling hands, stared at the white gleam of her body as she slid out of her nightgown.

The sensuality he had hidden for years emerged now: his mouth, his hands, his tongue exploring her body with open hunger, inciting her to do the same to him, groaning with closed eyes as Sophia caressed him. She lay twisting restlessly, her throat trembling in a stifled moan, as his head travelled over her. Parting her thighs gently, his mouth invaded between them and she cried out in acute pleasure, "Stonor, Stonor."

He laughed huskily and came back to kiss her moaning mouth, winding his fingers into her tangled hair. "So long, I've wanted to do this to you for so long," he muttered. "It could be enough, my darling, don't you think? And no risk to your life. There are many ways we could make love without risking anything."

She arched passionately against him. "No, take me, Stonor. I want to belong to you."

For one second he hesitated, then the silken brush of her body against him tilted the balance. They both groaned as Stonor at last took possession of her body. He lay, breathing thickly, as though that moment were enough, almost unwilling to move now that he had finally merged with the slender, sensuous little body he had needed for years.

Sophia had a feverish look, her blue eyes wide and vivid. She felt as though every bone in her body was being played at an intolerable pitch, her nerves flickering with fire. All thought of Wolfe, of the past, had gone whistling down the wind. There was desire in her eyes as she looked at Stonor. With a supple twist of her body, she invited him, her arms clinging round his neck.

He moved fiercely, the hard male demand rhythmic and quickening, her body eagerly receptive, matching his motion, their skin damp with perspiration, gliding against each other. "Darling, darling," Sophia groaned, kissing his neck, and Stonor looked at her with the blaze of passion in his eyes unmasked at last, all the coldness, all the control gone.

Her fingers dug into his back, she sobbed breathlessly, wildly, crying out without words against his smooth shoulder, and the tautened agony finally snapped. Stonor's hot face burned against hers as he fell through the descending spirals of pleasure and satisfaction, his voice hoarse as he moaned her name.

He lay on her, heavily relaxed, breathing as though he had just climbed a mountain, a ragged intake of air that made his chest heave. At last he lifted his head slowly and looked at her. "Oh, God, I needed you," he muttered wryly. "If you knew!"

"I do know," she said, a dimple at the corner of her mouth.

"Wanton," Stonor said, laughing, amusement in his eyes. The smile went. "My darling, how long before you know if I've made you pregnant? How long must I wait?"

She eyed him wryly. "If you mean what I think you mean, no, Stonor. Once will not be enough. Now that we have begun, we shall go on."

"Sophia," he said pleadingly.

"I mean it, Stonor. Good heavens, do you think I'm going to live that life forever? I'm not afraid. I've no intention of dying. I'm going to enjoy life too much. I fully intend to live until I'm a white-haired old lady, and I'll see that you make love to me like that every night of our lives.''

He laughed, then shook his head. ''I don't like it.''

''Liar, you loved it,'' she said, her eyes wicked.

''Darling.'' He kissed her laughing mouth adoringly. His head lifted and she saw his face change, grow sombre. ''And Wolfe?'' he asked, his eyes moving away restlessly.

''Leave Wolfe to me,'' she said.

His eyes came back to her, narrowing, jealous and hard. ''I'll shoot him if I see him near you again.''

''No need for anything so drastic,'' Sophia said, looking amused. ''Wolfe has one asset you'll never have, Stonor. He knows when he is beaten. You knew before we were married that I loved Wolfe, that we had been lovers, that I did not want to marry you, but you just refused to let go, didn't you?''

''I couldn't,'' he said hoarsely. ''I couldn't live without you.''

She gave him a wry, tender smile. ''So you hung on, and in the end you got what you wanted. Now Wolfe in your position would have shrugged and walked away. Can you see Wolfe chasing a woman he knows is in love with another man? His pride wouldn't let him.''

Stonor whitened and winced. ''I have no pride where you're concerned. Do you think I'm proud of it?''

She shook her head at him. ''For a man who hates taking risks, darling, you've taken a good many for me in the past. You're stronger than Wolfe, Stonor. I've said that Wolfe is ruthless. So are you, and where I'm concerned you've been far more ruthless than Wolfe ever has—when I was ill Wolfe went away and left me, because in the last resort he was less of a gambler than you are. You married me knowing I could never be a real wife to you, because you just would not let me go. You have no sense of defeat, have you, Stonor?''

''I thought I'd lost you when he came back,'' Stonor said heavily.

She had mockery in her eyes. ''Did you? I wonder. I think you took a last gamble.''

She saw his eyes and grinned at him. ''Yes, I'm not blind. You hoped I wouldn't take the risk of getting pregnant again, didn't you, darling? And then there was Daniel. You thought I wouldn't leave him to go to Wolfe. You went away, but you left two hostages behind, myself and Daniel. One of your very calculated risks, wasn't it, Stonor?''

He watched her frowningly. "It was a risk, though. You might have gone."

"The world well lost for love? Yes, I might have, but by going away you put my honour at stake too, didn't you, darling? As I say, you are more ruthless than Wolfe. Now he does not recognize honour, but he does recognize defeat when he sees it. Once he knows I've followed you to London, he will know the rest of the story. Wolfe and I understand each other. He knows I've refused him."

Unconvinced, Stonor said sharply, "He's in love with you, Sophia. He won't just forget you."

"His wife will distract him." Sophia shrugged.

"She's madly in love with him, poor damned woman," Stonor said with a grimace. "She looked like death when she sat in my office and told me how she felt."

Sophia's brows arched. "She came to see you?"

Stonor flushed. "Yes."

Her eyes amused, Sophia said, "You asked her to, of course? My word, Stonor, you leave no stone unturned, do you? When Wolfe realizes that he isn't going to get me back, he'll go back to her. He married her. That must mean he cares more for her than he realizes. She's beautiful, and I think she is just the sort of wife for Wolfe—someone who won't be hurt or shocked by his unscrupulous amorality, someone experienced and broadminded. Wolfe is ambitious. He'll be busy with his newspaper. You'll see I'm right. Wolfe will shrug and accept defeat."

"God, I hope so," Stonor said. "Or I'll have to kill him."

"Don't talk like that," Sophia scolded. "You must learn to understand and appreciate Wolfe. He's a wicked scoundrel but he has such charm, Stonor. He can't hurt us now. He can't hurt you. I won't let him, and if there is one person in this world who can threaten Wolfe, it is me."

Stonor looked into her eyes, his face grim. "Because he loves you," he said.

She smiled. "You must learn to accept that."

"I can't," he said angrily.

"Can't you be generous, Stonor?"

His face still, he stared at her.

"You've won. Can't you find it in you to be generous to him now?"

Stonor gathered her close into his arms, his head on her hair. "Oh, my darling, my love," he whispered, and she smiled as she snuggled against his chest.

# PART TWO

## CHAPTER NINETEEN

Louise Stonor Whitley was six years old before she first really looked at her mother. Throughout her childhood the warm, beautiful figure of her mother had come to the nursery each day to lift her and kiss her, to hold her on the comfortable silken confines of her lap, to stroke back her black hair and tell her fairy stories, and for that delightful personage Louise had had a special place, unique and labelled "Mama," for which there would never be a substitute. But she had never really noticed her mother as a human being outside this special context. To Louise her Mama existed just to be her own special corner of loving comfort.

She first realized that others had a share in her Mama during the autumn of 1885. Her brothers, Daniel and Edward, had shared her nursery playroom until then, their noisy squabbles over toys and personal possessions making havoc whenever Nanny Dorcas took her eye off them long enough. One day Daniel wickedly threw a cricket ball at Edward and gave him a black eye, and that evening Papa came to the nursery, stiff and menacing in his business clothes, his face and carriage coldly angry, and taking Daniel by the chin, stared down into the boy's eyes. "You will come to my study tonight and take a beating," Papa said in icy tones. Louise, on a nursery wicker chair, her small thumb in her mouth, watched in dismay. Apart from Mama, Daniel was her favourite person in the world, also her protector, bully, master of her every waking hour. At Daniel's long-legged stride she would wobble in her frilled skirt and call him to wait for her, and he would wait, his mouth fondly contemptuous. "If you're coming, keep up, Louise...."

She would then run after his thin figure admiringly, tagging along behind him to play Red Indians or pirates, usually permitted grudgingly to be a squaw or a captured lady who had to walk the plank. Daniel always allowed her to play with them. Edward never did. "Oh, not her," he would groan as her plump little legs twinkled after Daniel, and Daniel would cuff him to the ground, jerking a shoulder at her to follow him.

That evening when she saw Papa's angry eyes on Daniel's upturned face she felt a curious sense of alarm, but Daniel did not flinch. He never did. Papa had beaten him before when he had broken the cucumber frames twice, and when he had helped Louise to climb the lower branches of one of the apple trees and she could not get down. Daniel had taken those beatings without shedding a tear, although he had permitted both Edward and Louise to admire the raw red stripes on his white bottom afterwards, and Louise had known she would have screamed with agony if they had been inflicted on her.

As if Daniel's silent acquiescence maddened him, Papa then caught him by the ear in one hand and shook him violently. Daniel set his teeth and uttered no sound.

Then the door opened and Mama came in, her long skirts rustling softly. Papa released Daniel's ear, a faint flush coming into his face, and turned towards Mama. Quietly, her great blue eyes took in the scene, and Mama said to Daniel, "Have you apologized to Edward yet for what you did, Daniel?"

"I told him I was sorry at once, Mama," Daniel said, his blue-green eyes meeting hers. "I wish I had not lost my temper, but it was over so quickly...."

Mama bent down and kissed him gently on his stiff, white cheek. "Run along, then, dear, and sit with him in his bedroom. You could read him some of his favourite adventure stories. Poor Edward, he looks as if someone had been at him with a paintbox, and it will hurt him to read for a few days...."

Daniel went out and Mama turned towards Papa, unaware of Louise's curious gaze from her corner. Papa looked down into Mama's face with a faint grimace.

"He must be beaten, my dear," he said, as if apologizing.

"No, Stonor," Mama said very firmly. "You may punish him some other way. Stop his pocket money or deprive him of his Saturday sweets, but no more beatings."

Papa opened his mouth to speak, then closed it, and Louise realized with a shock that even Papa, so strong and powerful that the servants spoke of him with respectful awe, had to accept her mother's edicts.

"It is time Daniel went to school," Papa said after a pause.

"He is old enough. Jenkins is a good enough tutor for small boys, but Daniel is beyond him now."

Louise felt a pang of terrible grief at the thought of her beloved Daniel going away, and she looked hopefully at her Mama to hear the lovely, all-powerful mouth speak against the idea.

To her horror, Mama sighed and said, "Yes, perhaps you are right. You and he are best apart."

"I have tried, Sophia," Papa said almost pleadingly. "It is just that when he looks at me with those eyes of his I feel. . ." His voice broke off huskily, and Mama gently patted his arm.

"I understand, Stonor. These things cannot be helped. Come down to tea, then."

Turning, she caught sight of Louise and looked at her with a loving smile. "Why, darling, how like a little mouse you are in your corner. Have you kissed your Papa?"

Louise took her thumb out of her mouth with a sulky face. "I hate him," she had said, her blue eyes stormy. "I do not want Daniel to go away. I love Daniel."

Papa made a sound under his breath, and Mama shook her head at him, as if warning him. She rustled over to pick up Louise, and kissed her cheek, the delicious fragrance of her perfume filling the little girl's nostrils.

"We all love Daniel, darling, but he is getting too big for the nursery. Why, soon he would be like Alice in the White Rabbit's house, an arm and a leg stuck through the window and his head up the chimney. . . ."

Louise began to giggle at the picture, and somehow, as Mama made her little jokes, Papa began to laugh too, and Louise gave him his evening kiss without remembering her anger with him. Only in bed later did she remember, and then she thought curiously: Papa has to do what Mama says because she is a special person. . .and the thought was so strange that afterwards she began to notice other things about Mama. She noticed that the servants always obeyed when Mama spoke in her soft voice, their faces eager, as if they enjoyed doing what she told them to do. She noticed that although Papa was master of Queen's Stonor, Mama had the last word about everything that happened there. Slowly Louise realized that, far beyond the four walls of the nursery, Mama reigned over the whole of life on the estate, and she did it so gently and sweetly that Louise had never heard her raise her voice in anger. She had heard Papa shout. He shouted whenever

Daniel annoyed him, and that was quite often, but even when Daniel had spilled a bottle of bright blue ink over Mama's new green walking dress, Mama had only sighed and said, "Oh, butterfingers." Daniel, covered in chagrin and self-contempt, had walked for two hours through the Stonor woods to find a large bunch of Mama's favourite violets to put beside her plate at dinner. Louise had come in to give Papa his evening kiss just as Mama was pinning them into her belt, her face soft, and she had seen Papa look sharply at them, as if he resented Daniel's silent gesture of love. Once, when Daniel had knelt and kissed Mama on her hand, in a secret little movement not meant for anyone to see, Louise had seen Papa look around at them with a cold face, and had been puzzled. If she kissed Mama, Papa only smiled fondly at her, and when Edward hugged Mama as he said good night, Papa would ruffle his brown hair affectionately....

Daniel took the news of his approaching departure for school with a calm shrug, but Louise sensed that he did not want to go. Tucking her hand into his, she said miserably, "Oh, how I wish you were not going away, Daniel."

"It will be great fun," Daniel said gruffly.

"No girls there anyway," Edward had muttered, giving Louise a sulky look.

She stuck her tongue out at him, ducking behind Daniel as he tried to hit her, and Daniel pushed him away with one hand, holding him at bay.

"While I'm away, Ned, leave Louise alone," he said firmly. "If I find you've been bullying her once my back is turned, I'll beat you black and blue...."

"And Papa will beat you," Edward shouted.

"Mama won't let him," Louise said triumphantly, and both boys looked at her in curiosity.

"Mama can't stop Papa hitting Daniel," Edward said scornfully. "The father always does that."

"Mama can make Papa do anything," Louise said certainly, and remembered something one of the maids had whispered once in the kitchen: "She can make him jump through hoops if she smiles at him."

Daniel's blue-green eyes smiled down at her, "Yes," he said softly. "Mama can make anyone do anything...."

Then Louise was sure she was right. Her mother was the

most powerful, as well as the most beautiful, creature in the whole world.

A year after Daniel went to school, Edward followed him, to Louise's great relief. Although the house seemed quieter and emptier without the boys, she was glad to escape Edward's scornful looks. He had left for school with a swagger, wearing his new uniform proudly, and Papa had given him a whole guinea to spend at the school tuck shop. Daniel had got a guinea, too, but it had been given brusquely, as though with resentment.

Louise settled to her quiet life without the boys quite contentedly. She now had Mama to herself—as well as a governess, a thin young woman with dull brown hair and myopic brown eyes, who seemed terrified of Papa, but adored Mama passionately. Mama had frowned, shaking her head, over the girl's cheap clothing when she arrived, then ordered a whole new wardrobe for her—not plain quiet clothes, as she had worn before, but elegant, well-made dresses in pretty colours, which gave the girl a totally changed appearance.

"Asking for trouble," Louise heard one of the maids remark as she scrubbed the kitchen floor. "Young miss will find herself an admirer and then we'll have trouble...elopements if not unwanted babies...."

Cook hushed the girl, remembering Louise's silent presence, and the subject was hurriedly changed. They bribed Louise with a piece of shortcake to hold her tongue about anything she heard, and Louise was happy to stay silent.

Leaving the kitchen, she bent to tie her trailing waist ribbon and heard in a muffled whisper, "Well, madam has no fear the master would look twice at the girl—or any other woman, come to that. Besotted is what he is. I've never known the like...."

Louise asked Mama next day, "What does 'besotted' mean, Mama?"

The bright blue eyes had opened wide. "Why do you want to know, darling?"

"I heard someone say it," Louise said evasively.

Mama's eyes delved into hers, as if she could look straight through her daughter's blue gaze and read her mind. Then she smiled softly, and said, "Shall we look it up?" Fetching a great tome of a dictionary she turned the pages. "Here we are...besotted...mental stupefaction. That is what it means."

Louise frowned. "But what does that mean, Mama?"

Papa came in then and bent to kiss her mother on her soft, smooth cheek, touching her black curls with a lingering hand. "What does what mean, Louise? I am glad to see that you have a lively curiosity."

Mama looked up at him with a strange, teasing little smile. "Louise wishes to know what besotted means, darling."

Louise was surprised to see a flush come into her father's usually pale face. His eyes switched to her briefly, then he looked back at her mother. "Where on earth did she hear that?"

"Best not to ask," Mama said softly.

"What does it mean, Papa?" Louise persisted.

Papa was staring at Mama in a strange way, his eyes filled with a smile. "It means to love someone so much one is without willpower," he said huskily. "It is a delightful form of madness, Louise, and one from which there is little hope of recovery."

Louise lay in her bed that night, thinking anxiously about her Papa. Did that mean he was going mad? Was that what the servants meant? Poor Papa.

Miss Culpepper was a good enough governess. She took her tone from her mistress like an obedient child, and taught Louise quietly, without pressure, making sure she had plenty of rest and fresh air. Each day they went for long walks in the park, or drove in the carriage with Mama. Sometimes to Louise's great joy Mama told Miss Culpepper she might take the day off, and then Mama would take Louise with her on the drive to Bristol, to pay calls and have tea with people.

One day they left the carriage and walked in a gay, flower-filled park, strolling along the gravelled paths admiring the borders of roses, carnations and pansies. Mama sat down on the stone-walled surround of a circular pool and pointed out to Louise the goldfish lurking beneath the dark green lily pads. Louise ran around the pool, gaily laughing, her short frilled skirts flying in the wind, while Mama sat on the stone wall and watched her, smiling, waving her lilac-gloved hand from time to time, to reassure Louise that she was still there.

From the other side of the pool Louise looked at her mother and thought passionately that she was undoubtedly the most beautiful person who had ever been born. In the pale lilac dress she wore, with its high collar and tight bodice, her waist was so tiny Papa could span it with both hands. Her full, swathed skirt was pinned back with a huge black bow to reveal the purple underskirt. A bunch of violets was tucked into her bodice just below her neckline, and Louise thought lovingly that they were almost the same colour as her mother's eyes.

Running back, Louise suddenly saw a man advance towards her mother and bow. Mama looked around with a start of surprise, and Louise saw her face very clearly. She looked oddly unlike herself, a faint blush coming into her cheeks. Louise had never seen the man before. He was very tall, with black hair that grew down beside his face, and he had a curved black moustache above his smiling mouth.

Louise joined them and stood there, her small feet planted apart, an odd sensation of hostility in her blue eyes. The man was looking at her mother in a way she resented, although she could not quite put her finger on what it was that annoyed her.

Taking his eyes off her mother's face, the man glanced at her, and she had a shock of surprise as she realized that his eyes were strangely familiar. They resembled Daniel's beloved eyes, and instinctively Louise softened, reminded of her brother.

"This must be Miss Louise Stonor Whitley, as I live and breathe," the man drawled. He bowed again, taking Louise by the hand, and bent to kiss her hand, taking her by such surprise that she giggled. Nobody had ever done such a thing to her before. He looked up at her, smiling again, and the charm of his smile further softened her.

His eyes slowly ran over her lifted face. He put a hand to the thick black hair beneath her small yellow hat with its cheerful feather.

"A mirror image, by God," he said below his breath.

Louise frowned. "What does that mean?"

"She asks questions and persists in finding out the answers," her Mama said to the man softly, with an odd note in her voice.

Louise sensed that the remark had hidden meanings she could not fathom, and she looked from one adult face to the other probingly.

The man looked down at her with a wry smile. "I meant, Louise, that in a mirror you might be your mother." With a hand he drew her and her Mama to the lily pool and pointed into the flat, cool green water. Louise stared intently and saw her own face reflected beside her mother's, and with a gasp of incredulous joy she saw that they were very alike. She turned and gave the man a wide, childish smile of delight. "Shall I be as beautiful as Mama when I grow up?"

The man glanced over her head at her mother. "With luck," he said lightly.

Mama rose and gave Louise her hand. "We must go," she said politely.

"Not yet, surely," the man said, in a voice that held something that sounded like mockery.

"The carriage will not be back yet, Mama," Louise said, surprised her Mama should make such a mistake. "You said I might have a turn on the swings. . . ."

"Certainly she must have a turn on the swings," the man said, taking Louise's hand. "Come, I'll push you, darling."

"Mama calls me darling," Louise said, walking contentedly beside his long striding legs. "She calls Papa darling, too, and Daniel . . ."

"She calls Papa darling, does she?" the man asked softly. "And does Papa like that?"

"Oh, Papa is besotted about Mama," Louise said cheerfully.

An odd silence followed the remark, then the man said in his drawling voice, "Her vocabulary is as extensive as her eyes are sharp."

"Servants never remember not to talk in front of little ears," Mama said drily.

"So Papa is as besotted as ever, is he?" the man asked.

"Here are the swings," Mama said quickly, and Louise ran forwards to sit on one and the man pushed her until she was swinging at just the right height, neither too high nor too low, just as she liked it. She smiled at him over her shoulder, but he was standing beside Mama, staring down at her face, and as Louise looked at them she saw him detach the pinned violets from Mama's dress and trail them softly across her lips before pinning them into his own jacket. Mama looked at him without speaking, her eyes tolerant, and Louise thought that that was just how Mama looked at Daniel, with that warm, loving indulgence.

While Louise swung, her small feet stuck out straight, she heard the two adults talking in low voices. Snatches of their conversation came to her disjointedly.

"How is my dear, dear half-brother?"

"Very well, thank you."

"You rarely go to evening parties lately. Is he keeping you in purdah?"

"Stonor prefers quiet evenings at home."

"How annoyingly uxorious of him."

Uxorious, Louise thought. What did that mean? She must ask Papa.

Mama was laughing softly at something the man said, her face alight in a way Louise had rarely seen. Turning her head to look at him, Louise said plaintively, "Will you push me again, please, sir?"

"Certainly, Miss Whitley," he said with his charming smile.

She wiggled her toes in pleasure as the swing soared upwards, holding the ropes tightly. "That's high enough," she said quickly, afraid he would push harder. "That's as high as Daniel ever pushes me."

"Do you like your brother?" the man asked her, leaning on the upright post to her left, his arms crossed.

"I love Daniel," Louise said eagerly.

"And Edward?" the man enquired drily.

Louise made a face. "He's a pig. When he is mean to me Daniel beats him. Daniel is much stronger and braver than Edward and Edward is frightened of him. Daniel is the best-looking, bravest boy in the world."

The man turned and looked at her mother with a strange, bright look, and her mother turned away with what sounded like a sigh.

"No doubt Daniel is very like your father," the man said with a queer intonation.

"Oh, no," Louise said, laughing. "He is not at all like Papa, is he, Mama? But Papa never beats him now because Mama said he must not."

The man looked at Mama with a dark frown on his face, and Mama said almost apologetically, "Stonor does his best, but Daniel is very high-spirited. He is a wild, clever boy. They are chalk and cheese. Stonor would never hurt him, though."

"My God," the man said in a thick, angry voice. "He had better not."

"How is your little girl?" Mama asked him softly, looking into his eyes.

His mouth softened into a smile. "Would you believe that

she is not unlike yours? Alice has black hair and blue Stonor eyes, and she is as wild as a young bird. Eleanor has no idea how to deal with her, so she leaves her to me.''

Mama smiled at him, then, so lovingly that Louise felt almost jealous. ''How is Eleanor?''

His smile faded. ''She's taken to drinking in secret,'' he said.

''Oh, no,'' Mama said, shocked. ''Oh, Wolfe, what have you done?''

''I? Good God, nothing. I have given her a lovely home, four beautiful children, respectability, her own carriage, jewels, fine clothes. . . and she drinks.''

''You have not tried,'' Mama said sadly. ''You might have tried.''

''Why the hell should I?'' the man said aggressively, in a masculine violence that frightened Louise. ''Can I help the way things are?''

''She loves you very much. You could have been kinder.''

''Be kind to me,'' the man said in a suddenly strange voice, staring into Mama's blue eyes intently. ''And I'll be kind to her.''

Mama stood very still, flushing. ''We must go now,'' she said, turning away. She lifted Louise from the swing, took her hand, and they walked away. The man did not follow them, although Louise could feel his eyes watch them until they were out of sight.

Two days later, while Papa was reading a book of fairy stories to her, Louise remembered that she had meant to ask him the meaning of a word. ''Papa, what does uxurious mean?'' she asked, interrupting.

Mama looked up from the embroidery she was doing, and her eyes flashed to Papa's face with an odd anxiety.

Papa smiled at Louise. ''It means that a husband loves his wife,'' he said cheerfully. ''Which is very right and proper.'' Then he looked at Mama, his eyes twinkling. ''I suppose she has been listening in the kitchen again. Can they talk of nothing else?''

''No,'' Louise said indignantly. ''The man said it. . . he said you were annoyingly uxurious.''

Papa's smile vanished and he looked at Mama, his face as stiff and pale as if he were angry. ''What man?'' he asked Mama.

''The man we met in the park in Bristol,'' Louise explained

quickly, afraid she had made him angry. "He was very tall and had black hair and his eyes were just like Daniel's."

Papa put her down from his lap abruptly. "Run back to the nursery, Louise. I will finish the story another time."

Louise looked at Mama anxiously, realizing that something was wrong. "Mama..." she said pleadingly, and Mama kissed her cheek very gently.

"Yes, darling, run back to the nursery. I will come up and kiss you good night later."

Louise dragged her feet reluctantly to the door. As it closed, she heard Papa say, "Why didn't you tell me you had seen him?"

"It was only for a few moments," Mama said. "He pushed Louise on the swing and then we went."

"But you didn't tell me," Papa said, his voice angrier than Louise had ever heard it. "How often has this happened, Sophia?"

"It was the first time," Mama said. "Don't be ridiculous, Stonor. I have not seen him for years."

"No?" Papa sounded almost as if he doubted her. "Perhaps I should ask the child what else he said. So he finds me annoyingly uxurious, does he? Do you, too, Sophia?"

"Stonor, must I make you kneel and beg forgiveness, or will you apologize for that now?" Mama asked him, her voice very soft, as if she were smiling.

There was a movement, a rustling, and with her ear against the almost closed door, Louise heard a soft laughter.

"Oh, Sophia," Papa whispered, "my darling...."

Relieved that the cloud of anger had blown away, Louise went up to the nursery. Mama was like a magician, she thought, smiling. She only had to wave her magic wand and Papa's angry growling became soft and gentle again.

When she was eight years old Papa gave Louise a new pony, a small fat dumpling of an animal with mischievous habits and dark eyes. She rode in the park that summer with Daniel and Edward, learning to jump over low hedges, with Daniel shouting instructions patiently, applauding her when she did well, sighing when she failed.

Edward made a rude face. "Oh, come on, Dan...this is boring...let's gallop through the park. Leave her to practise on her own."

"It is too dangerous," Daniel said. "You gallop, Ned. I'll stay with Louise."

"Girls make me sick," Edward said crossly, sticking his tongue out at her. "Oh, all right. You stay with her. See if I care...."

That evening, Papa shook hands with both boys before they went to bed. He smiled at Edward, and gave Daniel a brief polite nod. Louise lifted her cheeks for his kiss, thinking that he was never as nice to Daniel as he was to Edward. She dropped her spinning top in the hall as she followed her brothers, and ran back to pick it up. Bending, she heard Papa say angrily, "He gets more like him every time I see him. I think fate has an odd sense of humour, Sophia."

"Then Eleanor must laugh often when she looks at her little Alice," Mama said gently. "Because I gather she is a pure Stonor and more like our Louise than her mother...."

Papa was silent. Then he said, "Oh, God, I'm sorry, Sophia."

"Never mind, darling," Mama said comfortingly. "I know you do your best." Then she laughed softly. "Odd how the face skips from generation to generation. I've no doubt their friends think the child looks like Wolfe, just as our friends think Daniel looks like me."

"He does," Papa said quickly. "He often does."

"He is my son," Mama said.

"Forgive me, Sophia," Papa replied oddly.

Louise went up the stairs, frowning. The names they had used were vaguely familiar, but she could not place them. She was sure she had heard them before, though, but where?

The following spring she went with Mama to take tea with one of Mama's friends, Mrs. Hunt, a rather thin, stiff woman with brown hair already dusted with grey, and beady dark eyes. Her husband, Louise gathered, was very wealthy, but so recently that their beautiful new house had an over-rich elegance that Queen's Stonor, in its mellow loveliness, would never have. Seated on a deeply comfortable sofa, her feet fidgeting, Louise listened as the little circle of women talked. Mama looked at her kindly, and said, "May Louise run out and admire your beautiful rose garden, Mrs. Hunt? She has heard how fine it is...."

"Of course," Mrs. Hunt said enthusiastically. Louise had noticed long ago that all the women her mother visited were eager to please her mother, and had put this down to the charm of her mother's lovely smile.

Eagerly, she went out through the conservatory and wandered around the smartly laid out gardens, observing the stiff neatness of it all with an eye accustomed to Queen's Stonor's time-enriched loveliness. The straight, clean lines of the beds, the squared lawns with their level, green turf, the rows of shrubs and trees, were somehow dull and lifeless, unlike the wild profusion of flowers and trees at her own home.

She found the sunken rose garden and dutifully admired it for a moment, then went on to find a tall hedge, in which a rough hole gaped. Squeezing through it, Louise found herself in another garden, one with fascinating arbours and grey-bronze statuary in it. She looked around it curiously.

Wandering along the hedge she turned a corner into a wilderness of grass and apple trees. A swing hung beneath one of the trees, and she sat down on it, swinging idly for a while. Tiring of this she went back towards the hedge and began to squeeze through, catching sight of her mother coming towards her. Suddenly a hand pulled at her skirts and she turned back to find herself facing a tall, thin dark boy, who grinned at her.

"What have I caught? A gatecrasher...."

"I'm sorry," Louise said, flushing. "I was curious."

"What's your name?" the boy asked, eyeing her curiously.

"Louise Whitley," she said.

The boy's eyes opened wide, their green-blue oddly familiar. "But that's my name."

"What? Louise?" She giggled.

"No, silly. Whitley," he said impatiently.

They stared at each other. "Quick," he said, "someone's coming...come on."

Without pausing to think she followed him and he swarmed up a rope ladder into a flat tree house hidden among the branches of one of the apple trees. Louise swallowed, and he hissed, "Come on, stupid."

She followed gingerly, and he pulled the ladder up after them, and grinned at her. "There...safe aboard."

"You look just exactly like my brother Daniel," Louise said, staring in fascination.

"And you look just exactly like my sister Alice," he said, with a wide smile. "Funny, isn't it?"

Louise nodded, awed. "If we've both got the same name, maybe we're long lost relatives."

"Or something," he said. "My name's Jerome, by the way. This is my house. Where do you live?"

"Queen's Stonor," she said, her smile beatific.

"What a funny name for a house," he said, frowning. "Is it near here?"

She shook her head, but before she could answer she heard her mother calling her anxiously, a queer note in her voice, and Jerome put a hand warningly over her mouth, shaking his head at her.

She peered down through the branches of the tree and saw her mother walking below. A hand on the swing, Mama looked around, frowning. Then she hesitated and suddenly sat down on the swing, a soft chuckle of laughter coming from her. Jerome raised his dark eyebrows at Louise. "Who is it?" he whispered very softly.

"My mother," Louise whispered back.

He looked at her strangely. "She's very pretty," he said, and a sadness came into his eyes.

They stared down at Sophia. She was swinging smoothly, the full, soft dark blue of her skirts flying back to reveal her slender ankles, her small feet pointing at the sky.

Suddenly a man came through the trees and stood very still, staring at her. Louise felt a flicker of recognition. For a moment she could not recall having seen him before, then with a flash she remembered the park in Bristol and the man smiling at her mother and stealing her violets.

He came softly up behind her mother and as the swing flew back towards him, his hands caught it and held it still, while Mama bent her head back and stared at him. Louise saw the shadow of the apple tree on her mother's beautiful face. She saw the warm mouth curve into a delightful, impulsive smile, and the dark blue eyes brilliant with laughter. The man made a strange sound and bent his head, and with a shock that went right through her, Louise saw him begin to kiss her mother. She had never seen two people kiss like that, not even when Papa kissed Mama. Their mouths seemed to devour each other, and the man's hands left the swing ropes to slide around Mama's slender, inclined body and curve over her bodice in a way Louise found embarrassing.

Suddenly remembering Jerome, she turned and looked at

him, and found him watching the two below with a dark, savage scowl on his face.

When she turned back, she found her mother standing beside the swing, a hand up to hold the man away.

"No, Wolfe," she was saying unsteadily.

"You looked all of ten years old," the man said in a husky, smiling voice.

"I'm thirty-two," Mama said. "And I'm a respectable married woman, so behave yourself."

"You shouldn't smile at me like that if you want me to keep my distance," he replied. "Respectable married women shouldn't be so seductive and inviting."

"You took me by surprise," Mama said, almost ruefully.

"I'll have to do it more often."

"I'll have to be more careful," she said softly.

He grinned at her and advanced. Mama backed against the tree, shaking her head at him. "Stay where you are, Wolfe."

The man placed a hand on the trunk of the tree and leaned there, staring into Mama's face. "I thought I was dreaming when I saw you just now, swinging like a child in the sunlight. What are you doing in my garden, Sophia, apart from giving me seductive smiles?"

"I was looking for Louise," Mama said, suddenly standing straight. "I was sure I saw her through the hedge. You haven't seen her?"

"Not a sign," the man said. "Are you gossiping at Luther's house? Isn't his wife the biggest bore you ever met?"

"Poor woman, she has no taste—but she means well," Mama laughed.

"Do you like my statuary, Sophia?" the man asked with a sound of amusement in his voice.

"Very Continental," Mama said drily. "Did you buy it while you were in Italy?"

"Yes," he said. "There's an insect on your neck. Keep still."

Peering down, Louise saw him softly brush something from Mama's throat, then his hand returned to it and moved round under Mama's thick black hair, stroking her skin.

"Stop it, Wolfe," Mama said sharply.

The man leaned forwards very slowly and began to kiss her again, and suddenly Mama gave a groan and her arms went up round the man's neck and she seemed to sway towards him as if she were fainting.

The man caught her against him, and the kiss went on and on while Louise felt a pain in the pit of her stomach and knew she was going to be violently sick in a minute. Her face had become very flushed and she was shivering.

Then Mama pulled away, gasping softly, and the man looked down at her and said in a very deep voice, "My dearest love, my dearest love...."

"I've got to go," Mama said, pushing him away.

"Sophia," the man said in that strange voice. "We've got to see each other. I've barely seen you for the past ten years. How many times have we even exchanged a word? Stonor keeps you locked away as if he was afraid someone would steal you."

Mama said nothing, and the man laughed harshly. "And someone damned well would if you would come," he said.

"It is over, Wolfe. Long ago. Don't try to breathe on the ashes." Mama sounded angry.

"Ashes?" The man threw back his head and laughed, but there was no amusement in his voice, and his face had a dark look to it. "You know as well as I do that the flames are fiercer than ever. You can keep them covered nearly all the time, Sophia. You can fool Stonor all you like. But just once in a while I catch a glimpse of them, and whoever else you may fool, you can't fool me. I know you. God, if I don't, who does? We were forged in the same fire. Your mind is as familiar to me as my own. You don't even have to speak. I know what you are thinking, what you are feeling, and by God, Sophia, I know what you want."

"Then you know that I want to make Stonor happy," Mama said. "I want to keep my children safe and secure. I want to see Queen's Stonor every morning when I wake up and be certain that it is always the most beautiful place in the world."

"Damn Queen's Stonor," the man said, and his voice surged with rage. "I could burn the place down happily."

"I would not let you," Mama said, and she smiled, but without her usual sweetness. "I would not let you harm or hurt anything of mine, and you know you would not dare to try, Wolfe."

"Wind Stonor around your little finger as if he were a skein of silk," the man said strangely. "But you will not do that with me."

Mama was silent, staring at him. When she next spoke her voice was totally unfamiliar to Louise, a strange pulsing ex-

citement in it. "I can make you do whatever I want you to
do," Mama said, as if she were giving him a provocative challenge.

The man lifted Mama's hand and bent his head over it, kissing the palm, turning it up and dropping light kisses in the
small pink hollow. "My dearest love," he whispered. "Don't
you think I know that? Just as I know that you hold me deliberately, despite your pretence that you have let me go. You
want us all—Stonor, myself, the house—but at least you give
Stonor and the house a part of yourself. Me, you refuse to
give anything to, except a look, a smile, enough to keep me
waiting like a lost dog, Sophia, but not enough to satisfy any
man."

"Then go," Mama said softly. "How many times must I
tell you?"

He dropped her hand and stared at her without speaking,
and Louise could not see his face because of the shadows the
tree threw over it.

Mama moved away, her skirt rustling, and the man stared
after her, his black head lifted, the faint streaks of silver
among his thick hair shimmering in the spring sunlight.

Suddenly he said to Mama's departing back, "Shall I give
Eleanor your compliments? If she is sober enough to understand me."

Mama halted and looked back at him. "Oh, God,
Wolfe. . . be kind to Eleanor. I like her so much, and she is
your wife, the mother of your children."

"Not all mine," the man said oddly.

"Don't," Mama said quickly.

"At least I do not beat my little Alice," the man said.

"I am glad of that," Mama said, smiling. "I should hope
not."

"She reminds me too much of you," the man said. "Every
time I look at her I see your lovely face and I want to kiss
her." A pause, then he asked, "Do you kiss Daniel?"

Mama flushed. "He is growing very tall, Wolfe. Almost as
tall as myself, now. I feel quite old when my big son sits beside
me."

"Does Stonor hate him?" the man asked abruptly.

Mama sighed. "He irritates Stonor, I'm afraid, Daniel
is. . ."

"Too much like me?" asked the man sarcastically.

Mama sighed again. "Far too much." She halted as she

turned again, and said sadly, "Wolfe, please, try to be kinder to Eleanor. A few smiles cost nothing. You married her. It is your duty to be good to her, and she deserves much better than you have given her."

"Oh, God, I know that," the man said, his tone irritable. "I cannot change my nature."

"Perhaps if you kept your mistresses less openly it would help," Mama said in a voice that, for her, sounded quite sharp.

"You have long ears," the man said softly, mockingly.

"All of Bristol is aware of them," Mama said.

"And Stonor makes sure you hear every word of gossip," the man retorted.

"I hear it through other channels," Mama said. "Stonor is not mean-minded." She gave an odd laugh. "And anyway, he never mentions you to me if he can avoid it."

"I can believe that," the man said, laughing at her.

"Kind friends doubtless make certain Eleanor hears the gossip too," Mama said. "If you must take these women, do it more discreetly."

"What a wife you would make me, Sophia," the man said with a slight drawl filled with mockery. "You would turn a blind eye to my pleasures, would you, so long as I was discreet?"

"You would not need them if I were your wife," Mama said.

"No," the man said huskily. "No, my dearest love, I would not—which is why I am as kind as I can be to Eleanor. She has all I have to give her. I can give her no more."

"For your children's sake you must try to," Mama said. "Think of your sons. What must they think of you? Boys adore their mother."

"I've no doubt your boys do, but mine. . . I think not."

"Nonsense," Mama said almost fiercely. "Jerome was a dear little boy, devoted to his mother."

"Jerome," the man said with a sigh. "He is the most like me. He has my eyes."

"Is he at school?"

"He has been, but he was expelled last term for smoking in the school grounds," the man said and laughed. "The little devil was stupid enough to get caught."

Mama laughed. "He sounds like Daniel. Daniel is forever in hot water. He is as wild as a hill pony and twice as much

trouble as my other two children put together. I see Stonor
looking at him and thinking that it is his bad blood that makes
him that way...."

"No doubt it is," the man said softly. "My sons are all out
of the same mould." There was a silence, then he said, "I
have seen him, you know. I saw him during the summer at a
cricket match. Stonor was with him and ignored me, but I got
a look at the boy, and he is amazingly like me." He laughed.
"God, how that must infuriate Stonor."

"More and more it maddens him," Mama said sadly. "He
began by loving him, but as he grows more like you Stonor almost hates him."

"Well, I shall always love my little Alice," Wolfe said
mockingly. "You asked me once if I was less of a man than
Stonor because I refused to accept the child, but it seems I am
proving him superior in this matter."

"Your reasons are different," Mama said.

"Yes," came the reply. "I love her because she looks like
you."

Mama turned away. "Goodbye, Wolfe," she said softly.
The slow rustle of her skirt among the grass disappeared. The
man sat down on the swing and idly moved back and forth,
his head bent, staring at the grass. Softly, he whispered,
"Goodbye, my dearest love...." Then he got up and walked
away.

The moment he was out of sight Louise got up and scram-
bled down the rope ladder. Jerome whispered, "Hey,
wait..." then stopped as, bending in the grass, Louise was
violently sick for several minutes.

When she had finished, she began to cry. Jerome hesitantly
put an arm around her and led her into the dense shade of a
cluster of the trees, pushing her down onto the grass. He
sprawled beside her, chewing a long stem of grass, staring at
nothing.

"What did you make of all that?" he asked her.

Louise cried softly.

"Oh, stop it, you little fathead," he said scornfully.
"Come on, what did you make of it? I tell you what, we *are*
relatives, you know. Your father must be something to do
with mine, having the same name, and us all looking so
alike...."

Louise looked at him with tear-drenched violet eyes. "I hate
your father. He is beastly and...and I hate him."

"He's a bastard," Jerome said agreeably. "I know that because I heard the servants talking."

"What do you mean?" Louise stared, baffled.

"It means his parents weren't married," Jerome said. "I looked it up once." He looked darkly angry. "And he's rotten to my mother."

"My mother will make him be nicer to her," Louise said.

"Your mother's a whore," Jerome said, getting up.

"Oh!" Louise stood up, staring at him, her face growing more hectically flushed. "You pig!" She knew what that word meant. She had heard it before in the kitchen and in a context that had enlightened her without recourse to a dictionary.

"Kissing my father like that. Flirting with him. Letting him call her his dearest love..." Jerome sounded as if he felt as sick as she did and his eyes were black with rage. "Who does she think she is? Telling my father to be kind to my mother in that patronizing way? They made me sick, both of them, with their kissing and looking at each other.... I'll tell my mother and she'll throw a bottle at him. She did once. He ducked and it went through a window and he was very angry."

"Your mother is sick," Louise said with certainty. "My mother would never do such a thing. If my father gets angry my mother only has to smile at him and say, 'Oh, Stonor,' and he starts to smile back and kiss her...."

Jerome looked at her furiously. "The way she did to my father just now, you mean—twisting him round her little finger, he said. And she said she could make him do anything she wanted. I hate women like that."

"I love my mother," Louise said, beginning to cry. "Everyone loves my mother. Papa does, and Daniel does, and the servants do—they say Papa is besotted with her. She's soft and warm and loving and she smells of French perfume and when she walks she rustles. And when she laughs you feel like laughing, too."

"I hate her," Jerome said sickly.

"You hate her because she isn't your mother," Louise said angrily.

And then Jerome hit her hard across her face, and she was so taken aback that for a second she just stared. Then she ran crying across the garden and dived through the hedge again. She was still crying when she got to the house and Mama and Mrs. Hunt's servants were anxiously searching for her.

"Darling, what's wrong?" Mama asked anxiously, turning a pale, frightened face towards her. "Where have you been?"

"I climbed a tree over there and fell down and hurt my face," Louise said, pointing towards a clump of trees behind the neat vegetable garden.

She saw relief in her mother's eyes as she told her the first real lie she had ever told in her life, then Mama put her arms around her and cuddled her, and Louise felt her nostrils fill with that sweet, musky perfume Mama always wore, and she pushed herself against Mama's warm, slender body and cried without stopping.

# CHAPTER TWENTY

Louise remembered the summer of 1887 for the rest of her life as a peculiar time of mingled delight and misery. It was a heavenly interlude, during which time she spent every waking hour of the day in Daniel's company. At home from school, he seemed to have shot up overnight, a long-legged sixteen-year-old with a thin, gawky body and a voice that ranged oddly from high to low in a sentence. He found this maddening, and flushed each time it happened, but Louise was impressed by the occasional hoarse masculinity of his tone. Edward had been invited to London to visit their Aunt Elizabeth for a few weeks to keep her son, James, company. Her invitation had included both boys, but Papa had sent Edward alone, a decision that had delighted both Daniel and Louise, and one that Louise suspected strongly had emanated in the beginning from Mama. Mama knew very well how deeply Louise adored her brother Daniel, and she seemed happy to see them together. It was a content not shared by Papa, Louise soon realized. When she and Daniel met him, riding in the park on the ponies, or talking as they walked in the gardens, Papa would eye them with an unsmiling severity that puzzled Louise, almost as if he resented and was jealous of her love for Daniel.

While Edward was away, Thomas, Luther Hunt's eldest son, would turn fourteen, and his proud parents decided to throw a very grand, grown-up party for him, to which the Whitleys were invited as a matter of course. There was no party given in the Bristol neighbourhood to which the owners of Queen's Stonor were not invited. Louise had lately begun to realize the beauty and fame of the house in which she lived. Born and bred there, she had not been aware for a long time of how the house was regarded. The great, dark-beamed hall with its suits of armour, the wide staircases, the high-ceilinged rooms with their tall windows looking out over the park, were sufficiently admired for people to wander past and gape in awed delight during the summer. Papa had spent a large part of his fortune in maintaining the house at its finest, and the elegant furniture he had bought added fresh lustre to Queen's Stonor's mellow beauty. The possession of it gave the Whitley family a position in local society which no amount of wealth could otherwise have done. Sophia Whitley, as a direct descendent of the family who had owned it for generations, was treated almost as a queen, and her husband's notorious adoration of her, combined with her own well-preserved beauty, made her position well-nigh unassailable.

Sophia took Louise to a Bristol dressmaker to have a special dress made for the Hunt party. Louise sat on a small gilt chair, watching excitedly as Mama chose materials and patterns, smiling at the eager dressmaker, her slender body graceful as she bent to inspect the cloth offered to her. Louise knew now that Mama was almost thirty-three. Her birthday fell in September, and Papa, was already planning to celebrate it with a ball at Queen's Stonor, although Mama smilingly protested. "At my age there is nothing to celebrate in becoming a year older, Stonor," she had said, and Papa had looked at her with that special, melting look and shaken his head. "A year more beautiful," he had said softly, and Mama had laughed.

It astonished Louise to consider that her mother was thirty-two. Looking at her as she moved to and fro, her movements so elegant and graceful, Louise marvelled that she should still look so lovely. Age seemed to add to her, rather than detract. The fine-boned delicacy of her small features grew yearly more pronounced. The black hair had no tinge of grey. The blue eyes were as brilliant as ever, although fine lines of laughter and tenderness radiated from them now in a strong sunlight.

When they left the shop Mama announced gaily that they would eat some ice cream in a smart nearby tea shop, so they crossed the road, weaving through the carriages and wagons, to enter the gold and white rooms and sit at a table, slowly savouring the creamy white food in silver bowls into which fan-shaped wafers had been pushed. Louise shut her eyes, her mouth full of melting cold sweetness, a beatific smile on her face.

When she opened them she glimpsed a woman with gaudy red hair and an over-bright green dress leading a girl of her own colouring past the table. Louise saw Mama glance away, and was astonished and puzzled by the glacial, sharp-mouthed look the other woman gave Mama. Surely Mama could not know such a common person, she thought, staring at the rich yet vulgar style and colour of the woman's clothes. As she stared the woman glanced at her, and Louise saw a peculiar stunned glaze come into her face. She had a high colouring, a fine network of blue veins on her cheeks and nose, and something sad in her green eyes that made Louise uncomfortable.

The little girl with her was about Louise's own height and age, her dress far more pretty and suitable than the one her mother wore. She dropped a meshwork purse on the floor, bending to pick it up, and Louise saw her face for a few seconds, and was immediately aware of its resemblance to her own, and with that awareness came another sudden thought, a memory of sick anger and bewilderment in a sunlit garden, of puzzling words and looks, of a tall, dark man holding her mother in his arms and kissing her in a terrifying way, which Mama not only seemed not to resent but seemed to enjoy.

Mama got up quietly and Louise followed her from the tea room, her mind occupied with the strangers she had seen. All the way home Mama was quiet, gazing out of the windows with a withdrawn, sad expression, and Louise kept her thoughts to herself.

The party at the Hunts' house was given on a warm late summer afternoon. Parents were invited to stay and take tea with the Hunt parents while their children took part in the celebration in the marble-floored room set aside for them and cleared of all its fine, expensive, vulgar furniture.

Daniel was scathing as he and Louise watched some of the younger children running and sliding on the floor. Thomas Hunt, Daniel's junior by two years, was a stockily built boy of vigorous character and a slightly intense nature. Intelligent, forceful, he organized the party with his bellowing voice, irritably aware of Daniel Whitley's sarcastic smile. At sixteen Daniel had a personality not easy to ignore. He was becoming darkly good-looking, his features distinct with arrogance and pride, put down by his enemies to his birth as heir to Queen's Stonor.

Thomas and Daniel did not hit it off together. Both boys were inclined to dominate the company they kept, and together they were like two aggressive young stags, butting their heads together in an attempt to achieve supremacy. Thomas gave Louise a flushed grin as he sorted the younger children into a separate group.

"We could dance if you played for us, Louie—"

"Her name is Louise," Daniel said, resenting this use of his own personal nickname for her.

Thomas ignored him. He seized her hand, dragging her away from Daniel's side. "Come on, Louie—you play very well. A polka would be best—"

Flushing angrily, Daniel caught him by his collar, shaking him as if he were a dog. "Let go of my sister, Hunt—"

Thomas turned a hot, angry face on him, and shoved his hands away. The next moment both boys were locked in a struggle the more savage for being inexplicable and unrestrained. The room fell into silence as they fought, and Louise, unable to bear it, fled from them into the silent hall. The adults, mainly women, were drinking tea in the drawing room. She heard their high-pitched social voices as they sipped tea and talked their polite small talk. Louise stood, looking around, then slipped through a small ante-chamber into the glass-domed conservatory that ran the whole length of the great house. In here it was quiet and shadowy. She pushed her slender body into a gap between a tall palm in a green pot and the angle of the wall, a sick sob in her heart. Violence terrified her. Edward's spiteful attentions in their childhood had always had this result, making her hide in misery until Daniel found her and comforted her.

For a few moments she cowered, shivering, wondering what was happening between Daniel and Thomas. Although she would never dare admit it to Daniel, she liked Thomas, who whenever they were alone showed her a side of his character he kept well hidden in company. Thomas's liking for her was part of his charm, in fact. It was flattering when he smiled at her and told her things she knew he would never tell anyone else. It was a secret relationship she knew Daniel would resent, and since in a straight choice between the two there was no doubt in her mind that she would choose Daniel, she kept her liking for Thomas a secret.

She had just recovered enough to think of sneaking back to see what had happened, when she heard the slow rustle of skirts and peered through the palm leaves shyly to see, with a joyous relief, that the newcomer was her Mama. Softly Louise watched her, smiling, enjoying as she always did that strong sensation of pleasure in her mother's beauty and warmth.

The white and green printed dress Mama wore was so tightly fitting that her slender body seemed to sway like a flower stem in it, and her black hair was as bright in the sunlight as a blackbird's wing, catching the light and reflecting it like a dark glass.

Louise was about to run out and hug her when she heard another step. Mama did not turn round. She stood beside a row of pots, her thin white fingers almost nervously plucking the leaves.

Louise felt that queer sick feeling in her stomach as she recognized the man. She gathered up her courage to run out and surprise them, feeling an urgent need to interfere between them before they even looked at each other.

Before she could move, Mama spoke, without even looking around, as if her senses told her who was standing behind her. "You should not be here."

"I brought Alice to tea with her cousins," he said softly. "Did you think they would not invite her? You forget, Luther is not only my cousin, but he is also my partner."

"Go back to your own house now," Mama said, still standing with her back to him, her voice very low. "We must not be seen alone together."

"When are we ever alone together?" the man asked sardonically. "A few times in a few years. A word. A look. The last time was two months ago at the theatre, and then you never looked in my direction once, in case Stonor noticed it."

"Go away, Wolfe," Mama said quietly. "Don't make me angry with you."

The man moved, pulling her around to face him, his hands on her shoulders. "God," he said in a hoarse voice. "Be as angry as hell, Sophia, because you know I've got to do it." Then his mouth was consuming Mama in the same hungry way that Louise had been so shocked by before, and Mama was pushing at his chest with both hands, twisting in his arms, before suddenly, without warning, going so limp Louise thought she had fainted. The slender white-and-green-clothed body fell against the man's hard figure, and Mama's arms went round his neck. The silence was so deafening Louise could hear the sick beat of her own heart and the distant song of birds in the garden.

Mama suddenly seemed to pull herself away, breathing very quickly, her bodice rising and falling, her blue eyes very bright in her white face.

The two adults stared at each other for a long time. Then Mama turned and walked away quickly. The man leaned against the cold glass windows, his hands clenched, and

Louise had a horrified feeling he was crying. She had seen Daniel in just that attitude now and then, bitterly fighting down tears, his thin body vulnerable in a moving way. Daniel hated above everything to be seen to any emotion. He hid everything if he could—his love for Mama, for Louise, his pain when he was hurt, his instinctive knowledge that Papa did not love him. Now she stared at the man's lean back and silvered dark hair, and felt the same compulsive, wild emotions inside him that she had felt in Daniel, and it frightened her deeply. Adults were stronger, more in control, than children. Men had no business to be as weak as this, she thought, her face alarmed.

The man turned, his face a stiff mask, no emotion showing now, and then he too vanished. After a while Louise stole out of the conservatory and returned to the party. Searching around the crowded room she found the girl for whom she had been looking and stared at her intently. The girl looked around and stared back. Louise walked over to her and said, "You're Alice Whitley, aren't you?"

The girl's blue eyes, so like her Mama's, smiled curiously. "Yes. Who are you?"

"I am Louise Whitley," she said, holding out her hand. "How do you do? I've met your brother Jerome."

Alice smiled then, her small teeth very even. "Jerome is reading in the corner," she said. "He hates parties and he only came because Papa made him."

Louise looked at her, flushing. Then Alice pulled her by the hand into a corner behind one of the floor-length silken curtains, pulling it back to reveal Jerome, curled up on the deep window seat, reading a large book in which Louise could see etchings of human bones.

"Whatever are you reading?" she asked him, so fascinated that she forgot everything else.

Jerome looked at her, and in his blue-green eyes she saw the hardness of recognition. "Anatomy," he said flatly.

"Why are you reading that?"

"Because I'm going to be a doctor," he said, his mouth obstinate.

"Papa will not let him," Alice confided. "He wants Jerome to be a partner in the firm."

"I am going to be a doctor and Papa can go to hell," Jerome said in a harsh voice. Then he looked at Louise and she saw that hardness in his bright beautiful eyes. "Is your Mama here?"

She stared back at him, flushing. "Yes."

He smiled, his lip curling. "So is my Papa," he said, and his tone had a nasty ring. He glanced at Alice sideways. "Fetch me a glass of that lemonade, Alice, will you?" The casual authority of the tone made it plain that Alice was his slave, and the ease with which she obeyed him underlined it.

Louise sat down beside Jerome, arranging her pretty flower-sprinkled skirts elegantly. He turned and looked at her, speaking very softly. "I've found out all about our families, you know. Have you?"

She shook her head, frightened at what he might tell her.

"Our fathers are half-brothers," Jerome said. "My father was illegitimate, though, and your father threw him out of their home when their father died. A real swine, your father. They hate each other like hell. That's why we've never met, even though your father does a lot of business with my Uncle Luther. Uncle Luther is my father's cousin and they're partners, you see, so in a way our fathers deal with each other, although indirectly. But it is a family feud, all the same."

Louise was indignant. "Papa is not a swine." Her face grew more flushed. "And he certainly would not try to...to touch...your mother the way your father does mine...."

"It may interest you to hear that my father can get any woman he wants by snapping his fingers," Jerome said hotly. "Your mother likes it when he kisses her. You saw that as well as I did."

"He shouldn't do it," Louise said with a cry of pain and shame. "My Papa loves my Mama so much—"

"That's probably why he does it," Jerome said sneeringly. "Papa likes to hurt and he knows exactly how to hurt most." His eyes had a brooding, bitter look. "He hurts my mother. One day I'll hurt him."

"Is that why you won't go into his firm?" she asked shrewdly.

Jerome grinned coldly. "I want to be a doctor anyway, but if it annoys Papa, that's all the better."

Louise stared down at her small black shoes. "Does Alice know?"

"That there's a family feud and we have half-cousins who live at Queen's Stonor, yes," Jerome said. "I've never told her about your Mama...."

Louise looked at him in gratitude. "Don't, please..."

"Do you think I want to?" Jerome's mouth twisted. "It made me sick."

Louise said politely, "I saw your Mama the other day, I think, with Alice in a tea shop. You are nothing like her, are you?"

Jerome looked sullen. "None of us are," he said. "We are all Papa's children." He gave Louise an odd look. "Except Alice. . . and she looks just like you, doesn't she?"

"Just like me," Louise agreed. "We could be sisters."

Jerome's eyes watched her in that curious, secretive way. "So you could," he said.

Daniel came up to them at that moment, his left cheek flushed and bearing a dark graze. Louise exclaimed in pity and sorrow. "Oh, Daniel. Did Thomas do that?"

"He's in the bathroom washing," Daniel said, grinning. "His nose is bleeding all over the place." The fight seemed to have pleased him, and Louise gave him a reproving look.

"It is his birthday, after all. You shouldn't have fought him."

Daniel glanced at Jerome and then looked again, a frown on his face.

Jerome gave him a cold, unfriendly smile. "Hallo, Cousin Daniel."

Daniel looked stunned, and then Louise had to explain the whole thing to him, carefully leaving out any reference to her Mama.

Oddly Daniel seemed taken with his newfound cousin. They fell into swaggering talk, grinning secretly over some of the illustrations in Jerome's book, and Louise was jealous until Thomas came and asked her again to play the piano so that they could have dancing, then she went and sat down on the velvet piano stool, playing a succession of polkas while Thomas leaned on the piano and turned the music for her, watching her small fingers fly and staring at her pale, pretty profile. Looking up at him once, Louise met his eyes and smiled, her wide impulsive smile, which she was unaware was the image of her mother's, and Thomas smiled back without speaking, as if they were such old friends that there was no need for them to talk. The rest of the party went so happily that she had no time to notice Daniel and Jerome in permanent, secret talk on the window seat, or to be jealous that her darling brother should like the company of someone other than herself. Only as she finished playing did she think, looking at them, that the family likeness between them was so strongly marked they could almost be twins, although Jerome was several years younger than Daniel.

Several days later as Daniel and Louise rode in the shadowy depths of the park they met Jerome on a black pony. He hailed them cheerfully, waving his cap, and Daniel grinned back at him.

"What is he doing here?" Louise asked in amazement.

"Visiting us," Daniel said. "Oh, look, Louie, just because our parents keep up some silly old feud doesn't mean we can't be friends, does it? I like Jerome and it will be fun to have company now and then."

Louise was disturbed, shaken and jealous at these words, but as the afternoon wore on she relaxed in Jerome's company. His earlier hostility and sullen moods had gone. He was friendly, open and cheerful with Daniel, and gradually Louise grew to like him too. Over the following weeks before Daniel returned to school, Jerome came often and they saw him each time with pleasure. A firm friendship grew between the two boys, as if they shared something beyond mere distant kinship. Louise might have felt left out of it had Jerome not adopted Daniel's attitude to her. Unlike Edward he never tried to exclude her or complain of her presence. He seemed, indeed, to enjoy it, and when he spoke of his sister, Alice, Louise guessed that he and Alice had a relationship as close as Daniel and she did.

It was understood by the three that they would keep Jerome's visits entirely secret. They always met and played out of sight of the house, and none of them risked any reference that might be picked up in their homes. Their summer friendship, to Louise, had a golden light that was compounded partly of the long, warm days, the scent of the grass and the trees and partly of the intimate secret they shared, giving their friendship a mixture of danger and excitement that made it special, and that made Louise more sad than ever when Daniel and Jerome both returned to school. But alone in the great, beautiful house she saw more of her Mama, and was pleased to find herself encouraged to become a companion to her in the afternoons.

The morning of Mama's thirty-third birthday dawned bright and crisp. The leaves on the oaks were beginning to turn yellow and the air had a wine-like coolness. The ball that evening was to be the event of the year. The great hall at Queen's Stonor had been polished until it shone, the floor had been cleared for the dancing, and there were brilliant flowers everywhere. An orchestra was coming to play. Caterers moved into the kitchens, annoying and offending the staff. An excited thrill ran through the house as the day wore on.

Mama had had an exquisite new ball gown fashioned, in a cream silk so smooth and soft it clung to her slender body like a second skin, the underskirt of embossed matching satin ending in a short train. The neckline was very low, draped across her pale shoulders, plunging so that Louise blushed to see the soft skin of her mother's breasts just visible, their high shape separated by a shadowy hollow that somehow made her look almost embarrassingly alluring, even to Louise's eyes. The new growing pressure of awakening adolescence had given Louise a frankly curious view of her mother's beauty, an awareness of the way her father looked at her mother when he thought himself unobserved. Under her calf-length short skirts, Louise was sensitive to the changes beginning in her own body. Her flat chest had swelled with small buds of breasts, which made her hot with shame. Her skin had a new tendency to burst into bright flushes. She was angrily aware of the ending of childhood and resistant to the coming of the future.

She had heard her parents arguing about the ball for weeks, and she knew on the morning of it that one of the causes of their arguments had been her mother's insistence on inviting Papa's half-brother and his wife. The realization was borne in on her as she heard her father say in a savage, bitter way, "If you think twelve years will have made any difference to him, you're mad, Sophia. How do you think he sees this invitation, the first we've ever sent him? What the hell do you think he sees behind it?"

Mama sighed. "We could not exclude him and Eleanor, darling. You conveniently ignore the fact that you trade cheerfully enough with Luther and Wolfe. If you invite Luther, you must invite Wolfe."

"I do not see any necessity for it," Papa growled. "Everyone knows there's no friendship between us. People would not expect it."

"Eleanor is rarely invited anywhere these days," Mama said oddly. "Do you think she does not feel that? With everyone coming to our ball, she would feel we had insulted her."

Papa sounded angrily embarrassed. "She's not invited anywhere for a damned good reason. Lately her drinking has become an open scandal, and the clothes she wears are more like a whore's than those of a respectable married woman... which is no doubt why she buys them—to annoy and embarrass him.''

Mama sighed again. ''All the same, we had to invite them. I do not imagine they will come, however. Eleanor would not dream of doing so, I imagine. But at least she could display the invitation card on her mantelpiece so that everyone knows they were invited. That will do no harm.''

''He'll come,'' Papa said hoarsely. ''You know he will. And I shall have to shake his damned hand in my own house and pretend I wouldn't like to beat his brains in.''

Louise had heard no more because, eavesdropping outside the morning-room window, she saw one of the maids staring at her through the scullery window and pretended to be taking a stone out of her shoe before walking on through the garden. She felt a queer prickle of sick excitement at the thought that Wolfe Whitley was coming to Queen's Stonor. She wished Jerome and Daniel were there so that she could discuss it with them, but she dared not even write of it to Daniel because although her parents never read her letters to him, she knew that the masters at his school had no such compunction.

Mama came to her bedroom that evening before she went down to greet her guests in the hall, and Louise adoringly gazed at her in her clinging cream silk. Mama opened the black, almond-blossom-scattered fan she bore and fanned herself elegantly, smiling teasingly at her daughter.

''Well? Will I do?''

''Oh, Mama,'' Louise said softly, knowing there was no way she could tell her mother just how lovely she looked.

Apparently, Mama read her voice and face clearly enough, however, because her blue eyes smiled tenderly back and she kissed Louise before she turned to go.

Louise crept out onto the minstrels' gallery later, hearing the music begin, and saw the guests arriving, met at the door by Papa and Mama. In his evening suit Papa looked very handsome, she thought, even though his fair brown hair was rapidly thinning and turning grey. He smiled, shaking hands, speaking, while Mama gracefully stood beside him.

Suddenly Louise saw a never-to-be-forgotten face and a pair of wide shoulders in the doorway. She sensed the peculiar excitement that ran through the hall as Wolfe Whitley, darkly handsome in evening clothes and with the silver threads in his

hair shining in the lamplight, moved forward to shake hands
with Papa. Papa looked so stiff and cold he barely seemed
able to speak. Wolfe Whitley eyed him insolently, his dark
head arrogantly tilted back, a mocking smile on his strong
mouth. Louise saw at once that he was alone, as Mama had
predicted. His wife had not come. Then he moved past Papa
towards Mama and Louise felt a hot tightness in the pit of her
stomach.

She could sense it in her Papa, too, in the taut unsmiling
way his grey eyes followed his half-brother's dark figure as he
bent slowly, his eyes on Mama's politely smiling face, and
carefully, slowly, taking his time, kissed her hand.

It was over in a second. He had moved on, but Louise could
feel the reverberations of it inside herself, inside her Mama
and inside Papa. Everyone else seemed unaware of it. The
family feud had been a topic of gossip for years. Now Wolfe
Whitley's presence in this house seemed to have ended it. It
was logical enough. With his partner and cousin, Luther
Hunt, he had been financially involved with his half-brother
for some years. Tonight conferred respectability on the business relationship, which had been almost furtive until tonight.

The other guests flowed on past host and hostess until all
had arrived. The dancing was general, the beautifully gowned
and jewelled women sweeping around in their partners' arms
among the massed flowers and glittering chandeliers.

Secure in her hiding place in the minstrels' gallery Louise
sat on the floor, her chin in her hands, her long white nightgown warm enough, watching, entranced as the couples slid
fluidly around the hall. There were two large mirrors hanging
on the walls, reflecting the dancing, reflecting the light of the
chandeliers and the flowers. As the air grew warmer the scent
of the flowers rose headily to Louise's nostrils, and the evening had a fairy-tale brilliance for her as she observed it in
secret.

Then suddenly she saw Wolfe Whitley walk slowly towards
her Mama, who was laughing in a circle that included Luther
Hunt and his wife. Mama was unconscious of his approach,
but Louise, looking anxiously around for her Papa, saw him
already dancing with a plump young woman in a bilious yellow gown, staring fixedly across the room towards them.

As the dark head loomed beside her, Mama turned very
slowly, fanning herself as if nervous.

Louise saw the bright look of Wolfe Whitley's eyes as he

spoke. Mama smiled very politely, shaking her head, fanning herself and gesturing. Louise saw Wolfe Whitley's eyes narrow and flicker dangerously, and even at that distance she could feel his anger. He bowed, moving away, and looking at Papa, Louise saw his face almost collapse with relief as if he had held his muscles tense while the brief exchange went on.

The supper interval was announced. The couples left the hall in a smiling, chattering throng. Mama and Papa led them, arm in arm, and Papa looked lovingly down at Mama as he walked beside her.

Louise sat dreamily, her hands around her knees, staring at the quiet empty hall. The musicians had stopped playing. They were eating and drinking, wiping their hot faces. From the supper room came a babble of laughter and talk, the clatter of knives and plates. And it was over an hour later that they all returned and the music began again.

There was a new atmosphere, Louise sensed, staring down at them all. The men had flushed faces, the women's smiles and laughter were easier. The champagne that had flowed during the supper interval had softened them all. Some of the older men withdrew to play bridge in the card room. The dancing grew more hectic and livelier. Louise saw Papa slip out to play a hand or two of bridge with some of his business partners, and she saw Mama, in one pair of arms after another, whirling lightly, provocatively, her cream silk dress giving her swaying body a supple smoothness that denied her thirty-three years.

Fanning herself, laughing, she sat out and watched for one long bout of dancing, then as the music began again she was face to face with Wolfe Whitley, and Louise felt that nervous prickle inside herself again. This time Papa was not watching, not aware, and Louise knew with a sinking heart that although Mama did not speak as the man extended his hand, this time she was not going to make a polite excuse.

She felt her skin grow hot, as though in bright sunlight, and her stomach muscles tighten nauseously. Mama swayed in the strong dark arms and said no word to him. He stared over the bare, creamy shoulders against which the soft silk lay so closely, and his face was controlled and expressionless. To the rest of the room it might look as if Mama and he danced a polite duty dance, hardly caring to speak to each other. But to Louise that dance was endless. The music gaily played, the couples revolved, the mirrors reflected brightness and beauty, and in Wolfe Whitley's possessive arms her Mama seemed to dance in a trance. Louise knew then that she hated Wolfe Whitley beyond any feeling she had ever had in her life before. She hated him because of the danger he presented to herself, to Papa, and most of all to Mama. She hated him because Mama looked so unfamiliar, so withdrawn, as though he had stolen her into a world they shared alone. He turned his head briefly, looking down at Mama's face, and Mama looked up at him, as unsmiling as he was, her blue eyes so brilliant they seemed like blue stones. Then slowly his blue-green eyes ran lower, touching the smooth sheen of Mama's throat and shoulders, delving into the shadowy hollow between her visible breasts. Louise blushed hotly, but Mama merely looked up at him, her lids half-closed, as though the way he was looking at her were a caress she enjoyed, and her small white hand, clasped on his dark shoulder, softly moved, her fingertips in their gloves pressing down on him.

When the dance ended he took a long time to release Mama. She smiled, a cool, polite movement of the mouth without expression, and she walked her back towards the walls against which rows of chairs were arranged. Mama sat down, and he bowed, still not speaking, then he turned and walked away. It was almost discourteous. He should have sat down, or brought Mama a glass of lemonade, or stood talking to her. His withdrawal seemed to Louise so much a part of the whole queer terrifying intimacy between him and her Mama that she pressed a balled fist into her mouth and shook. She turned and fled back to her own room then, and lay in bed, shivering, excited, angry, anxious.

The ball went on below for hours. It was in the early hours of the morning that Louise heard her parents' voices, low and yet filled with anger.

"Did you have to dance with him? For God's sake, couldn't you have refused?"

"I refused once. To refuse again would have been too pointed," Mama said softly.

Louise slid out of bed and crept along the landing, the coarse matting beneath her feet prickling her bare skin. She listened at their bedroom door, shivering.

"You waited until I was not there to see it," Papa said, his voice shaking.

"He waited," Mama said, and there was that strange thread in her voice that came only when she spoke of Wolfe Whitley.

"Oh, God, he waited, yes," Papa groaned. "He has been waiting all these years. Do you think I don't feel him like the shadow of my own grave behind me? Waiting, waiting.... He will never give you up...."

"He will never get me," Mama said, and she laughed softly. "Stonor, when will you learn to trust me?"

"You still love him," Papa said wildly.

"Have I ever lied to you and said I didn't?" Mama asked him in the soothing voice she used when he was angry. "But not as I love you, Stonor. I would do nothing to hurt you, don't you know that? Trust me, darling. I told you I had danced with him because if I had not you would have imagined all the wrong things...."

"I cannot bear the thought of you in his arms, even in a ballroom," Papa said. "Do you think I don't know it meant more than you want me to believe? You did not see the insolence, the triumph, in his damned eyes as he looked at me before he went. He wanted me to know that something had happened; he wanted me to suspect...God knows what."

"We danced," Mama said. "That is all."

"I've seen you dance with him," Papa muttered. "You dance together as if you made love in public."

Mama sighed. "You hurt me when you refuse to trust me, Stonor. If I were ever seriously tempted by Wolfe, I would be the first to tell you."

Papa was silent. Then he said huskily, "I want Daniel to go to a German university, Sophia, instead of to Cambridge."

Mama's voice was stiffer. "Stonor, Daniel is heir to Queen's Stonor. You swore it to me."

"He isn't my son," Papa said with a fierce madness in his voice. "Every time I see those damned eyes of his I want to kill him."

"Oh, Stonor, no," Mama said, and she began to cry, weak, weary tears that sounded like a child's. "Don't shut Daniel out. You swore to me that he would have Queen's Stonor."

"Is that why you've stayed with me, Sophia?" Papa asked bitterly. "So that your bastard should get Queen's Stonor? Do you deny Wolfe Whitley for his son's sake? That is the reason, isn't it? Don't you think that occurred to me long ago? You care nothing for Edward. You never have. It is Daniel, Daniel, Daniel with you all the time. Even Louise loves him more than she does her own real brother."

"Daniel is her brother," Mama said in a high, strained voice. "He is my son."

"And *his*," Papa said furiously. "And his. Was it a scheme between the two of you to get control of the house, Sophia? Have you kept apart all these years so that Daniel should get my house?"

"Daniel is a Stonor," Mama said, and suddenly for the first time Louise heard anger, real anger in her mother's voice. "A Stonor and my son, and if you try to take away his inheritance, Stonor, I *shall* leave you."

"At last we come to it," Papa said with that increasing wildness in his voice. "Leave me and go to whom?"

"You're hurting me," Mama said with a wince in her voice.

"I'd like to kill you," Papa said. "In my own house you let him hold you in his arms...under my own roof, you whore...."

"I have not been unfaithful to you, Stonor," Mama said faintly.

"You mean you haven't let him have your body," Papa said thickly. "Your heart he has always had, hasn't he?"

"Yes," Mama said, with a strange shivering emphasis. "Yes, Yes, Yes—"

Louise heard with disbelief the sound of blows, sharp cracks of the hand as they landed on her mother's face. Her father was breathing as if he were dying. She crouched, shuddering, listening with a white face and tear-filled eyes. The very thought of her adoring Papa striking Mama made her terrified and incredulous. The wounding blows seemed aimed at her, too, making her face quiver with pain. Mama was making soft sounds, groaning. Louise heard the sound of material ripping. Mama gave a faint cry. There was a heavy thud near the door and then the unmistakable sound of rustling, breathing, a heavy thick sound filled with emotions she could not understand.

Her mother's voice, so close Louise jumped, came in a long sigh. "Stonor," she moaned. "Stonor..."

Louise could not understand what was happening behind the closed door. Was her father trying to kill her mother? She bit her lip, wrung her hands tightly together. She dared not go into the room, nor go away, only listen anxiously, uncomprehendingly at the strange sounds she heard. Her father's breathing was so fast and choked. Her mother was sighing and moaning his name. Then a new sound began, one that made Louise feel oddly excited and sick. She had never in her life heard such sounds. Her parents sounded as if they were both dying, yet there was a fierce pleasure in their mingled voices.

"Oh, my dearest love," her father said thickly. "Sophia, my love...forgive me..."

She heard the sound of kissing, then her mother, with an excited laughter in her voice, said, "It is a very long time since you last raped me, darling. Don't leave it so long next time...."

Incredibly, Papa began to laugh huskily. "Oh, God, I ought to be shot! I've hurt you. Your sweet little face is bruised and I've torn that beautiful new gown that cost so much money..."

Mama's voice had a shivering softness. "I don't give a damn, my brutal, passionate idiot...come to bed and show me how sorry you are."

Louise crept back to her own room and sat on her bed feeling her body covered with heat and a strange excitement. Rape. The word made her shiver. She knew what that meant. Daniel and Jerome had enlightened her in a brief, terse boyish fashion as they lay reading one of Wolfe Whitley's popular newspapers that summer. A rape case had been reported, and the boys had seemed fascinated by it. Louise had not fully understood the exact nature of the crime, but the thought of her father, of all people, so controlled and formal, doing such a thing to Mama... And Mama had not swooned or screamed, or even, Louise thought, fought him. She had said soft, laughter-filled, excited things to him afterwards, as if she had enjoyed every second of it, even the blows Papa had viciously given her. Louise could not believe it. It opened a whole new vision of her parents.

A coldness shot through her as she remembered the other stark fact she had heard. Papa's violence had driven it out of her head, but now it came back with the impact of a thunderbolt. Daniel was not Papa's son. He was a bastard... Mama's bastard...and Wolfe Whitley was his father.

Louise wrapped her arms around her cold body. The silent, intense intimacy between Mama and that man had had a long history, then. Going back before Daniel's birth. She shut her eyes. Did Papa mean it when he said he would disinherit Daniel? Oh, my poor Daniel, Louise thought with aching compassion.

The autumn air grew more chill that week. Louise looked back on the glorious summer during which she, Daniel and Jerome had been so close and happy, and saw the night of the ball as a great abyss dividing that time from the time that was to follow. Looking back in later years she felt that that was the first great leap of realization she was to have—the discovery of those hidden, dark depths behind the mellow façade of her family life. All the tiny, disconnected memories of her childhood, starting with her vision of Mama as the most perfect being in the world, seemed to come into focus at that time. Wolfe Whitley's involvement with her mother, which had puzzled and disturbed her for years, took on an ominous appearance from then on, undermining Louise's life at Queen's Stonor as though he mined the very ground on which the house stood.

On the first of October, Papa, Mama and Louise rode in the park together on a fine morning before breakfast. Mama rode gaily, daringly, laughing at Papa to tease him, and Louise was relieved to see the old besotted adoration in Papa's grey eyes as his wife galloped away, her blue eyes inviting him as she glanced backwards.

All was well again, Louise thought, sighing. Then Mama's mare took a fit of temperament and bolted, with Mama trying hard to control the animal. Papa gave a long hoarse cry of terror. "Sophia, my love—" Louise saw his face illuminated by stark dread as he galloped after them, bent over the neck of his mount, urging it on. "Hang on, Sophia," he shouted. "Try to turn her."

Louise, alarmed, watched tensely in her own saddle. Papa came to the water hedge that kept the cows from straying into the park. Instead of taking the gate, as Mama's mare had done, he took the fence to save time, and Louise screamed as she saw his mount disappear, and heard the sounds of a horse floundering in water, and a scream from Papa, which was silenced almost at once.

She rode wildly forwards, taking the gate, and flung herself off her horse. Mama had glanced back and seen what had happened. Louise heard her start to scream. "No, Stonor, no...oh, God, no..."

# CHAPTER TWENTY-ONE

Stonor lay in the darkened bedroom, his broken body unmoving beneath the linen. On the mantelpiece behind her Sophia could hear the regular sound of the clock ticking, a tiny shivering metallic clicking that was like the sound of nails driven into her heart. Three days, she thought. Three days, three long, cold, hopeless nights, and he had not moved or spoken or shown any sign of returning consciousness. She had not slept or eaten during those days and nights. She had sat there, on a chair, watching him out of dark-ringed, weary eyes, and nothing the doctors or nurses, her servants, Louise or her two sons, brought hurriedly back from school, could say would move her or even penetrate the thick waiting silence of her concentration on her husband.

They had coaxed her to eat, but she had turned her white face relentlessly away. They had spoken gently, begging her to sleep, and she had been deaf.

Now Louise sat on a stool in a corner of the room, watching her mother's stiff, tense body with eyes that were raw with weeping. From the moment of her father's fall, and the carrying of his bloody, trampled body into the house, Mama had been in this white wilderness where none of them could reach her. Louise longed to kneel and put her head on her mother's lap, but Mama, she sensed, would not even be aware of her. Even Daniel had been unable to reach her. Her whole being was fixed upon her husband.

Daniel and Edward had taken their ponies and gone riding ten minutes ago, inviting Louise to join them. They had been worn down by the hours of waiting in the silent house, and the need for fresh air and exercise had driven their boys' bodies out into the park. Louise had refused, preferring to stay close to her mother. She watched her with love, compassion and fear. The strong, gentle, smiling woman who had run this house so smoothly for years had overnight become totally immersed in a pain that was stripping away her youth's last remnant, leaving her looking suddenly old and drained.

The door opened. Looking around, Louise saw the excited, confused face of one of the maids. She was beckoning, her eyes on the still figure seated by the bed. Louise rose to go out there, but even as she did so the man behind the servant pushed abruptly past her and moved into the room, his blue-green eyes not even seeming to see Louise, swerving across the room to find Sophia.

He stood, watching the white intensity of her profile. Louise nodded to the servant and closed the door, leaning against it, her heart angrily, bitterly thudding. How dared he come here? she thought.

He crossed the room with his long, graceful strides and his hands seized Mama's slender shoulders, pulling her up out of the chair by force, turning her without a pause into his arms, his hands around her slight body. Louise stared at them, waiting for Mama to push him away, but after a long shudder, her small hands pushing at his chest, Mama seemed to fold up like a weary child and lean herself against him, her eyes closing, her cheek against his chest.

Over her head Louise saw the shaft of the blue-green eyes resting on Papa's still body. His hands stroking Mama's hair. "I would have come before but I was out of Bristol when it happened," he said. "They tell me Stonor's injuries are very serious."

Mama's voice sounded threadlike, but it was the first time she had spoken for so long that Louise felt a surge of gratitude towards this man who was her father's enemy. "He was badly trampled," she said. "The water fence...just where Papa was killed...and my fault again.... I will have killed them both."

"If Stonor did die for you, he would die happily," Wolfe Whitley said without irony. "Stop blaming yourself, Sophia. It was an accident. He is still alive, after all. The doctors can work wonders these days. We'll get the best."

"They have told me that if he does recover consciousness he may have brain damage or be paralysed, or both," Mama said. "His eyes, too.... He may be blind. They cannot be certain. But it will be the end of everything for him. Blind, paralysed—what sort of life would that be for my poor darling?"

Wolfe Whitley looked down at the top of the black head, his arms tightening. "He never gives up, Sophia. Cling to that. Stonor's tenacity has stood him in good stead in the past. It will again. If he wakes up to see you at his bedside he will crawl and fight his way back to life somehow. You know that."

Mama gave a muffled cry, a sob. "I know. Why do you think I have sat here day and night since it happened?"

"Without eating, drinking or sleeping," Wolfe said wryly. "That is foolishness, Sophia. You'll do Stonor no good if you become ill yourself." He turned, holding her, and looked across the room at the silent, watchful girl, taking in with his strange eyes the stiffness of her attitude. "Louise," he said quietly. "Sit here by your father. I am going to see your mother has a meal and gets some rest. If your father needs anything, ring for the nurse. If he recovers consciousness and calls for your mother, hold his hand and try to hold him awake until she can get here."

"No, Wolfe," Sophia said, struggling to break away. "I will not leave him."

Wolfe lifted her slender, resisting body into his arms lightly, as though she were no older than Louise. "Do as I tell you, Sophia," he said firmly. Then he walked out of the room, carrying her, and Louise sank down on the chair beside her father. She watched the bandaged head on the pillow. Stonor was like a mummy, wrapped in bloodstained bandages from head to foot. If he knew that his wife had just been forcibly carried from his bedside by the man he hated most in the world, he would not lie there so still and silent, she thought. She felt a yearning, angry compassion for her father. Slowly she put her head down on the pillow next to his, her eyes closing, as if her nearness might comfort him.

Wolfe carried Sophia into her bedroom, ignoring her protests, then he rang the embroidered bell-rope violently, and a maid scurried into the room with a pale face that hid curiosity, fascination and alarm.

"Bring your mistress some beef broth and a light meal," Wolfe commanded. "Some milk, too."

As the girl, awed, curtsied and turned to go, Wolfe added, "And a bottle of brandy."

Sophia struggled to rise as the girl went out, but he pushed her back, kneeling on the bed, holding her shoulders down. She pushed at him angrily and he bent his head and began to kiss her violently, with a searing brutality that first made her wildly resistant, and then slowly weakened her, until she lay back, her mouth weakly open to his long hot exploration.

At last he pulled away, looking down at her. The whiteness had gone from her face. She was flushed and there was a glazed look in her blue eyes. "I would not have done that if you had not made me," he said almost fiercely. "Do as you're told, for God's sake, Sophia. Stonor will need you more in a day or so when he recovers consciousness. You must be strong, and to be strong you must look after yourself."

She had become submissive, as if the passionate struggle between them had been necessary for her. Wolfe gave her a curious, rueful, loving look. "I'll see you eat your meal, and then when you are asleep I'll sit with Stonor."

She looked at him, her eyes widening.

He grimaced. "For God's sake, he is my brother.... I have known him all my life. Hate each other, we may, but the damnable tie of blood is unbreakable, Sophia."

She smiled at him then, a sweet intimate smile that was echoed from his mouth, their eyes held in silent understanding.

The maid hurried in with a tray. Wolfe dismissed her curtly, then turned and began to spoonfeed Sophia, as though she were a child, his arm around her shoulders, his head close to hers as he sat on the bed. She drank some of the strong beef broth, shuddering. It was so long since she had eaten that she had no appetite. Wolfe forced her to eat some of the thinly sliced cold chicken and rice that had been sent up, allowing her at last to end the meal with some milk into which he poured a stiff measure of brandy. She shuddered at the taste and he grimly made her finish it. Then she lay back and he drew the quilt over her body, bending to kiss her gently on the mouth.

"Now go to sleep, my darling. If there is the slightest change, I'll fetch you immediately. I promise."

She looked at him, her eyes already drowsy after the brandy. "Do not sit too near him, Wolfe," she whispered.

His eyes had a grim smile in them. "No," he said. "I'll stay out of his sight." He knew she feared that Stonor, finding him present, might become so bitterly jealous that he grew worse rather than better.

Louise was still lying with her head on the pillow beside her father's when Wolfe entered the bedroom. She sat up, quickly, looking at him, and for a few seconds his strange eyes gave her a tender, gentle smile, then he sat down out of range of the bed, his hard body relaxed. Louise was anxiously puzzled.

What should she do? Ignore him? After a few moments the silence in the room settled into a peaceful pattern, and the two watching Stonor Whitley lying so silently seemed to be unaware of each other once more.

Nanny Dorcas caught Edward and Daniel as they came back upstairs after their ride, and crossly upbraided them for going out of the house. "Your father may die any moment... Edward, you look sick again. Go and wash your face and then rest on your bed for half an hour." Edward had been sick three times since his return from school. It had been borne in upon Daniel, with surprise, that his brother deeply loved his father. That his father loved Edward he had always known, but Edward took him by surprise in returning the love.

Edward now turned violently upon Nanny Dorcas, who had been his best-loved person for so many years as a small boy. "I'm not going to rest with my father dying."

Dorcas looked sheepish. "He is no worse," she admitted, flushing. "I was worried, that is all.... Edward, go and rest."

Edward would have argued, but the taut sickness in his stomach suddenly caught him, and he fled to be humiliated and shamed in private. Dorcas made a bitter sound. "Poor boy...and that man in the house just now, of all times—the insolence of it: walking in as if he owned the place—and owned her too, carrying her into her own bedroom, feeding her as if she were his wife, which God help her if she were. He's been a bitter enough husband to his own poor wife...." She suddenly closed her mouth, seeing Daniel's strange blue-green eyes upon her, and looked dazedly horrified. In her anxiety for Stonor, her fear for the future, her love for Sophia, she had forgotten what ears would hear her wild outburst.

Without a word Daniel turned and walked towards his father's bedroom door.

Wolfe was lounging casually in his chair, his legs crossed, his long fingers playing with the glittering gold watch chain that hung across his waistcoat. He did not give a sign by look or word or movement, but the two pairs of blue-green eyes surveyed one another curiously.

Louise turned from her contemplation of her father to see them stare silently at each other, and her heart began to beat rapidly, sickeningly. Father and son, she thought, shivering. It was all there to read in the two similar faces.

Wolfe was thirty-five now. The slim, arrogant insolent boy

Sophia had first met twenty years ago was now a well-built, lean, hard, fit man of mature years and startling experience. Years of fierce living, ambition, knowledge had toughened his features into a barbaric mask of pride and arrogance softened only by mocking humour. His shoulders were wide and powerful, his casually seated body still fiercely attractive. The silver in his thick black hair gave him an added charm.

Daniel seemed to straighten his thin shoulders, the thin gawky boy's body held stiffly. His black hair was ruffled by the wind in the park. His face was very pale and held none of Wolfe's hard-learned self-confidence. He looked coldly, proudly back at Wolfe, all the pride of birth and position in his vulnerable young face.

"It is very kind of you to call, sir, to enquire about my father, but we would not wish to take up too much of your time," he said icily.

If he had hoped to insult Wolfe, he failed lamentably. Leaning back, his eyes filled with laughter, Wolfe grinned at him, all his considerable charm in the glance of his eyes.

"Here I stay, and I'll not budge until my brother shows signs of life," he countered coolly.

Daniel flushed hotly. "My father did not want you in his house while he could deny you entry," he said rudely. "Now he is unable to speak for himself, I'll speak for him: Get out of my house."

Wolfe's mouth curved as if he was delighted, but the blue-green eyes mocked the boy. "How do you mean to force me to leave, Daniel?"

"I'll get the servants to throw you out," Daniel said between gritted teeth.

Louise got up and flew at him, her arms flung round his thin body, clinging to him. "Don't, Daniel," she whispered. "Oh, please, don't argue with him." She was afraid. Afraid that Wolfe Whitley might tell her brother to his face the hidden truth that Daniel must never know.

Daniel held her, his hands tender on her thin shoulders. "Father would not want him in this room," he said.

"How do you know what my brother would or would not want?" Wolfe drawled smilingly. "Young man, you've a lot to learn about human nature."

"I know he hates you," Daniel said bitingly. "Just as your wife hates you, and Jerome."

Wolfe sat up abruptly, his eyes narrowed on the boy's face.

"What?" The tone had harshness in it. Louise felt it in her own mind, and guessed that this man could be hurt by the idea that his son hated him.

She turned and looked anxiously at him, her blue eyes torn between fear and pity, and he turned his head and looked into her eyes slowly, his own narrowing in speculation. She felt dizzy as if he read her mind. His brows rose sharply.

Daniel was glaring at him, all fierce young pride and hatred. Louise wound her arms around her brother to hold him immobile, while her blue glance begged Wolfe to go quietly without saying any more, and Wolfe coolly read the shifting expressions on her pale young face.

Then the door opened and Sophia came in, her face flushed from sleep, her hair tidied, her dress changed. She looked quickly at Stonor, then sighed. Only then did she take in the tense situation between the other three in the room.

"Daniel, Louise," she said quietly but firmly, "go and change before you have dinner."

"Mother, you know Papa would want this man out of our house," Daniel said, although his tone was softened by the passionate love he had for her, and his concern and anxiety for her because of his father.

Sophia looked at him, sighing. "Leave the situation to me, Daniel," she said gently.

He was reluctant to go, shuffling his feet. Louise was equally reluctant, looking from her mother to Wolfe Whitley with silent fear. Sophia rustled softly to Daniel's side and pulled his own head down, kissing him on the mouth very briefly. "Be a good boy, Daniel," she said. "I shall need you very much from now on. . .show me I can rely on you."

Daniel looked very flushed, half-smiling, touched and delighted. He put an arm around his sister and led her from the room.

When the door had closed behind him, Sophia looked measuringly at Wolfe. They exchanged a long silent glance.

Then he stood up. "Very well, Sophia," he said. "If I must go, I must. I wanted to be here with you in case you needed me, but since it is to my son you turn I'll not insist."

She smiled at him, then, her eyes brilliant with unshed tears. "I am sorry he spoke to you like that, Wolfe."

Wolfe grinned. "Oh, don't fret. I took no notice. He's a chip off the same block. I understand Daniel." His eyes gleamed. "I'm proud of the boy." Then a new look came into his face and he turned away, his hands in his pockets. "Sophia, somehow they know."

She frowned. "Who knows what?"

He glanced at her. "I'm not sure exactly who knows how much, but certainly Daniel knows my son Jerome well enough to tell me to my face that Jerome hates me. No news to me, but it shows a certain intimacy, don't you think?"

Sophia shrugged. "They've met at Luther's house, of course. It is not surprising if the family skeletons were taken out of the cupboard and rattled a little."

Wolfe shook his head. "There's more to it than that. Louise looks at me..." He lifted his wide shoulders, his smile rueful. "In such a way! Afraid, anxious, suspicious...she's aware somehow of us, Sophia."

Sophia frowned in disturbed surprise. "Louise? She cannot be! Why, Wolfe, how could she know anything?"

"She was a sharp, quick-eared little creature, I remember," Wolfe said drily. "Quiet and thoughtful...not a wild gypsy like you were, my love. An odd mixture of you and Stonor, that child...."

Sophia smiled lovingly. "Oh, she is Stonor's child, that's true..."

"I know that, damn you," Wolfe said in sudden harshness.

She looked at him, shaking her head. "You've imagined all this, Wolfe. She loves Daniel deeply. No doubt she was afraid you might be angry with him."

"Perhaps," Wolfe said. He frowned. "I'd swear she was afraid of something when he was insulting me like a young cock on a barn door."

Sophia sighed. "She and Daniel have always been so very close. Seeing them together makes me feel happy. I think she is one of Stonor's reasons for resenting Daniel. It sounds foolish, but I think he is jealous because she loves Daniel so very much. He looks at them and he sees..." Her voice broke off.

Wolfe moved close, standing in front of her, not touching her, his eyes on her face, a curious smile on his mouth. "I saw it, too," he said softly. "I saw us, my darling. She is your image and he mine. You do not need to tell me why Stonor hates to see them hand in hand; their love for each other must remind him every minute of the day."

She looked at him, her blue eyes passionately tracing his face. Her lids drooped and he kissed her briefly, with a hunger so deep it burned her mouth, laying the mark of his possession on her as if he branded it there, then drawing away, as if he dared not linger over it.

"I'd better go—before Daniel bursts in to insult me again," he said wryly. "What about the business, Sophia? Is it in hand? Anything I can do?"

"Stonor's chief clerk is capable of running things," Sophia said. "When Stonor is better..." Her voice broke off.

"He will get better," Wolfe promised gently.

He opened the door and turned to look back at her, unaware of Daniel sullenly looming on the landing, staring with taut dislike at the tall, dark figure. "If you need me for anything, my darling, send word at once. I'll come, night or day. You're sure Stonor's doctors know what they're doing? I could get a specialist from London..."

"We have one," Sophia sighed. "The best. He says we can only wait to see how much damage has been done."

"Sophia," Wolfe's voice was urgent. "Stonor will get better. You must believe that, darling. We both know him. Stonor will not die if he thinks he would be leaving you to me. He will fight and cling onto life by every means in his power. All he will need is you at his side to make the fight worthwhile."

Her voice was filled with a sudden fierceness. "And I will be there, Wolfe."

"Do you think I doubted that?" His voice was dry.

He turned to leave and came face to face with Daniel. The two countenances, so deeply imprinted with the same nature, stared at each other. Wolfe gave his son a casual, mocking grin and sauntered away.

Daniel moved into the bedroom and looked at his mother with suddenly adult, accusing eyes. For a few seconds she met his glance smoothly, gently, all her usual warm maternity in her eyes, then slowly the look changed and she took in the stiff way he stood, the hardness in his face. She sighed, her head bending almost submissively, the slender droop of her body weary. Daniel moved forwards, watching her. He stared at her, standing directly in front of her, and Sophia swayed softly forwards, leaning her head on his thin shoulder. She was all feminine weakness in his arms, yieldingly weak, the fragrance of her musky perfume hanging on her skin. Daniel was unyielding for a moment, anger in his face, then he put his arms around her and held her, his heart beating.

"I'm so relieved to have you with me now, Daniel," she whispered. "It has been so much to bear alone."

"I'll look after you, Mama," Daniel said, his face alight with love and pride. Never before had she made him feel so adult and strong. He wanted to protect her, guard her, carry the burden of her fear and sorrow for her. His shoulders straightened as he looked ahead and saw that she would need him more and more from now on, and he forgot Wolfe Whitley's insolent way of speaking to her as if she belonged to him instead of to Daniel, he forgot his anger with her for permitting it while his own father lay so ill. He was only aware of the warm, soft beautiful weakness of her in his arms, and her need of his strength.

Stonor's illness changed that night. He clawed his way out of the dark clouds surrounding him to open his eyes and look feebly towards Sophia, sitting at his side, her hand holding his. Daniel, Louise and Edward stood at her shoulders, staring at him in joyful relief. Stonor ran his eye briefly over them, the faintest smile on his face, then he looked back at his wife and sighed, his hand faintly moving inside hers. "Sophia," his mouth shaped silently. "My love. . ."

She bent and kissed his mouth lingeringly. "My darling," she whispered, and Stonor closed his eyes, slipping back into darkness with a sigh.

Louise gave a wrung cry of fear. Her mother looked around at her, still holding Stonor's hand. "He will be stronger soon," she said comfortingly. "He is not going to die, Louise. But he is tired and he needs sleep. Go to bed, all of you. I will stay with him."

"You need rest, Mama," Daniel said, bending over her. "I will stay with Papa."

"Not tonight, Daniel," she said. "I slept this afternoon. I will do very well. You can take over from me tomorrow."

Daniel smiled and nodded, accepting that, and the three of them left the room. Edward gave a last glance back towards the bed, seeing his mother's eyes fixed on his father's bandaged head. She bent and kissed the pale mouth that had been left free of bandages, then she lifted her husband's hand and held it to her cheek.

Edward left the room, his face sullen. He loved Stonor with a silent, dark love that he hid from everyone in case they mocked him. His father, he had always felt, was the only person in the house who truly loved him. From early childhood

Louise had stolen Daniel from him, and he hated her for taking his brother from him. Only Papa had smiled at him with that special look. Even Mama, gentle and kind though she was, loved Daniel and Louise far more than she did him, and Edward felt that he, among them all, was isolated, a stranger, unwanted. He had felt so for years. He was jealous of Daniel, who would inherit Queen's Stonor. He was jealous of Mama, whom Papa loved more than anyone in the world. He was jealous of Louise, whose birth had ended his own reign as baby in the nursery and who had soon enslaved Daniel. Edward was subconsciously aware that Papa preferred him to both Louise and Daniel, and it was his one comfort. Papa was his. . . yet it was Mama who had the right to kiss his hand and sit beside him all night to protect him at the borders of life and death. Excluded, miserable, sullen, Edward went to bed and his grey eyes had Stonor's grim tenacity as he stared into the darkness. Papa must not die. Because if he did Edward would be truly alone. He must not die.

As the autumn wore on it became clear that Stonor would not die. His will to live pulled him slowly from the grave, but even his willpower could not restore muscles and sinews to his shattered limbs. He was partially blind in one eye, although he saw well enough to recognize faces and to read with a magnifying glass. He was unable to move, and his body gradually grew thin and white with weakness and inactivity.

"He will be paralysed for the rest of his life," the doctor from London told Sophia gravely. "He is lucky to be alive at all. I had serious doubts of his recovery at first, but he is a healthy strong-willed man. You must face the facts, Mrs. Whitley. Your husband will never again get out of his bed. He will be a permanent invalid. He must not be worried by business affairs. His heart will not take the strain. He must rest quietly all day, at least for the first few months."

Sophia told Stonor the truth herself. She sat on the bed, holding both his hands, looking at him lovingly, and Stonor braced himself for the cruel facts, his face coldly controlled. Even so, a cry burst from him, smothered at birth, and his lips shook.

"You are alive, my darling," she whispered. "That is more than we dared hope for at first. At least we will be together."

Stonor's eyes were bitter as he looked at her lovely face. "How long will you be able to bear living with a shattered cripple who can never hope to share your bed, Sophia?"

"For as long as it takes to live my whole life," she said lightly, smiling at him. "Oh, Stonor, you bore with all I imposed on you during the first years of our marriage. Do you think me less capable of love than yourself?"

Stonor's eyes burned on her face. "You have never loved me the way I love you," he said flatly. "During those years I fed my needs by kissing your hands or being able to look at you because even the tiniest crumb of solace was enough. I know I've kept you because you want Queen's Stonor for your son."

"No," she denied fiercely.

"Very well," he said wearily. "You have stayed partly because you did not find our hours in bed unsatisfactory."

She lifted his hand to her mouth, kissing the palm, her tongue moistly caressing his skin. "You are an exciting lover, Stonor, especially when you are violent—don't you know how much I want you?"

He caught his breath, his eyes flaming. "Sophia. . ."

"I think I always wanted you. From that day at Kew when you kissed me and touched my body. I was shocked by how much I liked it." Her eyes teased him. "And after Daniel was born I was even more shocked to find myself eager for you to touch me even more intimately. . ." Their eyes held, and a strange wry look came into Stonor's face as they both remembered when he had taken Daniel's place at her breasts, hungry to take nourishment from her body, wildly desiring to enjoy her somehow, some way.

Sophia blushed as she knew he remembered it, too, and Stonor laughed very huskily.

Daniel, entering the room, heard his father's laughter with a shock of surprise. It was the first time in weeks Stonor had given any sign of being free of endless pain. Unaware of his silent presence, Stonor put a hand up to Sophia's bodice and his fingers delicately stroked her breast, his eyes warm with memory.

Sophia said unsteadily, "We will find ways, Stonor, my love."

Stonor's eyes jealously darkened. "Swear to me now that you will not go to him, even if I die."

"I swear it," she said levelly, staring into his eyes.

Stonor sighed. "Thank you, Sophia."

She was alarmed by the white weariness of his face and ran a finger over his mouth to awaken him to her again. "But that does not mean that you can release your hold on life, Stonor," she said softly. "If you want to keep me, you will stay alive...."

Then Stonor laughed again, his mouth crooked. "Oh, my darling," he whispered, and she bent to kiss him.

Daniel withdrew, a dark frown on his face. Silently he went to the morning room where Louise was neatly writing letters of gratitude in reply to the many letters of condolence they had received. She looked up, her tongue between her lips.

Daniel stared at her intently and her eyes widened, taking in the expression on his face. "What is wrong?" Alarm darkened her blue gaze. "Papa?" She half-rose.

"No," Daniel said gruffly. "Louie...my father's half-brother—you remember what Jerome told us about the family feud?"

She looked wary. "Yes?"

"There's more to it than that, I suspect. I just overheard Papa talking to Mama, and I'd swear he was jealous of his brother because of Mama.... Do you think they quarrelled over her? Perhaps before she married Papa, Wolfe Whitley was in love with her too?" Daniel's face tightened jealously. "He treats her damned insolently, as if..." He broke off, his mouth angry.

"He has an insolent manner," Louise said carefully. "That is all."

"There's more to it than that," Daniel said. "Papa made her swear that if he died she would not go to...to him."

Louise went pale. "And did she swear?"

Daniel searched her face. "Yes," he said. "Louie, you know something! Tell me. What is there between that man and our mother?"

Louise hesitated, not knowing how to answer. Daniel waited, then said bitterly, "If you will not tell me, I'll ask Jerome. I'd swear he knows. He's very knowing. I think he gets it from his mother when she has been drinking. She says wild things, Jerome told me: shouts insults at his father, threatens him. Poor Jerome, it must be terrible. He picked up the story of the family feud from her when she was too drunk to know what she was saying. God knows what else she has told him. If you will not tell her, I'll ask Jerome—"

"Don't ask Jerome," she cried, fear in her face. "Daniel, please— Don't ask anyone. Leave it alone."

He stared at her. "I'm going to find out somehow—"

"Don't," she pleaded in terror. "Daniel, it would be best if
you did not know."

"I'll be the judge of that," he said, scornfully, his nineteen
years outweighing her, then he turned and walked out of the
room. Ten minutes later she saw him ride along the drive on his
pony towards the park gates. She was relieved when he returned, sullen and absorbed. Jerome was still at school, thank
God, and by the time Daniel next met him he might have forgotten his desire to ask questions.

The autumn faded into cold, grey winter, and Stonor slowly
recovered his strength to talk and read. Now it was almost
Christmas and the first chill flakes of snow sifted down over
the park, turning the grass into stiff white spears, and glisten-
ing on the eaves over the windows.

It was a subdued Christmas. They had their tree, their customary presents, their capons and plum puddings, but
Stonor's presence was absent from the family festivities, and
it threw a shadow over them all. Sophia left them to sit with
her husband that evening, and the three children gloomily
played cards and squabbled over accusations of cheating. Edward spent an hour each morning sitting with his father, reading business news to him from the paper, content to know that
he shared his father's interest in the rise and fall of the
markets, the changing pattern of trade. Stonor smiled at him
from time to time, happy to have him there, and Edward
would give him a look from glowing, possessive eyes.

Seeing them, Sophia thought how alike they grew year by
year, and wished she found it in her heart to love Edward as
much as she did Daniel and Louise, but the boy's strange
nature made it hard. He was as prickly as a hedgehog, she
thought wryly. Only his father softened him. Seeing how
much good his presence did for Stonor, she suggested that Edward should play chess with his father in the evenings while
she sewed beside the bed. For a moment warm gratitude stood
in Edward's grey eyes, then he looked eagerly at his father.
Stonor was watching Sophia adoringly. Thinking his father
had not even heard, Edward's mouth drooped sullenly. Then
Stonor looked at him, catching the jealous expression on the
boy's face, and he smiled. "I would like that, Edward," he
said. "It will keep my brains working to have to pit myself
against you."

When Edward, walking on air, had gone, Stonor said to

Sophia, "You are an angel, my darling. I abase myself in front of you."

She did not pretend not to understand him. His dislike of having Daniel in the room, his warm preference for Edward, had to be accepted, and since his illness she had realized how much Edward could help him.

All through those winter holidays Edward was constantly with his father, and the relationship between them deepened. Stonor had given Sophia power of attorney to deal with all his affairs, since the doctor had said he must not even think of the business, and she went each week into Bristol to visit the firm and see the chief clerk. Understanding nothing of the business, she left it all to him, and only made the trip to be able to tell Stonor all was well.

When the time came for the boys to return to school Edward was crushed by the prospect. Stonor, to ease the parting, suggested Edward should write to him as often as possible. "I shall be so bored in this bed, my boy. I shall look forward to your letters." He made no such request to Daniel, and Edward was comforted.

Daniel had had no opportunity to see Jerome that Christmas. Because of Stonor's illness, Sophia had made no attempt to take the children to the usual crop of children's parties. The only other possible meeting-place was the Wolfe Whitley household, which Daniel hated to consider. And so he returned to his studies still unaware of the reason that Stonor disliked him and preferred Edward.

When the boys were gone the house grew into a regular, peaceful pattern of living that centred around Stonor's bed. Unable to move to dress or lift himself, he had a nurse to attend to his physical needs, a fact that galled him and wounded his pride. He liked to have Sophia near him all the time, but when the nurse came in to attend to him, he made Sophia leave. His helplessness in the other woman's hands must never be viewed by Sophia. His pride would not permit it. He would die rather than have her see this woman treat him as a child, washing and changing him with cool brusqueness. As the weeks passed Stonor felt his bodily weakness more and more. Returning health in other ways made it much more intolerable. Stonor brooded in his bed, his grey eyes bitter. Sometimes, when he would wish he had died, he would imagine Sophia back in Wolfe's willing arms, and his mouth would grow anguished with jealousy.

# CHAPTER TWENTY-TWO

On a bitter February night the Whitley warehouse in Bristol was burned to the ground by a drunken night watchman who had accidentally knocked an oil lamp to the floor beside a bail of cotton waste. The flames had exploded so suddenly, with such violence, that the man had been killed instantly. By the time the fire engine had raced to the scene, the black harbour water had been alive with the orange reflections of the flames, and a buzzing crowd had gathered to watch from a safe distance.

Distraught, Sophia next day sat in the office at Bristol and learned that the insurance covering the warehouse had been insufficient to bear the loss of the goods it had held at the time of the fire. Stonor's chief clerk had embezzled some of the money intended for the insurance, then had accepted a crowded shipload of valuable goods, which were now destroyed. The firm had lost an enormous sum at one stroke, and she was faced with the fact that their bank balance would not cover it. She had a polite interview with the bank manager, who refused to give her the sum she needed. Only then did Sophia realize how delicately balanced the family fortune had been. Stonor had spent money freely on Queen's Stonor all these years, juggling to keep the firm and the house afloat, and the blow of the warehouse fire had destroyed his financial stability.

She dared not tell Stonor. She kept from him any news that might disturb him. He knew of the fire, but he thought the insurance must cover it.

Faced with disaster, she finally borrowed the money she needed from a financial house who specialized in such matters, mortgaging Queen's Stonor as the collateral they required. Dismissing the chief clerk contemptuously, since she dared not institute proceedings against him for fear it came to Stonor's ears, she told Stonor that the man had had a better offer and left. For the moment, she said, she would deal with the firm, with Stonor as her advisor. She had expected Stonor to protest, but he accepted her decision, and only later did she realize that he was hoping to control the firm through her from his bed.

Each evening they would sit together, going through the papers she had brought home, and Stonor would seriously discuss the business with her, telling her what to do, which firms to deal with, what prices to pay. Sophia had a quick, sound brain but Stonor's knowledge was invaluable. Together they began to refloat the firm on a sound footing, without Stonor ever knowing of the great debt they had to repay, or of the mortgage on Queen's Stonor. Having power of attorney, she had been able to deal with it discreetly, hiding it from him.

She realized slowly that the disaster had had happier results than she could have hoped. Stonor grew much more cheerful. His mind had food during the long, tedious days, and each evening his eyes glowed as she arrived to go over the day's business with him. It had relieved the appalling uselessness he had begun to feel, and it ended the bitter wariness towards her that she had noticed in him lately. She had seen his hatred of his own bodily weakness, his wounded pride, and she had been helpless to heal him. Now he seemed easier in his mind.

Sophia worked in the oak-panelled office looking out over the busy Bristol harbour area, and with Stonor's evening tuition, her ability to deal with the work grew rapidly and she began to find her feet in this strange new world. She acquired a new chief clerk, George Blare, a sober, quiet man of impeccable references, and Sophia soon learned to trust him. Her presence caused some shock and consternation at first, and the male bastions of business meant that she was forced to use George Blare in many of her dealings, but her soft hand still guided the firm, with Stonor at her back to oversee everything.

George Blare was a bachelor with obsessively neat habits, who lived alone in a small house with two silk-flanked cats that he adored. At first he showed wary courtesy towards Sophia, then slowly he developed a silent admiration and embarked on a mission to save her any anxiety, hardship or trouble, masking his feelings from her as far as he could because he was embarrassed by them. Sophia was the first lady of her class whom he had ever known, and he thought of her as a unique being out of his reach. As for Sophia, she had no suspicion that the thin, quiet little man regarded her with anything but courtesy. She was unaware that her impulsively bestowed smiles, her lingering French perfume, her silken rustling skirts, filled his dreams; that he would rather die than fail her in anything.

Two months after Sophia took control, Wolfe Whitley was announced as she sat poring over a large copperplate-inscribed ledger. She looked up, her eyes narrowing. "Show Mr. Whitley in," she said expressionlessly, and the clerk backed out, his eyes curious.

Wolfe and Luther had been in America for the past few months visiting the vast, growing trading centre there to get in touch with new business methods and learn what they could of American drugs. Sophia had not heard of their return. She had been so immersed in the business that she had had no time for social calls or gossip.

Wolfe came into the room, as darkly handsome as ever, his hair curling to his collar in silver-threaded blackness. He stood, grinning at her, his eyes amused. "My God, Mrs. Whitley, are you becoming a businesswoman?"

"Needs must when the Devil drives," she said lightly.

He sat down in the chair opposite her, his gloves in his long hands, and eyed her insolently. "I've been hearing a great deal of gossip about you since I returned. It seems you have outraged decency by taking over the Whitley empire and running it efficiently. Petticoat government is never popular in business circles, Sophia. You should know that."

"Stonor advises me," she said flatly. She closed the ledger and surveyed him coolly. "What do you want, Wolfe?"

His eyes were mocking. "You know that."

Her face did not alter. "Why are you here?"

"For the same reason," he murmured, mockery in his every line.

"Stop playing games and tell me outright," she said, her lips tightening.

He flapped his gloves against his lean thighs. "Stonor is a permanent cripple, it seems," he observed calmly. "Unable to move a muscle. . ."

"He's alive," she said levelly. "That is all that matters."

Wolfe's mouth twisted sardonically. "You little liar—what matters is that after all these months of frustration you must be going out of your mind. . . ."

The words brought a dark flush to her face. She met his eyes angrily. "That's enough, Wolfe."

"I haven't started yet," he said bitingly. "We know each other too well to lie. While Stonor was able to keep the fires banked down by satisfying you in bed, you were safe. But now things have changed, haven't they?"

"Nothing has changed," she said, her mouth a tight line. "Don't even think it, Wolfe."

"You came a cropper over the warehouse fire, didn't you, Sophia?" he asked, changing the subject.

She looked unrevealingly at him. "Did I?"

"I know about the mortgage on Queen's Stonor," he said drily.

She looked sharply at him. She had hidden the news successfully, she had thought. The fact that Wolfe knew alarmed her. She watched him silently, trying to read the thoughts in the blue-green eyes. Usually she had no need to guess at them, but today his face was a mask she could not penetrate.

Wolfe took out a cigar case. "May I smoke? Or do you ban it from your office?"

"As you wish," she said indifferently, aware in every nerve that he was deliberately postponing the moment when he told her what he had come to tell her.

He slowly, carefully lit the cigar and puffed blue smoke into the air, leaning back, his hard body relaxed and casual.

She waited, controlling the warning bells that were ringing in her head.

Wolfe surveyed her through the smoke, a mocking smile on his mouth.

It is coming, she thought with a shock, tensing to bear whatever it was.

"It was my company who lent you the money," he said softly. "I hold the mortgage on Queen's Stonor, Sophia."

She grew white then, and her face had a hard, glazed shine to it as she stared back at him. She had had no idea that Wolfe was involved in financial circles, and the news struck her as a terrible blow.

He lifted the cigar to his mouth, watching her, a gleam of enjoyment in his eyes. Somehow she managed to sit still, looking back at him.

"So now," he murmured smoothly, his face bland, "I have a delightful choice. I can either take possession of Queen's Stonor...or of you, Sophia."

Her body was rigid with rage and resentment. She stared, unable to say a word.

She knew as well as he did that she had a low bank balance. The firm was only just keeping afloat after the blow that had crippled it, and the banks were unlikely to offer to lend her any money. With Queen's Stonor mortgaged and the firm in low water she was caught in a trap, and Wolfe was deeply enjoying her helpless inability to escape.

He rose to his feet, taking her by complete surprise. Smiling, he bowed towards her courteously. "I will give you twenty-four hours to make up your mind, Sophia," he said. "The day you come to me as my secret mistress, I'll give you the mortgage documents back. I know we can trust each other." His smile was wicked. "Stonor shall never know of it. I have already taken the apartment. You need it now, admit it or not, and I am giving you the chance to take what you want without feeling guilty." His eyes mocked her. "You see, I know your odd ideas of integrity towards my dear brother. I realized I would have to force you to do what you would not let yourself do. You have no choice now, my darling. You would not want to see me in possession of Queen's Stonor, would you? Or even to know I had the ability to take it from you. So you must come to me to save the house." A strange brightness filled his eyes. "You sacrificed yourself to Stonor for the damned place. It seems only just you should do so again for me."

She watched blankly as he strolled towards the door. Wolfe glanced back at her, his mouth curving in a grin. "My God, you look as if you could do with a glass of brandy, my love. I'll see you tomorrow at the same time for my answer."

When he had gone she sat rigidly, her back straight, her face hard. The thought of his holding Queen's Stonor in his power was so bitter that she could have screamed. His threat against the house was intolerable. All her life she had loved the house with a deep, abiding passion, which she knew would never change. Anything Wolfe did to her she could have borne, anything but this. He must not be allowed to reach out those hard hands towards Queen's Stonor. It never even entered her head to think of his alternative. Her anger that he should have seized the house was too deep for her even to consider it.

She wrote a brief note and despatched it by messenger at once. An hour later she was facing Luther Hunt across her desk. When he had been in America with Wolfe, during the January snows, his wife had died of pneumonia, and he now wore black for her, his stocky body seeming denser in the heavy cloth.

Sophia smiled at him, using every ounce of her femininity, her blue eyes charming. Luther Hunt admired her. She had

known that for years. In his quiet, polite fashion he had never
hidden the fact that he enjoyed her company, but unlike
Wolfe, he was known as a man of domestic virtue. He had
never been heard of keeping a mistress or abusing his wife. He
drank little and was a tireless worker.

"How can I help you, Mrs. Whitley?" he asked courteously.

Sophia lowered her lashes, her small white hands fiddling
with the ledgers on her desk. "It is very hard for me to tell you
this, Mr. Hunt. You are your cousin's partner and friend."

Luther looked sharply at her. "Wolfe? It has to do with
him?"

She bit her lip, her small white teeth glimpsed against the
warm pink of her mouth. "Mr. Hunt, I love my husband very
much. I am trying to safeguard my home and my family by
running the firm in his absence."

"And I have heard you have done very well," Luther said
politely.

She sighed. "Unfortunately, I was faced with a crushing
blow." Quietly she outlined the story of the fire, the need for
money, the mortgage on Queen's Stonor. "Today your cousin
informed me that he owned that mortgage," she ended quietly, her eyes lowered.

Luther smiled. "Ah, it was his finance company who
helped you? Well I'm glad of that."

Sophia looked up, lifted a trembling hand to her lips. "Oh,
Mr. Hunt..." Her acting was superb, her eyes all embarrassment and shame. "He has threatened me with.... Either
I...become h...his mistress, or he will foreclose on my
home."

Luther sat upright, exclaiming in disbelief. "Good God!"
He was genuinely shocked, appalled. "I know Wolfe is not a
moral man but that is—" He faltered, cutting off his words.

"It is terrifying," Sophia wept, putting her face into her
hands. The tears that spilled were real, although they were
tears of rage and bitterness rather than fear and shame.
Luther Hunt came around the desk and anxiously, gently,
patted her heaving shoulders. She lifted her tear-stained face
pleadingly. Softly, he wiped her eyes and wet cheeks with a
white handkerchief, unconsciously enjoying the soft weakness
of her slender body as it leaned against him, filling his nostrils
with her alluring scent.

"Do not cry like this," he said harshly. "I'll see him and
stop this—"

"No," she said urgently, putting a white hand on his sleeve. She gave him a soft, pleading look. "He would be angry that I told you, and then who knows what he might do? I cannot risk my husband hearing a whisper of it. Oh, Mr. Hunt... give me your advice. I cannot borrow more money on Queen's Stonor to pay him back. How can I raise the sum I need? That is what I need to know."

Luther Hunt stared down into her lovely, pale face, his eyes suddenly shrewd. "What about the firm?" he asked her. "Have you tried to raise money on that?"

She shook her head, her eyes submissive. "Is that a way, do you think? If I took a partner?"

Luther Hunt stroked his chin. "May I look at your books, Mrs. Whitley? Assess your financial stability?"

"Of course," she said at once, ringing for George Blare.

Luther Hunt and Sophia's chief clerk went over the books for the next hour, their heads together. Sophia waited patiently, her nerves prickling. At last Luther looked at her thoughtfully.

"Your husband may dislike the idea of selling part of his firm to me, Mrs. Whitley," he said.

She met his eyes. "He would dislike the alternative far more," she said huskily.

He flushed. "Yes. Yes, of course."

When Wolfe returned next day, his handsome face was alight with his coming triumph, with the urgency and desire for his long-delayed possession of Sophia. As he walked into the office, his eyes flashed and she felt a sweet yielding hunger deep down inside her own body, but she looked down, forcing it out of sight.

He lounged opposite her, his hands driven into his pockets, his hard features only just masking the passion he would not yet reveal to her.

"I've come for my answer, Mrs. Whitley," he drawled, looking at her between hooded lids, his mouth only just held in restraint.

She put her white hands on the desk and stared at them, her head lowered. There was a silence.

"Don't do this, Wolfe," she said huskily. "I beg you, don't force me to make such a choice...."

"You want me as much as I want you," he said harshly. "We both know it. We belong together. You've forced me to blackmail you by your stupid desire to keep that damned house intact, and to do that you have stayed faithful to Stonor. I've always known that Queen's Stonor was my real rival. I've no doubt Stonor knows it too. He used the house ruthlessly to get you. Now it is my turn. I am only doing what he did.''

She lifted her head slowly, her white neck quivering under the black hair. Her eyes were brilliant in her white face. ''I am begging you on my knees, Wolfe, don't do this.''

His eyes flashed furiously, bitterly. ''You've wasted my life because of that house. I loved you from the moment I saw you and you loved me. I'll do anything—manipulate, trick, black-mail, cheat—to get you, Sophia. I'm nearly thirty-nine years old. My life is slipping away from me, and the loss of you has made it a hollow, empty life for years.'' His voice held a burn-ing, bitter hunger. ''I've got to have you before it's too late. I will not let you waste any more of our precious lives. You will come to me.''

''Have you considered what this would do to Stonor? Wolfe, we can't do it to him. He is a cripple, his life in ruins. How can you aim such a blow at him?''

Wolfe's eyes were savage. ''Do you remember how he told you I was dead? You asked me how he could do such a thing, and I said all was fair in love or war. Do you doubt for a second that in my position Stonor would hesitate to do what I am doing? He did it, Sophia, you know he did—he taught me how to manip-ulate you by using that damned house as the lever to get you.''

She looked at him wearily, then she drew out a piece of paper and handed it to him without a word. He looked down at it blankly, read it, then stared at her, his mouth sardonic.

''You must think me a fool, Sophia—your bank does not have enough funds in your name to cover this.''

''It didn't,'' she said calmly. ''Now it does.''

Wolfe's hands slowly clenched, his eyes reading her face with a wild rage. ''What have you done?'' he asked hoarsely.

She smiled. ''Sold myself to someone else,'' she told him.

He gave a deep, raging cry of protest. ''Tell me the truth,'' he asked harshly. ''Where did you get the money?''

She leaned back and gave him an insolent look. ''Do you think I could not find a man to give me any sum I cared to name, Wolfe?''

Wolfe came around the desk so fast she was too late to evade him. Then she was in his arms, her mouth twisting to escape him. After a moment he held her, his hands a vise around her head, and she stood still, looking up at him.

They stared at each other in silence. "You stupid, obstinate little fool," he said bitterly. "Why have you done it? Why have you thrown away our last chance of happiness?"

"You shouldn't have touched Queen's Stonor," she said on a note of cold anger. "I could forgive anything else from you, Wolfe, but not that."

"Oh, Christ—that house," he said savagely. "You've used my own weapon against me."

There was another silence while their eyes fought. Then Wolfe slowly lowered his mouth, trapping her head so that she could not escape it, and as it touched her lips they parted hungrily, the taste of her tongue on his, the sound of her breathing growing faster. Her arms clung to him, her body pressed eagerly against his, and the silence deepened as they took sustenance from each other. Sophia closed her eyes and felt the whirlpool of her blood driving her. Wolfe's hands were shaking as they held her face, and his heart was racing against hers.

Wolfe sighed as they drew apart. He looked down into her flushed, aroused face with eyes that ate her. "Come to me, my darling. . . I need you."

She shook her head without replying.

He groaned angrily. "I ought to beat you for your pigheaded stupidity. Stonor does not deserve you."

"It would kill him to find out," she said unsteadily. "I cannot do that to him." Her eyes were sad. "And if he even suspected it, he would disinherit Daniel."

Wolfe's eyes narrowed. "So that's it," he said flatly. "My God—defeated by my own son." A queer smile curved his mouth. "You devious, unpredictable bitch, do you know I shall love you to the day I die?"

She smiled back, a tremulous laughter in her voice. "There is nothing about you I do not know, Wolfe."

"There is one thing I still do not know," he said. "Where did you get the money, Sophia?"

She laughed, teasing, mocking him. "Find out."

"Oh, I shall," he said blandly. "And if your benefactor has any personal motive for his generosity I'll kill him."

She still laughed, her eyes amused. "Oh, I think not," she said lightly.

His amusement sobered. He eyed her. "Tell me it is a straight business transaction, Sophia."

She caught the warning note in his voice and laughed again,

enjoying the jealous anger in his eyes. "I'll tell you nothing."

"Then I shall make it my business to find out," he said, his mouth grim. "If you think I would let you find your consolations in some other man's bed, you're wrong. I will put up with your celibacy, Sophia, but not your fulfilment in another man's arms."

"You've no right to object if I chose to do it," she said, still amused.

"As your brother-in-law, I've every right," he said, his eyes insolent.

Sophia laughed openly. "You hypocrite."

He moved to the door, glancing back at her. "I'll find out, Sophia, never fear," he said softly. "And when I do... beware."

Two days later Wolfe returned, a grim look on his face, and stared at her from the doorway. She looked up from her ledgers and leaned back, waiting for him to speak.

Closing the door he said softly, "You cunning little bitch... Luther. My upright, virtuous cousin.... He told me frankly when I asked him if it was true.... Sophia, did you have to tell him everything?"

"It suited me to do so," she said steadily.

"Revenge, Sophia?" he asked grimly.

She didn't answer, and he grimaced.

"Luther is appalled, he tells me. How could I treat such a lovely, sweet, virtuous young matron so disgustingly, attempting to force her to cater for my depraved desires by common blackmail...." His eyes were angry, even as he spoke lightly. "I've had a good partnership with Luther all these years, but you've built a wall between us. He ignored my women and my treatment of my wife—but I've a shrewd fancy he desires you himself, Sophia, and, being Luther, the thought that I had tried to take so blatantly what he secretly wants himself has made him view with disfavour what he merely winked at before. What will you do if Luther tries to take you?"

"He will not," she said clearly. "I assure you, I am certain of that."

"Tell me I'm wrong about how he feels, then," Wolfe said drily. "Tell me Luther has not looked at you with desire?"

She smiled, her eyes mocking. "Oh, he has looked, but as you say, he is basically virtuous. He will not lose his head."

Wolfe grimaced. "I hope not—or I might make sure he loses it permanently."

She leaned back in her chair, staring at him, feeling the clamour in her blood like an illness. Her long months without Stonor's lovemaking had left her starving for fulfilment. She wanted Wolfe so badly she could only just hold herself on a leash. Since they had parted and she had given herself entirely to Stonor, she had suppressed all her love for Wolfe. Their few meetings, stolen kisses, touches of the hand, had been a heady delirium throughout those years. She had suppressed it by force, and Stonor's passion had helped her. Her deeply growing love for her husband had coupled with her sensual enjoyment of their nights together to make a firm wall that Wolfe could never break down. Now that Stonor could not give her the relief her body needed, the wall was weakening rapidly, and Sophia knew it. Her reasons for breaking with him were unchanged; only her weakness for him was no longer kept in check.

As Wolfe turned to go Sophia clenched her hands on her desk, biting her lips to silence the cry of need that might emerge. She wanted desperately to feel his mouth on her own, to feel the hard masculinity of his body pressed against her. Instead, she forced a polite smile, and Wolfe went, leaving her struggling against desires she could only hope time would allay.

Sophia's partnership with Luther Hunt made a dramatic difference to the firm. His brilliant business sense and flair brought a change to the way in which the Whitley empire had been moving. Sophia and he spent hours with George Blare, discussing plans, going over ledgers, probing the future. Sophia confessed to Stonor what she had done that summer, and Stonor reacted with angry bitterness.

"How could you do such a thing to my business? Luther Hunt will slowly absorb it into his firm, you stupid woman."

Sophia glanced at him, seeing his physical weakness and mental embitterment with sadness. She hesitated, then decided to tell the truth. "I had no choice. I . . . I had to mortgage Queen's Stonor. . . ." She told him everything then, and he listened with eyes that turned to flame as she went on.

She omitted Wolfe's offered alternative, merely telling Stonor that when she discovered to whom she had mortgaged their home she had looked desperately for a way to free it from Wolfe's grip. Stonor was not deceived. He stared at her blindly, his face white.

"He wanted you, that is what you are not telling me," he said. "He had the house and that meant he had you."

"Stonor," she said anxiously. "It is over now. You see why I had to sell to Luther..."

Stonor groaned. "Oh, I see, I see it all: the scheming, twisting bastard. Oh, God, if I were not a cripple...."

She held his hands, urging him to believe her. "I did not hesitate even for one second. I was so angry I could have killed him—"

Stonor's mouth twisted wryly. "Angry because he threatened Queen's Stonor, not because he threatened our marriage, Sophia?" he said.

"I would not break my oath to you," she said steadily.

Stonor laughed. "Oh, take back your oath, Sophia. I'll not bind you with words. I regretted asking you the moment I had done so. If you chose to go to him, no oath could hold you and I know it."

"I do not choose to go to him," she said.

"No," Stonor said in that wry voice. "You do not choose to go. I do not blind myself to the reasons why."

They were alone in the bedroom, as they were each evening before Sophia retired to her own room. The nurse had put Stonor to bed an hour earlier and had gone to her own couch in a room across the hall. Stonor had a bell with which he could summon her if he needed her in the night. Sophia looked down at him, reading his disillusion, his weariness, his despair, and her heart ached for him.

She sat down on the bed and began to stroke his hair, her eyes warmly inviting. Stonor stared at her, his eyes shifting restlessly over her slender body. "How do you manage to look so lovely at your age?" he asked her. "As you get older the bones in your face seem to take on a beauty that takes my breath away. Your skin is so good you must use witch-craft...."

Sophia slowly let down the black silk of her hair and Stonor moved his hands to touch it, his eyes closing. He felt her hands stroke over his chest, sliding beneath the high collar to find his skin.

"It is so long," he groaned. "So bitterly long since I held you in my arms, my darling...."

"Stonor," she murmured, her eyes half-closed, sensual longing in her face.

He looked up at her, reading with deep hunger the look on

her features. From beneath her lids her eyes glimmered down at him. Slowly she began to unfasten her dress, and Stonor watched, his breath thickening. She stripped while he watched, looking back at him, deliberately provocative as she moved to fold her clothes on the end of the bed. Then she arched her body over his and Stonor made a hoarse, suffering sound of desire. "Christ, you know it is impossible, Sophia.... Are you trying to drive me mad?"

"Please me, Stonor," she said huskily. "Touch me...I need it...oh, Stonor, I shall go mad...touch me...."

Stonor's hands trembled as he began to stroke her white body, hearing her muffled cries of pleasure and relief under the caress of his fingers. When his mouth touched her breasts she twisted hungrily, gasping. Inch by inch she exposed her flesh to the warmth of his mouth, the probing, arousing exploration of his tongue. Stonor was sweating, his eyes moving over her. She swung suddenly out of his reach and he saw her pull the bedclothes away from the limp immobility of his body. "No, Sophia," he muttered, wincing. She gave him a quick look, then turned and put out the lamp. In the stuffy darkness Stonor felt her hands pull back his night shirt, then she softly touched him, her small fingers kneading his pallid, lifeless skin. "Can you feel it when I touch you, darling?" she asked him.

Stonor was torn between an acute pleasure in feeling her hands on him again after so long, and his dislike of having her know the true state of his shattered legs. The scars and wasted muscles revealed themselves to her slowly searching fingers, and Stonor was helpless to disguise from her any longer the loss of his strong, fit limbs. The weak shrunken body that he now had made him almost sick with hatred and disgust, and he was afraid she would feel the same. Stonor's pride would not permit her to know how he felt. He lay and suffered as she discovered in the dark that the powerful male body she had known during their marriage had become a pale wreck.

Sophia read his mind as if she could see it in front of her. At her finger ends she learned Stonor's bitter loss and anger. Slowly she bent her head and her mouth trailed over his skin. Stonor gave a sudden gasp, a hoarse cry, almost a groan of shocked disbelief.

Her mouth incited him softly and he pushed at her head with his hand shaking. "No...."

"Yes," she said, her tongue silken on his skin, feeling the sensitive, hardening flesh under her mouth.

"Oh, God," Stonor moaned. "I can't let you do this. . ."

"I want to," she said softly against his body. "I am enjoying it."

Stonor abandoned any attempt to stop her. He lay with closed eyes and incredulous pleasure, feeling her mouth as it tortured him to an extremity of sensuous need. "Sophia, my love, my dearest love," he gasped, unable to hold back as the almost forgotten agony overcame him.

Sophia lay beside him, her warm body curved against his, her head on his shoulder, hearing the wild racing of his heart slow and the suffocating hoarseness of his breathing calm.

"Did it tire you, my darling?" she asked him, a hand on his chest to test the pace of his heart.

"It should not have happened," Stonor said. "I should not have let you do it. My God, my darling, you know you should not have done it. . . ."

She laughed, brushing his skin with her flushed cheek. "I wanted to see if you had lost all feeling. You haven't, Stonor. Have you?"

"No," he said shakingly. "Oh, God, Sophia, no." He kissed her, his mouth trembling. "You almost drove me out of my mind, you know that. I've wanted you so long. I've been so afraid I would lose you. But this. . .I cannot let you. . . ."

She laughed. "You cannot stop me," she teased, bending her head to kiss his mouth softly. Her tongue teased his lips sensitively. "I can do what I like and you cannot stop me. . . ."

"I adore you," he said hoarsely. "I worship you."

"Still my slave, Stonor?" she asked him gently.

"Utterly," he whispered.

"Then I am content," she said, leaning her head upon him. After a moment she tidied his bed and picked up her clothes.

"Light the lamp," he said drowsily. "Let me watch you dress. . . ."

She obeyed without comment and with half-closed, smiling eyes he watched her as she resumed her clothes. After she had kissed him good night, and gone out, the slow night enveloped Stonor as if swallowing him, so that for the first time since his accident, he slept like a happy child.

The resumption of their private life, even on such an occasional level, changed Stonor. The bitterness vanished; he bore his pain, his helplessness, without the grey tension. When Sophia was lying in bed beside him, exchanging slow sensuality with him, she knew that he had begun to live for nights like this. Her own needs were eased; her fear of Wolfe was penned in again. While Stonor could relieve her physical hunger, Wolfe ceased to be ever present in her mind, a dark figure prowling on the borders of her life, waiting for his chance to take her, and Stonor knew it too. His hourly terror of his brother faded again as he guessed that Sophia was his once more, and with his fear of Wolfe eased his moods became softer.

He even tried to be kind to Daniel when he and Edward came home during the school summer vacation. At twenty Daniel was suddenly almost a man, his shoulders filling out, his face now unmistakably that of Wolfe—dark, handsome, arrogant. He looked at Queen's Stonor as he rode in the park with the eyes of a future master, his blue-green gaze blazing with possession. Louise was delighted by his return. While Edward spent most of the day hovering near his father, happy to wait on him, to read to him, play chess or talk to him, Louise and Daniel rode together in harmony, talking and laughing, totally at ease together.

When Jerome appeared in the park one August morning, Louise was petrified. She dreaded the questions Daniel would ask him, and waited for them, but they never came, and the three of them spent the morning lying in the grass laughing, watching the hot blue sky with lazy eyes. When Louise went in to luncheon, she expected Daniel to follow her, but he never came.

Sophia was arranging white roses in a silver bowl on the drawing-room table. The soft light of an oil lamp gleamed over her black hair. The dove-grey dress she wore was of a filmy material that fluttered seductively as she moved, outlining her slender figure. Louise, seated on the brocade sofa watching her, turned to stare as Daniel flung open the door and looked wildly at his mother.

Sophia turned in mild reproval at the crash of his arrival, and then took in the look on his face, and went pale. Daniel stared at her, the beautiful strange eyes in his white face filled with bitterness.

"Is it true? Am I Wolfe Whitley's bastard?"

Sophia swayed in shock, catching the edge of the table to support herself. "Who told you that?" Her mind went at once to Stonor, stunned by the thought that he had told her son the truth.

"Jerome," Daniel muttered through his shaking lips. "My half-brother, it seems. Oh, Christ, so it is true! You cannot even deny it! That is why Papa has never cared for me, why I have always felt I shared no part of him—" He stopped, looking at her as if he had never seen her before, his wild eyes running over the exquisite picture she made in that elegant room, her sleek black hair and fine-boned, delicate face filled with the fastidious refinement of her birth and nature.

His face quivered. The depths of disillusion and distaste in his voice rang out clearly. "You let that man—" He broke off, as though even to say what was festering in his mind might burn his lips.

All his life he had worshipped her without question. Stonor's open adoration of her had set the pattern in the household long ago. Sophia ran Queen's Stonor with such gentle, smiling sweetness, and in return all those under its roof had treated her reverently. Daniel's romantic view of his mother had been shattered for ever. The thought of her in the arms of the insolent, mocking stranger whom he had detested on sight, permitting him intimacies Daniel felt sick to consider, made him want to scream. He had been violently sick after Jerome had calmly told him. He had asked for the truth, and Jerome had given it to him, with the cold steel of the surgeon's knife. Jerome had lived with hatred, disillusion and scorn for so long that he had not expected the violent depths of Daniel's reaction, perhaps even a little alarmed by the way the other boy had looked afterwards.

Sophia moved towards Daniel, pleadingly, but he backed away, as if her touch might contaminate him. His face was half-mad with misery and pain. Suddenly, he cried wildly, "I will kill him!"

Sophia ran after him as he tore from the room, but he had gone through the front door into the dark night, leaving the door wide open, the fragrant summer air breathing warmly into the house as she heard the sound of his horse's hoofbeats departing down the drive.

Sophia stood for a moment, trying to think, her mind thrown into terrified confusion. Louise had followed her into the hall, watching her anxiously, and as Sophia turned she met the girl's blue eyes, and saw the compassion and alarm in them, and knew that Daniel's discovery had been no surprise to her daughter. Louise gently took her hand, smiling at her.

"He will come back, Mama," she said soothingly.

Sophia felt tears prick at her eyes. "Louise, my dear," she said, the soft murmur of her voice filled with gratitude and love, replying to the look and tone rather than the words. She drew herself up. "I must go after him. He is unstrung. God knows what he may do." She looked at Louise, trying to speak calmly. "Stay here, and if your father asks where I am, tell him I have a headache and have gone to lie down. He will not wish to disturb me. I will get a jacket. Tell Russell to fetch the carriage round at once."

Louise flew to obey her. Returning to the hall a few moments later she found her mother already there, a velvet jacket covering her grey gown. "Let me come with you, Mama," Louise begged. "You may need me."

Sophia shook her head. "You must stay here with your father. I will come to no harm." She kissed her daughter warmly, held her for a moment in tight arms, then went out into the dark summer night.

# CHAPTER TWENTY-THREE

Wolfe lounged on a deep, silver-brocade chair in his elegantly furnished drawing room, staring at a new marble statuette he had bought that morning, a figure of a young girl, bathing in a shell-like fountain, her slender naked limbs exquisite, her hair caught by a fillet on the top of her poised small head. It reminded him of Sophia. His half-lowered lids disguised the hungriness of his eyes as they roved over the pure line of the girl's body. He would keep it in the bedroom, he thought, his lips twisting wryly. He could look at it as he lay in bed at night. He had lately felt no drive to seek pleasures in strange beds. Either, he thought with dry amusement, he was getting old, or purchased sex had lost its appeal for him. For years he had taken his strong sexual drive for granted, indulging it at will. Yet he felt no sense of loss now that he had ceased to feel it.

His marriage to Eleanor had ended physically after the birth of their youngest son, Jonathon. She had almost endangered the child's life by her drinking, and Wolfe's irritated demand that she stop had only made her more determined to go on with it. Drink had coarsened her features, blurred her once shapely figure, made her distasteful to him. She had taken his absence from her bed badly for a while, and the scenes had been shocking. Then she had relapsed into sullen oblivion, drowning herself in gin, as if it helped her to forget. Wolfe's open liaisons with a succession of kept women had brought an occasional obscene bitterness into their relationship, and her open drunkenness had meant that she had ceased to be invited when Wolfe went out to other houses. Gradually, he had ceased to treat her as his wife at all. He now furnished and ran the house himself, and Eleanor was rarely seen outside her room, which he had made into a boudoir of restrained elegance and she had turned into a stinking gin palace, deliberately leaving empty bottles everywhere, leaving her vulgar, crudely coloured clothes lying on the floor and hanging out of open drawers. She often never dressed at all, slouching in a loose, stained wrapper, her hair dishevelled and gaudy, her coarse-featured face heavy with stupor.

Wolfe had long ago begun to take care that his children saw as little of their mother as possible, and had ordered their nurse to keep them away from her. A quiet, discreet woman, she had shown no sign of comment as she had nodded. As soon as Jonathon and his two elder brothers James and Martin were old enough, they had gone off to school, and each holiday they went away together, to play and be free under the nurse's watchful eye at an expensive hotel on the Devon coast, which was where they and Alice were now.

It had been more difficult with Alice. Wolfe had been forced to keep her at home, but he had seen to it that she too, was, as far as possible, sheltered from Eleanor's presence.

He regarded his children with possessive affection. Even Jerome, his difficult, sardonic son, aroused pride in him. It was for them that he worked to build a vast fortune, and he protected them as far as he could from the damage of their home environment.

Jerome was in the house now. In his room, Wolfe thought drily, reading his everlasting medical tomes. Jerome's unmoving insistence that he wanted to be a doctor had irritated him. Wolfe wanted him to come into his business—the choice he offered him was wide enough, God knew. He had spread his interests more and more widely in the last few years. Newspapers, property, finance, trade—Jerome could have started anywhere. Yet the boy obstinately, grimly, refused even to consider the idea. Wolfe was under no illusions as to how his eldest son regarded him, and he even felt pity and regret for the life the boy had been shown as he grew up. Eleanor's drunken, coarse rages made her no mother for any sensitive child. Wolfe had succeeded better with his younger children in filling the empty space Eleanor had left in their lives, treating them with loving fondness himself. But for some reason, he had never been able to show Jerome the same warmth. Eleanor had got at him at too early an age, filling his ears with sick tales of his father's cruelty and evil. Wolfe guessed Jerome no longer believed all his mother told him, but the damage had been done by then. Jerome hated both of them. He found his mother embarrassing, distasteful and sick. His father he despised and loathed.

Wolfe's blue-green eyes again roved over the white marble body of the bathing girl. He sighed deeply, running his hands through his dark hair. Why had Sophia thrown away their last hope of a brief happiness? The futility of it had left him scarred. He had felt no desire for any woman since. He had been so sure, so eager.... And now that he had failed to get her he felt despair.

Thirty-nine, Wolfe thought. Soon I shall be forty. The thought made him wince. His one night with Sophia had become an elusive horizon of bliss that he had sought endlessly, hungrily, despairingly. She had felt the same, he knew it. Even though she had clearly grown to love Stonor and openly admitted that she enjoyed going to bed with him, Wolfe was not deceived. Only the two of them could know the piercing agony of the lovemaking they had shared for one night. It had had the dimension of a dream. No other woman in his life had reached that pitch with him, nor he with anyone else. It had been an act of total merging. Wolfe had not taken her—they had taken each other, their minds as united as their bodies, exchanging souls. He had told her, as if by premonition, that it was a sacrament as binding as marriage. He had meant it then, and he meant it more each hour of each day.

When she had decided to end their secret hours together, he had accepted it, worn out by the long frustration of never possessing her body totally. He had had his long climb to wealth before him. He had wanted to cement the future with sons and a respectable background, and at the beginning he had thought Eleanor might make the right wife. He had achieved the financial success he had sought. He had had four sons. But he had found the victory bitter: his personal life had been empty; pleasure had palled. He had tasted the emptiness of wealth and had turned away, feeling cheated.

Many times in the past years he had looked with bitter envy towards Queen's Stonor. His half-brother's notorious contentment, the success of that marriage, had almost driven Wolfe insane. He had seen Sophia so rarely, often only in the distance. Their few meetings had had a charged, electric bittersweetness he found haunting. To know she still loved him, to feel the bond between them unbroken, had made it worse. He had lived for a year on a kiss, for six months on the brief touch of her hand. Weeks when he did not see her were deserts. He understood perfectly why she stayed with Stonor. He read her thoughts without difficulty. She could not place a barrier between their minds. He could always read her.

Stonor's accident had called out all Wolfe's tenderness towards her. Knowing her fondness for his half-brother, he had thought only of her pain, hoping Stonor would live, certain that if it were humanly possible, Stonor's driving passion for her would pull him back to life. Only afterwards had Wolfe begun to consider the future. He had begun to glimpse his chance, and his wild eagerness had almost made him crazy for a while.

"Oh, God, I was so sure," he muttered, his face grim.

Jerkily, he leaned forwards and poured himself a glass of port. He drank little these days. Eleanor's example had been a warning. As he sipped the rich, red liquid, he heard a sudden outburst of knocking at the front door, and frowned, glancing at the silver French clock on the mantelpiece. It was late for callers. Could something be wrong?

All the servants except Rogers, the butler, were in bed by now. He heard the baize door to the kitchen open, then heard Jerome call, "I'll see to it, Rogers. Good night."

"Good night, Master Jerome," Rogers said in his polite cold voice, and the baize door closed again.

Wolfe lounged back, sipping his port, his eyes on the white girl's body again. He heard Jerome speaking, heard a muffled sound that seemed to be that of a blow, and began to rise. Before he had moved, the door was flung open and a slim boy rushed into the room, his face white and strained, his hair windblown. Wolfe stared at him, instinctively leaning back to give himself time to think, his casual, insolent good looks hardening in thought.

Daniel stared at him. "You...you swine..." His roughened tone shook with wild emotions. "I'll kill you."

Jerome appeared in the doorway, a bruise darkening on his cheekbone, a curious ironic smile on his mouth. Wolfe glanced at him, eyes narrowed.

"Good evening, Daniel," he said coolly. "Does your mother know you are here?"

As if the bland question loosened all Daniel's rage and hatred the boy ran towards him and began to shower Wolfe's unguarded face with slashing blows from the riding crop he carried. For a moment Wolfe was so taken aback, so startled, that he merely sat there, feeling the stinging of the blows with disbelief. Then he grew annoyed, twisting the weapon away from the boy with a flick of his strong wrists. Daniel punched him, his fists swinging wildly, and with a grim look Wolfe was on his own feet and quickly caught Daniel by the shoulders, pushing him relentlessly back until the boy stood against a wall, flailing with fists and kicking feet, sobbing, his eyes flashing with grief and hatred.

Wolfe stared at him, feeling a queer weakness in his own body. The boy looked so much like himself. He was Sophia's son. The passionate love he bore Sophia had given the boy life.

"Daniel," he said gently, lovingly, his hands holding him away. "Don't, my son—"

There was a silence so intense the room seemed stricken with it. Daniel stared at him. Wolfe's blue-green eyes were filled with a light only Sophia had ever seen before. Daniel would have had to be blind not to read the love in the hard, dark face. Slowly a wash of crimson ran up his face.

Lounging in the doorway, Jerome watched them, and an incredulous anger came into his eyes. His father had never looked at, spoken to him like that. Or to his brothers, or even to Alice...indeed, the last time Jerome had heard that tone in his father's deep voice had been when he had seen him with Daniel's mother in the garden of his home. He remembered as if it were yesterday the depth of passion he had sensed in his father then, and the jealousy, rage and hurt he had suffered.

Into that silence came more knocking. Jerome turned and walked down the hall, his face bitter. Opening the door, he looked icily at Sophia.

She read his face quickly. "Daniel is here?"

Jerome jerked the door open wider and gestured without speaking, his attitude contemptuous.

He followed her graceful figure down the hall, watching the sway of her slim body, the poise of her dark head, with a peculiar hunger. This, he thought, might have been my mother....

He had had the thought first as he watched her in his father's arms under the apple trees. She had been the most beautiful woman he had ever seen, and the combination of her alluring body and the warm loving maternal feelings she had shown towards her own children had angered him into hating her for being out of his reach. He had known the sick taste of treachery as he looked at her and wished she were his mother. Eleanor, for all her drunken coarseness, was his flesh...and Jerome had felt bitter in betraying her, even in thought. Ever since, when Jerome saw Sophia, he had felt the same contest between attraction and hatred, and felt it now, redoubled by his father's unexpected, loving way of speaking to Daniel.

Sophia walked into the room and saw her son pushed against the wall, held there stiffly by Wolfe. She saw the red slash marks on Wolfe's hard face, the cut at the corner of his lip, the faint trickle of blood on his chin. Daniel's face was confused and wild. He did not look at her; he stared at Wolfe instead.

Wolfe looked round and his eyes touched Sophia. Both the boys saw the emotion in his look and both flinched from it.

"How did he find out?" Wolfe asked her levelly. "Stonor?"

"No," she said quietly. "No, not Stonor."

"I told him," Jerome said insolently. "He asked if I knew anything, so I told him.... It was time he knew what any mirror could have told him years ago."

Wolfe's eyes were dangerous as he surveyed his son. "Go to your room, Jerome. I'll deal with you later."

Jerome smiled coldly. "Don't you want to know how I found out, Father? Aren't you curious as to who told me all about your secret mistress, the special one you kept locked away while you paraded all the others openly?"

Sophia winced at the sting in his voice, and Wolfe released Daniel abruptly, turning instinctively to take her into his arms, forgetting his watching sons, only concerned with the white misery of her face.

"My darling, don't," he said hoarsely. "Don't look like that. He gets it from his whore of a mother...."

Jerome laughed. "Talking about whores," he said conversationally, and Wolfe's eyes grew violent, his face so black with rage that he looked terrifying as he moved from Sophia towards Jerome.

Sophia caught at his arm. "No, Wolfe," she said, tears in her eyes. "No—"

Wolfe halted, breathing hard, his fists clenched. He stared at Jerome menacingly. "Speak of her like that again and I will knock you to the floor...."

"You should not have said such a thing about Eleanor," Sophia said huskily. "It was wrong, Wolfe, to speak like that in front of her son. He loves his mother."

"He hates his mother," Wolfe said impatiently.

Sophia winced, remembering the sick distaste and hatred Daniel had shown on hearing the truth. Until now, he had adored her, and she had valued his love even above that of

Stonor. She had built her whole life around him. Daniel was to inherit Queen's Stonor. For Daniel her love for Wolfe had been thrown away. The thought of his new feelings for her made her sick.

Wolfe saw the pain in her face, and he caught her into his arms, his cheek against her black hair. "Oh, God, my dearest love, don't...."

Jealously, Daniel leapt forwards to push him away from her, his eyes filled with hate. Wolfe released her and caught Daniel, pinioning the boy's flailing arms easily.

He looked into the hate-filled face with a sigh. Sophia was crying softly, her head in her hands.

"Listen to me, Daniel. I am not ashamed of having fathered you on your mother." Daniel's breath raged furiously. Wolfe smiled at him. "I am proud of it. We fell in love before she agreed to marry Stonor. We were going to elope, but we were so wildly in love I couldn't wait.... It was all my fault—I needed her. Can you understand that need? We had one night together, then she fell ill. They said she could never have a child or she would die. I was almost crazy with grief, but I knew I lacked the control to marry her and never make love to her. So I went away, and she married Stonor after all. He loved her enough to do what I wasn't man enough to do. He even accepted you, knowing you were my son. Your mother swore to him she would never tell a living soul that you were not his child. I will not have you despise your mother. Any blame is mine, but I—" Daniel struggled suddenly, interrupting, his face wild.

Wolfe held him, his fingers possessive. "Yes, Daniel, I know you are hurt and angry now, but your mother and I loved each other." His eyes flashed. "We still love each other. And we both love you, my son."

"How touching," said a voice from the door, the tone indistinct. Eleanor stumbled into the room, her coarse face flushed between straggling gaudy hair, an unkempt wrapper flung around her clumsy body. She held a bottle in her hand, and looked as if she had consumed most of its contents.

"What a beautiful love story, my dear husband," she mocked. "But you've left out a few things, haven't you? Like how you and your secret whore met for years while her husband ate his heart out for her, or how you've been trying to get back into her bed ever since by every filthy trick you know.... Oh, don't think I know nothing about the way you've wanted her for years—''

Wolfe made a violent move, but Sophia held him back, shivering. Eleanor gave Daniel a bitter, malicious smile.

''Your dear father, my boy, lusts after the elegant Mrs. Stonor Whitley night and day, particularly at night. She has that effect on men, your lovely mother. Her husband crawls on his knees if she smiles at him, and she knows how to keep him on his knees, don't you, Mrs. Whitley?'' She laughed coarsely. ''Oh, Christ, if the upright citizens of Bristol knew the truth about the mistress of Queen's Stonor...'' She swept an ungainly, lurching curtsey. ''Oh, she's the admiration of Somerset, so refined and beautiful, of such an aristocratic family, the perfect wife and mother, kept on a pedestal by a husband who would sacrifice anything to keep her.''

Sophia winced at this mention of Stonor, and Wolfe's arm tightened, responding to her pain with a searing anger. His eyes raked Eleanor bitterly.

''Jerome, take your mother upstairs,'' he said bitingly. ''She is in no condition to know what she is saying....''

Jerome did not move, his head bent, a curiously sick expression on his face.

Eleanor laughed, swaying, raising the bottle to her lips and swallowing some of the spirits. ''Oh, I know what I *am* saying! The boy's learned the truth, and it's time he knew all of it—'' She hiccupped, patting her mouth. ''Why the hell not? He's no child any more. I've no doubt he has swallowed the lies his mother's fed him all these years, and it's time he learned what a cheating, two-faced little bitch she really is.''

''Shut up,'' Wolfe said, starting forwards, his hand raised to hit her, but Sophia clung to him, saying, ''No, Wolfe,'' and, looking at her, he groaned and put his arms about her, holding her openly, protectively, possessively.

Eleanor stared, her flush darkening. ''You see, Daniel? Your lady mother burns for my husband the way he does for her. They lust for each other like trapped animals. You have only to see them together to know that. Look at them, boy. You should see them dance together. My God, a blind man could see that they're aching to go to bed. My dear husband can hardly keep his hands off her, and she looks at him, openly yearning to have him rip her clothes off, but you see, Daniel, she hasn't got the guts to leave the elegant fleshpots of Queen's Stonor for him. That's why they haven't run off together long ago. Oh, she'll feed you a pretty tale about being faithful to Stonor Whitley, but the truth is she cannot bear to lose her place as queen of the county. What a come-down to be known as Wolfe Whitley's little whore—all the romantic trappings come off if you look closer, my boy. It isn't a fabled love affair. It is a sordid little lusting they haven't the courage to admit. . . ."

Wolfe would have moved to shut Eleanor's mouth in the first sentence, but Sophia stopped him, holding him tightly. As the vile words poured out, his face turned to stone, and Sophia grew so white she was clearly on the point of fainting. Daniel stood in anguished, sickened disbelief, staring at Eleanor as the loose, wet mouth ranted on. Jerome thrust his hands into his pockets and stared at the floor. Even his bitterness could not bear to hear Eleanor's outburst.

When she stopped there was a long silence. Eleanor looked from one face to another, laughing. Suddenly her laughter died and her green eyes raged with a surge of jealousy.

She stared at Sophia's slender, graceful body, seeing the protective way Wolfe shielded her, his arm holding her.

"You bitch!" she screamed suddenly, her real hatred breaking loose. "Get away from my husband—" Her clumsy body flew towards Sophia, the almost-empty bottle held as a weapon. "I'll ruin your lovely face for you, by God," she shrieked, and the bottle slashed downwards at Sophia with a sudden movement that took Wolfe totally by surprise, so that he only stared, shattered to rigidity.

It was Daniel who reacted first. A hoarse cry broke from him as he saw the bottle flying at Sophia's pale face. He leapt forwards, striking Eleanor bitterly, throwing himself between the bottle and his mother instinctively, taking the blow meant for her upon his face.

"Daniel!" Sophia cried in terror and grief, turning to catch him as the blow struck.

Eleanor fell backwards too, her body clumsy. She struck her head upon the corner of the black marble fireplace and lay still. Nobody even noticed. Jerome, Wolfe and Sophia were gathered around Daniel in shared anxiety. He lay very still, his white face marred by a long bleeding cut that ran across his temple. Jerome pushed Sophia gently away and lifted Daniel's wrist. He knelt, frowning.

"His pulse is just a little fast," he said, after a moment. "We will have to get a doctor for him."

"Oh, God," Wolfe muttered, his hand tender as it touched the unconscious boy's cheek. "He's so cold."

Jerome got up. "I'll fetch Dr. Waring," he said, then turned and caught sight of his mother. A grimace of distaste crossed his face. He bent and touched her wrist, too. Sophia was gently wiping the blood from Daniel's head with a handkerchief. Tears ran down her face. Wolfe watched her, helpless.

Jerome stood up. "Father," he said quietly.

Wolfe looked around, his eyes narrowing. He moved over to Eleanor's body, looking down at her, his mouth hard.

"She's dead," Jerome said flatly.

Wolfe looked blank. "But—"

"She hit her head hard," Jerome said.

Daniel was stirring, his eyes fluttering. "Lie still, my darling," Sophia whispered, stroking his black hair.

The blue-green eyes opened wide. Tears leapt into them. "Mama," Daniel cried like a child, "Mama..."

Sophia kissed him passionately on his cheek and his eyelids. "Rest there, darling," she muttered huskily. "Don't try to move...."

Jerome and Wolfe both turned to look at them. Tender, melting, loving, she knelt at the boy's side, stroking his hair and kissing him. Daniel was looking at her weakly.

"I love you, Mama," he said.

"Oh, my darling, I know you do," she said brokenly. "I love you too."

Daniel's eyes closed and he sighed wearily.

Jerome felt a sick envy in his stomach. He glanced obliquely at his father and saw his own jealous, hungry look in the man's face.

Below his breath, Jerome said, "We can't have Dr. Waring here to see them both—it would cause talk. She will have to take Daniel away and get their own doctor to see him. When they've gone, we'll call Dr. Waring and say Mother tripped while she was drunk. There'll be no surprise to Waring in that—she is always falling over."

Wolfe nodded grimly. He moved to Sophia and bent, lifting Daniel like a child. "You must take him home," he told her. "It must not be known this happened here...."

Sophia followed without question as he bore her son out of the room. Left alone with his dead mother, Jerome looked at her once, then looked away, his face convulsed. "Oh, God," he said under his breath. "Oh, God..."

When the carriage delivered them back to Queen's Stonor,
Sophia sent to the village for the doctor, who discreetly attended to Daniel's cut, shaking his head over it. "There'll be a
scar," he said. "Can't be avoided, I'm afraid." He smiled at
the boy. "It will spoil those good looks of yours for a few
weeks, then it will fade, with luck." He winked. "I'm sure the
young ladies will find it very dashing and romantic."

Left alone, Sophia looked nervously at her son. He lay in his
bed, his bandaged head on the pillows, his eyes on her face.

"Daniel, I know it is hard for you to understand," she said
huskily. "I wish I could have spared you ever knowing. Your
father did not mean you to know. . ." She halted, flushing.
"Stonor did not mean it. You are still our eldest son, Queen's
Stonor is yours, darling. . . ."

"I know about his promise," Daniel said thickly. "Jerome
told me. His mother knew all about it. But I can't. . ." He
swallowed. "I can't live a lie all my life. Queen's Stonor is Edward's house, not mine. I don't want something that does not
really belong to me."

"Don't say that," she winced. "Darling, all these years. . .
The house is yours, not Edward's. Stonor wants you to have
it."

"He wants you to be happy," Daniel said. "He has never
liked me. He hates me. If it were not for his dislike of making
you sad, he would long ago have thrown me out."

"No," she said wildly.

Daniel lay still, his eyes closing. She bent over him lovingly,
unhappily. "Darling. . ."

"I want to go to sleep now, Mother," he said without opening his eyes.

She had no choice but to go, terrified of what was going on
inside her son's mind, yet powerless to do anything. She did
not go to Stonor's room that night. She lay awake until dawn,
trying to think of a way of reaching Daniel before he did
something that might ruin both their lives. All her planning,
her dreams, her hopes were centred on the boy. She could not
face the thought of losing him.

Next morning she went to his room and found it empty.
Desperately, she searched for him. He was not to be found
anywhere, and when she looked again in his bedroom she
knew he had gone. Some of his clothes and an old valise were
missing. He had left no word of explanation. Silently he had
left the house on foot some time during the night.

White-faced, she went into Stonor's room. He was reading his morning newspaper and looked at her in concern, seeing the pallor of her face. "Darling, have you still got a headache? You look quite ill."

She faced him, her hands trembling. "Daniel has gone," she said starkly.

Stonor's brows drew together. His eyes darkened.

"He found out...the truth," she said. "Last night. This morning he has gone." Her voice was dry with pain. "And he is not coming back. I know it."

Stonor flinched, a burning fear in his eyes, staring at her. "How did he find out?"

Her mouth moved in a white smile. "Eleanor told her son Jerome, and Jerome told Daniel," she said.

Stonor swore under his breath. "That bloody woman again..." He looked at her desperately. "We will get him back. He's only a boy. He will not go far."

She shook her head without a flicker of expression. "No, I know he has gone for good. I think I knew last night. I could not reach him. He looked at me, and he was out of my reach." Turning, she walked out of the room, ignoring Stonor's urgent cry for her to come back.

Stonor had never felt his crippled helplessness so strongly. He knew only too well how much Daniel had meant to her. He knew she had lived to see her son master of Queen's Stonor. Daniel's disappearance had blown a great hole in the wall with which Stonor had held Sophia. He was terrified.

Briefly, he was filled with pity for the boy. He lay, remembering the day of Daniel's birth, when Stonor had almost wrenched him from his mother's body and had held him triumphantly in his hands. He had forgotten the feeling he had had for the child then. The long years while Daniel grew more and more like Wolfe had destroyed that emotion. As had Edward's birth. Now, he thought, now Edward will have Queen's Stonor, and a sharp pleasure pierced him. Then he thought again...if Edward has Queen's Stonor, she will leave me and go to Wolfe...and his heart beat with anguish. He loved Edward deeply, but he loved Sophia more. He stared at the wall, his face torn.

They heard next day of Eleanor's death. An accidental fall while she was intoxicated, gossip said politely. Less politely there were shrugs. "Drunk as an owl," people said. "It was bound to happen..."

Stonor received the news almost as a death blow. Wolfe was free. His wife out of the way, he was totally free to take Sophia.... Stonor lay, deathly white, waiting for her to come to him and tell him she was going, waiting because she did not come at all that day. She had a headache, he was told. Stonor cursed silently, grinding his teeth. Would she just go? Would she even come and tell him? He lay awake all night, his heart beating as if each beat was a stab of pain.

Louise sat at her mother's bed that night, holding her hand, while Sophia wept. They both knew Daniel had gone forever. They had not even talked of it. They looked at each other in misery and grief, and Sophia could not stop crying.

Stonor sent for Sophia in the morning. Louise went to him, her pale face strained. "Mama is too ill to come," she said quietly. ·

Stonor could see she knew. He stared at her hopelessly. His mouth shook and he held it firmly. "Tell her I will never alter my will," he said huskily. "Daniel shall have Queen's Stonor. He will come back one day and he will have the house."

Louise looked almost sick, her face quivering. She bent and kissed her father, crying. "It is no good, Papa...it is no good...."

When Louise had gone Stonor turned his face to the wall. It is no good. The words went on and on in his head.

# CHAPTER TWENTY-FOUR

It was three days before Stonor saw Sophia. She came into the room quietly, her face pale and expressionless, the light totally dead in her blue eyes. Stonor's heart leapt wildly. He hurriedly dismissed his nurse and held out his hand pleadingly towards his wife.

She took it and stood looking at him dully. "I am just leaving for the office," she said in a flat voice.

Stonor searched her face incredulously. "Yes," he said, playing for time. He longed to ask her questions, but he dared say nothing. She had not gone. She was not going. That was enough for the moment.

Sophia returned to work, sinking herself into it as Eleanor had done with drink. She worked long, exhausting hours, dragging herself home with a face like a stone and eyes that never smiled. The whole house felt the change in her. Even Edward was worried and alarmed. Daniel's disappearance had not been explained to him. All he knew was that his brother had run away. Stonor had made an exhaustive search for his missing son, sparing no expense, refusing to give up, but there was no clue, no word, no hint as to where Daniel had gone. His mother's sufferings were written on her face. Edward felt pity for her.

The weeks passed. Stonor said nothing, watching hopelessly as Sophia's lovely smiling grace failed to return. In its place he saw a woman as cold as death, lifeless, unreachable. She barely spoke to him these days. He rarely saw her.

Stonor was desperate enough, in the end, to send for Wolfe.

The summons came like a thunderbolt. Wolfe read the brief, unilluminating note with curious, thoughtful eyes. He had heard, of course, that Daniel had vanished. He had even been to the Whitley office in an attempt to see Sophia, but George Blare had three times denied him entry, and he had given up.

Now he drove out to Queen's Stonor, wondering what desperation had driven his half-brother to send for him.

Stonor lay alone, his face pale, his eyes expressionless. Wolfe stood looking down at him. A qualm of compassion crossed his face as he realized the full extent of Stonor's condition.

Stonor waved a hand to a chair. "Sit down."

Wolfe sat down, crossing his legs. A wry smile touched his hard mouth. "This is an unexpected occasion, Stonor—"

No flash of answering humour crossed the cold, pale face on the bed. Stonor said flatly, "I am frightened about Sophia."

Wolfe sat up, his eyes narrowing. "Why?" he asked brusquely.

"She is ill. . .never speaks, rarely eats, works from morning to night. . ." Stonor spoke huskily. "Oh, God, I think she's dying—"

Wolfe stared at him. "Because of the boy?"

"She has lost her reason for living," Stonor said flatly. "I knew she loved him deeply, but I never knew how much. She has given up caring about anything. I think if the house burned down tomorrow she would not even try to save it."

Wolfe flinched. His mouth tightened. "Why have you sent for me?" he asked his half-brother levelly.

Stonor looked away from him. His lips were white. "You were my last hope. . . ."

There was a long silence. Stonor glanced reluctantly back at his half-brother and found Wolfe regarding him with a curiously compassionate, almost admiring expression.

"You awe me, Stonor," Wolfe said ruefully. "My God, how you love her. . . . Would you really give her to me to save her life? I would not do as much. . . ."

"Wouldn't you?" Stonor sounded curious.

Wolfe made a slight face. "Oh, perhaps. When I left her with you in the beginning, I thought I could bear even her marriage to you rather than her death. . ."

"There is a condition," Stonor said roughly.

Wolfe looked at him hard, then smiled mockingly. "Ah, there is a catch, after all. . ."

Stonor flushed at that. "I cannot live without her," he said, and there was admitted pain in the cry.

Wolfe's eyes surveyed the helpless ruined body of his half-brother pityingly. "No," he said after a moment. "I see that. Well, Stonor? What is your condition?"

"She must never know I am aware of it," Stonor said huskily. "It must be secret. And she must not leave me."

Wolfe stood up and walked to the window, shivering. "Christ, you ask a good deal," he said. "If she found out about this she would think us both cold-blooded, disposing of her as if she were a chattel..."

"Do you think I am finding this easy?" Stonor's voice shook. "It is killing me. But I cannot stand by and watch her as she... She is dying under my eyes and I am helpless. I cannot offer her anything to hold her. She does not care if the house falls down. She never looks at me, let alone speaks to me. I could bear her hatred, her reproaches. I cannot bear this."

Wolfe sighed. He had thought at first that Stonor was releasing Sophia entirely. He had thought that at last she would be free. Now he saw that Stonor was trying to hold her anyhow, any way, despite the bitterness of the cost.

His mouth was crooked. "Now that you have told how things are, what is to stop me taking her for good?"

Stonor looked at him. "Nothing," he said.

Wolfe looked puzzled. "I do not understand you."

Stonor smiled, his mouth wry. "If she decides to go, I cannot hold her. She has not come to you, though. I waited. I thought she would. She did not. She just started to die silently. So I knew I had to let you know that she needs you now. I could not bear her to know what I had done. You must make her think I am blind to it. In exchange, let her stay with me. She will not go to you if you do not press her to. I'm sure of that. I've told you; you owe me something."

"Oh, Christ, brother mine, you are a master of intrigue," Wolfe said half-angrily. "So, out of my gratitude that you have told me your wife is now without defence against me, I am to promise not to take her from you?"

"Yes," Stonor said flatly. "That is it."

"God, have you no pride?" Wolfe demanded bitterly.

"None," Stonor said hoarsely. "Just make sure nobody ever hears of it. It must be the best kept secret in the world...."

"Are you so sure I'll agree?" Wolfe sneered.

Stonor held his eyes. "I am certain."

Wolfe's brows drew together. "Why? For God's sake, why?"

Stonor smiled drily. "Because I am where you have always wanted me, Wolfe—on my knees. And your pride will make you agree."

Wolfe stared at him for a long time. "I have never loved her that much," he said at last. "I always knew you were mad about her, but to do this..."

Stonor's eyes flashed with sudden, violent, intolerable passion. "You have no conception of love," he said fiercely. "Sophia is the breath of my life. I would sacrifice pride, life, my children—anything. There is literally nothing I would not do for her. I've starved for her, suffered for her, died for her, and I will go on doing it. I will bear anything if she will stay with me."

Wolfe gave a long groan. "Oh, very well," he said. "You win, Stonor. I'm a fool, but you win...."

When he had gone, Stonor stared at the room with pain-blind eyes. He pushed his knuckles into his mouth and bit them to stop the cries of jealous anguish that were tearing at him, and for a long time he did not move.

Wolfe went to the Whitley office next evening after the staff had all gone home. The night watchman let him in with a surly growl. Wolfe gave him a guinea, and the man touched his hat to him more politely. Wolfe quietly entered Sophia's office and found her seated at the desk, the lamp showing him her white stiff face, reading a file of letters. She looked up at him without expression.

He said nothing and reached for her jacket and hat. When he lifted her to her feet she pulled away from him rigidly. Wolfe held her with a struggle, forcing her into her outdoor clothes.

"What do you think you are doing?" she asked him wearily.

He took her arm and dragged her out of the office, past the staring, curious watchman, into the dark street. He had dismissed her carriage and his own waited. Wolfe put her into it and the carriage started off at once.

"Wolfe!" Irritation made her voice shake. "Where do you think you are taking me? I have to go home."

The carriage trotted quickly down a quiet side street, stopping at a small white-painted house. Wolfe helped her down and dismissed his driver, then led her, struggling, up the short path. He let them in at the door and closed it, leaning against it.

Suddenly her face came alive. "Daniel," she said hoarsely, "he is here?"

Wolfe's face quivered. "Oh, my darling," he said, and lifted her into his arms.

She lay quiescent in his arms as he carried her up the stairs, and sadly he could feel the tension in her body, the eagerness, the hope that Daniel would be waiting there for her. Bearing her into the small bedroom he put her down, holding her close, and said gently, "No, my love, he is not here...but we are...."

She gave a cry of grief. "No," she screamed, pulling away from him. Her frail hope of finding Daniel gone, she turned almost mad. As Wolfe tried to put his arms around her, to comfort and soothe her, her nails raked down his face, her fingers like claws.

"Don't, Sophia," he said huskily, but she hardly seemed to hear him. Animal rage possessed her. She struggled, her body twisting, striking his face violently.

A sudden storm of answering rage blew up within Wolfe. He thrust her backwards brutally, sending her tumbling onto the bed. Before she had recovered her balance, he was beside her, pushing back her skirts. She fought him silently, scratching, biting, kicking. Ruthlessly he caught her arms and bore them back above her head. She stared at him with wild eyes, hatred in her face, using her body and legs to keep him at bay.

Wolfe flung himself astride her, his superior strength controlling her. She writhed helplessly, arching her back, trying to throw him off, and the wild movements of her body beneath him sent a hot wave of sharp desire coursing through him. The love and gentleness he had longed to show her was submerged in a hunger so deep it burned inside his loins, driving him mad.

Wrenching her arms downwards, he leaned the full weight of his upper body upon them, releasing his own hands. While she struggled to free herself, he tore her underclothes away, his hands roughly parting her thighs before he undid his own clothes.

"No," she screamed bitterly, trying to evade him. Holding her thighs apart, Wolfe took her with such savage violence that he felt her whole body shudder underneath him. Her thighs were trembling as the hard, muscled body began to drive into her in an act of elemental possession while she clawed at his face and neck, sobbing wild hatred. He was deaf, ignoring her cries, her blows, using her body without tenderness or love, sensuality or gentleness, making himself full master of it with barbaric force. She had denied him for years. Now he would not be denied.

He saw the change in her take place as he stared down at her. The white, angry stiffness dissolved as though under water. A choked groan came from her parted mouth. He ripped her gown open, his teeth biting into her white breasts, his hands holding her throat, the thumbs hard on her soft skin. His body rammed into her like a tilt hammer, tireless, savage. She began to writhe, moaning. Wildly, she tore his shirt back, digging her nails into his bare chest, raking her fingers down his body, and at last the resistance of her flesh turned to hungry reception.

Burying her face in his throat, her mouth opened, she devoured his flesh, groaning. Heat burned between them, as if fire consumed their bodies, the bitter violence of their love-making at last melting her white grief for their son.

Wolfe could almost believe he felt the tearing membranes of her sorrow. He had wanted to make warm, sweet love to her, to ease that pain with tenderness, but he knew now that instinct had prompted him to do what she needed more—to assert the life force that had been dormant in her since Daniel had left, to force her to accept that she was alive and must go on living.

Wryly, he recognized, too, that he had needed this—he had been hungry for her so long, held at a distance, permanently haunted by her, filled with a persistent, nagging ache that he could not satisfy.

In the darkness their eyes met, hers filled with wild hunger, an explosive desire that was mindless, as if she barely knew who he was, only that the brutal rape of her body was easing the long agony of her sorrow for her son.

He felt her erotic movements quickening, her hoarse gasps of pleasure as her flesh ignited faster and faster. Sweat ran down his back and dewed his face as he thrust himself deep into her, fondling her full breasts with shaking hands.

She arched with bitter pleasure, her mouth open in a tortured cry of need, and Wolfe bent his head to take her mouth with the same ramming brutality he was using between her thighs, his tongue forced into her mouth, his lips hard and ruthless.

He was waiting now, knowing that his body was poised for the last agony, but refusing to release it until he took her with him. When at last her body quickened, shuddering, writhing, he slid his hands beneath her back, lifting her, and their bodies were one driving hunger, their voices hoarse with passion. When she lay still at last, the tears came in such a flood he thought they would never end.

He lay above her, still inside her, feeling her shake with the wildness of her pain. Softly he kissed her wet face, the tears under his own lids too.

"All these years for nothing," she said wildly. "I gave up my love for him . . . Queen's Stonor was for Daniel . . . and he's gone . . . all ended . . . nothing. . . ."

Wolfe kissed her without tiring, his mouth moving gently over her lids, feeling the tears squeeze out beneath his lips; over her wet cheeks, her nose, her ears, her chin, her quivering, moaning mouth.

At last she lay still, breathing huskily, and he lay down beside her, pulling her into his arms. Gently, he removed the last of her clothes and then his own. Naked, they lay close, silent, listening to the beat of each other's hearts. He stroked her body with his warm hands lingeringly.

"It's been so long," he said. "I've dreamed of this for years. I need to touch every inch of you."

She did not answer. He took her hand and placed it on his chest. For a second it lay without moving, then instinct made it flex softly, her fingertips stroking the black hairs on the skin. Her other hand touched him slowly. They faced each other, their eyes staring into one another's, and languorously let their hands wander at will, without passion. In the days when they had lain naked together unable to fulfil their desire properly, there had been an insane, burning pleasure in such exploration. Now there gradually grew a prickling, electric realization that they could abandon all inhibitions, all controls, and the warm, unhurried caresses began to grow fevered. Wolfe heard her groaning.

"Again, Wolfe," she whispered hoarsely. "Again. . . ."

They stayed all night, hardly speaking, wearing out each other's bodies with hunger that seemed insatiable. In the dawn light she lay yawning, her black hair tumbling over his shoulder, her hand on his body as if to reassure herself that he was there.

Suddenly she looked at him, her eyes enormous. "Wolfe. . . Stonor will go mad . . . he will wonder where I am . . . or not wonder . . . guess, which is worse."

"I told that driver of yours that you were staying in town to dine with the Winverns," he said casually, watching her. "I said you would stay the night with them."

"Stonor is bound to suspect, though," she said anxiously.

"Lie to him," Wolfe said. "You are going to have to learn to lie to him, my darling. If you think I will ever let you go again, you're wrong...." His hand pushed back the black hair, which was damp with the perspiration of their long love-making, and lovingly touched her cheek. "Either you come to me for good, or you lie to Stonor."

"I cannot leave him," she said slowly. "He...he could not bear it, Wolfe. I think he might die."

Wolfe's face did not change. His opalescent eyes watched her sad face thoughtfully. "Then you must lie," he said firmly. "This is our home, my darling. I've bought it. Here we will make love every day, and you will lie to Stonor."

"Oh, how can I?" she asked, but weakly, as if needing to be ordered.

"What the eye doesn't see, the heart does not grieve over," Wolfe said. "Stonor will never know. That is what matters."

She looked at him helplessly. "I cannot...."

"Can you tell him that you have lain in my arms all night?" he asked her wryly. "Can you look at him and tell him how many times I have had you during the hours we have been here? You have no choice but to lie, Sophia. Because you know as well as I do that this time we can never part again." He put a possessive hand upon her thigh, leaving it there, the fingertips caressing. "We have to have each other."

She closed her eyes in submission, sighing. "Yes," she admitted. "It has all been my fault. I have always been yours. I threw it all away for Daniel, and he has walked away without even saying goodbye."

"We'll find him again one day," Wolfe said gently. "Daniel loves you, darling. He will come back."

"He will not have Queen's Stonor," she said. "Not now."

"Damn Queen's Stonor," Wolfe said bitterly. "It is just a house, Sophia. We are alive and we need each other."

She gave him a bright, wild smile. "Oh, God, Wolfe, I could not give you up again. I must have you now."

And Wolfe felt his heart leap with response.

Stonor had lain awake all through that night. It seemed to him endless. He knew what was happening as if he were present. He had known from the moment he heard she had not re-

turned from Bristol. Wolfe had moved faster than Stonor had
somehow expected, and although he had accepted the necessity of what would happen, he could not stem the pain. He
thought of them together, the sweet white body he loved so
deeply in his brother's arms, and he groaned.

Before he had discovered how passionate a lover Sophia
could be, he had been wrung with jealousy of Wolfe. Now,
with so many years with Sophia behind him, he was eaten
alive with the agony of it, as if insects crawled beneath his
skin, driving him insane. Pictures formed in his brain. He
knew only too well the warm sensuality, the hot passion, of
which she was capable. He tried to close himself to those
flashing images, but all through the night they came: Sophia's
eyes shut, her body arching, her throat trembling with soft
wild cries of pleasure. It was so long since he had been able to
enjoy her body fully. She would be eager for Wolfe's passion,
fully receptive, her slender limbs aflame.

When Louise saw her father next day she was shocked by
the grey tinge of his skin, the haggard, devil-driven look of his
eyes. His nurse had her day off, by chance, and Dorcas took
over her duties, leaving Louise to fulfil the more pleasant
ones, like reading to her father and waiting on him during the
day.

"Have you had pain all night, Papa?" the girl asked anxiously.

"A little," Stonor said evasively, trying to smile, his mouth
crooked.

"Shall I send for Mama?" Louise wondered if her mother's
unusual absence in Bristol had been the cause of her father's
deathly colour.

"No," Stonor said hoarsely.

Seeing her stare, he added in a tone he tried to make normal, "She has enough worries to contend with, darling."

"When she sees you she will be upset," Louise pointed out.
"Papa, you look so ill. . . ."

Stonor said nothing then, but later, as the hour for Sophia's
return from the office approached, he said, "Louise, your
mother must not see me like this. . . bring me some brandy,
child."

She was shaken. "Papa, you know you are forbidden—"

"Do as I tell you," he said fiercely, his eyes flaming.

She flushed and went. Under her reproving stare he drank
two glasses of brandy, bringing a flush into his cheeks and a

fevered brightness to his eyes. He had not taken spirits for so long that the stiff measures almost made him drunk.

"That is enough," Louise said, removing the brandy before he could take more.

She returned the bottle and rinsed out the glass in the bathroom, then went back to sit beside him. As he heard Sophia's steps upon the stair Louise saw his eyes flash, and his hands tighten upon the sheet, and suddenly knew that her father was in terrible dread of what he would see as her mother came into the room. What instinct prompted her to guess, she did not know, but her hours of quiet observation of her parents had taught her to know them well.

The door opened and Sophia came into the room. With surprise, Louise saw she was wearing a new dress, one she had never seen before, an exquisite, tight-waisted, full-skirted white dress printed with coils of deep blue flowers. Her eyes rose to her mother's face and widened in disbelief. The white, stiff mask that she had grown to know over the past weeks had gone. Her mother had returned from the desert of the heart to which she had seemed lost forever, and her warm, smiling grace was astounding. Mama looks ten years younger, Louise thought in wild incredulity. Her eyes are laughing and her skin is so flushed.

Sophia came across the room to sit on the bed beside Stonor, her hands taking both his, the enormous sapphire eyes filled with love. "Darling, did you miss me? I am sorry I could not get home, but it was so late when the dinner ended, and I was so tired..." Her voice had a gentle sweetness that was calm and soothing.

Stonor smiled drowsily, the brandy working in him. His grey eyes moved over the exquisite cameo of her face. "You are home now, darling. That is all that matters."

"Shall I eat up here with you tonight?" Sophia asked him. "We could have a picnic...then I'll play cards with you and cheat you, shall I?"

He lifted her hands to his mouth, kissing them, trying to control the wild shaking of his mouth. "Please, my love...."

She bent down, the scent of her perfume filling him with aching desire, and the tenderly curved mouth brushed against his lips. Stonor had to control a savage urge to hold her, kiss her fiercely, burn the mark of his own possession where he knew his brother's mouth had so recently lain. Instead, he smiled coolly.

"Your dress is extremely pretty, dear. Did you buy it to-day?"

She glanced down at it, a curious, sensual, remembering smile on her mouth. "Yes," she said softly. "I am afraid I had an accident and the one I was wearing was torn...beyond repair, I think. It was old, anyway. No point in mending it."

Louise was burning with shame and embarrassment. Only now had she noticed the strange marks upon her mother's face and throat—faint bluish bruises, tiny red stains like burns...and instinct told her that her father had seen them, too. His grey eyes stared as Sophia turned to glance out of the window at the dusk. Louise saw him looking at the marks. She saw his whole face quiver as if he were suppressing a cry of anguish.

When he spoke, though, he sounded normal. "You will need to bathe and change, my dearest. You must be tired."

Mama laughed, her voice filled with radiance. "Oh, I am worn out... How lovely the park looks tonight. I have never seen Queen's Stonor look better. As I rode up the drive it seemed to shine like a beacon in the sunset."

"I think the house is always glad to see you return to it, Sophia," Papa said huskily. "As I am...."

Then Mama looked down at him quickly, her blue eyes wide. She was silent for a moment, then her smile shone out again, filled with a dancing, enchanting sweetness. "I shall always come back to you, Stonor, you know that...."

Then she went out of the room, and Louise watched as Papa's calm smile died and pain ran like fire over his features. She could not bear to watch. She left the room too, and Stonor closed his eyes, biting his lips. He had bought Sophia's happiness at a price that almost bankrupted him. One glance at her had told him everything. For a second he had been blindly happy to see her as she used to be...then his heart had cried out in jealous rage because that lovely, tender face was restored only because of his brother's passion. Wolfe had been the one who had ridden into the wasteland of her grief to bring her back, not himself. He had read the scars of Wolfe's hunger on her body, and known she had belonged to him all night. It was one thing to guess, to suspect, to dread. It was another to see for himself.

Then he exerted his last ounce of willpower, forcing himself to fight his jealousy. He had wanted this, planned this, begun this.... Sending for Wolfe had been his last desperate throw of the dice. He had not been able to bear her dead, white face a moment longer. It was selfish folly to protest against it now that his brother had restored her to life. If she had been drowning, and he unable to save her, would he have wished Wolfe to leave her to die?

He firmed his lips. It must be borne. Then a last wild jealous voice cried out inside him: did she have to come back from his arms with that smile of delight on her mouth, that brightness in her eyes? She was surrounded with the ambiance of love, her slender body bathed in it, as though she were flaming. Oh, God, Stonor thought, her very skin rippled with pleasure, with memories of the night. . . .

He wished Louise had not removed the brandy. He needed it badly as he waited for Sophia to return.

Stonor was never able to see her in the white dress printed with blue without a sick shudder of distaste from then on, reminded by it of that first night. But although Sophia made no more overnight stays in Bristol, Stonor was not fooled. He knew as well as if he were present that she and Wolfe met somewhere each day. Sophia's beauty glowed like the last of a dying sunset, her body radiant with pleasure and happiness. Sometimes Stonor saw her rapt in thought, her mouth curving, her blue eyes shining, and he knew she thought of his half-brother. That look only came for Wolfe. With a final wrung pain, Stonor accepted that Sophia belonged to his half-brother. He knew that, despite their happy marriage over the years, he himself had never brought that brilliance to her. Wolfe's love, the long delayed surrender to each other, had clothed her in light. She was all flying brightness, her smiles enriching the house, her eyes always dancing.

Towards Stonor himself she showed warm tenderness, the loving, caring warmth she had always given her children, but their bodies had no sensual contact whatever. Stonor never asked for any, and Sophia did not offer it. Gradually, he adapted to his changed life, bearing the crucifixion of her love affair with Wolfe without complaint, never letting her know he guessed.

At least, he told himself, she is still here. He could see her, talk to her, kiss her, however briefly. It was enough. He could never be her lover again himself. Fate had seen to that. But he had not lost her altogether. She was still his wife. He could not have lived if she had left him.

# CHAPTER TWENTY-FIVE

Jerome Whitley entered the drawing room of the Hunt house with a sensation of intolerable, driving boredom. His father had insisted on his presence tonight. Since his eighteenth birthday, Jerome had been a very junior member of the firm of Hunt & Whitley, bitterly nursing his grievance against his father for having insisted that he enter the business world rather than that of medicine, as he had so long desired. Jerome would have gone to medical school, regardless of his father's wishes, if he had been able to find a way of doing so, but Wolfe had refused to give him any financial help whatsoever, and short of living in penury, Jerome had seen no way of reaching his goal. He was a young man who had grown up in the lap of luxury, had been showered with the good things in life, and he had felt no inclination to grub in a garret, studying by day and working by night, which was the only alternative open to poor students. He knew his own character by now. Sardonic, cold, contemptuous, he was aware that wearing fine linen, well-cut suits, drinking good wine and smoking good cigars were hedonistic pleasures in which he revelled, and which he would miss if he disobeyed his father and was deprived of them.

Over the two years since his mother's sudden death, his hatred and contempt for his father had, without his realizing it, spread to himself: he had a low opinion of human nature, and, being very well aware of his own humanity, therefore of himself.

Jerome also detested his cousin Edward, whose own father had not insisted he come tonight. Edward had also begun to work in Bristol, nominally under the direction of his mother, but in fact spending the day working under Luther Hunt, as Sophia and Luther had sensed that Edward would not take kindly to a woman's rule. Though Edward disliked both his mother and his sister, and his manner was offhand with them, and though he accepted Luther Hunt, he resented Luther's involvement in the Whitley firm, despite the vast improvements this had brought about, and he had dreams of retrieving the share of the firm Luther had bought. Oddly, Edward got on very well with Thomas Hunt. The aggressive spirit in Thomas, which had made Daniel curl his lip and sneer, only attracted Edward. Often in the evenings he and Thomas went out on the town together, pursuing young male pleasures secretly. Edward's only bone of contention with Thomas was the other young man's unhidden interest in Louise. Edward had always disliked his sister. He grimaced whenever Thomas brought her name into the conversation. Thomas, in no hurry to tie himself down, bided his time. He saw, if Edward did not, the common sense of binding their two families by marriage, and quite apart from that, he found Louise deeply attractive. Her quiet, graceful gentleness drew him like a moth to a moonlit copse. Bristol had become dominated by the Whitleys over the past few years. Luther and Wolfe together owned dozens of firms in the city. The Whitley import business, now part-owned by Stonor and Luther, made up the triangle. Thomas had far-reaching schemes for consolidating and building upon the partnership. Money and business should be kept in the family.

Completely indifferent to the glances of interest he was receiving from some of the assembled young ladies, Jerome glanced around the room, bowing to various acquaintances whom he recognized. Cousin Luther, he thought, a sneer on his extremely handsome young face, had come up in the world of late. There were no more sniffed asides from the gentry about his lack of background, his vulgarity, his *nouveau riche* appearance. Since his wife's death, with the aid of the lovely Mrs. Stonor Whitley he had totally renewed the decor of his house, giving it an elegance that the old, overcrowded, stuffy, plush-curtained, ornately decorated rooms had never had. Most of the best-respected citizens of Bristol were here tonight, to celebrate Thomas Hunt's twentieth birthday. Jerome despised and disliked his cousin: while he himself was bored and irritable in the commercial world, Thomas was at home in it, his aggressive, driving energy finding an outlet in the cut and thrust of the profit motive.

Several people wandered over to speak to him, and Jerome, impeccably elegant in a tight-waisted dark suit that offset his rather saturnine dark looks, exchanged polite, bored small talk with them, while his eyes, so like his father's, wandered across the room to alight upon the still ravishing Mrs. Stonor

Whitley, her softly pleated dress in a bluey grey shade that reminded him of autumn smoke, the enormous sleeves like the
wings of some tropical bird, their width and delicacy exquisitely emphasizing that slender body. Unconsciously
Jerome's eyes lingered, his mind irritated by the fact that he
could not help but admire a woman he detested. The bodice,
plunging discreetly, revealed a skin so white and still smooth
that Jerome marvelled at her ability to maintain such textural
magnificence at her age. Did the woman have the power to
make time stand still for her? He wondered grimly. He
thought of his mother, dying squalidly at his feet unnoticed,
and distaste for all mankind wrenched at his hard young
mouth.

He watched as Sophia talked to Luther Hunt, her blue eyes
smiling tranquilly up at him. Jerome's dry gaze did not miss
the way Luther was watching her. How did his father like to
see that? he wondered nastily. Still, since his mother's death,
the spark of enjoyment seemed to have gone out in his father.
Jerome glanced around for him and saw him at the other side
of the room, speaking in his incisive way to a business acquaintance, who listened respectfully. Men did now when
Wolfe Whitley spoke. His commercial octopus had spread its
tentacles across the south-west of England right to the heart
of London. His wealth grew without any apparent effort on
his part. Everything he touched turned to gold.

Jerome's nostrils flared. It pleased him in some subterranean fashion that in recent years his father had ceased to have
sexual adventures. Jerome had been puzzled at first, incredulous, seeing his father spend evening after evening at
home, quietly reading, talking to his other children. The unexpected spectacle of a reformed rake had baffled him. Then it
had amused him. His father, he told himself, was burned out.
Old before his time. His vibrant sexual energies all dried up. It
had amused Jerome, the more so because, becoming a man
himself, he was beginning to appreciate the very thing his
father was losing.

His eyes returned to Sophia Whitley. Around her slim
throat a wide choker of black lace made a curiously seductive
shadow on her white skin. He felt his mouth go dry suddenly,
watching her. This woman, he thought, had been his father's
mistress, the love of his life. It gave him an odd frisson to
think that she was still desirable, despite her forty years. Old
enough to be my mother, he thought wryly. His mind flashed

to his half-brother, Daniel, who had borne him such a strong resemblance, and he looked vaguely uneasy. He had told Daniel the truth thoughtlessly, scornfully, and then felt a peculiar remorse, seeing the pain and horror he had inflicted on a helpless innocent. The moment still haunted him, that and the subsequent moments, when his drunken mother had ranted at Sophia Whitley, when he had seen Daniel struck down and his mother die. They formed a permanent pattern in his head. From that moment he had felt as if he himself had precipitated what happened. He blamed himself and hated himself.

Luther Hunt was joined by a thin, pinched man in rather old-fashioned evening clothes, and Sophia drifted politely away towards a group of women. Jerome stepped into her path, bowing.

"Mrs. Whitley—" Unknowingly, his tone held insolence, a hidden taunt, his blue-green eyes lifting to her face with a strange mixture of admiration and contempt.

Sophia considered him calmly, a soft light in her blue eyes. "Jerome, my dear," she said, smiling, the way her pink mouth moved giving her a warm, gentle sweetness that made the young man almost flinch.

He took her hand in mock gallantry, intended for those who saw them, and kissed it lightly. "How ravishing you look," he murmured.

A light of amusement suddenly lit in her eyes. "And how fast you are growing up, Jerome," she said lightly, teasingly.

Jerome felt a flicker of anger at her amused glance, the patronizing tone. "I have wished to speak with you, Mrs. Whitley," he said, making a lightning decision which had been very far from his mind. "I have some news that I think you would wish to hear. . . ."

"Oh?" Still her blue eyes held that tantalizing amusement, as if she saw him as a small boy whom she indulged.

"I have heard from Daniel," he said, watching her deliberately, and saw the colour leave her face, the soft smile fade from the lovely mouth. It was with some remorse that he caught her as she slid senseless to the floor. The room hummed. Luther Hunt was there at once, fussing, concerned, staring at Jerome accusingly.

"Why did she faint?" Wolfe Whitley caught his son's arm, his fingers hard, his eyes fierce on the young man's face.

"I told her I'd heard from her son," Jerome said, knowing

it was useless to lie now, kicking himself because he had been pricked into telling her anything.

She had been carried from the room by now, attended by her daughter, Louise, whose quiet gentle presence Jerome had never even noted. Wolfe moved after her, taking his son with him, a tight look about his mouth and eyes.

In the wide, stone-flagged hall he surveyed Jerome coldly. "Now, what's all this about Daniel?"

Jerome lifted a cool eyebrow. "I've had a letter from him."

"When?" Wolfe demanded. "Why didn't you tell me? Why keep it to yourself and then spring it on her in public? You damned little bastard—" The last word died in his throat.

Jerome laughed sardonically. "Do go on, Papa," he said, his tone derisive. He knew his father's hatred of the word bastard and all it implied.

Wolfe raised a hand to hit him by instinct, driven to temper. Then it froze, mid-air. He was still a strong, violent man, his forty-two years lying quite lightly on his powerful shoulders, his face as darkly attractive as ever, although his dark hair now had more silver in it and his features bore the lines of pain, experience and knowledge.

Jerome faced him, daring him to strike him, willing him to do so, as if he wanted only the opportunity of striking back. Wolfe glared at him, real dislike in his face.

Then the door to a small morning room opened and Louise Whitley stood framed in the doorway, her glance moving between the two.

She was her mother's image, Wolfe thought, looking at her tenderly. Alice had grown up, had changed considerably, her temperament far more like that of the dead woman who had been her mother, and holding a curious cold tenacity at the core, which she had, Wolfe thought wryly, from him. Louise, however, had grown more and more to be a gentle echo of her mother, and for Wolfe, bathing daily in the graceful smiles and loving warmth of Sophia, it was not strange. Her black hair was softly waved over her small head. Her blue eyes held none of Sophia's brilliance and charm, but they had a tenderness that gave her face great appeal.

Now she said huskily, "Jerome...will you please come to my Mama?"

Jerome moved forwards, his father at his heels.

Louise looked politely, rather coldly, at Wolfe Whitley. "If you please, Mama would like to see Jerome alone,'' she said, excluding him.

Jerome gave his father a strangely triumphant look and walked into the room. Louise closed the door, leaving him alone with Sophia. Wolfe, his face blank, stared down at the girl, reading her dislike of him in her blue eyes. Strange, he thought, drily, that this young creature of whom he was deeply fond, should loathe him for her father's sake. He had known for a long time that Louise was aware of his relationship with her mother, that she knew of it, resented it, hated it.

In the morning room, Sophia lay weakly upon the chaise-longue, her head upon a cushion. She held out a pleading hand to Jerome, who knelt on one knee to take it, a hot sensation in his throat as he did so. He looked into the white, troubled face, his eyes running over the separate features, wondering what it was that made such beauty out of such very human material: the fine, high fleshless cheekbones, the exquisitely modelled nose and curved pale mouth, the high temples and the long neck.... Beauty, he thought...one could not predict it or confine it. It caught one by the throat, just looking at her. Her daughter did not have it. She was merely a shadow of her mother. Her youth and sweetness could not add up to this.

''Daniel...tell me, Jerome...where is he? What has been happening to him? Where is his letter?''

The questions poured molten out of her, her voice trembling, and he held her hand between both his, enjoying the feel of the smooth skin between his palms.

''I do not have the letter with me,'' he murmured, staring at her. ''He wrote to me from London. He is well. He asked me to write and let him know how you are....''

''He did?'' Wild colour rushed in a blinding wave up her face, as if she were a young girl whose lover had sent her a message.

Jerome stared, blinded, incredulous. My God, he thought thickly. No wonder Papa could never forget her. She is... His thoughts broke off from the brink of admitting how he felt.

''What is he doing?'' she asked, her eyes fixed eagerly on his face.

''He has joined the Army,'' Jerome said.

The colour drained away. She looked at him in consternation, her blue eyes terrified. ''The Army? Oh, no...he might be killed...where is he? What barracks? We must get him out of it—"

Jerome said regretfully, "That will be impossible. He is in India by now. He was just leaving.... I wrote to him giving him news of you all—"

"But when did he leave?" she asked, her lips shaking.

Jerome hesitated. "Two years ago," he said.

Her eyes widened. "And you never told me?" The accusation, the grief, was shivering in her voice.

Jerome flushed, then. "I promised not to do so...." He had sworn in his letter that he never would admit to knowing Daniel's whereabouts. A wild impulse had made him break his word, a desire to shatter the amused, indulgent smile on Sophia Whitley's face. He was furious with himself. For years he had cherished the secret of Daniel's presence in the Indian Army. He had enjoyed knowing something his father would have given much to know. Now on some whim he had betrayed it.

The blue eyes studied him, tears in them. "Why didn't you tell us? We could have saved him—brought him back—"

Jerome gazed back at her. Strange, ungovernable desires were raging beneath his cold surface. "He asked me to give you this," he said thickly, leaning forwards.

His mouth brushed over her lips lightly. So close up she had a sweet scent, a delicate nostalgic fragrance, like a potpourri. It tingled in his nostrils. He could not move away, and continued to stare into her blue eyes. "Do you want to see his letter?" he asked her, merely in order to find some way of prolonging the moment.

"Yes," she said eagerly. "Oh, please, Jerome." She smiled at him, forgiving him his long silence. "At least we will know now where to look for him—"

"I will bring it to Queen's Stonor," he promised.

"He wrote only once?"

"Just once." His heart was thudding. She lay so close, that perfume filling his lungs, sending waves of heat to his head. He was searching for an excuse, however thin, to kiss her again, unbearably driven by the desire to feel her soft mouth under his once more. Again he thought, my father loved her once...she was his mistress...this is no dull, cold matron who lies there, all whalebone and corsets...this woman is totally desirable still, passion in the curves of mouth and body, knowledge in the depths of the blue eyes. Jerome was already sufficiently a man of the world to read the signs. He suddenly imagined her naked in his father's hard arms, and a flush mounted to his forehead.

"Forgive me for my silence," he said clumsily. "Daniel was insistent that I should not tell you until some time had elapsed...."

She looked at him, seeing his hot face and oddly restless eyes, and misunderstood the reasons for it. Gently, tenderly, she smiled at this boy who had Daniel's eyes, her hand patting his flushed cheek. "I do not blame you for your loyalty to my son, Jerome dear. I am glad you have told me now, at least. You will bring his letter?"

"Early tomorrow," he swore, looking at her with those blue-green eyes filled with brightness.

She leaned forwards then, impulsively, and kissed him. She intended to kiss his cheek, but Jerome turned his head and caught her mouth, still restraining himself, merely enjoying the taste of her lips on his.

Wolfe came into the room at that moment, having been freed from Louise's restraint by Luther Hunt's son, Thomas. He halted, stunned, watching as his son, on his knees, deliberately turned his head to make Sophia kiss his mouth. He saw Sophia's look of surprise, indulgent amusement. He saw the back of his son's neck glow with colour. He saw, as she did not, the boy's hands clench at his sides, saw one of them come up to brush her cheek. Suddenly Wolfe became deeply aware of Jerome's emotions. Like a fox in a covert scenting the hunt even though he cannot view it, he stiffened, poised and alert.

Jerome heard the door close and jumped up, growing more flushed than ever as he saw his father. Without a word he walked across the room and went out, ignoring Wolfe. All the lazy sardonic coldness had gone from his handsome young face. Wolfe saw the look in his eyes and he was shaken.

Quickly, Wolfe looked at Sophia very intently. She was lying there tensely, her face alight. "Daniel is with the Army in India," she told him rapidly. "He wrote to Jerome two years ago, but made him promise not to tell us—"

Wolfe's brows drew together. His face became a cool mask. "Why did he choose to tell you now of all times, in public?"

Sophia brushed the question aside, smiling, so alight with relief she cared nothing. "He has told us," she said. "At least now we can find Daniel! We know he is alive, where he is, how we can reach him—"

"I will set enquiries on foot in London at once," Wolfe said. "The Army will tell us all we need to know; it will be easy to find him, my darling, and we will get him home to us again."

Sophia held out her hand, so happy she forgot to be careful lest someone walk in, forgot to be wary. Wolfe went to her and knelt, as his son had done, to kiss her, but their mouths lingered hotly, caressing, needing each other.

"Shall you tell Stonor?" he asked, watching her. He did not even begrudge Stonor his share in her. Stonor, God knew, had little else. He knew all marital exchanges between her and Stonor had ended. Stonor seemed to be content with what he had—and Wolfe knew himself to be in possession at last of the thing he had needed all his life.

Sophia shook her head, her face briefly sad.

"Why not?"

"Stonor would not care," she said, almost harshly. "He did not love Daniel. Edward will have Queen's Stonor, and Daniel's return cannot affect that now. He is our son." Her blue eyes shone up at him. "Yours and mine. We are the only ones concerned in this."

Wolfe's face was alight with tenderness. "Yes, my darling," he said, deeply touched. "Our son has no need of Queen's Stonor...."

"I did not say that," she said, her mouth tight. "Daniel loved the house. I know my son. It hurt him deeply when he lost it. But it is lost—we have to face that. Daniel is not. Not now." She smiled at him. "Oh, I could have kissed Jerome!"

Wolfe watched her through his dark lashes. "You did," he said lightly.

She gave no sign of consciousness. "He is an odd boy... and so like Daniel they could be twins. He is often very sarcastic and rude, but tonight he was kindness itself to me."

"Was he?" Wolfe was thinking hard, his face taut. She had no suspicion, he thought. She was blinded by the boy's youth and look of her son. What the hell was he to do? It was a damnable position to be in....

Next morning Jerome rode out to Queen's Stonor with Daniel's creased and much-read letter. Sophia received him eagerly, kissing him on the cheek, unaware of the effect that brief contact had on the boy.

She was wearing a simple morning dress of lavender and

black, the bodice barred with pleated frills of white, and her black hair shone in the sunlight. Suddenly he saw a few fine threads of silver among the black, and found it moving, increasing her beauty, conferring upon it the kiss of time.

"Sit down, dear," she told him. She rang a small bell and Louise came into the room, girlish in a pleated white dress with a tartan underskirt that showed around her ankles like a frill.

Sophia and Louise read the letter, their eyes filling with tears. Daniel wrote briefly, his tone very adult, but they read between the lines, and were saddened. "May I keep it?" Sophia asked Jerome pleadingly.

"Well..." he said, pretending to be unsure.

She took his hands, pressing them pleadingly. "Please, Jerome..." The blue eyes were filled with that brightness of tears, that sweetness of her love for her son.

Summoning all his nerve, he leaned forwards and kissed her on the mouth. "Daniel would want you to have it," he said, with a pretence of casual kindness.

"Thank you, Jerome," she said, sinking down on the sofa to read the letter again with hands that shook.

Louise was staring at Jerome closely. He glanced at her, coolly sardonic with her as he never was with her mother, and was astonished to see scorn and dislike in her eyes. A flush rose to his face. He was angry with her, and gave her back the hostility she showed him.

Louise was completely aware of his feelings. She had begun to sense them last night, and this morning she knew intuitively, as she watched him staring at her mother, exactly how he felt. At fifteen she was deeply sensitive to the atmosphere around her. Her life at Queen's Stonor had bred in her a strong instinct for emotions. She had watched her parents, and learned to read their feelings over the years. Now she watched Jerome Whitley and saw the way he looked at her mother, and was bitterly, contemptuously angry.

She remembered him striking her face, when he was a boy, for saying that she wished her mother was his mother...she remembered him at Thomas's party drawling biting words about her mother...she remembered very well watching him staring at her mother at the party last night, reading the look in his eyes, so like Daniel's they made her feel sick.

At times now she felt as if the whole façade of Queen's Stonor might crack open and reveal the dark life behind it to the world. Her father's long agony over her mother's relationship with Wolfe Whitley did not grow easier as time passed. Rather, it grew worse. Only Louise knew that he resorted to the aid of brandy at times to help him through the long night. Only Louise read the white lines of jealous bitterness in his thin face as he watched his still-beautiful wife turn away from him each morning to go to Bristol to work and secretly meet her lover.... Louise marvelled at her Papa's capacity to bear the pain. He hid it from Sophia as if she were a stranger. Over the three years he had ceased to hide it from his daughter. She showed him compassion and love when he needed it, and he had to have someone who did not need to be deceived. He needed at least the luxury of open grief.

Sophia looked up, smiling, at Jerome. "You must be thirsty after your long ride. Louise, take Jerome and find him some lemonade...."

The tone stung him. He turned a curiously darkened look upon her, his eyes flashing, giving him an odd likeness to his father suddenly, taking her aback. "I am eighteen years old, Mrs. Whitley, not twelve," he said through taut lips.

She met his glance, her own eyes widening. "I am sorry, Jerome," she said quietly. "I keep forgetting how grown-up you are...."

Yes, thought Louise bitterly. You cannot see what is right in front of your face. Papa would see it. Your lover would see it. You only see Daniel's eyes, Daniel's face.... And she gave Jerome an oblique, half-pitying look.

Sophia got up, her skirts rustling softly, and rang for a maid. She gave Jerome a teasing, smiling glance. "What would you like then, Mr. Whitley?" she said softly, her mouth curving with unconscious flirtation. "Sherry?"

"Thank you," he said stiffly, his face a little red, feeling foolish in the face of her bright eyes.

The maid brought him some sherry. He nervously lifted the glass to his lips, sipped it, while Louise and her mother watched him. Jerome felt like an idiot. Resentfully, he gave Louise a cold stare. Little bitch, he thought furiously. Why is she looking at me like that?

He put down his glass at last, thankful to have finished it. "I must go," he said brusquely, in boyish rudeness. He gave Louise a brief indifferent nod. "Miss Louise..." Then he turned to Sophia, quite intending to do the same.

Somehow his body did not obey his mind. He bowed, taking her hand, kissing it, consumed by a wild, sick ache for something he had never had. Then he turned on his heel and strode out of the room, very tall, very slim, still a boy yet with that dark presence that his father had bestowed on him at birth.

Sophia sat down again suddenly, a dreaming look on her face. Her daughter eyed her, wondering if at last she had seen what had been written so plainly on Jerome's face. But Sophia was miles away.

"I must go to Bristol," she said. "Daniel must be found soon...."

Louise's mouth tightened. "Will you tell Papa?"

Sophia's face hardened. "No. Nor will you, Louise. This is nothing to do with him."

"Anything to do with you matters to Papa," Louise said, even her love for her mother pushed to the limit by her instinctive loyalty to her father.

Sophia shook her head, unyielding. "Not Daniel," she said firmly. "Daniel is my business."

And Wolfe Whitley's, Louise thought, bitterly angry.

When Sophia had gone she went up to her father's bedroom and found him reading a book, that weary grey look on his face, which came after lost sleep. He looked at her tenderly. She had become his chief comfort since he lost Sophia. She was so like her mother, a soft blurred image of what Sophia had once been.

"Who was here? I heard visitors arriving."

"Jerome," Louise said, shaking up his pillows.

Stonor froze. "What is he doing here?" Anger entered his voice.

Louise lied. "He came to visit me, Papa." The blush that entered her face was from awareness of the lie, but Stonor, staring at her, read it differently, and was filled with a bitter rage.

"I will not have that boy on my land," he said through white lips. "Louise, are you encouraging him? I will not have it."

She stared, then gave a faint, amused laugh, ironic and tinged with incredulity. "Oh, no, Papa... nothing like that... Jerome would not look at me in that way...."

Stonor sighed, believing her. He lay back against his pillows in relief. The thought of Wolfe Whitley's son with his daughter was so violently repulsive to him that he forgot to

enquire further about Jerome's visit, his face filling with the
bitterness that came whenever he thought about his half-
brother.

Louise later found herself flushed as she remembered her
Papa leaping to that odd conclusion. Jerome interested in
her? She smiled angrily. Jerome could not even see her in the
shadow of her mother. What man could? At evening parties
she felt she was invisible, her very personality submerged,
standing beside Sophia, watching her hold court, ringed with
eager, obsequious guests who competed to gain her attention.
Louise still loved her mother, unable to hate the warm, tender
woman who had never changed towards her since her childhood. She had no memories of unkindness, spite or pain to
spoil the glowing image Sophia had flung over her childhood,
but at times she felt restless, sensing herself to be in danger of
losing her identity beneath the brilliance of her mother's
domination.

In her bedroom she looked at herself in the mirror. Even the
way she dressed was quiet, restrained.... It was not Mama's
fault, she admitted irritably. Mama shook her head over
Louise's choice of clothes, begging her to be a little more daring. Louise was grimly aware of playing down her own looks,
almost giving herself a cloak of invisibility in which she could
hide, as if she actually feared to seem to compete with her
mother. As well might a pale prism from the chandeliers try to
compete with the moonlight, she thought wryly. What chance
had she against Mama?

Sophia sat with Wolfe on the sofa, her hands held tightly in
his, leaning her head upon his shoulder. "You will go to London yourself and see if you can trace him? At least you might
get news of him."

"I'll go tomorrow," he promised, gripping her small hands
between his. "Just be patient, my dearest. I'll find our son if I
have to move heaven and earth."

"I know you will," she said sighing.

Wolfe's hands released her, moving to stroke her hair,
pushing her back towards the cushions. She looked up at him,
smiling, distracted from her eternal thoughts of Daniel by the
way he was looking at her.

"Not now, Wolfe... I have to go to the office."

"Now," he said huskily, his voice determined, his hands at
her dress. Ever since he had seen his son kneeling at her feet

and had caught the backwash of the boy's emotions he had felt oddly uneasy. Jerome puzzled and alarmed him. He had always been out of Wolfe's reach, sardonic, withdrawn, contemptuous. Wolfe was proud of the boy's good looks, his intelligence, his brilliant, hard cold mind. It irritated him to see the boy waste his chances in the business world, turning his back with a shrug on what his father provided for him. Jerome's dislike of him had often stung, but now Wolfe was conscious of something deeper, a personal, secret jealousy that he found shameful and ridiculous. Jerome was a boy, he thought...and then remembered himself at eighteen, burning with a man's hunger for Sophia, enjoying her body with all the formidable drive of maturity. His face took on a deep, hard flush as he looked down at her. She was well past thirty-five, he thought, and still whenever he saw her his heart moved in his body. For the first time he saw himself in an impossible position. He dared not warn her, put the thought into her head. Her total blindness was a form of security. Jerome would not dare to make a frontal advance...a boy of his age would not have the nerve. And if he did? Wolfe looked at her searchingly, taking in the soft sensual curves of face and body, the warm, lovely femininity she still wore like a banner. Oh, God, he thought...would she be tempted? Jerome was a handsome young devil, and Wolfe knew how much like himself the boy looked...it was ridiculous, he told himself. But he wondered, and while he wondered, his hands eagerly undressed her, touched her, reassured that secret voice in his head as he felt her passionate response.

He left for London the next day to follow up on Jerome's information. Sophia waited, concealing her hungry impatience from Stonor's eyes, working and following her usual routine. Several times during Wolfe's absence Jerome called in at the office to see her. The first time she was surprised but pleased to see him, accepting without question his excuse that he had been curious as to whether she was succeeding in her search for Daniel. Jerome was all politeness, friendly interest, and she smiled at him gratefully. When he called again, with a thin excuse of having left his gloves behind, Sophia felt for the first time a faint tremor of unease. His gloves were discovered, hidden behind a row of dusty ledgers, where he had previously hidden them himself. He did not leave, however, and talked lightly to her of Louise, of Queen's Stonor, of Luther Hunt, his voice so like his father's that it almost made her shiver. Turning to look at him she caught his eyes on her profile, and saw with astonishment the deep flush that swept up his handsome young face. Then Sophia began to sense something behind his visits that she had not even suspected. It was absurd. She was deluding herself, she thought wryly. Good God, she was old enough to be his mother... indeed, she might well have been his mother...that was not the first time such a thought had occurred to her. So like her dearest Daniel that her heart leapt whenever she saw him, it was a disgusting idea to have entertained even for one second....

Jerome saw the flicker of surprise and then incredulity that came into her lovely face, and his heart plunged. He had no idea how to proceed. His emotions were driving him as if he were a blind horse, whipping him on without any idea where he was going. Breaking off what he had been saying, he muttered that he must go, and came to kiss her hand. She gave it to him slowly, looking at him curiously, and bending to kiss it he caught the soft fragrance of her perfume and was filled with a wild emotion he found uncontrollable. It was the first time in his life he had ever felt the merest brush of it and it overthrew him, knocking him off balance.

He had never loved another human being in his life. Eighteen years old, cold, bitter, warped by his family background, he had shut himself off from the rest of mankind since early childhood. He had hated this woman, despised her, condemned her. Now, as if his feelings were a thin silver coin of which he had seen just one side, he felt the coin of emotion spin wildly and land with the reverse side showing; and passionate love, like a flame, consumed him. He had been so totally unprepared for emotion that he had no idea what to do or say. He had prided himself on self-control, on a clever cold tongue, a sharp mind...now he had lost them all, existing in a wash of confused feeling, as if he were driftwood flowing in and out with a tide that was irresistible.

Sophia stared up at him, alarmed and bewildered by the strange flux of emotions on his handsome young face.

He was on his knees before either of them had anticipated it, his black head bent over her hands, kissing them wildly, muttering muffled words she could not hear.

She did not need to hear now. She could feel it. And she was shattered.

Jerome looked up once, his face darkly flushed, his eyes

hot. She stared at him, her lips parted in a soundless cry of disbelief and shock.

The boy leaped up, horrified himself, and shot from the room as if he were on fire, leaving Sophia sitting astounded, wondering what on earth she was to do.

Wolfe returned from London two days later, and called at the office to see Sophia, finding her deep in a great mound of paperwork, her dark head thoughtfully bent over it.

She looked up as he closed the door and fled into his arms, her hands outstretched.

He held her, kissing the top of her sleek black head.

"You found out where he is?"

"Come out, my dearest," he said gently. "We must be alone for a while. Get your hat and come for a drive in the country."

She was anxious at once, looking up at him, but he smiled very reassuringly, his eyes tender, so she fetched her hat and they went out together, walking calmly through the outer office under George Blare's watchful eye. Over the last years Wolfe had paid rare visits to her place of work. They had been very careful to keep their relationship a total secret from everyone. Their visits to the little house in a back street were always separate, always discreet, and since nobody there knew either of them they were able to escape detection so far.

Jerome stood on the opposite side of the street. He had just tied up his mare in preparation for going in to see Sophia, with the excuse that he had come to apologize for his behaviour last time. Now he froze, incredulous, watching as his father handed Sophia into a hansom cab. Rapidly he remounted and followed on horseback at a discreet distance.

"Tell me," Sophia said to Wolfe in the cab, turning eagerly to him.

"When we are alone," he said gently. He produced a straw hamper from under the seat and grinned at her. "We'll have a picnic by the river. What do you think of that?"

"Is this a celebration or a wake?" she asked him huskily, watching his face.

Wolfe kissed her nose. "Not a wake," he said quietly. "Daniel is safe, my dearest."

She relaxed, her eyes brilliant. "Oh, thank God! When you did not tell me, I thought—"

"Try to be patient," he said soberly. "I have too much to tell you to begin before I have you to myself. . . ."

He paid off the driver when they reached a bend on the river road, and ordered him to return in three hours to the same spot. Then, taking her hand, he walked with her through the long, waving, seeding grass of a meadow, and down to the willow-swept river banks. They sat down on the grass, and Wolfe opened the hamper and laid out the food he had brought.

"I could not touch it," she said in a choking voice. "Tell me at once. Please, no further delays—I cannot bear it."

He took her hand, gazing at her. "Daniel is in the northwest of India, my love, at a rather remote fort. He is in the ranks. . . he was recruited in the streets in London. . . took the shilling and sailed within weeks. They tell me he has done very well. Promoted already to corporal. He showed great bravery under fire during a native skirmish and seems set for a fine career."

"We must get him out," she said, barely listening. "We must get him back."

"I have done what I can," Wolfe said sombrely. "The officer I saw was most kind, most helpful, but Daniel is no boy now, my darling, to be rescued by his mother. He is of age. We cannot make him do anything."

"He must come home to me," she said wildly, shaking her head. "He will want to. . . ."

Wolfe looked at her, sighing. "Of course he will want to, Sophia," he said gently. "He loves you."

She lay down under the cool green shade of the willow, her eyes open, filled with dreaming thoughts. Wolfe sat in the long grass, picking buttercups with slender stems and weaving them deftly into a long chain, the metallic enamel of their brightness gleaming on his skin. Quietly, stealthily, Jerome crept through the grass, hiding behind some bushes, from where he could watch them.

He saw the cloth, the litter of untouched food, his father, looking incredibly young and unlike himself, intent upon the long chain he was making, and at last his eyes moved to the slender figure of Sophia in the shade of the willow. Her skirts blew lightly in the summer breeze. The outline of her body was half-hidden by the grass.

Jerome watched as his father turned, the chain in his hands, and lifted her hat from her head, dropping it on the earth. With one hand he rapidly let down the thick black hair until it hung in shining strands, which the sunlight touched with palest silver. Wolfe took her shoulders, pulled her up until she sat next to him, then he threw the chain of buttercups around her head, the lustre of the petals like fairy gold on her black head.

"You look sixteen," he murmured, just audibly enough for his son to hear.

"I am forty, and I am getting old," she said, but lightly. "My hair is turning grey."

Wolfe laughed. "Witch! You mean you have captured moonbeams in it.... Those little silvery streaks are captivating, and you know it...." His arm slid around her waist, and she languidly leaned against him, her fingers starting to undo his shirt. Jerome saw his father watching her as she did it, and his own heart beat violently with jealous rage.

He was incredulous, wild, sickened. Now Sophia's hands were sliding over Wolfe's skin in open pleasure. She took the chain of buttercups from her head and threw it round his neck, laughing at him. "There, I have you on a chain," she teased.

"Haven't you always had me on a chain?" he asked, not quite lightly. "Since the day I first saw you, my dearest...."

"You escaped your chain long enough to pleasure half the women of Bristol," Sophia said, her eyes mocking. "I should have made a cage for you long ago."

"I've been caged ever since the night you came back to me," he said. "There would have been no other women ever if you had been my wife...."

"Liar," she said, laughing, and leaped up and moved away.

Wolfe came to his feet to follow. She ran and he pursued, their laughter gay and thoughtless, as if they were children. Jerome felt older, far older, as he watched and listened. He felt tired and grey and sick.

He watched as she let his father catch her and pull her down into the grass, and heard the soft sounds of their kisses. The wind lifted her black hair and blew it upwards. It mingled with Wolfe's hair, as if the two were twining together.

He knew as he watched and listened that this was no brief, chance meeting. He felt the warm intimacy of old lovers between them. Even their lovemaking had none of the urgency of novelty. They kissed and touched each other slowly, pleasurably, like those who have the world before them and mean not to hasten through the present.

He heard his father murmur her name, saw her white hands in the silver-streaked dark hair above her body.

"I love you," she whispered. "Oh, Wolfe, I love you. . . ."

Jerome turned then and quietly went away. He rode to Queen's Stonor like a demon, set upon destroying everything in his path, his eyes blazing with jealousy and hate.

Louise saw him coming, and went down to greet him coldly. "I wish to see your father urgently," he said, walking towards the stairs.

She dismissed the curious servant and caught Jerome's sleeve as he mounted the stair. "No," she said sharply.

He turned upon her a face like white lightning. "It is time he knew that your mother is my father's mistress," he said between his teeth. "It is time he knew what manner of whore he has for a wife—"

Louise slapped his face hard, as he had once slapped hers. Jerome moved furiously to hit her back, but she hit him again, and so wild was her temper that for a moment she looked incredibly like Sophia, flushed, heaving with emotion, fighting like a savage for her father's peace.

"You will not go up there! He is too ill to see you—"

Jerome turned to go, ignoring her, but she pulled at him as he trod up the stairs, jerking him backwards. He fell with a crash and she stood in his path, barring his way. Getting to his feet, flushed, his head aching, he glared at her.

"They are there now, in the river meadows, doing it in public, in the open air, like animals," he said hysterically. "Christ, why shouldn't he be told? Hasn't he a right to know his bastard brother is cuckolding him?"

"And you are sick with jealousy," Louise cried furiously. "Don't come here whining like a little boy who has found out the toy he wanted belongs to someone else. . . . Leave my father alone. Take out your jealousy on your own."

Jerome was crimson, his eyes flashing. He stared at her for a long moment in silence, for the first time seeing her as a young woman, her blue eyes as brilliant as Sophia's in her temper, her face flushed a wild pink, her mouth trembling with anger.

Driven to an extremity of violence, he took her by the arms and shook her cruelly, glaring down at her. "I'll tell the world—I'll tell the whole world that your mother is a whore—"

She slapped him again, wrenching her arm free, and Jerome

rammed her back against the wall and began to kiss her savagely, hurting her, biting into her shaking mouth. She gasped, angry and astounded, twisting against him. His hands moved from her arms to her breasts, touching her. Jerome had lost all sense of where he was, who he was, who she was. Sophia was in his arms and he took what he wanted, his mouth demanding, his hands urgent.

Louise groaned. The hard thin limbs pressing against her were staggeringly exciting. Her hands curled round on his shoulder, her nails digging into her palms, then she groaned again, excited, heated, and her mouth opened under his and her arms went round his neck.

The air around them seemed to be full of drugged incense. They breathed hoarsely, deeply intent on what was happening between them. Louise was trembling, her lips bruised and tender under the hard boy's mouth, but her eyes were closed and she had surrendered. Jerome could sense his victory. He felt her body yield to him and his own was pulsing with the desire to take her.

Suddenly he heard the clock strike and came back to reality, to where they were and who they were. He leaped away from her. She opened her eyes and stared at him, suddenly deeply white.

Jerome stared and stared as if his eyes ate her. Then he turned on his heel and went out of the front door, and Louise burst into shattering, silent tears.

# CHAPTER TWENTY-SIX

Louise waited next morning until her mother had left for Bristol and her father was being attended to by his nurse before she went out of the house and took a horse from the stables. She rode in the park, her mind totally occupied with what had happened yesterday between herself and Jerome. She had been stunned by it. For a long time she had been aware of Jerome, finding him maddening, his cold sardonic stare affronting her, yet never quite being able to ignore him because of that odd resemblance to Daniel. Her love for her brother had never wavered, never lessened, and Jerome was a permanent reminder of it. Since she was six she had been aware of him on the outskirts of her life, his name familiar to her, his presence like the dark shadow of a threat, linked indissolubly with his father's existence, a slight echo of Wolfe Whitley's influence on their lives, a threading counterpoint to it.

She rode into the trees, brooding, her eyes on the horse's white mane, riding easily, thoughtlessly, almost born in the saddle, totally at home there.

When another horse moved out of the shelter of some trees she heard the crack of a twig underfoot and looked up.

Her heart stopped. Instinct took over from thought. She turned her horse and rode away, fast, and heard the other coming behind her. The rider was more daring than she. As they wove through the trees the other spurred round her in a semicircle and came up to catch her bridle, halting the animal strongly.

Blind with anger and fear, Louise raised the small silver-handled whip she carried and struck Jerome across the face. He wrenched the whip from her, pulled her forward out of the saddle and dropped her to the ground. Before she had a chance to mount again he was beside her, his hands violent as he took her into his arms.

"Let me go," she shouted, struggling fiercely. "How dare you do this! You disgust me."

Jerome was smiling that sardonic smile, his eyes flaming.
"So I saw yesterday," he said unpleasantly.

Hot colour rolled into her face. She caught her breath,
angered and incredulous. "Have you no gentlemanly instincts
at all? But what else could I expect from the son of a bastard—"

"You could expect this," Jerome said thickly, and began to
kiss her.

She barely struggled. The touch of his mouth was what she
had wanted again since yesterday and Louise was past caring.
She let him pull her to the grass and wound her arms around
his neck, kissing him back hungrily.

At last they lay still, their heads on the grass, breathing
hard. Louise began to think again, and her thoughts were bitter. "I am not my mother," she said insultingly.

"Damn your whore of a mother," Jerome said languidly.
He rolled onto his face and picked a long stem of grass, tickling her ear with it, his eyes mischievous. "When you grew
angry yesterday you grew beautiful, too," he said. "Why do
you sneak about like a little white mouse when there is a wild
cat inside you?"

She looked at him sideways. The opalescent eyes like
Daniel's were smiling at her, and suddenly she smiled back.
"Cats scratch," she said lightly.

"So I've observed," he said, fingering the red line she had
laid across his face with her whip. "Kiss it better. . . ."

"Make me," she said, her voice excited.

He pushed her back into the grass and said coolly, "Kiss it,
Louise. . ."

Slowly she raised herself and her lips slid along the cut.
When she lay back, he stared into her eyes. "Your mouth has
my blood on it," he said huskily.

As he lowered his head her lips parted eagerly, and for a
long time there was silence. Only when he moved his exploring
hands to her skirts did she stiffen, and push him away. "No."

Jerome grimaced. "Little virgin."

"And mean to stay so," she said flatly.

"Then you are not your mother's daughter," he sneered.

"If you came here looking for a substitute for her, look
elsewhere," she said bitterly.

"Do you hate her?" he asked curiously.

She stared at him, then shook her head, tears in her eyes.
"How could I? I wish I did. Oh, God, I wish it was so easy."

Jerome groaned. "Yes...."

They stayed silent, looking at each other for some time, their eyes locked in thought.

"You are in love with her," she accused, bitter at the thought for a reason she could not explain.

He flushed. "God, how do I know? I was...until I saw her with my father. How long has she been meeting him? I wonder. Since my mother died, no doubt. I thought it was long over, but it has gone on secretly all this time.... The hypocrisy of it sickens me."

"What did you want from her then?" Louise asked coldly. "Kind words?"

Jerome slapped her face and she was suddenly wild with rage, hitting him back violently. They rolled in the grass fighting like wild dogs, kicking and scratching each other. It ended with her lying spread-eagled on the grass while he lay on top of her, holding her down, his chest heaving with the exertion of the fight. The warm pressure of his body excited her. She was flushed and breathless too, and when he stared at her she could only look back, waiting.

"Let me," he said suddenly hoarse. "Let me, Louise...."

"I will not be used to comfort you because you cannot have my mother," she said, her mouth firm.

"I can take you and there is nobody to stop me," he said, still breathing unevenly, staring at her.

"If you want a whore go to Bristol," she said icily.

"I want you," he said.

She shook her head. "I am well aware that you want my mother," she said.

Jerome stared down at her, his eyes feverish. "Damn you," he said bitterly. "Keep your virginity until you are too old to tempt anyone."

She laughed, suddenly, her eyes bright blue. "Didn't you know? I am going to marry Thomas."

He had not known. It had never entered his head. He stared at her, his eyes narrowing. "You little bitch," he said angrily. "You have been teasing me all this time...."

"Did I ask you to lay a finger on me?" she asked, her glance mocking. She found it oddly exciting to see his scowl, his darkened look. He was looking at her now, she thought, and seeing her, not her mother.

He got up, brushing the grass from his clothes. Louise rose, too, tidying herself, then he caught her round the waist, deliberately holding her too tightly, and threw her onto her horse with a rough gesture.

She gave him a downward smile, her head tilted. "Goodbye, Jerome," she said, turning towards the house.

He did not reply.

In their little house in Bristol, Sophia and Wolfe were eating cold chicken and drinking champagne, lying together in their bed, their bodies resting against each other. They had made love slowly for half an hour, gently and without haste. Now they were both happy, still naked but feeling the heavy relaxation that came after love, hungry for food once their need of each other had been sated.

"Wolfe..." she murmured, sipping from her glass, her brow concerned. "I forgot to tell you...something strange occurred the other day...Jerome came to see me and behaved so oddly...."

She felt his body stiffen against her, and with her sixth sense where he was concerned knew at once that the news she was about to give him was no surprise to him. Turning her head she looked into his eyes.

"You knew," she said, her mouth wry. "Why on earth did you give me no hint?"

He gazed at her, his face restless. "What happened?"

"Oh, nothing much," she shrugged. "He started to kiss my hands in a distinctly amorous fashion...." There was laughter in her voice, a note of mischief that he found disturbing.

"What did you do?"

"I? I did nothing," she said, hearing at last the jealous note he had been trying to hide from her. She looked round at him again, her blue eyes mocking. "Afraid I might encourage him, Wolfe? Even give myself to him?"

He bared his teeth in a snarl of rage. "I'd kill him," he said.

"Your own son?" Her eyes were amused.

"Torment," he said, trying to speak lightly. "Now, tell me the truth—what did you do?"

"Stared in amazement," she said, smiling. "He ran like a deer when he saw my expression. Good Lord, he looked so young, so flushed and excited! Like a child caught trying to steal a lollipop."

Wolfe's eyes darkened. "God, what a tangle. How dare he even look at you!"

"He does not know about us," she pointed out. "Does he?" Her eyes flew to his face in alarm.

Wolfe shook his head. "Not about the present. About the past, yes, of course."

She shuddered, remembering. "Yes, of course. He told Daniel....." Her eyes were suddenly wet. "He told Daniel...."

Wolfe put down his glass and drew her into his arms, his hand on her black head. He looked down and saw her body lying close to his and felt his heart turn over, as it always did, seeing them lying together.

"Ssh...my darling...my dearest...." He drew out the long black strands, staring at them as they strayed across his own bare skin. She never failed to delight him, to arouse him. Even now, having had her so satisfactorily for half an hour, he felt himself wanting her again.

Jerome, he thought, was a threat. He must be dealt with. His eyes narrowed speculatively. Jerome must be got rid of somehow, and Wolfe's strong mind at once came up with the answer. Jerome hated the whole of his father's business. He wanted to be a doctor. It was a simple equation, Wolfe thought, his mouth wry.

Wolfe brought up the matter that evening over dinner. Jerome was in a dark mood, his eyes brooding. The other boys were still away at school, and Alice was having dinner with the family of a young man who was paying her some interested attentions. It was not a match Wolfe particularly cared for—the other family were not quite wealthy enough for him, but Alice showed signs of liking the boy, so Wolfe shrugged and let her choose for herself. He had no wish to ruin her life if she knew her own mind.

Passing the port to his son, Wolfe leaned back, his gold watch chain glittering in the lamplight. "How do you feel about the business now, Jerome?" he asked casually.

Jerome lifted his mouth in a sneer. "I detest it," he said, giving his father a defiant glance.

Wolfe fiddled with his watch, his eyes on the face so like his own. "Prefer medicine still?"

"Yes," Jerome said curtly, sipping his port.

"Well, you've given it two years," Wolfe said coolly. "We might as well call it a day. You can start at medical school in September."

Jerome slowly put down his glass, staring at him. A dark flush grew in his face. His eyes were suddenly filled with flames. "She told you, did she?" he asked thickly. "Getting me out of your way, Father?"

Wolfe's face hardened. A tight cold band grew around his mouth, a white line of rage. "What are you talking about? Don't you want to go to medical school after all? I thought you were so sure...."

Jerome leaned forward, his face quivering. "Beautiful, isn't she, Father? I want her. Did she tell you that? Why not? You've had her long enough. I thought you believed families should share...."

Wolfe's hands were at his throat before he had finished and they struggled together, the young man still no match for his father but his temper so high he was violent enough to hurt. They crashed across the room, kicking and punching each other. Wolfe smashed his fist suddenly into Jerome's face and the boy fell, blood streaming from his nose, his skin white against the dark colour of it.

Too angry to care now, Wolfe looked down at his son. "I could stave your ribs in like firewood," he said tersely. "You'll never speak of her or to her again in that fashion. For now, you'll pack and go to London to a hotel. In September you'll start medical school. You will put anything else from your head."

Jerome's eyes hated him. "Why not kill me the way you did my mother?" he asked sneeringly. "Your mistress would enjoy that, the thought that you had killed to keep her...."

Wolfe's mouth twisted. "Do you think I wouldn't?"

Jerome stared at him, taken aback by the flat reply. He stared at his father in a totally new light, seeing the blaze in the opalescent eyes, the hard structure of the bones, savagely intent on him.

"I'll give you just one warning," Wolfe said levelly. "Next time I'll break your neck."

"She's another man's wife," Jerome said huskily. "What if I told him the truth?"

Wolfe smiled then, his eyes devilish. "Tell him... you will be astounded by the reaction you get."

Jerome was shocked now, reading the amusement in his father's eyes. "He knows," he said slowly. "Good God, he knows...."

"Of course he knows. Do you think it could be kept a secret from him all this time?"

"And he lets it go on? I thought he hated you."

"He loves her," Wolfe said, sighing suddenly. "Oh, God, how my poor brother loves her. If you imagine you know anything about love, Jerome, take note of Stonor Whitley. He would be torn limb from limb by wild horses to save Sophia one instant of pain."

"And yet you cuckold him?" Jerome sneered. "Knowing how it must hurt him?"

Wolfe looked at him drily. "You young fool, has it never occurred to you to wonder why she does not leave him and come to me? Do you think I do not want that? I have her for a short time every day, then she goes home to him. No doubt he suffers knowing she sleeps with me, but she goes home, Jerome...that is what matters to Stonor now. He could never touch her again. You know that, surely. He is impotent. This is the only bargain he could strike with fate—to have her come back to him each day, even though she has been mine."

Jerome sat up, fumbling for a handkerchief with which to stop the flow of blood. He cleaned his face and stood up, swaying, his face bruised and puffy.

"You've knocked out one of my teeth," he said, his tongue feeling for the place.

"Perhaps it will teach you to keep a civil tongue in your head," Wolfe said calmly. "I will say this once and never again: Sophia is the woman I love, the person I love most in the world. Stay away from her, Jerome. No doubt you thought to amuse yourself by taking the woman you thought I once loved. Forget it, I'm warning you. Nothing and no one shall ever come between us again."

"Damn you, keep her," Jerome said sullenly. "I'll want a good allowance while I'm at medical school...."

"You insolent young hound," Wolfe said, grinning. "Very well."

"You'll find the other boys more amenable, Papa," Jerome said with a sudden, sardonic grin. "Dull as ditchwater but very well brought up...."

Wolfe grinned back. "At least they'll know how to behave like gentlemen."

Jerome sauntered to the door. He turned and glanced at his father strangely. "At the risk of having my other teeth knocked out, Papa, she is the most beautiful woman I've ever seen and it would be very easy to love her."

Wolfe studied him coolly. "Then you must try not to," he said flatly.

"I think I must be too much your son to knuckle down to an unkind fate," Jerome said. "Try not to fall under a hansom cab, Papa, or I swear I'll take your place in her bed within six months."

Wolfe's mouth snarled at him. "Get out before I lose my temper again."

"I look so much like you," Jerome said conversationally. "It would be so easy to forget, don't you think, that I was not you, Papa?"

He saw the look in his father's eyes and was gone before Wolfe had reached him. Wolfe swore beneath his breath for some time, his body clenched with jealous rage. The boy had put his finger on the very thing that Wolfe had feared. After a moment he grinned. Well, it showed skill in diagnosing, he thought wryly. Damn the boy.

Jerome did not leave for London immediately. He went, instead, to Queen's Stonor. Louise saw him this time before he reached her, but she made no attempt to escape, eyeing him consideringly as he rode out to meet her.

When she saw the condition of his bruised and battered face she was astonished and alarmed. "How do you come to look like that?"

"My father," he said drily. "Your mother kindly informed him of my interest in her and he beat me into a cinder."

"Serves you right," she said flatly.

"He's sending me to medical school in London," Jerome said. "He is frightened your mother may find my attentions too flattering to resist...."

She flushed. "Shut up."

"You know very well I've no further interest in her," Jerome said. He looked compellingly at her. "It was a lie about Thomas Hunt, wasn't it?"

"No," she said calmly. "He wants to marry me...there is no engagement yet, but in time no doubt there will be."

Jerome caught her hand. "Run away to London with me. Papa will support us. I know he will. He'll give me a good allowance, more than enough to keep us both...."

"Do not talk such nonsense," she said shakily.

"Marry me, Louise," he said.

She looked at him sadly. "What do you hope to achieve by marrying a poor copy of my mother, Jerome?"

"I want you," he said stubbornly. "Do you doubt it? Let me show you how much I want you—"

"I know how much you want me," she said. "You want to do to me what my mother will not let you do to her."

"Bitch," he said furiously. "Do you think I don't know you want me to do it? You made yourself very obvious, you know."

She was scarlet, her eyes shamed. "Perhaps I want your father," she retorted. "Had you thought of that? Perhaps all these years I've wanted him to treat me the way he does my mother...."

Jerome laughed then, and she laughed too. After a pause, she said, "Anyway, I could never do it. Papa would die. You have no idea how much he hates your father."

"Oh, haven't I? I think he hates him almost as much as I do," Jerome said sourly. He looked at her, sideways. "Your father knows, Louise...he knows about your mother and my father. Papa said so."

She was white now, her eyes steady. "Do you think I wasn't aware of that? If you could see him sometimes, drinking himself into a stupor to kill the pain of seeing her after she has been with that man.... Those are the times when I hate her for what she does to my poor Papa.... I could never, never marry you, Jerome. Papa would not forgive me, and I could not forgive myself."

Jerome shrugged. "Yes, I see that now. After all, Louise, there is more of the white mouse than the wild cat in you."

"Perhaps that is safer," she said flatly.

"Marry Thomas, then, and be safe," he said coldly. "Just do not invite me to your wedding."

Then he turned and rode away. When he had gone she cried for a long time in the shelter of the trees. She had known yesterday that she was in love with Jerome, and she had known, too, that there was no future for her with him.

The days wore into autumn and Louise heard that Jerome had gone to London to study medicine. Everyone said how kind his father had been, how understanding with the boy. Louise thought of Jerome's eyes as he talked of her mother, and she winced. Wolfe Whitley was only ever kind with a purpose, she thought, unless it was towards her mother.... There all the kindness of which he was capable spilled out in a golden shower. Louise envied her mother for that ability to make the men in her life so totally adoring. It was a quality she herself didn't have.

Late that autumn Wolfe gave Sophia news of Daniel. It cut her to the quick. Daniel had received the letters she had sent him, but had refused to leave the Army and come home. He wrote her a brief, kind note in reply. The very kindness of it made her shake with pain.

"A stranger," she wept. "I am a stranger to him.... I could have borne his anger, but how can I bear this distant kindness?"

"One day he will come back," Wolfe said soothingly. "One day, Sophia, my darling."

That winter, death carried off their family doctor, who had cared for Stonor ceaselessly for years, and a new young man arrived to take over the practice. Stonor was restless and disturbed, angered at the thought of strange eyes viewing his wasted body, strange hands examining him.

The young man was filled with new ideas. He nodded soberly over Stonor's condition. "Why do you lie in bed all day?" he asked him. "Get a bath chair."

Stonor was taken aback. The old doctor had told him his heart would not stand the strain of any exercise at all.

"One of the old school," the young doctor said carelessly. "A walk each day will soon fill out your lungs and give you a good colour. You'll see. One day we will have you looking quite a healthy man."

Stonor was trembling with excitement when Sophia came home. He launched at once into the tale, his face bright. She smiled happily at him, her eyes dancing.

"And when you are used to walks in the park, perhaps he will let you come for drives with me, darling? We could visit our friends in Bristol together again. You could come out of your little hermit shell and live a real life once more...."

Stonor was tense enough to lie awake all night. Within days the bath chair had been ordered and had arrived, and he took his first walk in the cold winter air, wrapped up like a mummy, but bright-eyed and hopeful.

As one of the servants pushed the chair, Sophia walked beside it, smiling at Stonor, utterly delighted with this new turn of events. He stared across the park, his lungs filling with crisp air, and his face was filled with new life.

After that, his progress was spectacular. He was able to drive in the carriage, dressed for the first time in years. Nobody in the world, he thought, as he stared from the window, could imagine how it felt to be seeing all this once more. He felt like Lazarus risen from the dead. Newborn, he began to slavishly follow his young doctor's advice. When the young man said, ''Buy some exercise weights,'' Stonor did, and spent a quarter of an hour each day lifting them carefully, feeling the blood flow once more through disused limbs.

When the young doctor advised massage, immediately Stonor commanded that a masseur be sent out from Bristol to rub his attenuated limbs. He found the treatment effective within days. ''I can feel the blood flowing around my body,'' he told Sophia. ''It is working, my darling. I am getting better.''

The first evening party he attended was at Luther Hunt's house. He caused a sensation when he first arrived, already accustomed to his bath chair and enjoying himself enormously as he was wheeled into the room. Across the drawing room Wolfe stood watching him. Suddenly he felt a flicker of alarm as he saw his half-brother's grey eyes flick over him. Stonor paused and stared. A long, cold smile lifted his mouth. Wolfe stared back. He sensed the thoughts in Stonor's head as if they were written on his face, and his body tensed.

Sophia bent down to speak to her husband, and Stonor lifted a hand to her neck caressingly. It was the first time in many months that he had made such a gesture. She was conscious at once of the deliberate nature of it, and looked into the cold grey eyes.

Stonor stared back. ''You look so lovely, Sophia,'' he said softly. ''Kiss me, dearest.''

She hesitated so slightly that anyone but Stonor might have missed it. Then she brushed her mouth over his lips, drawing away again at once. As she straightened, her eyes met Wolfe's. He was pale.

Stonor watched them exchange that look and his cold eyes flashed. He looked down, pretending to arrange his covers. A chill intensity of determination was filling him. He had borne enough. He would bear no more.

# CHAPTER TWENTY-SEVEN

From the moment that Wolfe saw his half-brother's cold grey eyes across the drawing room, he had been waiting for Stonor to move, aware, as Sophia was, that Stonor had made up his mind to intervene again between them. His returning health had given him a new impetus. He had long ago abandoned his struggle to do more than hold Sophia, but now his tenacity had returned with his physical reawakening.

There was, of course, no question that he would ever walk again, ride again, ever be the fit, athletic man he had once been—but he had come out from the four walls that had held him so long, and he was charged with the pent-up energies of years of inactivity, burning to enforce his will once more.

It took him three months. During that time he concentrated fully on recovering his health. He watched calmly as Sophia went on with her own life, meeting Wolfe as before, but she knew that beneath his withdrawn quietness something else lurked now, and she was anxious.

"He spends long hours each evening with Edward," she told Wolfe, frowning over the problem. "On weekends they walk out in the park. I never hear what they are saying. Edward has never liked me much. We are poles apart. He dislikes Louise, too. For Edward it is only Stonor."

Wolfe knit his brows thoughtfully. "Perhaps for Stonor it is only Edward now," he said.

She glanced at him through her lashes. Their eyes met and a glance of wry comprehension passed between them. They knew they both lied.

"Perhaps," she said. After a silent pause, she added, "Wolfe, if Stonor has discovered our secret, what shall we do?"

"What do you want to do?" he asked levelly. "It is your decision, my darling. For my part I would say come to me, openly, freely, at last... but you know what I wish. I will not try to bind you to me. I ask only that you remember I am nothing without you."

She sighed. "We are nothing without each other," she said. "Hollow, without point. I will not go back to those years."

"Then we will face Stonor when he makes his move," Wolfe said.

"You think, as I do, that he will?"

"We both know he will," Wolfe said flatly. He looked at her, his mouth hesitant. "Sophia, he does know, my love."

She glanced at him, her brow wrinkled. "You're sure? How long has he known? He has never said one word to me—when did he find out? How?" Her blue eyes widened. "Jerome—is that it? Jerome told him?"

Wolfe shook his head wryly. "Stonor has always known," he said, watching her.

For a moment her face was blank. "What do you mean? Always?"

"He gave you to me," Wolfe said calmly.

She sat very still, her face frozen.

Quietly Wolfe told her of his interview with Stonor, and the bargain they had struck, watching her intently, fearing her reaction.

She was very stiff, her face deeply flushed, when he finished. "So he gave me to you as one might a toy one can no longer use," she said bitingly. "Well! Thank you, Wolfe, for telling me the truth at last. I am glad to know it. How self-sacrificing of him, and how noble of you to take me all these years and let me go back to him each night."

"I knew you would see it that way," Wolfe said drily. "I told Stonor so at the time."

"How else am I to see it? My husband gives me to another man?" Her face was darkly flushed. "Am I to have no will of my own?"

Wolfe's opalescent eyes glittered. "You and I were left free to love each other, that is all."

Sophia stared at him bitterly. "Wolfe, can you not see? Stonor by what he did controlled us as if he were a voyeur watching us through a hidden window. All these years when I have lied to him, he's known, known everything, and said nothing. What does that make of us but his puppets?"

Wolfe's face slowly grew dark. "I had not seen it in that light...."

"Then see it now," she said huskily. "And see this: when Stonor decides to end the puppet show, what then? Are we to get back into his box and turn back into creatures of wood?"

Wolfe swore under his breath. "Come to me now, Sophia. Come to me."

Her eyes were very bright. "I must think before I decide...."

"Think of what?" His voice grew harsh. "Of what you sacrifice? Is Queen's Stonor still my rival? I thought we were agreed the house means nothing."

Her eyes shifted, confusedly. "Wolfe."

"It is bricks and mortar, nothing else," he said bitterly. "I am alive, Sophia, and I need you."

She looked at him levelly. "This time I shall decide what I need, Wolfe. The house, Stonor, Daniel and yourself have all been placed before my own needs in previous times. This time I shall choose for myself."

Wolfe relaxed, his face gentle. "Yes, dearest love, choose for yourself. Remember, you have a right to freedom and life.... Duty is an empty word. You placed your duty to our son before me time and time again, and when he grew up he walked away without a word. This time, choose the thing you need most."

He was certain of her choice at that moment. Her love for him was as strong as his for her, and since Daniel had gone and Edward was to be the next master of Queen's Stonor, he was very well aware that the house had lost its power over her. Stonor's power, since she knew of his decision to give her to Wolfe, had been lessened too. Wolfe left her that day with a leaping heart and a certainty of final victory.

A few months later Stonor gazed around the dining table at his home, his glance resting briefly on his son, who looked back at him with a calm, secretive expression. Sophia was smiling at Louise, her blue eyes teasing. "That dress is fit only for the rag bag, darling. Please, as a favour to me, buy some new gowns. Your summer clothes are so dull. I want you to shine at the tennis parties this year."

Louise quietly smiled back. "Yes, Mama."

"Sophia, I have been thinking," Stonor said casually, and she was abruptly alert, catching the nuance in his tone, conscious of a secret vibration from Edward which put her on her guard.

"Yes, dear?" Her face was tranquil as she stared back at him, none of her thoughts allowed to show on her face.

"Dr. Stewart assures me that I am now strong enough to

take up my business life again," Stonor murmured. "You have borne my burdens long enough, my dear. Edward and I will take over the business together from now on, I think."

So, thought Sophia, this is his plan. A clever one. She looked at him gently. "Just as you wish, dear, of course. I do not want you to overtax your health again, though. Edward, you must do all you can to help your father at first."

Stonor's cold grey eyes held a faint flicker of confused surprise. He had expected her to protest, to delay. "You will no longer need to go into Bristol every day," he said, pretending to smile. "I think you have been looking rather tired lately. A business life is not suitable for a woman. You will be much happier at home here at Queen's Stonor."

"I shall be very willing to give up my business life," Sophia said softly, looking at him directly. "I only took it up to save it for you and our children. Now that you can take over again I am glad to hand it back to you."

Edward looked satisfied. He and his father had spent months in planning this change. Stonor had expressed to him openly his fear that Sophia might object to being excluded from the firm once more. Edward had waited for his mother to attempt to hold onto the power she had, in his opinion, seized. His jealousy of Sophia was hostile even now. She had run his firm long enough, he thought. A woman should be in the proper place—her home.

He glanced at his father, eager to see Stonor's quick smile at him, the scent of victory in his own nostrils. Stonor was watching Sophia, though, with a fixed intensity, his facial muscles stiff.

What was she thinking? She must know that he was making it well nigh impossible for her to meet her lover daily in future. Their meetings would be strictly curtailed, if not ended altogether. Yet she looked so calm and unmoved. Stonor was troubled.

Sophia smiled at Louise. "It is fortunate that Papa's health has improved just now, when it is time we were thinking of your future, my darling. It is time you made the right impression in society. You will need pretty clothes, some suitable escorts—oh, Louise, what fun it will be! All the evening parties to which we may go, the dressmaker's visits, the milliner's . . . I shall have all the time in the world for enjoying myself at last, as other women do."

Stonor's hands clenched on his lap. Sophia glanced at him,

her face filled with open mockery. "All the time in the world for pleasure," she said softly, watching as her husband's face turned grey.

Edward encouraged her, unaware of any undertones in the conversation. "Quite right, Mama. Time we got Louise off our hands." He gave his sister a cold look. "She is old enough to be married now."

"Thank you, Edward dear," Louise said bitingly. "Have you chosen me a husband yet?"

Edward shrugged. "Poor fellow. I am sorry for him. But there it is. I've no doubt we'll find someone suitable."

Sophia looked at him thoughtfully. "Time you were married, Edward, too," she said. "You are twenty-three now—more than old enough for the married state."

Edward's heavy face looked red. "I've no desire to marry yet," he said flatly. "There are enough females in this house already...."

Sophia raised her brows. "Oh? But if you married, you would leave home, silly boy. Married couples do not live with their in-laws."

Edward's jaw jutted. "But this will be my home all my life," he said. "Queen's Stonor is mine...."

"Edward!" Stonor spoke harshly, staring at his wife with grey eyes that were tormented now. He knew far better than his son just how Sophia viewed the house. Edward's aggressive statement of his future ownership stated the truth too bluntly, and Stonor was alarmed.

Edward misunderstood his reaction. Quickly he turned to his father in loving dismay. "Oh, not for many years yet, Papa, please God. I would rather never have the house than have it through your death."

"How dutiful you are, Edward," Sophia said quietly. "Your father is very fortunate to have so loving a son."

Stonor watched in silence as she rose from the table. "Well, I think I will go to bed early," she said. "No doubt you will wish to take up the reins at once, Stonor, so I need not go to work tomorrow. I may spend the day completely in dedicating myself to the pursuit of happiness."

"Sophia...." Stonor's voice was a hoarse cry. "I must talk to you. Edward, Louise, leave the table, please."

Astonished, Edward went out, his brow heavy. Louise quietly followed, and Sophia paused, staring at her husband.

Stonor looked at her in silence for a while. "Come here, my darling," he said at last, holding out his hand.

Sophia walked towards his chair and stood just out of reach, staring coldly into his face.

Stonor drew a long breath. "Sophia, I will say no word of blame for what has lain between us all these years, but now I beg of you to return to your family duty. Queen's Stonor, Louise, Edward—we all need you here each day... let the past be forgotten without a word, but let the future begin tonight...."

Sophia studied him without expression. "You cannot take back what you have once given away, Stonor," she said.

His features quivered as though she had struck him. "That bastard broke his word!"

"Only when it became clear that you were about to break yours," she said.

"I wanted to help you," he pleaded. "You were dying in front of my eyes and I could do nothing...."

Sophia's face softened very slightly. "Why do you think that was, Stonor? Since you pretend not to guess, shall I tell you? You could do nothing because I belong to Wolfe and always have, and you knew that when you forced me to marry you instead of him. You used Queen's Stonor then, you used it again later... you used any weapon that came to hand to keep me. When all your weapons were useless, you turned to Wolfe at last, and he, out of pity for you, struck a bargain with you. There was no time limit on your agreement, Stonor. You left me free to go to Wolfe.

"I went. I shall never leave him again. Take your choice, Stonor. Either I go to him tonight forever, or you put up with it as you have done for so long."

Stonor looked at her, defeated and helpless. Agony came into his voice then. "I cannot bear it," he said hoarsely. "I have suffered the tortures of the damned for years, Sophia. Don't inflict them on me any longer."

"I am sorry, Stonor," she said quietly. "You made a bargain with me once before—do you remember? Daniel was to have Queen's Stonor and you swore to love him. We both know what came of that. You hated my son and you let him see it, so that when he found out the truth he went away rather than face your hatred knowing the reason for it. You drove Daniel away. He would have forgiven me if you had ever done so. You pretended to forgive me, but you took out your jealousy on my son for years, and I bore with it for the sake of the house. Then you gave me to Wolfe quite shamelessly, as if I were a concubine for whom you had no further need. You let me lie to you, you pretended to be blind, you knew all the time that Wolfe was my lover.''

''I suffered,'' he groaned. ''Sophia, I died of jealousy....''

''You wove the web yourself,'' she said flatly. ''All this is your doing, not Wolfe's. You know, Stonor, you have always known, that I am his: I never lied to you; I never once pretended I did not love him.''

He glanced at her grimly. ''You were happy with me for years...''

''Yes, I admit that,'' she said. ''As happy as I could be with half my soul torn out of me.''

He winced.

''Wolfe and I are like the woven strands of a cloth,'' she said. ''Unwind them and they are nothing but a mass of tangled, torn threads. You kept us apart for years by every trick you knew. In the end the only way you could keep any power over us was to push us together, so you were even prepared to do that—anything rather than see me walk out of your life and into his forever.''

''You will not leave me?'' His face was totally defenceless now. ''You would not go? I will do anything, Sophia, anything.''

''I have not made up my mind,'' she said. ''I must see.... For the first time in my whole life I am free to choose for myself. I will tell you when I have chosen, Stonor.''

A few days later Louise was sitting beside her Mama in the elegant drawing room of the Hunt house, listening to Luther Hunt, standing upon the hearth, his thinning hair shining in the lamplight, talking of the worsening of world trade. Through the greenery of the conservatory she saw Thomas beckon to her and quietly she tiptoed out, grateful to be released from the boredom of Luther's idea of small talk.

''Coming to the tennis party on Saturday?'' Thomas asked her casually, smiling down into her quiet face.

''Yes,'' she said, watching him with affection. She and Thomas had a quiet understanding that she valued. Ever since childhood they had been close, not quite as close as she had been once to Daniel, but close enough, closer now than Louise was to any other human being.

Louise was feeling excluded now by her Papa—since he had recovered his health he had turned so much to Edward, leaning on him, planning with him, turning all his considerable powers of cool intelligence into mapping out the future of the Whitley firm and Queen's Stonor. And, Louise was aware, without ever having been told, that her father had hoped to put a stop to her mother's meetings with Wolfe Whitley. She was aware, too, that he had failed. She was aware, equally deeply, of his agony of mind as he waited for his wife to make her decision whether to stay or go. She felt as if, at last, the long threatened destruction of her home by Wolfe Whitley had come close enough to be clearly visible. He had undermined the house so long. Now Louise waited for the final collapse of everything she had ever known. If Sophia went, she was aware, Stonor would die of grief, the house would be without a heart and she would be left alone in a cold mockery of a home.

Thinking of all this, rather than of what Thomas was saying, she missed his opening remarks, carefully long rehearsed in front of a mirror for days. She only heard him say suddenly, in mumbled excitement, "Will you, Louise?"

She turned blank blue eyes on him. "Will I what, Thomas?"

He flushed deeply then, looking wounded. "I was asking you to marry me," he blurted out, his voice filled with anger and hurt.

Louise smiled at him, her face soft. "You know I will, Thomas," she said affectionately. "Why do you need to ask?"

Thomas's anger and pain vanished. He was grinning now, holding both her hands. "Louise. . ." He had nothing to say but that. "Louise. . ."

She kissed him quietly. "Yes, Thomas. . . ." For years she had been the gentle confidante to whom he whispered all his secrets, his thoughts, his dreams of the future. She had known perfectly well for a long time that he wanted to marry her. Thomas had never said as much, but it had been there for her to read plainly.

He took her hand tightly, squeezing it. "Let's go and tell them now," he said excitedly.

She followed him into the drawing room, her cheeks a little flushed. Luther Hunt broke off what he was saying and turned to survey them both, seeing, as Sophia did, Thomas's glowing triumph and Louise's shy smile.

Luther glanced at Sophia quickly. He had not broached the matter to her, although he was sure she must be aware of his son's long admiration for her daughter, and he was not yet certain whether she would react favourably or not. The Stonors were an ancient family. They were no longer as rich as the Hunts, but their pedigree conferred a mystical crown upon them in the county.

Sophia looked into Louise's blue eyes. Thomas cleared his throat, preparing himself for this momentous announcement. He was, Sophia thought wryly, already an alderman in the making, with a tendency to being pompous on occasion, but he was a clever, shrewd young man with an aggressively competitive spirit, and would no doubt go far. Louise could have done much worse. Apart from that, she thought, her eyes amused, the Hunt family were climbing rapidly, and their fortune would be useful to the Queen's Stonor family in the future. Yes, Louise had chosen well, she thought.

Thomas launched himself into his little speech, glancing from his father to Louise's mother. "Of course, I realize we must approach Mr. Whitley before we can seriously consider the future," he said, "but Louise has accepted me..." Then with an unpremeditated lapse into young happiness, he said again, "Louise has accepted me...." And in his voice Sophia heard the accents of real love, and was touched.

Luther, equally touched, still watched Sophia for her reaction, unwilling to appear to be pushing the young couple into anything in case the Stonor family proved unreceptive to the idea. But Sophia stood up gracefully, her skirts swaying, and held out her arms to Louise.

"Darling, I am very happy for you."

Louise kissed her gratefully, her nostrils filled with that sweet delicate fragrance that was Mama.

Sophia turned to Thomas. "Dear Thomas...welcome to my family."

Luther beamed, relieved and delighted. He shook his son's hand, kissed Louise and, greatly daring, kissed Sophia on the cheek, enjoying this privilege for the first time with a sensation of delight.

Stonor, when he heard, was angry that Sophia should have given the young couple tacit acceptance without consulting him. "I will not have my daughter marrying into the Hunt family," he said coldly. "Over the years Luther Hunt has encroached too far into our circle. As soon as I can, I intend to buy back his share of the firm. Louise will not marry young Hunt.''

''You cannot do this to her,'' Sophia said angrily. ''She loves the boy.''

''She will do as she is bid. Louise is a very biddable child.''

''I will not permit it,'' Sophia said.

''Since you plan to leave this house, you have no say in any decisions I may make about my daughter's future,'' Stonor said.

Sophia was silent. He watched her from beneath a veil of anxiety. She turned her head and looked down at him.

''Stonor, do not try to use my child as a weapon in the struggle between us. It will rebound on your own head.''

A flush grew on his face. ''Do you really think I would let Louise marry the cousin of the man who took you from me? Do you really think she could do so? Are you blind? If you leave me and go to him, all communication between yourself and any member of this household will be ended. Louise will never speak to you again. She will never speak to any member of that family again, let alone marry into it.''

Sophia walked out without a word. She went to Louise and told her bluntly what her father had said. There was no need to disguise the truth now. ''He will never permit you to marry Wolfe's cousin,'' she said.

Louise nodded without replying, her face calm. Sophia stared at her incredulously. ''Have you nothing to say? Do you intend merely to accept it?''

Louise looked at her in silence. Sophia felt her cheeks burn at that look. In that moment she felt her daughter reject her, refuse to confide in her, refuse to talk to her at all. Slowly she went out, her black head bowed.

Louise sent an urgent note to Thomas. He came, in surprise and bewilderment, to meet her in the park. ''Thomas, my father will not let you marry me,'' she said directly, looking at him.

Thomas was struck with dismay and anxiety. ''Then we will have to wait until he changes his mind,'' he said after a moment. ''I will be patient, Louise. There will never be anyone for me but you.''

Louise sat down on the damp evening grass and began to undo her buttons. Thomas stared, flushing and looking horrified. ''Louise, what are you doing?''

''You must make me pregnant, Thomas,'' she said coolly. ''It is the only way.''

Thomas energetically pulled her to her feet and shook her. "Are you mad? Do you think I would do such a thing to you?"

She looked up at him oddly, her blue eyes very bright. "Don't you want me, Thomas?"

Thomas stiffened. "As my future wife," he said, looking angry. "I have too much respect for you to...to..."

"Papa will never relent," she said. "He hates your family. Did you not know that?"

"Edward is my friend. He'll persuade his father to agree to the wedding," Thomas said, sure of his ability to triumph.

She sighed. "Thomas, Papa will never consent...never. Either you want me or you do not. Tonight you must make up your mind. If we do not do something quickly, he will marry me to someone else."

Thomas stared at her. "You cannot be serious. Who?" A flush mounted to his head as he considered that possibility.

"Does it matter?" She was contemptuous. "It will not be you, Thomas. Edward cannot sway my father in this, believe me."

Thomas looked down at her. "Louise," he muttered, suddenly believing her. "I cannot be so criminal as to ruin your good name...but if you are prepared to do that, will you be prepared to elope with me? We can be married in Scotland."

Louise relaxed. "Yes, Thomas. We can be married in Scotland. Why did I not think of that? I was so filled with anger that I saw only one way."

"You were not thinking," Thomas scolded. "Suppose I had made you pregnant and then been killed before I could marry you? My darling, any number of things could have gone wrong with such a plan. No, no, the only sensible thing for us to do is elope."

She laughed. "Yes, let us be sensible and elope, Thomas."

He talked for a while of how they would set about it, then broke off suddenly, saying in a queer thick voice, "Although it was wrong of you to suggest it, Louise...do not be hurt that I refused you...I...I would have given anything to..." His words blurted out, hot and stammered, but his eyes were filled with a passion he had never shown her before. "I...I love you too much to do such a thing."

Louise looked at his square-cut, steady, aggressive face, her eyes warm. For a second the vision of Jerome flickered in her mind and a mental wince ran through her. Jerome's wild passion was like a scarlet thread in the backcloth of her memory—he had not loved her, but she had loved him, and she knew she would never love like that again, never know the intolerable necessity such desire could bring. Her life with Thomas would be settled, secure, as warm as a seat by the fireside. Just for one moment she regretted all she would never have—then she smiled at Thomas lovingly. "I will always do what you think is best, Thomas," she said to him. "There is no other man in the world I would wish to marry."

Thomas drew her slowly into his arms and bent to kiss her, his mouth gentle and warm. Under the kiss she could not help but remember the savagery of Jerome's kisses, the unknown, unexpected arousement of her body, but she forced such memories out of sight. Never, Louise thought, never would she follow the path her mother had taken—seeking the wild emotion of the heart at the expense of everything else. Sophia had taught her to fear such traps. Louise wanted a quiet life, security within a good home. The dark mines beneath Queen's Stonor's mellow façade should never exist within her own home. Tenaciously she kissed Thomas back, responding to him with a feeling exactly equal to his, neither giving nor taking more than she knew he desired.

Thomas was satisfied. He looked down at her eagerly. "We will be very happy," he said. She brought him so much—a fine name, a rich background, a loving, dutiful, admiring wife. Thomas thought her perfect. He had thought so for many years. "We will always be very happy," he said, and Louise nodded without speaking, leaning against him.

They eloped two days later. When Sophia came into Stonor's room and broke the news to him, after reading the note her daughter had left behind, he was filled with bitter rage against his daughter, and against the whole Hunt family. "She will never enter this house again," he shouted, his fine-drawn face dark with rage. "She is no longer my daughter...if ever she was...." His grey eyes accused Sophia openly, the final taut a deliberate insult, which they both knew to be wildly false.

Sophia considered him with pity and contempt. "She was your daughter, Stonor," she said quietly. "Until you tried to destroy her to keep me. If you use human beings ruthlessly you will find they reply in kind."

Stonor could find no answer to that. Silent, he watched as she turned and walked out of the room, her dark head glinting with growing threads of silver but her body still graceful, still upright. He knew that she was leaving him. He had tried to hold her by blackmail again, using Louise as his tool, but he had failed. He had indeed precipitated the very thing he dreaded most.

Despair and anguish ate at his heart. Hours later he sat alone in his elegantly furnished room facing an empty future. From the first day he set eyes on Sophia he had become a man obsessed—she had shaped his whole life, she had become his own life. Everything he had ever planned had been for her. Now she had gone. Before his accident he had thought of the future as golden and settled. Queen's Stonor had been a happy home for years with Sophia as its glowing heart. Now the house lay empty around him. Louise had gone. Daniel had gone. And at last Sophia had gone. Only Edward was left to him, and his love for his son was not sufficient to make the years ahead bearable to him.

For a long while Stonor contemplated death. He had borne Sophia's infidelity with Wolfe because he had had the tenacity to cling onto what he still had of her, but to lose her entirely made of his whole life a mockery. Since the age of nineteen he had built his world around her. He had no idea how to fill the empty space in his life that she now left by going to her lover.

He stared at his own hands. Flesh and bone, living, capable of feeling, changing day by day through the miracle of nature. . . death would end that forever.

Through his mind passed memories of his life with her, visions of her as a young girl, practically a child yet bearing his half-brother's child in her womb, that slender little body heavy with the burden she bore, her eyes full of that child's future. From the first moment he had known that the coming child would hold her as a young sapling held eroding soil. He had used Daniel then, as he had used Queen's Stonor. He had used anything that had come to hand to hold her. A quiver ran over his face. She had been sixteen when they met. Seventeen when Wolfe's son was born. Eighteen when she bore Edward to him. A child, he thought bitterly. She had been a child then.

He thought of her beauty the night Wolfe had come home from America and she had gone into his arms without a word, like a lost spirit going home. He had known as he watched them that they were one mind, one heart, one body, yet he had tried desperately to keep them apart. He had tried to convince himself Wolfe only wanted her because it would harm him. . . yet his own honesty had compelled him to know otherwise.

Suddenly a hoarse cry came from his throat as his memory flashed another picture to him—the flashing image of Sophia as a young woman in his arms, returning sensual hunger for his passion, her body wax in the heat of his desire. Those were the years for which his whole life had prepared—the years during which he had possessed her, had known her for his own, had been able to look forward to each night as if it were paradise.

It had all gone now. All he had left was a choice of death. He could live on in this house, a slowly decaying thing without life, without hope. Or he could die tonight and admit he had lost.

And leave her to Wolfe Whitley, he thought, shuddering.

A hoarse cry came from him again. *"No!"*

Stonor could do neither. While there was life, there was hope, he told himself. He had gambled before. He had accepted anything rather than admit defeat. Why give up now?

Like a spider in a cold, grey web Stonor leaned back and began to look into the future. While she was alive, he must be alive, too. Once he had been sure that he would die if she left him. Now he admitted he must stay within the same world that held her—fate might yet give him the chance to take her back. . . or a chance to destroy Wolfe Whitley.

The hell of a world in which there was no Sophia was something he refused to contemplate. He was only forty-five. He might live for years. Surely he would find some chance to hit back at that bastard in those years. . . . His eyes flickered with tormented passion. Surely he would have a chance to see her, he thought in agony. Even to see her would be better than to be dead.

# CHAPTER TWENTY-EIGHT

During the next few years the marriage between Thomas and Louise Hunt grew in strength, despite the irritation of her father's continuing refusal to recognize it or them. Luther was angered by Stonor's attitude. Somehow, by dint of enormous effort, Stonor had raised enough to buy the Hunt family out of the Whitley firm. There were even rumours that he had mortgaged Queen's Stonor again to do it. Edward Whitley, his face growing more and more aggressive, worked like a slave from morning to night to keep the firm solvent. Stonor, familiar in the city now in his wheelchair, worked with him. Edward showed no signs of wanting to marry. His whole life revolved entirely around his home and his father, his business and his triumphant possession of all three.

After Sophia left Stonor, gossip ran rampant for months. She lived openly with Wolfe, expecting somehow that Stonor would divorce her, but Stonor was as determined to ignore the situation as he was determined to repossess the firm.

Sophia had, of course, entirely lost her reputation and her place in society. If anyone imagined that that would bother her, they were proved wrong. One only had to see her with her lover to know her to be too happy to care. At long last she and Wolfe were together, night and day, and in these years her face reflected the tranquillity of her decision.

Jerome, at medical school, had soon heard the tale. He had made it his business to make a return visit to Bristol to face them both. Sardonic, dry, he had arrived back from the station in a hansom cab, his powerful face filled with mockery.

It had been a letter from one of his brothers that had brought him back. Sophia's arrival at the house had thrown everyone in it into a complete state of disarray. Alice had married her dull, well-to-do suitor some time before, but the three boys, James, Martin and Jonathon, still lived at home, although they were at school for most of the year.

Wolfe calmly informed them that Sophia would be the

mistress of their home in future, and offered them the choice of accepting her, or of being made provision for elsewhere.

The three boys had debated the matter in privacy. All of them were very similar: well-mannered, sensible, calm in temperament—and lacking Jerome's wild originality.

Wolfe was astonished when they elected to stay. At first they were withdrawn in Sophia's company, but somehow, he never knew quite how, she won them over during his absence at work each day, and by the time they had known her for three months she had become the centre of the house for them. For the first time in their lives the three boys had a home instead of merely a house in which they lived. They only remembered their mother as a drunken embarrassment. Wolfe had never been able to draw a veil over Eleanor's behaviour sufficiently to disguise it from the boys. Their childhood had been one in which they had existed rather than lived, spending it in schools or hotels, far from home. Sophia changed all that. They found themselves seeking her out, singly, to tell her confidences, to hear her admire them, to watch her adoringly. She had them eating out of her hand, Wolfe thought drily. At least he need never fear, with them, as he had with Jerome, any rivalry. The boys were oddly immature. They viewed her as the mother they had never had.

At first there had been trouble from the servants. Sophia's arrival had been the signal for insolence, revolt, downright rebellion, but she had told Wolfe to ignore it, and quietly dealt with it herself. Not for nothing had she run Queen's Stonor alone since she was a young girl. A few of the servants were dismissed. The others knuckled under. Within weeks she absolutely reigned in the house as much as she had at Queen's Stonor, both servants and boys competing for her attention and interest, conspiring silently to revolve around her as if she were the sun and they her satellites.

Jerome sent no word of his arrival. Since he had begun medical school he had spent all his holidays in London, and Wolfe did not expect him home. When Jerome arrived, Sophia was alone. He stood in the elegant drawing room and surveyed her insolently with those hard, opalescent eyes, daring her to behave as if everything were normal, waiting to see colour rise in her face, consciousness in her eyes.

Instead she held out her hand, still as calmly amused as ever, saying softly, "Jerome, dear boy...why didn't you say you were coming home? I would have ordered a special dinner."

Jerome's mouth was mocking. "I may gather, may I, that my father's house has a new mistress?" He emphasized the last word insolently.

Sophia laughed. "I think Martin wrote to tell you so, Jerome." The blue eyes sparkled teasingly. "Martin shows me all his letters. . . ."

Jerome's brows lifted. "You are like moss, Mrs. Stonor Whitley. . . put you down and you will grow anywhere."

Her face reflected nothing but amusement. "I am very fond of your brothers. They are good boys. We get on very well."

His eyes flicked over her. "And will you be a loving mother to me, too, Mrs. Stonor Whitley?" His constant use of her married name was meant to wound but it appeared to make no dent on the soft plating of her armour, as though she were unaware of his deliberate attempt to insult her.

"You have no need of a loving mother, Jerome," she returned quietly, meeting his opalescent glance. "You are a man. Your brothers are still boys. I can be of use to them."

He moved closer. "You could be of use to me," he said, quite deliberately, staring hard at her.

Then colour did rise in her face and her blue eyes were angry. "That is enough, Jerome."

"Not for me," he said, his voice thickening.

She rose to leave the room, brushing past him, and he caught her arms and said harshly, "Do you think I am like my father, Mrs. Stonor Whitley? Do I remind you of him when he was young? How old were you when he first had you? You must have been a child. . . ."

"Let me go, Jerome," she said coldly. "I will not stay here to listen while you insult me."

"Stay for this then," he said, bending his head.

She tried to pull away, but he was too insistent. His mouth covered hers eagerly, urgently, his arms went round her, holding her. Sophia stood, passive, knowing that to fight him would merely excite him further. She was perfectly aware of the emotions contained behind that hard, handsome face, and she was bitterly sorry for him. Jerome kissed her long and deeply, breathing as if he were dying, shaking as he felt her in his arms.

At last he lifted his head, a drawn look on his face. There was silence between them. He closed his eyes, still holding her. "You should have been my mother," he said, as if accusing her of treachery. "I love you. . . . In the train I visualized this and I meant to hurt you any way I could. I wanted to see you cry. I wanted to shame and disturb you. But I love you...." He opened his wild eyes, looking at her miserably. "I do not even want to love you. I cannot help it."

Gently she freed herself and sat down on the sofa, holding out her hand. He sat on the carpet like a child and laid his head on her lap, his lids closing.

She stroked his black hair, her face tender. "You are so like Daniel," she said lovingly. "Jerome, accept me as your mother. The other boys have done so. We are all happy together. You have a place here if you will take it . . . as my son."

Jerome laughed, his mouth shaking. "You know I cannot."

She went on stroking his hair. "You are too young to know the meaning of the word cannot," she said smilingly. "Try, Jerome."

He turned his head, his cheek against the silken cloth of her gown. The opalescent eyes blazed. "I love you," he said, and the tone made her whiten. "When I found out you were my father's mistress again, I tried to tell your husband, did you know?"

She looked at him in perturbation. "What did Stonor say?"

"I never reached him. Louise would not let me." Jerome's mouth twisted. "She was so angry. She looked like you then, a fire in her blue eyes. She has always been so quiet and demure. Suddenly I saw you in her and I tried to take her. . . ."

Shock made Sophia stiffen. "Jerome!"

He grimaced. "Oh, do not worry . . . your daughter can take care of herself. She soon saw me off—although I think she wanted me to do it; I could feel it. There is a hard core in Louise, though. She refused me outright."

"So I should hope," Sophia said, thinking of her daughter sadly. She had not seen Louise since the day Louise had left with Thomas. Sophia had written to her and had no response.

"She's married to Thomas, I gather," Jerome said drily. "She said she would marry him." He sighed. "She is an odd girl. I was surprised by the way she responded to me. I do not see her doing so with Thomas. But if that is what she wants. . . ."

Sophia frowned down at him. "She loves Thomas," she said. Surely Louise had never felt anything for Jerome?

He shrugged. "If she had not known why I wanted her, I think she might have come away with me. . . ."

"No," Sophia said anxiously. Louise. . . and Jerome? She

had never had a suspicion. Beneath her daughter's quiet surface lurked things that surprised her. The girl's elopement with Thomas had been a shock. The deliberate refusal to admit her mother to her confidence had been another. From a loving child Louise had turned into a stranger overnight. Like Daniel, she thought miserably. I've lost them both. The two children I really cared for... both gone... because of Wolfe.

Jerome suddenly detached himself and stood staring down at her. "There is nothing either of us can do about it," he said flatly. "I love you quite desperately, and I could not stay in this house. I meant to stay. I meant to flay you alive if I could. I came to hurt as much as I dared." There were shadows beneath the brilliant blue-green eyes. "I thought if I stayed I might get to you somehow. I might as well admit it. If I could find a way of getting you I would take it...."

She was silent, staring at him in consternation. He was a complication she had not anticipated. Wolfe would go mad if he came home and found the boy here with that look in his face. She knew Wolfe would read it as he had before, as anyone who knew Jerome could read it.

He read her dazed, anxious expression with a wry look. "Oh, I will go," he said mockingly. "Papa will not need to fight me to keep you. He told me once he would kill to keep you, did you know? And so would I. Your husband too, poor swine. Helen of Troy... how does it feel?"

"You sound drunk," she said gently.

"Mad," he said, laughing recklessly. "Mad with love. You haunt my dreams. You have for years. I saw you under an apple tree in my father's arms and I was jealous, both of him and you. Jealous because I could see how he loved you. Jealous because you were the loveliest woman I had ever seen and I wished you were my mother. I grew up looking at you. I grew up wanting you. I think I will live all my life knowing what I have missed. Just as well Louise had sense enough to refuse me. I only wanted her for her echo of you, and she knew it. Hate me, Sophia. I told Daniel the truth because I wanted him to feel some of the anguish I felt whenever I thought about you. Hate me for that." He laughed bitterly. "You see, I would rather you hated me than smiled gently at me, as you do. As a mother I will never accept you. As an enemy I would at least arouse an adult emotion in you."

She could find nothing to say to him. His confession that he had wanted to hurt Daniel came from a hard, wild, reckless

unhappy young man with such passion in his opalescent eyes
that she was only filled with pity.

After a moment, she said quietly, "When you were born I
was already the mother of your father's first child. You are
the image of Daniel, Jerome. I cannot hate you because you
look so like your father and my son. When you are thirty, I
shall be over fifty—a woman well into middle age, past all
thought of romance, without beauty, no longer desirable to
anyone.... Be sensible, Jerome."

"Sensible?" His mouth twisted. "Have you forgotten already what it is like to be in love? Do you say to the flames
consuming a house, be sensible and go out? All you can do is
watch as everything burns. Every time I think about you I die
a little. I despised my own mother. I hate my father. I am indifferent to my brothers and my sister. In all my life only one
other human being has mattered to me...you."

She winced, stricken by his hard sincerity. "Oh, Jerome."

He pulled her up from the sofa, holding her shoulders. She
looked at him anxiously, her face pale and disturbed.

"I am going," he said. "I shall never come back. Tell Papa
that. Tell him I can recognize futility when I see it. I think I
shall never love another living soul again. Love is another
word for pain. I have seen enough pain in the hospital wards
to know the folly of permitting disease to cause it."

"Don't talk like that," she said quickly. "You are young.
You will grow out of this."

He shook his head, the handsome dark face sombre. "Do
you honestly think I have not tried? I have had girls in London in an attempt to shut you out of my mind, and each time I
have found myself crying out your name inside my head....
You've spoiled me for any other woman. It's hopeless." His
hands trembled as they touched her face, shaping it softly.
"Be kind for once," he whispered. "Kiss me goodbye...."

She flushed deeply, trembling. "No, Jerome."

He stared into her eyes. "It cannot matter to you, but to me
it will...just once..."

"No," she said wildly. "Please, don't ask me to."

A curious eager look came into his face. "Sophia..."

She tried to move away, but his hands controlled her.
"Shall I tell you why you refuse?" he asked her thickly. "You
dare not...in case you find yourself wanting me."

"Let me go," she said wildly, terrified.

"Do you want to make me beg? Do you think I wouldn't?

In front of my father, in front of the world...I love you...kiss me." He was totally out of control now, white to his hairline, trembling with passion.

Still she stood, disturbed and alarmed, staring at him.

"I swear I will go for good if you do," he said. "On my honour. I swear I will go at once."

Slowly she raised her face. He watched her, shaking. Her mouth brushed over his lips. Jerome's arms went round her and Sophia closed her eyes, her body suddenly taut with excitement. They kissed hotly, pressing closely. She put her arms around his neck and forgot everything. Jerome was murmuring her name, kissing her hungrily, deeply, possessing her and receiving all the response he wanted.

Behind her closed lids she saw pictures of a dark, moth-filled park, heard Wolfe murmuring to her, felt the fire of life burning within her body as she surrendered to him. In the years since that night she and Wolfe had aged imperceptibly day by day, but at the back of her memory the vision of that night was always alive. While Jerome eagerly, wildly, caressed her and enjoyed the yielding of her soft mouth, Sophia dreamed of his father and of her own vanished youth.

When he slowly, reluctantly released her, she opened her eyes, flushed to a deep pink, and looked at him almost without knowing who he was.

"Goodbye, Sophia," Jerome said deeply.

She watched him walk out of the room and felt her age press down upon her like the weight of the house.

Wolfe heard of Jerome's visit before he reached home. A spiteful, quick-eyed neighbour whom he met informed him of it, and he only managed to reveal none of his alarm by smiling and nodding before leaving the woman at once. He came home early, tense, expecting to find Jerome there, anticipating trouble.

Sophia looked at him, reading his expression. "He has gone," she said, before Wolfe had spoken.

Wolfe looked at her sharply. "What happened?"

"Nothing," she said. "Nothing that can be helped. He is very bitter, Wolfe, and very unhappy. Please, don't talk about it."

Wolfe walked to the window. "It is still the same?"

She did not ask what he meant. Huskily she answered, "Yes."

"God." Wolfe twisted restlessly. "What the hell are we to do? He cannot come here feeling like that."

"He won't," she said. "He told me to tell you. He will never come home again." A sob broke in her throat. "Oh, my darling. I have come between you and your son. . . . I'm sorry."

"There was nothing but hatred between us anyway," he said. "Jerome has never liked me—Eleanor saw to that." Wry irony echoed in his laughter. "God, how she would scream with rage to know how the boy feels about you, of all people; it is a damned, malicious joke."

"Don't," she said, covering her face with her hands.

He came over to her and sat down, his arm around her. "Dearest love, forget the boy. It is an accident of fate."

"I never took it seriously," she whispered. "Until I saw it today. . . like flames consuming a house, he said. Poor Jerome. . . he is black and twisted with it. I've hurt him so badly."

"Was he unpleasant to you?" he asked anxiously.

"Unpleasant?" She laughed hollowly. "Oh, Wolfe. . .he looks so like you when he talks like that. . . ."

Wolfe looked down on the bent black head, the gathering silver threads in it shining as she wept, his face paling. "Like what?" he asked carefully. "What did he say?"

She lowered her hands, her eyes filled with tears. They stared at each other in silence. Wolfe groaned.

"Oh, Christ," he said painfully. "He didn't touch you?"

She met his eyes honestly. "I kissed him."

Wolfe's mouth set. "And?"

She put her hands to his hard, jealous features, stroking them. "I forgot it was not you for a moment, my dearest; I felt sixteen again, in the park at Queen's Stonor, with all of life in front of us and the earth shaking under my feet." She smiled wildly. "And I opened my eyes and was a middle-aged woman locked in nothing but memories."

"And Jerome?" he asked, watching her.

"He went."

"He will get over it," Wolfe said without conviction.

She did not answer, remembering Jerome's face and voice as he said he would never admit love again.

A year later Jerome wrote to them that he had married a Lancashire mill girl whom he had met while he was working during his holidays. Wolfe increased his allowance without comment. To Sophia he said, "Well, he is over it."

Sophia made no reply. She could not tell him that she had received a brief letter from Jerome by the same post. She had burned it after reading it. Jerome had married because he found it tiresome, he said, to buy women when he needed them. Hannah, he wrote, was a level-headed girl who would make a good partner for a doctor. He meant to live in Lancashire when he had ended his training. He would work among the poor. They needed him. Those who have been in hell can always recognize it when they see it, he said. The slum dwellers of these mill towns are denizens of hell. He would do what he could to ease their pain, although their lives could not be made tolerable by any means he knew. Any more, he added, than mine can without you. I love you, Sophia. Always. Hopelessly. I dream of you at night. I think of you by day.

She answered the letter secretly. Her words were carefully chosen.

She told him that she hoped his marriage would prove a happy one. She hoped that he would get what he needed from the life he had chosen. She sent her love to his wife. She ended that she thought of him often very sadly. "You are so like Daniel," she wrote. "You are so like your father."

There was nothing else she could say to him. She knew that he would read into her admission that she thought of him often. She knew what he would think of her admissions, but she put both into the letter with deliberation. She knew it was wrong to do so, but Jerome wrote out of hell and she could not pass by on the other side and not try to ease his pain.

Over the next years peace seemed to hold her and Wolfe, the calm backwater of time slowly enfolding them. Smiling at him over their breakfast table she said lovingly, "We are getting old, you know."

"I am," he said. "Not you."

Her blue eyes danced. "A silver-haired old lady I shall be soon. Good heavens, darling, I shall be fifty before I know where I am."

"With your bone structure that will only make you lovelier," he said.

Their lives held happiness like a cup of wine. The urgency had completely vanished from their lives. They still made love warmly, happily, but without fire. The three boys had left school and each chosen one arm of the business to enter. They were without any spark of originality. They worked hard. They rose by dint of perseverance. They each began to look about for wives of their own. Sophia watched with wry amusement as they blossomed into manhood.

Society still ignored her position as Wolfe's mistress. She never went out with him to any social functions, and they were not able to invite anyone to their home. Even Luther Hunt held aloof, shocked and angered by her fall from favour. "Jealous, poor fellow," Wolfe grinned. "My God, how he envies me."

Of a child for Louise and Thomas there was no sign at all. Sophia had waited eagerly for news of a grandchild, but none came, and year followed year without any word of one. Luther was disturbed by this, she heard. He had eagerly awaited grandchildren, too. They would be the heirs to an enormous fortune. He blamed Louise for her failure to produce his awaited heir. Wolfe drily told Sophia that Luther, from being proud of his daughter-in-law, had become hostile to her.

Sophia was distraught. "My poor girl...Luther cannot blame her! It is unjust."

Wolfe shrugged. "Luther is brooding because Stonor has never forgiven him. He wanted Thomas to marry her so that one of his family could be part of Queen's Stonor...you must know how Luther has always envied you and Stonor that damned house. He would give his eye teeth to own it. As it is, Louise has brought him neither the house nor a grandchild. He dislikes her for it."

Sophia groaned. "I could kill Stonor for his obstinacy. If he would only forgive her..."

Wolfe grimaced. "He will forgive her the day you go back to him," he said drily.

She gave him a smiling glance. "Even for that I would not go back. You need not look at me like that...."

Wolfe grimaced. "I could almost pity him—if he were not so damned tenacious. He is behind every problem that confronts me. He would ruin me if he could. He outbids me shamelessly. He pours out a fortune to try to cut my prices, to force me into a loss—every trick he knows he uses, he and that damned son of his. They have tentacles everywhere for just one purpose. To destroy me."

"You are too big for them," she shrugged. "You've grown beyond Stonor's power to harm you."

"He irritates me, though," Wolfe said morosely. "He is like a fly buzzing around my head. He will neither go away nor harm me, merely drive me to distraction."

She looked sad. "It is all he has to live for."

"Sorry for him, Sophia?" he asked her wryly.

She looked at him. "Aren't you?"

Wolfe gave a faint sigh. "I suppose so...alone in that house, with his son, brooding eternally...yes, I am sorry for him." He looked at her passionately. "But he cannot have you back."

When the three boys were married, one after another, Sophia did not attend the weddings. The families of the brides would not agree to that, and she refused, despite Wolfe's anger, to insist upon going. The boys apologized anxiously. They retained affection for her despite their new allegiances. After their departure, the house was very quiet. Wolfe and Sophia settled to a tranquil happiness that needed nothing but each other. His sons visited them from time to time. As children were born to them, Sophia was gradually allowed some of the happiness of a grandmother. Jonathon's wife, Mary, in particular, grew very fond of her, and often brought her three children to visit her. A quiet, thoughtful girl, she had no intention of allowing the views of her parents to dictate her own behaviour. She felt herself to be very advanced and modern. "After all," she said to her husband, "she is quite an old woman. She is on her way to being fifty. It is absurd of my parents to talk as if she were a scarlet woman. She is a very fine lady and has such a kind face."

When the Boer War broke out it made a great stir in Bristol. During the years it continued many young men left the neighbourhood and never returned. One of them was the eldest of Wolfe's younger three sons, James. Married to a rather pretty blonde girl with a catlike smile, James found himself frequently the object of public amusement as his wife flirted with other men. Unexpectedly he joined the Army and was killed within months. His wife consoled herself before her period of mourning was up, and Wolfe ended her allowance furiously. "Shallow little bitch. James deserved better," he said to Sophia.

Just before the end of the war a letter came breaking the news of Daniel's death. He had been killed in an act of great bravery and daring. His commanding officer had written to Sophia instead of to Stonor at Daniel's own request, and she felt that this gesture by her son was intended as an act of forgiveness, a silent admission of unbroken love. She wept in

Wolfe's arms and she felt him weep, too. Daniel had been a living proof of their love and he was gone finally and forever.

"Will you tell Stonor?" Wolfe asked her later.

She silently shook her head. After a while she said, "Stonor has no rights in him. He was our son."

The twentieth century drew on with gathering speed, which seemed apparent to everyone. When the Boer War ended in 1902 there was general rejoicing. The political arguments it had spawned had split society into pro- and anti-Boer factions, and the final months of the war were marred by bitterness.

That summer Sophia was shopping in Bristol alone when she came face to face with Stonor. He was being pushed along the street by a thin young man whom she did not recognize. Stonor's eyes blazed as he caught sight of her. It was the first time they had met since she had walked out of Queen's Stonor years before, and without volition she halted, staring at him. The young man, not knowing her, was pushing past when Stonor sharply told him to stop.

His eyes on her face, he said coolly, "How are you, Sophia?"

The question might have come from a total stranger. She felt her colour rise. She had felt angry hostility towards him ever since the night Wolfe had told her of the bargain Stonor had struck with him. Nevertheless, she was glad to be wearing one of her most attractive dresses; the shade of blue that most suited her eyes, a delicate violet, with a high ruched neck that disguised the prominent muscles of her throat and gave her still-slender, graceful figure a distinction that suited it. Her hat bore violets, too, massed in silken profusion. Beneath it her black hair was wreathed softly on her neck, the silver in it merely like the reflection of light.

She felt a desire to wound him that surprised her. Rarely in her life had she felt such an impulse.

"I am very happy, thank you," she said, smiling deliberately, her eyes on his face.

He looked at her then with that cold, hard expression that, over the years, she had learned disguised anguish. As if to hit back at her, he said, "You will be fifty next year.... You are getting old, Sophia."

"Wolfe and I are getting old together," she said.

It was as if they threw knives at each other, watching to see the steel points find their mark.

He ran his grey eyes over her slowly. "Women age faster than men," he said. "He will find consolation when you are no longer desirable."

The young man behind his chair looked aghast, his face crimson. Stonor was beyond remembering anything but her, staring at her, willing her to feel pain.

"Would you, Stonor?" she asked him very softly.

The whiteness in his face grew deeper. He breathed harshly. "I am not my brother," he said through stiff lips.

"No," she said. "You are not." Twirling the pale grey parasol she carried, she gave him a careless smile. "Goodbye, Stonor."

As she passed his chair she brushed her skirts against his arm and felt his hand briefly move to touch her, hearing his intake of breath, knowing he suffered.

Stonor ordered his servant to take him at once to his carriage. He did not even see the young man's gaping curiosity. His mind was filled with images that drove him like the flies around a horse's head.

For days he thought of nothing else. Her very cruelty, so deliberately inflicted, moved him. She had wanted to hurt him. He had been aware of that, and it had pleased him. Had she been indifferent, even politely kind, he would have died of agony. She had been cold and carefully cruel, and it was as if she had answered passion with passion. He went over the words again and again. He closed his eyes, remembering her skirts brushing against his hand, the sensation he had had of touching her, of imagining her body beneath the material....

Would she tell his brother she had seen him? He ached to know. If she did not.... He clenched his hands upon the arms of his chair. If she did not tell Wolfe there would be some meaning in his life. Like a secret love affair, the barbed exchange of cruelty moved in his blood. He remembered the night of her birthday ball when he had raped her, and the bitter words they had spoken to each other then, the twist of the knife of anguish in his flesh. She had taunted him then, her blue eyes tormenting him, and he had used all the extremity of pain against her, as he had before in their first years together. Stonor's eyes glowed hotly. She responded to cruelty, he thought, his heart beating. She had often driven him to it quite deliberately, using the flick of her voice to start him into violence, as if she needed it.

He brooded over his need to see her again until he was

almost mad. That chance meeting had awoken buried emotions that haunted him. Then he heard of Daniel's death by a roundabout route—he had not been informed of it officially and it took months to percolate to him—and for some time he considered his course of action. Finally he gathered together all of Daniel's possessions, had them packed in a case and ordered his carriage. When he gave Wolfe's address to his driver he was aware of the man's gasp of disbelief, but Stonor showed no sign of having noticed. Cold, formal, precise, he leaned back in his carriage as they drove.

Wolfe's elegant house had matured over the years into something of great style and beauty. From his carriage Stonor considered it icily. Then he ordered the driver to ask if Mrs. Whitley would come out to speak to him.

Sophia, through her drawing room curtains, stared incredulously at the carriage. A dark flush mounted to her cheeks. What on earth was he doing here?

Ever since they had met in the street she had been uneasily aware of him hovering in the dark regions of her mind. She was as conscious as Stonor of the nature of their brief exchange. Sophia had rarely wanted to hurt as she had wanted to hurt him. She had astounded herself by her reaction.

She turned, as disturbed as a young girl by the arrival of a suitor, to stare at herself in the drawing room mirror. The black and white dress she wore was delicately pleated and exquisitely cut. She gave herself a wry glance. Fifty years old...was she insane to look at herself in mirrors? Like Queen Elizabeth I she should cover them up, she told herself.

Her white skin was at last beginning to show signs of time's attentions. She had resorted lately to a faint dusting of rice powder to disguise the lines and wrinkles. Her features retained all their old strength and charm—time could do nothing to mar that fine, modelled structure. Her hair was as thick, as shining as ever—even the silver in it was more a distinction than a debit.

Gracefully she walked out to the carriage and stood on the pavement, looking up at him. He had opened the door as she approached and looked back at her icily. Not by a flicker did his face reveal any of the wild emotions beneath.

"I wish to speak with you," he said, gesturing for her to join him.

Sophia glanced back at the house, aware of the servants who had clustered to stare in fascinated disbelief.

Her lips compressed, but at last she allowed his driver to aid her into the carriage. The door was closed. A moment later the carriage started off.

She was startled by that. She stared at him, her blue eyes hard. "Are you abducting me, Stonor?" she asked coolly.

His mouth twitched as if he almost smiled. "I have brought all of your son's possessions," he said quietly. "I heard of his death. I thought you might want them."

She was taken aback, moved. Tears rose into her eyes. "Oh..."

Stonor watched her deliberately. "His cricket bat, his books, his toys..." he said. "I packed them all."

She bent her head into her hands and wept. Stonor watched her, his mouth dry.

The carriage drew up slowly in a quiet close. Her tears ebbed gradually and she accepted the handkerchief Stonor handed her, carefully drying her face. When she looked up she gave him a long, unsmiling look.

"Why?" she asked.

He did not pretend not to know what she meant. "I wanted to see you," he said flatly.

She flushed, looking away. "Please, take me back to my house," she said.

He folded his hands on his lap. "Wolfe will be very curious when he hears of my visit, I suppose," he said casually. "What did he say when you told him you had seen me the other day?"

"Take me home, Stonor," she said.

"You did tell him, didn't you?" he asked.

She looked at him then. "No," she said as if she flung a bitter insult at him. "Why should I even remember I had seen you? It slipped my mind."

His cold grey eyes stayed concentrated on her face. He was breathing very fast. "Do you hate me, Sophia?" he asked thickly.

"Yes," she said, her voice shaking with it.

"Yes," Stonor said wildly. "Hate me...hate me, Sophia...."

Their eyes met in a long duel, silent, deadly, tense. He banged with his stick and the carriage started again. As they drove back he never took his eyes off her face. They drew up outside Wolfe's house. She rose to go. The horses moved restlessly and she stumbled, trying to avoid falling against him.

He turned, a hand moving to her waist, and she heard his indrawn breath.

She was wearing a bunch of her favourite silk violets in her belt. His hand deliberately detached them. She looked at him angrily.

"Give them back...."

He smiled icily, pushing them into an inner pocket. "I am taking them in payment for your son's possessions," he said levelly. "They are still warm from your body, Sophia."

Scarlet flowed up her face. "Stay away from me, Stonor," she said bitterly. "Stay away from me."

"Will you tell Wolfe I stole them?" he asked pointedly.

She gave him one look and left the carriage. The driver carried the case of Daniel's possessions up the path and she vanished into the house. Alone, Stonor drew out the violets and held them against his face. They bore her personal perfume, the sweet lingering fragrance she always carried around with her. His driver came back and the carriage drew away from the house just as Wolfe approached it. Stonor caught a glimpse of him, saw his startled, frowning, angry face, and a cold, satisfied smile came to his lips.

Sophia was in her own bedroom kneeling beside the opened case of Daniel's things when Wolfe burst into the room like a madman, his eyes blazing.

"What was he doing here?"

She looked up, tears in her eyes, holding a wooden toy which Daniel had had as a baby. "He brought Daniel's things to me," she said.

Wolfe looked at her, his eyes calming. "That was kind of him," he said.

Sophia looked down at the old, familiar, forgotten objects and felt her heart ache.

"He did not come into the house, I suppose?" he asked her gently, watching as she picked up the things one by one, touching them lovingly.

Sophia shook her head. "No."

"Did you speak to him?"

"Yes," she said.

Wolfe watched the bent dark head. "What did he say?"

"Very little," she said. "But to the point."

"Yes, he would," Wolfe muttered. "Did you speak to him for long?"

"I got into the carriage and he drove away with me," she

said, still not looking at him. If she did not tell him, the servants soon would. "For a moment I thought he was abducting me...."

Wolfe was tense, alert. "And?"

She shrugged. "You know Stonor...."

"What did he really want?" Wolfe asked, then, bitterly, "as if I did not know. Did he touch you?"

"He stole my violets," she said, then laughed a little hysterically. "Do you remember you did that once? Oh, my darling, so long ago...Louise was tiny and you smiled at me and kissed my violets, looking at me so lovingly...."

"Did Stonor look at you lovingly?" Wolfe asked tightly.

"Stonor?" Sophia looked round at him, her blue eyes wet with tears. "He came to hurt if he could. To take what he could. Wolfe, at times he frightens me...he would rather I killed him than ignored him."

"He is obsessed with you," Wolfe said. "He always has been. I've never known a man with the capacity to love as Stonor does...his love is like a frozen river under his mind...it flows on and on out of sight, filled with dark weeds."

"He gave me to you," she said in a wild flare of emotion. "He knew what he was doing."

Wolfe studied her with narrowed, speculative eyes. "That has always burned in your mind, hasn't it, Sophia? Why do you resent it so much? I thought it rather fine, myself. He suffered appallingly but he did it to save your sanity or your life."

She was holding one of Daniel's books, staring at the boy's name written in large, childish handwriting in the front. Her eyes were fixed, angry, filled with bitterness. She did not answer, but Wolfe was aware that she was silent deliberately.

Slowly she packed the things away. Wolfe stood watching her, wondering.

# CHAPTER TWENTY-NINE

The years between the end of the Boer War and the beginning of the war with Germany stretched in unbroken halcyon peace for Sophia and Wolfe. They grew old together in perfect happiness and were visited on Sunday afternoons by Wolfe's grandchildren. Both of his sons' wives had now accepted Sophia completely, Martin's wife, a rather level-headed and shrewd woman, having decided that if she allowed Jonathon's wife to monopolize the position of daughter-in-law to Sophia, she might one day wake up and find that Wolfe, in revenge, had left his fortune entirely to his youngest son. Martin was relieved that the division was over, for whatever reason. He was very fond of Sophia and liked to see his two children playing with her on the lawns of her home.

Of Louise there was no hint, no sign. Sophia had heard of her through Wolfe, and knew her daughter was unhappy in her marriage. Luther's cold anger towards her had somehow seeped into Louise's relationship with Thomas. Her failure to have a child had eaten bit by bit into the deep feelings he had had for her. "I almost think he blames her for it," Wolfe said drily.

The outbreak of war came like a thunderclap into a perfect summer day, although it had signalled its arrival to sharp eyes by continual drifting flurries of dark cloud. The early months of the war were a peculiarly heady time, and patriotism was high. Young men volunteered in a spirit of adventure, egged on by their girls and even their mothers.

When Jonathon arrived one Sunday afternoon wearing uniform, Sophia was struck dumb. She looked at him incredulously. He was no longer a boy, but a full-grown man with a young family; for him to volunteer seemed like lunacy. He grinned at her sheepishly. "I know," he said, seeing her anxious eyes. "It will only last a few months, though, and I do want to do something." He saw it as a crusade, an adventure, which he was afraid to miss. He had been so sensible all his life, a good boy, never misbehaving, always doing the right thing. Now he was eager to embrace life, to go off into the unknown of war and face the uncertainty of this battle with an enemy. It was as if he had never known the reality of being alive, of having manhood. Now he wanted it.

His wife was irritated, upset, scolding. She did not understand what had made him do it.

All over Bristol women were saying goodbye to their men with the same mixture of feelings. The heady euphoria of flag-waving and shouting carried on all over the city.

"I am glad you are too old," Sophia said to Wolfe, thinking that he would undoubtedly have gone.

He grinned at her, kissing the top of her silvery head. "Oh, you shackled me by the leg too many years ago, my dearest. I hope Jonathon will do nothing stupid, though. His children need a father."

"I need you," she said softly, leaning her head back against his shoulder. She was sixty-one now, a still upright, slender woman with her hair so thickly silvered that the light on it sometimes made her look almost blonde. Her face had that delicate fine-boned look even now. Age was giving her a luminous beauty she had never had before—less of woman, more of spirit.

Wolfe had aged more than she had. His lean fit body had thickened in the last five years. He still worked incredibly hard, and she worried at times because he breathed tightly, as though he found it hard to breathe at all. His financial empire had grown too large for him to know all its ramifications, and he left large parts of it to underlings now, some of it to his two sons, but even so he carried an enormous burden on his shoulders.

In the early years of their relationship there had been a blaze of awareness between them. Now it had become the comfortable warmth of a domestic fire, but it was still there, the link unbroken, unshakable, more of the mind than the body, and stronger for that.

In December 1914 she and Wolfe were working on the Christmas decorations in the drawing room, talking and laughing quietly. Their grandchildren were all to be present for the day. Wolfe had commanded it, and his two daughters-in-law had agreed. Wolfe still held the financial purse strings.

Suddenly the maid came into the room looking excited and strange. "Oh, sir...oh, madam," she burst out, giggling.

Wolfe, on a stepladder, looked round irately. "What's the matter with you, Maisy? Spit it out."

Sophia was kneeling on the floor by a box of coloured glass balls. She looked up, smiling, and then her smile faded as she saw the tall, dark handsome man in the doorway. The uniform he wore was new and immaculate. Without even looking at Wolfe, who had frozen on the stepladder, staring, he moved forwards slowly staring at Sophia.

She looked into the blue-green opalescent eyes almost dazedly. "Jerome!"

Wolfe's thick cry made them both turn. He had a hand to his chest, was swaying. As he fell, Jerome moved like lightning to catch him and laid him, supporting him with difficulty, on the couch. Sophia was distraught. "What's wrong? Wolfe, my darling? What is it?"

The sounds were suddenly terribly familiar. In a flash her mind went back more than forty years to the night Wolfe's father had died. She went so white her eyes were like black shadows. "Wolfe...no, Wolfe..." She did not even know she was speaking, kneeling beside him, too tense for tears, hearing the gasping, choking sounds with a heart that beat wildly.

Jerome gently moved her aside and bent over his father. Jerome is a doctor, she thought, with a relief that went deeper than words. Thank God, Jerome will know what to do.

The sounds had stopped. She opened her eyes in relief, wanting to kiss him...dear Jerome, she thought. He had saved Wolfe. She looked past his lean body at her love, her blue eyes searching for his return of warmth, and a deep terrible coldness washed over her.

Jerome turned.

"No," she said. It came out as a scream so fierce the hairs rose on Jerome's neck. "No...Wolfe, no..."

The servants ran into the room. Sophia stood screaming out her refusal to believe it while Jerome put his arms around her and tried to hold her, to stop her tearing herself to pieces with grief. "No, no, no," she cried again and again. "No, Wolfe. No..."

Jerome carried her up to her bedroom, aware with pity of the birdlike lightness of her slight body, and put her to bed, giving her a strong sedative which sent her into a dazed, nightmare-driven sleep. While Sophia slept, Jerome busied himself with the arrangements. His younger brother, Martin, was too shocked to believe the news at first.

"My wife will come over and stay with Sophia," he said.

Jerome looked at him coolly. "Louise must be with her. She is Sophia's daughter."

Martin grimaced. "Louise hasn't spoken to Sophia since she eloped."

Jerome stared at him. "I'll see her," he said grimly.

He drove to Louise's home and was shown into the drawing room. She faced him, a woman now of thirty-six, with all her mother's slender grace and black-haired beauty, yet the blue eyes in the oval features were cold and expressionless. Jerome studied her curiously. They had not met since they were adolescents. They were strangers to each other.

"What do you want, Jerome?" she asked him clearly.

"My father died this afternoon," he said in a crisp voice. "Your mother is in shock. You must come to her."

Louise's blue eyes flickered briefly. "I am sorry. My mother and I no longer see each other."

Jerome's hard mouth snarled. "For God's sake, woman... this is no time for petty grievances."

She flushed slightly, her eyes freezing. "I refuse to discuss the subject with you, Jerome. Good day."

He crossed the space between them, grasping her by the shoulders, shaking her. "Damn you, Louise, you're coming to her if I have to carry you every step of the way."

Mockery suddenly flared in her face. "My God, I believe you're still in love with her... a woman of sixty. Are you that much of a fool, Jerome?"

His cheekbones tightened into a barbaric, angry mask. "I'm a human being, Louise, not a cold, selfish bitch like you. Sophia is out of her mind over my father's death. If you will not come to her of your own free will I'll force you there if I have to break both your legs to do it."

"Let go of me," she said, a sudden dark colour in her cheeks. "How dare you manhandle me in my own drawing room?"

"I'll slap you silly in your own drawing room if you don't do as I ask!"

"You wouldn't dare!"

His hand stung across her face and she gasped in shock and disbelief. Over the quiet, slowly chilling years with Thomas she had insulated herself from feeling. The warmth between herself and her husband had died as she failed to give him a child. Luther's angry attitude had sapped Thomas's affection for her. There had never been wild passion between the two of them, but the love Thomas had once felt had faded out of all recognition, and the polite formality of their marriage had left her unprepared for the eruption into her elegant life of this lean, hard, angry man with eyes of opalescent metal.

"You bastard," she said, then bit her lip, hearing the word come from her mouth in shocked surprise. She never ever swore. Her blue eyes were dazed. Jerome had always had this effect on her—bringing up out of her depths emotions she refused to admit.

"Get yourself ready and come now," Jerome said shortly, reading her face.

"I refuse to go," she said flatly.

He twisted her arm up behind her back and wrenched it, making her moan in pain and surprise. "You'll do just as I tell you."

Looking at him she knew she would. He frightened her. She got ready and he drove her to the house she had never entered, the house where her mother had lived as Wolfe Whitley's mistress for the past twenty years.

Twenty years, she thought, as she walked with Jerome into the house. Twenty years during which she had led a sheltered, exclusive formal life as the wife of a wealthy businessman. Twenty years during which she had been an empty shell. While her mother was excluded from society, an outcast, ignored, she had assumed the flattered position in society that her mother had once had. She had danced, given dinner parties, smiled and been sympathetic, a quiet, elegant shadow. And her mother, disgraced and despised, had, Louise guessed, been radiantly happy, radiantly alive.

It was not fair. The cry came silently as she followed Jerome up the stairs in the quiet house. There was the sound of crying from the servants' hall. The blinds had been drawn down. The feeling of death filled the air.

Sophia lay asleep like a restless child, her lids quivering over the blue eyes.

Jerome bent and gently touched her wrist, listening with a closed face to her pulse. He drew up a chair and pushed Louise down into it.

"Sit there until she wakes," he said, his lips scarcely moving. "And when she does, you will be kind and loving to her."

Defiantly, Louise stared into his dark face. "I hate you," she said in a relapse into childishness.

He gave her an odd look. "Do you?" A sudden smile of amusement curved his mouth. "Not in a million years, Louise."

Wild, hot colour flooded her face. She stared at him, her mouth dry. Only to see him, she thought drowningly. Only to see him. The twenty years rolled away and she was weak with a long-buried desire she had never since known.

He walked out and she sat and faced her mother. The slow hours passed. Louise stared at this slight, silver-haired woman on the bed and learned with every look what she had always known: that she loved her mother, she envied her, was jealous of her....

Gradually Louise touched upon the thorn that had impaled her own breast for so many years. Jerome had loved her mother. Her mother had taken Jerome, as she had taken Papa, as she had taken Daniel. They all preferred Mama. They always had. It was Louise the shadow, Louise the little girl, Louise the unnoticed woman, who was left to watch as the sun of life burned down upon her lovely mother, so vulnerable and slight was she, touching, more like a child than an old woman even now.

Then the lids flickered and the blue eyes gazed vacantly at her. For a moment there was total lack of recognition. Then Sophia knew her, and knew too what had happened.

Louise had no difficulty in leaning forwards and putting her arms around the slight, trembling body. The tears gushed out onto her shoulder. Sophia groaned again and again. Louise rocked her like a baby, patting her hair, her shoulders, murmuring the incoherent words of sympathy, of love, of understanding that came so instinctively.

Jerome came in some time later and found them silent, hand in hand. Sophia's white face was tear-stained. Her eyes were rimmed with pink. Her mouth was shaking.

He gently bent over her, asked if she would eat or drink, was refused and firmly gave her another sedative. She was asleep within minutes. Jerome nodded to Louise.

"Come down and eat something. She will be asleep for hours."

Silently she followed him down and pretended to eat some of the light meal the kitchen had provided. Then she had to talk to Martin's wife, who arrived with Jonathon's wife. They spoke stiltedly, amazed to see her there, but keeping a polite mask on their feelings. They offered to stay and help, but Jerome coolly told them there was nothing they could do. "Your families need you at home. Louise will manage here."

"Of course, Louise is so lucky not to have responsibilities

at home," said Martin's wife, then caught Louise's flushed face and was horrified. "I mean...I...."

Jerome drily changed the subject and they talked for a while before leaving rather gratefully.

Alone, Jerome eyed Louise. "No children," he said flatly.

She turned on him, ready to spring angrily. "No," she said. "I'm barren. Sad, isn't it?"

Jerome was scathing. "You're lucky. You could be alive."

She was taken aback, not comprehending. "What?"

He moved, sitting down beside her on the couch, his eyes derisive. "Dead as stone, Louise...how many years have you been like that? When I saw you in that fine house of yours I thought you were one of Papa's statues for a moment. Is Thomas no good in bed?"

She slapped his face violently.

He laughed. "That's the second time today you've come to life for me. Have you regretted it all these years, by any chance?"

She was burning with rage. "I don't know what you're talking about. I'm going to bed."

As she stood up he jerked her backwards and pushed her down into the cushions, his hands holding her. She struggled to get up, glaring at him, feeling the thunder of her pulses with a sensation of total terror.

He leaned over her slowly while she twisted and tried to evade him. An inch from her mouth he said softly, "You cold little bitch..." But the words were inviting, almost loving.

As if the touch of his mouth was the signal she had been waiting for all her life she went quite crazy, her arms going round his neck, her mouth opening hungrily, her heart beating so fast she felt she would die of it. His hands moved over her and her body trembled with pleasure. "Jerome," she groaned. "Jerome...."

He took her on the couch ten minutes later and she was wild in his arms, so desperately, violently alive that Jerome was staggered by the response he got from her.

"I love you," she groaned, her body convulsive. "I love you...." Jerome felt a strange jerk of agony in his mind, as if something had torn inside him. He looked down at her flushed, passionate face with incredulity.

Gently he stroked her hot cheek and the blue eyes opened, staring at him wildly. "I am not my mother," she said hoarsely.

Very seriously, Jerome said, "No, you are Louise, and I love you...."

She was still, searching his gaze. Tears formed in her eyes and ran down her face. Jerome kissed her wet lids and her cheeks and then her mouth, and felt her kiss him back desperately.

They went to bed together, lying naked and silent. After a while Jerome said, "I've wasted our lives. My obsession with your mother was like an illness. It lasted so long, I took it for granted. It was wise of you, Louise, to refuse me when I asked you to marry me. I would have made you wildly unhappy. Now it is too late."

"I'll have tonight," Louise said. "If you hadn't come back I would never even have had that."

He kissed her hands gently. "Did you love me then, my darling? Was it always this way with you?"

"Always," she said.

"Oh, God, what a mess I've made of everything."

"It doesn't matter now," she said. "You're here."

"I'm only here for a few days," he said. "I'm serving in the Army medical corps. I'm going back to camp after Christmas."

"A few days...twenty years...they can seem the same at times," she said.

"It didn't work with Thomas?"

"How could it?" She was resigned. "He never loved me the way I needed to be loved. He wanted a submissive, gentle wife. I pretended to be what he wanted, but without children, our marriage fell apart years ago."

"It doesn't work for me, either," he said. "I never wanted it to. Hannah is a good wife. She works with me as a friend, but we have never been lovers."

She looked at him incredulously. He grinned, a faint mockery in his eyes. "Oh, we sleep together now and then, but that is not the same, is it, my darling? It has never been with her what it just was with you—the need, the wildness."

"No," she said, sighing. "Or with Thomas. So much time has gone by without even being noticed. I was tempted to go with you when you asked me years ago, but there was so much against it—Papa, Mama, yourself. Had you loved me I would have gone, but I knew you loved Mama."

He pulled her into the hard, lean curve of his body. "Go to sleep, Louise. You're tired."

She leaned, sighing, her heart racing at the feel of his body against her. Suddenly she began to laugh in half-hysteria. He shook her.

"What is it?"

"I'm an adulteress, like Mama," she said, giggling. "Is it in the blood, do you think? A fatal tendency? Or just an inherited weakness for bluey-green eyes that can smile and be savage all in a minute?"

He grinned. "God knows. I find I've a weakness of my own, Louise, for blue eyes and black hair." He sobered. "There's something I must tell you. Tonight is the time, I think. I'm thirty-nine years old and in all those thirty-nine years I've only ever loved one person—your mother. Now I find I love you. God knows what one makes of that. I'm too tired and too happy to care. I only know that for the first time in my life I've given and taken love. It is a heady experience, my darling. I'm old to have discovered what it can be like. It seems to have knocked me off balance."

They lay together peacefully until they slept. Over the next few days Louise spent each waking moment with her mother, tender now as she never had been in her life since she was a small child, totally loving, totally concerned. Sophia barely noticed the looks that passed between her daughter and Jerome. The funeral was to take place at eleven o'clock three days after Wolfe had died, and Thomas Hunt was unconcerned by his wife's absence at her mother's house, although Luther looked grim when he heard of it, and forbid Thomas to visit Sophia.

"Of course she will not attend the funeral," he said. "If she did it would make things very awkward for everyone. I imagine Wolfe's sons will see she is not present."

Wolfe's sons, conferring briefly, decided to leave the decision to Sophia herself. "She will not go," the two younger ones agreed. "She will realize the social embarrassment it would cause."

Jerome looked sardonic and said nothing. He knew her better.

He had already spoken to her sadly of his guilt over his father's death. "If I even suspected he had a weakness of the heart I would not have walked in like that...I was childish, wanting to surprise you both...." He looked at her gently. "After so many years I wanted to see both of you before I went off to war. Who knows? I might be killed and then I would not have said goodbye and that I would have regretted very bitterly."

Sophia patted his hand. "Wolfe would have understood. It was not your fault, Jerome. Anything might have triggered it off. I never knew. He kept it from me. He knew for months, the doctor tells me. He never said a word.''

"Didn't want to worry you," he nodded.

"He didn't want me to be afraid," she said, her voice trembling.

"You needn't be," Jerome said quickly. "We'll look after you, Sophia."

She looked at him oddly, her eyes glazed with tears. "Dear boy, that was not what I meant."

Jerome looked down at her, his mouth twisting. "No," he said. "I know what you meant."

Sophia looked away with a sigh. "I shall never get used to it," she said. "For a long time I lived without my soul, then I got it back. Now time has wrenched it from me again. . . .''

"Time," Jerome said bitterly. "Time has a lot to answer for."

She thought about his words later that night. He had given her a lighter sedative this time, afraid she might become too used to it, and she kept waking up from dreams of Wolfe. By the soft lamplight she saw her daughter sitting by her bed, deftly doing some embroidery.

Through half-closed lids Sophia considered Louise contentedly. She had lost Wolfe. But she had got Louise back. It was not an even bargain fate offered her—but at least it was not all loss. The slim figure of her daughter looked comfortingly permanent. This time, Sophia thought, Louise and I may have a chance to know each other. . . .

Then she heard Jerome come into the room. Her lids were almost closed now, flickering lightly. Jerome bent over the bed and she lay still, pretending to be asleep. The drug had hold of her mind enough to make her drowsy if not actually chaining her in unconsciousness.

Jerome turned away and Sophia faintly saw Louise look up at him. With a start of astonishment she saw the look they exchanged. Passion blazed between them. Jerome bent his head, his hand around Louise's nape, and began to kiss her with an unmistakable, open hunger.

"Come to bed, my darling," he whispered. "She will sleep now until the morning."

Louise laid down her embroidery and got up. Their arms around each other they went out and the lamp softly washed the bedroom in pale light. Sophia laughed huskily under her breath. "Oh, Wolfe, my dearest, how I wish you were here. . . .''

When it was seen that Sophia had every intention of being
present at Wolfe's funeral there was general consternation in
the social circle that surrounded the Whitley family. Dressed
entirely in black, a veil over her face, she walked with Jerome
on one side of her, Louise on the other. Closing ranks,
Wolfe's other two sons walked behind them, their wives,
flushed and embarrassed, falling in behind. The community
was outraged. It was, everyone agreed, typical Stonor arrogance. How did she have the nerve?

In silent agreement, the members of the congregation, after
some stiff flushed glances, nods, raised eyebrows, decided to
ignore her. They sat through the service like statues, concentrating on what they would do afterwards rather than listening
to the sermon. Wolfe's importance in the community meant
that few people of any note had felt able to stay away from
the funeral, but they were all furious with Sophia for attending.

Around the grave they stood, in their stiff black mourning
clothes, while Sophia silently wept beneath her veil and
Jerome held her with an arm around her shoulders, as if he
were her son. Oddly she almost felt it was Daniel, so conscious of this man who was flesh of Wolfe, bone of his body.

As the formalities ended, a chauffeur in a smart uniform
came up to the graveside with an enormous wreath of flowers.
Quietly he placed it in a prominent position. All eyes focused
in disbelief and shock upon the clearly written card. Sophia,
turning to go, stood, staring down at it. Jerome's brows rose
as he saw the name—no words of sympathy or greeting—just
the name written in a clear fine hand.

Sophia turned and stared through the gates. The other
mourners stared too, a faint whisper rising from them, like
the sound of far off waves rushing in on a lonely shore.

Sophia slowly moved down the path. Everyone watched in
sheer dazed incredulity as the door of the new limousine
opened and a thin, pale hand was extended. Louise felt tears
rise to her eyes. Jerome pursed his lips in a silent whistle.
Sophia paused, staring into the car, then she got into it. The
chauffeur resumed his seat and the car moved away down the
road.

It was as if a bombshell had exploded among them all. People broke into open, horrified, fascinated gossip. Luther Hunt
stared after the car as if he had just seen the end of the world.

"The old devil," Jerome said under his breath to Louise.

"My God, your father is incredible. I take my hat off to him—his timing is impeccable."

"He loves her," Louise said.

They stared at each other in silence. Thomas came bustling to his wife's side, more aldermanic than ever, a querulous look on his face. "What is your mother doing now? She is going to start all the gossip off again. How can she do this to me?"

"Because she doesn't give a damn for any of us," Jerome said sardonically. "And why should she? Do we give a damn for her? She has gone where she is most wanted...which of us is stupid enough to refuse to do that?" And all the time he spoke he was staring into Louise's eyes, and it was not to Thomas he spoke at all, but to her, and she read his message clearly.

In the car Sophia lay with her head on Stonor's shoulder, weeping bitterly, silently. He stroked her silvery hair, a smile of content on his cold face. There had not passed one word between them. There had been no need.

As they drove up to Queen's Stonor the house was bathed in a fitful winter sunshine, cold and brief, but touching the mellow stones to brightness. Sophia looked at it with a long wrenching sigh. She had not seen it for almost twenty years. Her heart moved painfully inside her.

The servants were as excited and incredulous as the church congregation had been. They could not believe it was happening. The kitchen talked endlessly of why Stonor had done it, of what their own attitude should be. Sophia was a fallen woman, disgraced, shameful. But she was the true Stonor of this house. They all knew exactly how much that weighed in the scales of social judgement, and for the moment they decided to wait and see.

Edward was almost speechless. Stonor had never hinted to him of his intention. Indeed, Stonor had not known whether she would come or not. Ever since he had heard of Wolfe's death he had been on tenterhooks of sick excitement, but he had not dared to move until he saw how his wreath was received. If she had ignored it, he would not have dared to open the car door. But she had not ignored it. She had turned and come to him, and he had silently invited her to return.

That evening Edward sulkily withdrew, leaving his parents alone all evening. They talked in fits and starts, their minds absent, and it was of Wolfe they talked. Stonor understood her need to speak of him. He shared memories of Wolfe no other living soul could share. He was too happy to have her back to care that it was of his brother she talked. He listened, and answered, and watched her, his cold formal features softening with happiness.

When he was taken up to bed by his manservant, Sophia came in to say good night to him. He lay in his great bed looking at her with those grey eyes, his face expressionless. "Stay with me, Sophia," he said, as she turned to go.

Between any other two human beings such a request might have seemed the height of insensitivity. Sophia turned, though, and closed the door, then she slowly undressed and in her simple white petticoat got into Stonor's bed. His arm came around her and she lay easily against him. There was comfort in that human warmth. She had slept alone since Wolfe died, and she was lonely. I may live for twenty more years, she thought, staring into the darkness. Twenty years without Wolfe. Stonor's fingers stroked her hair and she sighed, moving closer to him.

"I saw Louise at the funeral," Stonor said. "Shall we see her at Queen's Stonor again, Sophia?"

"You must ask her, Stonor," she said without surprise.

"She is our daughter," he said.

"Oh, Stonor, you fool," Sophia said, her tone wryly affectionate.

He did not pretend not to understand. "I was going to kill myself when you left me," he said. "But I decided to wait and see.... These have been very long, empty years, but I am glad I waited."

# CHAPTER THIRTY

Louise and Jerome met whenever he was able to get leave from his Army camp. They used hotels for snatched hours, walked in quiet parks, held hands like young lovers, and talked. Thomas went off in the spring of 1915 to America on business, and Stonor's invitation to visit Queen's Stonor gave the lovers a chance to meet far more often and privately.

Luther Hunt was delighted with Stonor's and Sophia's reconciliation, so delighted that he took it upon himself to be the first in the Bristol community to recognize Sophia as the re-established mistress of Queen's Stonor, inviting her to a quiet dinner party. People talked of little else but the scandalous behaviour of Sophia Whitley for months, but as the gossip palled and the news of war grew far worse, Sophia's position in society was quietly accepted once more. She would never again be queen of the county. She had blotted her copybook too badly for that. But few people were prepared to ignore a summons to Queen's Stonor if she gave a dinner party, and Stonor's magnanimity in taking her back was regarded so highly that people preferred to follow his example and pretend the whole shameful incident had never happened.

It was towards the end of 1915 that Stonor realized that his daughter was Jerome Whitley's mistress. At first he was deeply, coldly angry, but age had softened him to a large extent. He spoke of it to Sophia tentatively, and found her quietly aware of it, completely happy about it.

"And what if Thomas finds out?" he asked drily.

Sophia made a face. "Oh, he's such a bore these days, darling. An alderman with nothing on his mind but the making of money. Poor Louise—can you blame her?"

His grey eyes considered her thoughtfully. "In the circumstances, no...."

She laughed down at him. "With my blood in her veins, you mean? There is that, of course."

Stonor laughed too. "She is beginning to look quite lovely," he said, surprised. "She has changed out of all recognition."

"Love has that effect," Sophia gently agreed. "Louise is in love, darling.... I envy her. Don't you?"

"Yes," he said levelly, staring at her.

She touched his cheek. "All passion spent, Stonor?"

He had been reading Milton to her that morning. They often spent hours reading aloud to each other. It was a delightful occupation on a quiet morning at Queen's Stonor. He recognized the lines.

"Passion?" He murmured the word thoughtfully. "Perhaps.... Not love, though. That remains, like the evening star, steady and never diminishing. Didn't you know, Sophia?"

"Yes," she admitted, looking at him with blue eyes that smiled. "My brutal, passionate darling, yes. I knew."

"Why did you want to hurt me after you had left me?" he asked. "Why, Sophia?"

"You gave me to Wolfe," she said. "I could never forgive that."

"I did it for you," he said. "I was afraid. You were so white and cold, like death.... I knew only Wolfe could pull you out of it."

She nodded. "Yes, only Wolfe could have done that. But I am a woman, Stonor. I still resented the fact that you stood aside and let him take me. Wolfe thought it very noble of you. I was merely angry."

"Did you want me to let you die?" he asked, baffled.

She shook her head. "It is not so simple. I wanted you to fight, as you did when I nearly died of having Daniel. You fought for me from the moment we met, but suddenly you stood aside."

He was flushed suddenly. "I'll never understand you, Sophia," he muttered.

She looked at him and laughed. "Oh, you understand me well enough, Stonor."

In 1916 Jerome was ordered to France. He and Louise spent a last weekend together at Queen's Stonor. Sophia made it easy for them to be alone for every moment of the day and night. Stonor frowned over it, his head shaking. "This is very unwise, you realize...."

Sophia pinched his ear. "They have very little time left, Stonor. If it were us what would you say?"

He looked at her, amused. "Do you think I do not know

that you find it delightful to see Wolfe's son in bed with our daughter?"

She laughed openly at him. "Puritan."

"I ought to put my foot down and forbid it," he said without conviction. Since Wolfe's death he cared little about Jerome's paternity. Wolfe gone, Stonor was in eternal possession of happiness and he cared nothing for anything or anyone else in the world.

After Jerome had gone, Louise was gloomy and silent for weeks, and she spent most of her time at Queen's Stonor with her parents. As for Edward, he was rarely at home. He had taken, of late, to driving up to London in his car, acquiring a passion for the motorcar from his first moment of owning one. A telephone had been installed at the house and it was by this means that they heard that Edward had been killed in a car crash one summer night in 1916. Stonor was grief-stricken. Since his wife's return, he had neglected Edward, and guilt weighed heavily on him.

"Who will have Queen's Stonor now?" he asked Sophia some time later, his face drawn. "There is only Louise, and she has no child...."

As Wolfe had said to her once before, she said to him, "It is only a house, my darling. We are alive."

She had felt guilty over Edward's death too. She was aware that her return had broken the mould of closeness her absence had allowed him to build with his father, and in a way she felt she had caused Edward's death, just as Jerome felt he had caused his father's.

Three weeks after Edward's death Louise arrived at the house late at night, in terrible grief and with a swollen cheek, bringing the news of Jerome's death in France.

"Your face, my love," Sophia said, bathing it with witch-hazel. "How did you hurt your face?"

Louise looked apathetic. "Thomas did it."

Stonor stiffened. "He hit you?" He sounded so angry that Sophia glanced at him with dry amusement, remembering the times he had hit her in the past.

Louise smiled drearily. "I couldn't hide the way I took the news of Jerome's death," she admitted. "Thomas was angry. And then I told him I was carrying Jerome's child...."

Sophia's hand froze. She stared down into Louise's face,

her blue eyes breaking into wild flames of joy. "Oh, my dearest girl...how wonderful...."

Stonor was gasping in dismay. Louise looked at him, then at her mother, and began to laugh.

Gently Sophia put an arm around her. "Louise, darling, don't...."

Laughter turned to wild tears and then to a sort of stupor. Sophia put her daughter to bed and went back to Stonor, who looked at her with great concern.

"This will shatter the Hunts."

"Do we care?" Sophia shrugged. "Don't you see, Stonor? We have an heir to look forward to...."

Stonor's jaw dropped. "An heir...a bastard? Jerome Whitley's bastard heir to Queen's Stonor?" His voice held a furious anger.

Sophia shook her head at him. "He will be your grandchild, my dear man. There is Stonor blood in him. What do we care if he is Jerome's child or Thomas's child?"

"You care," Stonor said jealously. "You wanted this. You hoped for it. You gave them every chance to sleep together in the hope of it."

"Well, so I did," she said cheerfully. "Thomas proved incapable of fathering a child. We need an heir with Edward gone..."

"I won't accept it," Stonor said forcefully. "Do you think I'm soft in the head because I am old? I know what you want, Sophia. You want to see Wolfe's grandson reigning here at Queen's Stonor when I am gone."

"Your grandson, too," she said lightly. "And mine...he has all our blood in his veins, this child."

Stonor stared at her, his grey eyes considering what she had said. After a pause, his mouth sulky, he said, "It will probably be a girl."

Laughing, Sophia kissed him. "Oh, Stonor, my poor fool."

Thomas came to Queen's Stonor some weeks later. Sophia and Stonor received him together. He came in, bristling, full of anger and self-righteousness. "I shall divorce her, of course," he said. "She shall never have a penny of my money and this bastard shall not bear my name."

Stonor coldly nodded. "If you would be good enough to contact us in future through our solicitors," he said flatly.

Thomas flushed, staring at him incredulously. "You mean

to give her bastard house room? To encourage her? She's a whore! For months she was sleeping with him! Disgusting...."

Stonor rang the bell and ordered the servants to show Thomas out. Within a short time the divorce was set on foot, and Louise, already heavy with her child, merely shrugged over the papers she read.

Luther Hunt also made an attempt to persuade Stonor to exclude his daughter from the house. "You must realize the scandal this will cause." He glanced slyly at Sophia. "Even worse than before."

Sophia kissed Stonor after Luther had gone in angry silence. "I was proud of you. You sent him packing like a grocer, cap in hand."

"You are winding me round your little finger, Sophia," Stonor said drily. "I'm aware of it, but I must be too old and weak to do anything but obey you." Then his face became stiffly angry. "And anyway, I'll have no interference in my family affairs from anyone. If I choose to keep Louise here that is my business. Luther can keep his nose out of Queen's Stonor."

"Poor Luther," Sophia said. "He would have given anything to see his own grandchild master of this house.... Now he must watch as Louise gives birth to another man's child."

"Thomas was at fault," Stonor said scornfully. "Obviously, Louise was always able to have a child. The difficulty lay with her husband."

"Yes, poor Thomas...the divorce makes that plain enough," Sophia said. "If I were he I would not make such a public meal of my own impotence. He is telling the world that although he could not give Louise a child in all the years of their marriage, Jerome managed to quite quickly...." Her eyes danced with amusement.

Both of Wolfe's remaining sons had joined the Army by now, and in the early autumn Stonor and Sophia heard that both were dead, killed on the same day, in the same battle. Sophia drove to visit their wives and found them both together. All over England women were weeping now. Tears were a national pastime. The adventure that had begun so splendidly in 1914 had grown into a vast bloodbath that went on and on without ever seeming likely to end.

Louise was still technically Thomas's wife when she went into labour one winter night. Stonor was unable to relax as he waited for news of the birth of his grandchild. Sophia sat beside him, watching him with warm affection, perfectly aware that beneath his cold, quiet façade there were churning emotions of which he was only partly aware himself.

The baby was born at three o'clock in the morning. "A fine time to choose," Stonor said drowsily. He had kept himself awake with the occasional short glass of brandy, and was slightly drunk. Sophia would not have permitted it at any other time, but she knew when to relax her strict rules about his drinking.

It was the boy Sophia had known it would be—a long, thin baby with wild black hair and eyes the colour of the violets that were Sophia's favourite flower.

Stonor looked down upon the dark head, feeling a curious sensation of *déjà vu* . . . had this happened before? He had a flashing memory of Daniel's birth, the screaming baby in his arms, Sophia dying under his eyes until he dragged her back to him with all his willpower.

Weary and pale in her bed, Louise watched her father, wondering what he was thinking. She had not spoken to him much of Jerome, knowing the emotional abyss that must lie between them on that subject. Her child was Wolfe Whitley's grandson. . . . How did her father view that? She had no idea.

Sophia came in and smiled at her lovingly, delightedly. "Isn't she a clever girl. . . ." Her voice was soft with pleasure. "She has given us our heir, Stonor. . . ."

It shook Louise. She had not expected it. She had been fervently grateful that they had, despite the pressures of social opinion and the Hunts, taken her into the house. She knew how little she could have expected such kindness anywhere else. She had committed a terrible social crime. And now this—a spoken promise that her child should be the heir to Queen's Stonor. . . . It staggered her.

She looked at her father doubtfully. He was saying nothing. He put out a long, dry finger and the tiny baby hands, like soft starfish creeping over the bedclothes in the crib, fastened on it possessively, closing tight.

Stonor caught his breath. He looked at Louise. "What will you call him?"

She had not thought. Her face was blank. "I must think about it," she said.

"Daniel," Stonor said. "Call him Daniel."

There was a silence. Louise felt tears rise to her eyes.

She looked at her mother and saw the tears reflected there too.

Stonor looked round at Sophia, his cold face broken with emotion. "I will change my will today leaving everything to Daniel...."

Sophia said nothing. This time there was no threat, no bribe, no attempt to use the child as a pawn in the deadly game of chess Stonor had played all their lives in his efforts to keep her. She knew with deep certainty that Stonor saw this child as his own flesh and blood, she had felt it as the tiny fingers grasped Stonor's extended hand. Flesh of our flesh, she had told him. Bone of our bone. What do legal titles matter? What does the world matter? This will be our grandchild.

In the city the news that Stonor Whitley had made his daughter's bastard heir to everything he owned was treated with amazement and glee. The Stonor family had proved themselves an endless source of fascination to their neighbours.

The Hunt family were bitterly outraged. Luther sat thinking grimly of the obvious fact that had this child been Thomas's, it would have been his grandson who would inherit Queen's Stonor one day. Thomas, having realized the open amusement he was to suffer not only as an admitted cuckold but as a man who had failed to impregnate his wife only to have another man do so, turned in upon himself with rage.

"I will marry again," he told his father furiously.

Luther bitterly eyed him. "What's the damned point?" he asked flatly. "One woman's the same as another. You had years to get her pregnant and you failed. Why waste time trying with someone else?"

Desperate with temper, Thomas rushed off to Queen's Stonor, hardly aware of what he was doing, and by terrible chance met Louise and the baby. Louise was pushing the elegant little perambulator, cooing over the tiny pink-faced object inside it, when she heard the car stop. Looking round she saw Thomas and flushed.

He got out and walked over to her, stiff with bitterness. "Whore," he said wildly. "You've ruined my life, you whore...you and your bastard...and they will make it heir to Queen's Stonor...even my own father sneers at me openly...you've destroyed me, you bitch."

She said nothing. She had never seen Thomas so angry. He looked mad, his eyes bloodshot with hours of sleepless brooding.

He stared down into the baby's face with loathing. "I ought to put that pillow over its damned face," he said, and for a moment she thought he might actually try to do it.

She pushed him away from her child, a tigress defending her young. "Go away," she shouted at him.

There was nobody in sight to whom she could call for help. Thomas looked deranged, a man who meant trouble, and she was terrified for the baby's life.

Thomas completely lost his temper. He struck her violently, knocking her down onto the grass. She struggled to get up, terrified of what he might do to baby Daniel, but he had forgotten the child now, a male aggression driving him to other ideas.

She was alarmed as his body heavily fell across her and began to struggle, fighting him, but he held her down without difficulty, his breath coming fiercely. "If he could, I can," he said incoherently. "A whore will always do it without arguing."

"Thomas, if you dare—" Louise was unable to believe that this was the quiet, pompous husband who had bored her for years. His face had a square-cut aggression that reminded her of Thomas as a boy, fighting Daniel over her at his party, a compact, dynamic boy with force in his body.

Their bodies rolled over on the grass in an animal struggle that she had no hope of winning. Thomas held her, panting, while he took her savagely. Never in all their married life had he used passion towards her on this scale. Only public shame could have driven him to it.

He drove into her with brutal determination, his strong body clenched in a need to show mastery, staring at her with hatred. "I should have known, you bitch, when you offered yourself to me here in the park that you were nothing but a whore," he said, his voice thick. "I should have used you then and left you. I was a fool to treat you with respect and gentleness. Women like you only understand this—" His body rammed into her and suddenly she began to make a low moaning, keening noise, her eyes closing.

Thomas had never seen her in the daylight with that look on her face. During their married life their moments in bed had been quiet, discreet rituals in the dark, and his face slowly flushed darker.

Her arms came up round his body, digging into his shoulders, the strong broad back. She was no longer struggling.

Her body was arched receptively, meeting his downward drives with open eagerness.

Thomas put his hands on her breasts, staring at her. He fumbled with her gown, freeing the white flesh, touching it.

"Yes, yes," she groaned, writhing under him.

"Oh, Christ, Louise," he said, suddenly conscious of an incredible pressure of desire. "I want you." He had never said it, never thought it before. She had been his wife, gentle, submissive, discreet. The hot need driving him was a revelation to him, and her response threw him totally off balance.

The sweet, full curve of her mouth drew him like a magnet. He kissed her and found her mouth opening, her tongue inciting him. Gasping, he deepened the kiss. For the first time their mouths explored each other freely.

"I never knew," he said thickly. "I never knew...."

The words were unexplained but perfectly comprehended by Louise. She wound herself hungrily around him and they moved together in the only total act of love they had ever known.

Thomas was past thinking of anything. Indifferent to the chance of any audience, uncaring if anyone heard his wild cries, he rode to the peak of a pleasure he had never known existed, and Louise moaned under him, with him, engulfing him.

Drained, dazed, he lay on her for moments, his face buried on her smooth white body. When he moved she stretched out upon the turf, her arms flung wide in a gesture of life.

Thomas lay beside her, tidying his clothes, his face so flushed he looked as if he had sunstroke. The warm silence of the park poured down over them. Spring filled the air with a fragrance that was fresh with new life.

After a long silence, he said, "Come back home to me, Louise."

She did not answer for a moment. Then she said, "And Daniel?"

Thomas's jaw moved. "Bring him," he said.

She sighed. "I saw how my brother suffered all his life because he knew my father did not love him. I will not do that to my child."

"If it does not work out for us you can always come back here," he said. "Your parents will take you and Daniel back, you know that. Give me a chance, Louise."

She was silent, wondering what to do.

Thomas turned and sat up, laying a hand on her still-exposed breasts. "After this, I must have you back," he said. "We never had a chance before. I was a bloody fool. I had no idea. Louise, I want you...not as my wife, not as a suitable mistress for my home...I want you because you..." He broke off, his eyes hot. "You know how I want you. Once wouldn't be enough. I want you like that every night."

She laughed then, affectionately. "Oh, Thomas, how shameful of you...so you will treat me as a whore every night, will you?"

His face was filled with excited desire. "Yes," he said bluntly. "Yes, Louise."

Her heart began to beat suddenly. "Suppose I want to hear you say you love me?"

"I love you," he said angrily. "I love you and I've wasted years of not knowing how I love you."

"I loved Jerome deeply," she said, suddenly serious. "I always loved him even before I married you."

Thomas stared at her, his face revealing his jealousy and his pain. Then he said with the competitive instinct that had always driven him, "I'll make you love me."

"Oh, God, I think you may," she said, laughing abruptly. "You have shaken me, Thomas. I did not think you had it in you to do what you just did.... And make me like it...what else will you make me do?"

"I'll make you love me," he said obstinately.

"What about the scandal? The divorce?"

"To hell with the scandal," he said, his lower lip jutting. "I'll stop the divorce. Your father took your mother back. Why shouldn't I take you? People have short memories. A few years and it will be forgotten."

Louise looked at him through her lashes and remembered suddenly her mother saying, "I can make you do whatever I want you to do." Whom had she said that to? Wolfe or Stonor? Louise could not remember. But she could remember how she had watched her mother twist both men around her little finger, teasing them, enchanting them, holding them without effort. She could remember how she had grown into a quiet little shadow beside her mother because she could not bring herself to compete with her.

Now she said softly to Thomas, "Do up my dress, Thomas." And without a word he obeyed her, his eyes passionate on the slim body as he carefully did up her buttons.

Louise felt a heady rush of power to her head. She drew in a spring-filled breath of air and smiled at him, unconsciously flirtatious.

"Help me up. You were very brutal, knocking me to the ground like that...."

This was it, she thought, watching his intent face as he raised her carefully. This was the secret of her mother's power over the men who had loved her, and having discovered the secret Louise would hold it for as long as she could.

"You must come in and speak to Mama and Papa," she said softly. "We must explain that we are reconciled."

Thomas walked beside the perambulator feeling both older and younger than he was. The explosive experience they had shared had liberated him from shackles he had worn since youth. He glanced sideways at her and saw with astonishment that she had all her mother's beauty—a beauty she had never possessed before, as if she had entered into her inheritance suddenly, without his noticing it. The quiet, demure wife who had been at his side for years had overnight become a desirable, exciting woman, and he ached even now with his wild possession of her, looking forward with hunger to enjoying her again. As they entered the house, Thomas was totally indifferent to everything but Louise. He wore his chains of need and desire eagerly as he followed her into the morning room where her parents sat.

They stared in complete astonishment. Sophia's sharp blue eyes saw the grass stains and dishevellment they both showed, and her eyebrows rose.

Quietly, Louise said, "Thomas wants me to go back to him," her face wearing a faint smile.

"What about the boy?" Stonor barked, his brows jerking together.

"Thomas is going to try to be kind to Daniel," Louise said.

"If he isn't," Stonor said fiercely, "Daniel comes back home where he belongs. He is my grandchild and I'll have nothing hurt him, ever."

Sophia put her hand on his shoulder and he covered it with his own. Thomas flushed and said awkwardly, "I swear I'll do my best."

They talked for some hours, discussing the situation, then Thomas took Louise, Daniel and the child's nurse back home with him, unwilling to wait even one night before he resumed his married life.

"I'll never understand the women of this family," Stonor said, shaking his head. "I thought she hated him. . . ."

Sophia looked amused. "Darling," she murmured. "So blind. . . ."

Stonor laughed, his eyes adoring. "We're alone again, dearest. Will you miss them, Louise and the boy?"

"They'll visit us often," she said happily. "And we'll have each other."

Stonor looked content. "Yes," he said. "We'll have each other."

The reconciliation between Louise and Thomas broke upon Bristol like a thunderclap. Nothing else was talked about for months. Luther, raging, incredulous, was unable to believe it when his dutiful son told him to mind his own business. "And if you insult Louise you'll never be welcome in our home again," he said.

"I'll never have that bastard child as my heir," Luther said, his mouth hard. "Never, Thomas, do you hear? I'll leave my money to a home for cats before I do."

"Leave it where you damned well please," Thomas said. "Louise's son doesn't need your bloody money. He'll have Queen's Stonor."

"I'll never have her in my house," Luther said. "Have you no pride? Have you no manhood?"

Thomas laughed at that, loudly, and Luther was unable to believe his ears.

"I've just discovered, Father, that I have both," Thomas said. "A little late, but thank God, just in time."

Three months later Louise told him she was expecting his child. Calmly she said, "This one will be your father's grandchild. Daniel will not need any of his money. They will each have their own inheritance."

Thomas called on his father that night with a magnum of champagne. Luther stared at it as his son slammed it on the table in front of him, then he looked up at Thomas. Flushed, triumphant, glowing with pride, Thomas said, "Daniel will have Queen's Stonor. My son will have your money, Papa."

Luther let out a long sigh. "Are you sure it is yours?" he asked without intending to be cruel.

Thomas laughed. "Oh, I'm sure," he said. "I've been making sure every night for the last three months."

Luther laughed then, his eyes amazed and amused. Thomas broached the bottle and they toasted the baby triumphantly.

Luther drank deeply, ecstatic as he considered the future. He had been bitter over the lack of a grandchild for so long, bitter over the fact that Queen's Stonor was alien territory for him. Suddenly he said, "You've made sure Daniel is registered as a Hunt?"

Thomas stared at him. "Yes. I couldn't have the child bearing another man's name and calling me Papa."

Luther smiled. "Then there will be Hunts at Queen's Stonor one day...think of that...our name, Thomas. Our name."

During the long, ugly, terrible months of 1918 there was only one topic of conversation at social gatherings. The amazing fact that Louise Hunt had given birth to twin boys—and actually had the insolence to call them Stonor and Luther. Bristol grew accustomed to the sight of Luther Hunt proudly displaying his two grandsons, their small, compact little bodies bearing so remarkable a resemblance to Thomas that their paternity was in no doubt.

Luther showered gifts upon them and their mother. From being a creature he could hardly bear to name, she became his doted-on daughter-in-law, and Bristol noted with disbelief the fact that as she grew older Louise Hunt grew more and more like her mother, the notorious Sophia.

"They were always wild, the Stonors," they said to each other, beginning now to feel almost proud of the eccentric, unconventional, shameful behaviour of the women of that family. "It's in the blood."

And during the year of peace, 1919, Sophia and Stonor watched with delighted, adoring amusement as their eldest grandson sat shouting astride his first pony, held there by a smirking groom.

"See me, Grandpa," he shouted to Stonor. "See me..."

"I see you, Daniel, darling," Stonor said, smiling. The boy's grey eyes were blazing with triumph as he kicked his small heels into the pony's fat sides.

"He is so like you," Sophia said.

"He has your hair," Stonor told her, as he had done again and again.

What neither of them said to each other as the boy's strong, handsome wild features filled with triumph and he smacked his pony lightly to make it move faster was their secret thought: every feature was marked with Wolfe Whitley's stamp. It was true that the boy had Stonor's eyes and Sophia's colouring, but the overall impression he left upon the eye in a quick glance was that of Wolfe.

Later, as they walked back to the house together, Daniel tried to help to push his grandfather's chair. From early babyhood he had shown his grandfather an eager, loving affection, which Stonor returned without reservation. Now he wobbled along behind the chair, trying to push, saying proudly, "I'm pushing you, Grandpa...I am."

They all paused to look at the house. The early-morning sunshine fell over it like a golden veil. Tranquil, dreaming, it stood in its green setting and was filled with the births, sorrows, joys of centuries of human beings. Nothing of the violence, the tragedy, the heated desires of its past inmates showed on the mellow façade. It had survived all that weather, time and disaster could do to it. Around it the green park, the meadows, the rolling English counties spread like a sea of calm serenity. The war was over. Peace was to last for ever. Queen's Stonor waited to welcome beneath its broad, elegant roof the present and the future master of it.

Daniel peeped around at his grandfather, the face that was Wolfe's face bearing the marks that betrayed his blood, filled with the mingled lives of Stonor, Sophia and Wolfe, all coalesced into this one unique and adored human being who would one day rule at Queen's Stonor.

"We're home again, Grandpa," he said, as if Stonor had not noticed. "Well, nearly home..."

Stonor held Sophia's hand. "Yes, Daniel darling...we're nearly home."

# THE GOLDEN CAGE

## The first Harlequin American Romance Premier Edition
## by bestselling author ANDREA DAVIDSON

Harlequin American Romance Premier Editions is an exciting new program of longer–384 pages!–romances. By our most popular Harlequin American Romance authors, these contemporary love stories have superb plots and true-to-life characters–trademarks of Harlequin American Romance.

*The Golden Cage*, set in modern-day Chicago, is the exciting and passionate romance about the very real dilemma of true love versus materialism, a beautifully written story that vividly portrays the contrast between the life-styles of the run-down West Side and the elegant North Shore.

# Discover the new and unique

# *Harlequin Gothic and Regency Romance Specials!*

## Gothic Romance

**CASTLE AT JADE COVE**
Helen Hicks

**AN INNOCENT MADNESS**
Dulcie Hollyock

**RESTLESS OBSESSION**
Jane Toombs

## Regency Romance

**A GENTLEMAN'S AGREEMENT**
Deborah Lynne

**REVENGE FOR A DUCHESS**
Sara Orwig

**MIDNIGHT FOLLY**
Phyllis Pianka

# A new and exciting world of romance reading

## *Harlequin Gothic and Regency Romance Specials!*

# Enter a uniquely exciting new world with

# *Harlequin American Romance*™·ᴹ·

**Harlequin American Romances** are the first romances to explore today's love relationships. These compelling novels reach into the hearts and minds of women across America... probing the most intimate moments of romance, love and desire.

You'll follow romantic heroines and irresistible men as they boldly face confusing choices. Career first, love later? Love without marriage? Long-distance relationships? All the experiences that make love real are captured in the tender, loving pages of **Harlequin American Romances.**

What makes American women so different when it comes to love? Find out with **Harlequin American Romance!**

AMR-SUB-3X